© MEREDITH HEUER

About the Author

DANIEL HANDLER is the author of *The Basic Eight*, *Watch Your Mouth*, and *Adverbs*, and, as Lemony Snicket, the enormously popular children's novels in A Series of Unfortunate Events.

THE BASIC EIGHT

ALSO BY DANIEL HANDLER

Watch Your Mouth

Adverbs

THE BASIC EIGHT

DANIEL HANDLER

AN ECCO BOOK

HARPER PERENNIAL

NEW YORK • LONDON • TORONTO • SYDNEY

HARPER ● PERENNIAL

First published in the U.S. in 1999 by Thomas Dunne Books, an imprint of St. Martin's Press.

First Harper Perennial edition published 2006.

Library of Congress Cataloging-in-Publication Data

Handler, Daniel.
   The basic eight : a novel / Daniel Handler.—1st Harper Perennial pbk. ed.
       p. cm.
  ISBN-10: 0-06-073386-1 (pbk.)
  ISBN-13: 978-0-06-073386-5 (pbk.)

PS3558.A463B37 2006
813'.54—dc22   2006041095

18 19 20 21 ❖/RRD 18 17 16 15 14 13 12 11 10 9 8

The author wishes to acknowledge the following people:
Lisa Brown; Louis and Sandra Handler;
Rebecca Handler;
Kit Reed and Joseph W. Reed;
Charlotte Sheedy and Neeti Madan;
Ron Bernstein and Angela Cheng;
and Melissa Jacobs.

THE BASIC EIGHT

INTRODUCTION

I, Flannery Culp, am playing solitaire even as I finish this. Gifted children have always been good at doing two things at a time, and where I am I've played solitaire so much it's practically a biorhythm. It helps me think. When I can't tell which of two sentence arrangements sounds better, I just look over at the top of my neatly made bed where I've laid out the game and see something: red seven on the black eight. Why didn't I see it before?

Don't think I'm not aware of the metaphor (or of the double negative – in spite of all the hoopla, I did get a diploma). I'm alone here, sitting at this typewriter with my journal propped up to my left and a pile of typewritten papers to my right. I am a woman with a room of her own, just like what's-her-name, the writer. I am rereading my journal and typing my life here onto stark white paper. If I make a mistake, I just type back a few letters and write over it. It's one of those typewriters with white erasing tape, so whatever I write wrong, I can erase, except for some faint imprints which will be completely obliterated when I have this copied. Those shreds of misplaced facts and typographical errors will fade and vanish as I ready this to send to publishers. That's metaphorical too.

Can I just say something? (A rhetorical question.) Somebody down the hall is listening loudly to the radio and it is just driving me crazy. It's "the station that plays the hits of the nation," which are essentially greeting cards with guitar solos. I hate it. It's so inconsiderate of whoever-it-is, too. When I play music – and I mostly listen to classical music, like Bach – I play it softly, because I'm considerate of other people. I just had to get that off my chest.

Right now I have the suspicion that the ace of diamonds is trapped forever, face down, beneath the king of diamonds, which is sneering at me like Juror Number Five, and my whole life feels like a similar misshuffle. One more flick of the wrist and it could have been my math teacher who had been targeted, or some other teacher: Johnny Hand, or Millie. The Grand Opera Breakfast Club could have become the "important aspect" of the Basic Eight, and Flora Habstat could have ended up on the Winnie Moprah Show saying that we were some club of mad opera lovers rather than babbling about Satanism the way she did, though I guess in a slightly different set of circumstances Flora Habstat could have been one of us and actually known what she was talking about. With a slight shuffle there could have been somebody else sniffling into a handkerchief on the talk show, with a cult investigation citizens action group named after her child, and Mrs. State could have just shook her head as she watched the show, instead of participating in it, and then reached over to telephone her son Adam and his new fiancée: me. Things would be a different way. While at a bookstore, Adam would tell me to get lost while he bought me a present. I would wander down the uninteresting aisles: Gardening, Pets, Travel and finally, True Crime. I might glance at some slightly different book, there in this slightly different world, where my love for Adam worked out instead of ending in tragedy: The Basic Six, The Basic Seven.

But this is not some true-crime tell-all. This is my actual journal, with everything I wrote at the time, edited by me. The revisions are minor; I only changed things when I felt that I wasn't really thinking something that I wrote at the time, and probably would have thought something else. After all, I was only eighteen then. I'm almost twenty now. I learned lots about narrative structure in my Honors English classes so I know what I'm doing. Everyone's names are real, and so are their various nicknames. The radio was just turned up a notch, if you can believe it.

By process of elimination (too small, too big, won't stay up with regulation Scotch tape) I have only one picture of the Mislabeled Murderers, by which I mean my friends or, I'll just say it, the Basic Eight, that is on my wall. It faces me, and in a rare synchronous moment, everybody is looking at the camera, so everyone is looking right at me. Kate, leaning on an armrest rather than sitting on the couch like a normal human being, placing herself (symbolically, in retrospect) above us and looking a little smug, serving out a four-year sentence at Yale. Right next to her is V___, fingering her pearls. V___ must have snuck into the bathroom sometime that evening to redo her makeup, because she looks better than anyone else, better than Natasha even, and that's saying a lot. Lily and Douglas, snug on the couch. Lily between Douglas and me as always. Douglas looking impatiently at the camera, waiting to continue whatever it was he was saying. Gabriel, his black hands stark against the white apron, squashed into the end of the couch and looking quite uncomfortable. And there's beautiful Jennifer Rose Milton standing at the couch in a pose that would look awkward for anyone else who wasn't as beautiful. And stretched out luxuriously beneath us all, Natasha, one long finger between her lips and batting her eyes at me. I mean the me sitting here typing, not the one in the picture, who's looking right at me, too. That's also symbolic. Most of those people won't meet my eyes, now, but I'm not one of them. Every morning I get up, and while brushing my teeth, look at my showered self, calmly foaming at the mouth. Take out the photograph now. (I hope you can, reader. I want to arrange with the publishers to have a copy of it tucked into each copy of the book, for use as a visual aid and as a bookmark. Isn't that a good idea?) Look into each of our eyes and try to picture us as people rather than the bloodthirsty mythological figures you've seen on those tacky television shows about bloodthirsty events. Come on, you know you watch them.

Will anyone read this introduction? When this is published (with all proceeds, by law, going to charity), my own introduction will probably be buried among other prefaces and forewords by noted adolescent psychologists, legal authorities, high school principals and witchcraft experts, all of which will be ignored as readers cut to the chase. There is no getting around it: this is going to be marketed as a trashy book. Most readers will flip through these first pages, half reading as the flight attendants give the safety lecture, and by the time we're all airborne they will have forgotten them in favor of the actual journal, the real beginning. Perhaps they'll look at my name under the introduction with disdain, expecting apologies or pleas for pity. I have none here.

Perhaps, though, people will read the quote that opens the journal. I chose it from the limited library here, to reveal the dim-wittedness of the pop-psych gurus who look at people like me. Of course I'm neither fish nor fowl. I'm a real person, like you are. This journal is real. It is the reality of the photograph you're using to mark your place, a photograph that nobody ever got ahold of. It's more real than all those pictures the magazines used. Those were our school pictures, pictures taken of us when we were wearing appropriate outfits, smiling for our out-of-state relatives to whom our parents would mail them. What sort of image is that? This journal is the truth, the real truth. This book is as real as it gets. As real as – let me think – as real as the red queen I just overturned, or the black king I smothered with it.

Vocabulary:

HOOPLA   METAPHORICAL   RHETORICAL   ATROCITIES
NARRATIVE STRUCTURE   ADOLESCENT   DISDAIN

Study Questions:

1. What do you already know about the Basic Eight? How will it affect what you read here? Discuss.

2. Most people who keep diaries want to keep them secret. Why do you think this is?

3. If you were to reveal your diary to the general public, would you edit it first? Why or why not? (Note: If you do not keep a diary, pretend that you do.)

4. It is often said that high school is the best time of one's life. If you have already graduated, was high school the best time of your life? Why or why not? If you have yet to go to high school, how do you think you can prepare yourself to make it the best time in your life? Be specific.

One of the reasons the teenage years are so agonizing is that in most societies, particularly ours, the adolescent is emotionally neither fish nor fowl.

— Dr. Herbert Strean and Lucy Freeman,
Our Wish to Kill: The Murder in All Our Hearts

One may as well begin with my letters to one Adam State.

August 25, Verona
Dear Adam,

Well, you were right — the only way to *really* look at Italy is to stop gaping at all the Catholicism and just sit down and have some coffee. For the past couple of hours I've just been sitting and sipping. It's our last day in Verona, and my parents of course want to visit one hundred thousand more art galleries so they can come home with a painting to point at, but I'm content to just sit in a square and watch people in gorgeous shoes walk by. It's an outdoor cafe, of course.

The sun is just radiant. If it weren't for my sunglasses I'd be squinting. I tried to write a poem the other day called "Italian Light" but it wasn't turning out so well and I wrote it on the hotel stationery so the maid threw it out by mistake. I wonder if Dante was ever suppressed by his cleaning lady. So in any case after much argument with my parents over whether I appreciated them and Italy and all my opportunities or not, I was granted permission – thank you, O Mighty Exalted Ones – to sit in a cafe while they chased down various objets d'art. I was just reading and people-watching for a while, but eventually I figured I'd better catch up on my correspondence. With all the caffeine in me it was either that or jump in the fountain like a Fellini movie I saw with Natasha once. You know Natasha, right, Natasha Hyatt? Long hair, dyed jet-black, sort of vampy-looking?

I stumbled upon an appropriate metaphor as I looked for reading material in the hotel bookstore. Scarcely more than a magazine stand, actually – as always, I brought a generous handful of books with me to Italy thinking it would be more than enough to read, and as always, I finished two of them on the plane and the rest of them within the first week. So there I was looking through the bare assortment of English-language paperback pulp for anything of value. I was just about to add, if you can believe it, a Stephen Queen horror novel to my meager stack of mysteries, when it hit me: Is this what next year will be like? Do I have enough around me of interest, or will I find myself with nothing to do in a country that doesn't speak my language? I don't mean to sound like Salinger's phony-hating phony or anything, but at times at Roewer it seems that everybody's phony and brain-dead and that if it weren't for my friends and the few other interesting people I'd go crazy for nothing to do. To me, you're one of the "few other interesting people." I know we don't know each other very well and that you probably find it strange that I'm writing to you, if you're even reading this, but I really enjoyed the conversations we had toward the end of the year – you know, about how stupid school was, and about some books, and about your own trip to Italy. You were one of the non-brain-dead non-phonies around that place. I felt – I don't know – a connection or something. Well, luckily I'm running out of room on this aerogram, which is probably a good thing, but I'll seal this before I change my mind.

Yours,

Flannery Culp

P.S. Sorry about the espresso stain. All the waiters here are gorgeous, but clumsy and probably gay.

September 1, Florence

Dear Adam,

If writing one letter to you was presumptuous, what is two letters? It's just that I feel you'd be the only one who'd understand what I'm thinking right now, and besides I've already written everybody else too many letters and I have all this caffeinated energy on my hands, as I said last time.

But in any case, the only person who'd really get what I want to say is you, because this relates to the hotel bookstore metaphor I told you about before. Yesterday, when viewing Michelangelo's David I had the exact opposite metaphorical experience. I mean, I had of course seen the image of David 18 million times, so I wasn't expecting much – sort of like when I saw the Mona Lisa last summer. I stood in line, took a look, and thought, Yep, that's the Mona Lisa all right.

It was huge. From head to toe he was simply enormous, and I don't just mean statuesque (rim shot!) but enormous like a sunset, or like an idea you can at best only half comprehend. It simply took my breath away. I walked around and around it, not because I felt I had to, but because I felt like it deserved that much attention from me. I found myself looking at each individual part closely, rather than the entire thing, because if I looked at the entire thing it would be like staring at the sun. It was such an unblinking portrayal of a person that it rose above any hackneyed hype about it. It flicked away all my cynicism about Seeing Art without flinching and just made me look. I walked out of there thinking, Now I am older.

But it wasn't until I finished one of my hotel-lobby mysteries that night that I thought of my experience metaphorically. Unlike bringing books to Italy, I went to see David anticipating an empty, manufactured experience; instead I found a real experience, and a new one. I didn't think I'd have any new experiences left, once sobriety and virginity took flight. Perhaps that is what next year will hold for me. Not sobriety and virginity, but real new experiences. Maybe in writing to you, a new person in my life, I will embark on something new, as well. David has filled me with hope. And another biblical name fills me with hope as well: yours. Out of room again.

Bye,
Flan

And a postcard, written September 3rd, postmarked September 4th.

On the back:

Listen what my letters have been trying to tell you is that I love you and I mean real love that can surpass all the dreariness of high school we both hate, I get back from Italy late on the night of Saturday the 4th call me Sunday. This isn't just the wine talking.

F.

On the front:

A picture of the statue of David. Cancellation ink from a winking postmarker across the groin.

Vocabulary:

VAMPY   PRESUMPTUOUS   FAUX   HACKNEYED
SOBRIETY   VIRGINITY   POSTMARKED

Study Questions:

1. A Chinese proverb reads: "Never write a letter when you are angry." Are there other states of mind in which one should not write letters?

2. Most postal laws state that after one has given one's letters to the post office to mail one cannot retrieve them. Do you think this is a fair law? Think before answering.

3. Taking jet lag into account, how long would you wait to call someone who had just gotten back from another continent? If you had just gotten back from another continent yourself and were expecting a phone call, what would be the appropriate amount of time to wait before you could assume the phone call wasn't coming? Assume that you kept the line available as much as possible by keeping all other phone calls short.

Monday September 6th
Jet lag finally wore off today, so it seemed time to start my brand-new-expensive-black-Italian-leather-bound journal.

Historians will note that my bargaining skills were not yet sharpened when I made this purchase, which is why I'm trying to write costly sentences to justify my expenditure (i.e., "Historians will note . . ."). For the past couple of days since I got back I haven't been doing anything much, anyway; only sitting around my room trying to call my friends. My bedroom became a perfect decompression chamber between the European and American civilizations: I spent all my time talking to machines and was thus soon acclimated back to my motherland.

No one was home. I was sorry to miss them but glad to keep my phone time brief. I'm keeping the line open for Adam. He hasn't called. I'd like to think that he's on vacation, but school starts tomorrow so his parents must have brought him home by now to give him time to shop for new khakis.

Just when I was going over each of my letters in my head, Natasha called. "You know Natasha, right, Natasha Hyatt? Long hair, dyed jet-black, sort of vampy-looking?" What *stupid* things to write! I picked up on the third ring, but before I could speak I heard her breathy voice.

"Flan, are you waiting for some *guy* to call?" Reader, note here that she pronounces my nickname not as the first syllable in my name is regularly pronounced, but as "a pastry or tart made with a filling of sweet rennet cheese, or, usually, custard."

I put down *The Salem Slot*, the last of my hotel bookstore acquisitions. Once I've started something, I have to finish it, no matter how bad it is. "Hi, Natasha. How did you know?"

Natasha sighed, reluctant to explain the obvious. "You just got back from your European jaunt. You've left 'Hi-I'm-home' messages on everybody's machines, so you haven't gone out. You are therefore sitting on your bed reading or writing something. You can reach the phone without moving, but you waited until the third ring. Now, Watson, we need school supplies, ja? Let's meet for coffee and go buy cute notebooks."

"Cute notebooks?" I said. "I don't know. I sort of have to –"

"*Yes*, cute notebooks. We're going to be *seniors*, Flan. We have to play it to the hilt. If we can find pencils with our school colors on them, we're buying them. But of course we'll need coffee first. I'll meet you at Well-Kept Grounds, OK?"

She started to hang up. "Wait! When?"

"Whenever we get there, dearest. While on the Continent, did you forget how we operate? Did you forget us entirely? Nobody got even a postcard."

"Sorry."

"Yes, yes, yes. Leave the machine on in case he calls. And I'll want to hear *all* about it. The more you talk with machines and the more they talk with you, the more acclimated you'll get to American civilization. *Ciao*." The phone clattered as she hung up.

Only Natasha can make me move as fast as I did. I left the machine on, ran out the door, turned back, got my coat, ran out the door, turned back, got change for the bus and ran out the door. I forgot that San Francisco September can be chilly and that my July bus pass wasn't going to work two months later. Once on the bus I adopted the Blank Face Public Transportation Dress Code but by the time I got off I couldn't help beaming. I was happy to see Natasha again. It's often difficult to keep up with her Bette Davis-meets-Dorothy Parker act but underneath that she'd do anything for me.

Well-Kept Grounds is tucked into a neighborhood full of hippie preteens and bookstores dedicated to the legalization of marijuana, but the surroundings are a small price to pay for the cafe's collection of fabulous fifties furniture and for not charging extra if you want almond extract in your latte, which I always do. Natasha was there already. I saw her lipstick first, though her forest green rayon dress was a strong second. "*Flan!*" she called, sounding like she was ordering dessert. Men in their midtwenties looked up from their used paperbacks and alternative newspapers and followed her with their eyes as she cantered across the Grounds. She gave me a hug and for a second I was embraced by a body that makes me want to go home and never eat again. Natasha is one of those high school students who looks less like a high school student and more like an actress playing a high school student on TV.

"Hi," I said sheepishly, wishing I had worn something more glamorous. Suddenly a summer of not seeing each other seemed like a long time. She stood in front of me and looked me over. She swallowed. We both waited.

"I'll go get a drink," I said.

Natasha looked relieved. "Do that."

The men in their midtwenties slowly returned to their used paperbacks and alternative newspapers. What I would give to have someone in college look me over. I got my drink and went and sat down across from Natasha, who put down her book and looked at me. I looked at the spine of the book.

"*Erotica* by Anaïs Nin? Does your mother know?"

"Mother lent it to me," Natasha said, rolling her eyes. She always calls her mom "Mother" as if she's some society matron when in fact she teaches anthropology at City College. I thumbed through the book as Natasha took a sip of some bright green fizzy drink. *I can see you biting and scratching. She learned to tease him, too. The*

8

moans were rhythmic, then at times like the cooing of doves.
When people thumb through this book, those italics will
catch their eyes and they'll spot a pornographic sentence
before the page flaps by. A writer's got to sell herself.

"Why no latte?" I asked, gesturing to the green
potion. "I thought it was mother's milk to you."

"After this summer it's begun to taste like some other
bodily fluid," Natasha said, looking at me significantly.
Her eyes were very carefully done; they always are.

"Do tell," I said, happy to have arrived at a topic that
didn't involve my confession of love, written in a hurried,
Chianti-laced scrawl, on a postcard. Just thinking about
it made me want to hide under the table, which was
painted an unfortunate fiesta-ware pink.

"All right, I'll talk about *my* love life, but then we'll
talk about *yours*. But first, this Italian soda needs a little
zip." Natasha found a flask in some secret pocket and
added a clear liquid to the soda, watching me out of the
corner of her eye. She's always taking out that flask and
adding it to things. I often suspect that it's just water but
I'm afraid to call her bluff. She went on to describe some
guy she met at the Harvard Summer Program in
Comparative Religion. Natasha's always had a fascination
with what people worship. Kate says Natasha's actually
fascinated that people aren't worshiping *her* instead. In
any case, each summer Anthropologist Mom plunks
down her hard-earned money for Natasha to fly across
the country and make out with gorgeous men, all for the
cause of higher learning. According to Natasha, this one
was five years older than us and attended a prestigious
liberal arts school, the name of which I'm not sure I can
mention here lest its reputation become tainted due to its
association, however brief, with the notorious Basic
Eight.

"He was said to be brilliant," Natasha said, "but to be honest we didn't have too many conversations. It was mostly sex. It will be a while before I order any drink with steamed milk again." She drained the rest of her soda in an extravagant gesture and I watched her throat as she swallowed, taking mental notes.

I sighed. (How *perfect* my recall of these small details. I *sighed*, reader; I remember it as if it were yesterday.) "You go to the puritanical city of Boston and hook up with a genius who also happens to be an excellent lover –"

Natasha used a blood-red nail to poke a hole in my sentence. "More accurately, he was an excellent lover who also happened to be a genius."

"– and I go to Italy, the most romantic country in the world, and the only man who makes my heart beat faster is carved out of marble." I briefly described my experience with Michelangelo's David. She broke character for a full minute as she listened to me, shaking her head slightly. Her silver earrings waved and blinked. I was a little proud to have hushed her; even my best poems haven't done that. When I was done she remembered who she was.

"So this is the guy you're waiting to hear from?" she asked. "Can I give you a piece of advice? Statues never call. *You* have to make the effort."

"You have experience in this realm?" I said. "And here I thought you only slept with anything that *moved*." Natasha threw back her head and cackled. U.p. and a.n. went down again; the men all sat and wished they were the ones making her laugh like that. I jumped in while she was laughing.

"It's Adam State. I'm waiting for Adam State to call." Once I finally told someone it seemed much smaller, a problem made not of earth-shattering natural forces but of proper nouns: first name Adam, last name State.

Her cackling stopped like somebody pulled the plug. "*Adam State?*" she screeched. "How can you have a crush on anyone who has a name like a famous economist?"

"It's not because of his name. It's because of –"

"That *sine qua non*," Natasha finished, batting her eyelashes. She stopped when she saw my face. "Don't get angry. You know how I am. Underneath all my Bette Davis-meets-Dorothy Parker act I try to be good, really. There's no accounting for taste. Do you think it will work out?"

I bit my lip. "Honestly?"

Natasha looked at me as if I suggested she keep her hair natural. "Of course not. *Honestly*. The very *idea*."

"In that case, yes. It will definitely work out. I'm just worried about how 'Flannery State' will look on my stationery."

"You could do that hyphenated thing. Culp-State, say."

"Sounds like a university. Where criminals go after high school."

I finished my latte and paid careful attention to the taste of the milk. I didn't notice any real similarity, but my palate isn't as experienced. "This is a secret, Natasha."

"Mum's the word," she said. Her hair looked gorgeous.

"Don't say the word to me. My parents have vanished as far as I'm concerned."

"You have to stop traveling with them," she said, smiling slightly as her eyes met one of her admirers. "Get them to send *you* to summer school. You'd learn things."

"Thanks, but there's enough steamed milk in my life."

"Come on, you need to buy notebooks so you can write his name on them in flowery letters."

I rolled my eyes and followed her across the street to a stationery store. We opened our purses and bought things: notebooks, pencils, paper with narrow, straight lines. Our school colors weren't available, which is a good thing: Roewer's colors are red and purple.

She drove me home, which made me worry a little bit about the flask. I leaned back in the passenger seat and everything felt like a transatlantic flight again. I hoped I had enough interesting books, but for now I felt at ease, pampered even. It was almost dusk. I rolled down the window and felt air rush into my mouth. I stole a look at Natasha as she stole a look at me. Friends, we smiled and I closed my eyes again and let the sublime noise surround me.

"The music is great. Who is this?"

Natasha turned it up. "Darling Mud. They're all the rage in England."

It sounded great. It was all thundering percussion and snarling guitars, and the chorus told us over and over that one thing led to another. "On and on and on and on," the singer wailed, on and on and on and on.

As I opened the door to get out, Natasha touched my hand. "Listen, if you want Adam, you're going to have to *move*. I talked to Kate just the other day, and she had talked to Adam just the other day. He's apparently been getting crazy love letters from someone all summer. He wouldn't tell her who." Natasha's voice sounded too careless for these remarks to be well placed. I could have told her then that it was me, but I didn't. I could have told her I was in love, and didn't just have a crush, but I didn't. Maybe I would have saved us all the trouble in the next few months, but I didn't tell her. School starts tomorrow and with it the chattering network of friends telling friends telling friends secrets. On a *postcard*; I'm so stupid. I got out of the car and Natasha drove off. All I heard as she left was one thing leading to another.

Tuesday September 7th

So let it be noted that the school year began with the difference between authority and authoritarianism, and I have a feeling that the rest of it will be just as clear. My homeroom teacher is Mr. Dodd. It has always been Mr. Dodd. I cannot remember a time when my homeroom teacher wasn't Mr. Dodd, and my homeroom teacher will always be Mr. Dodd, forever and ever, world without end. While the rest of us took unknowing summer sips of coffee (and "steamed milk," in Natasha's case), Mr. Dodd was apparently at some Assertiveness Training program. He droned on and on about it after stalking into the room and writing "MR. DODD" in all caps on the blackboard, even though homeroom has been the same kids, with the same teacher, year in and year out, world without end. The gist of his speech was that thanks to Assertiveness Training we couldn't chew gum anymore. He told us of his vision of a new homeroom, "one with authority but not authoritarianism." I would have let it go, but he insisted we all look it up. He waited while we fumbled with our Websters. We knew he was waiting because he kept calling out, "I'm waiting!" Finally Natasha stood up, brushed her hair from her eyes and read out loud: "'Authoritarianism: a doctrine favoring or marked by absolute and unquestioning obedience to authority. Authority: the power to command, determine, or judge.'" Then she looked at Mr. Dodd and sat down. No one ever stands up in class and recites like that, of course, but I suppose if I looked like Natasha I'd stand up too. All the boys, Mr. Dodd included, gaped at Natasha for a minute before the latest graduate of Assertiveness Training for Homeroom and Geography Teachers said, "Does everyone understand what I mean?" Everybody thought, *No* (except for a sizable handful of homeroom kids who will never think anything, world without end), but only Natasha said it. I looked back and saw her take out an emery board that had a carved claw at either end. She didn't look at Mr. Dodd as she began to do her nails. Ever since Natasha and I read *Cyrano de Bergerac* in Hattie Lewis's freshman English class she's done everything with *panache*. Later this emery board will be very important in our story, so I introduce it now.

Mr. Dodd cleared his throat. Nobody at Assertiveness Training had prepared him for Natasha Hyatt. Nobody ever would be prepared for her. He opened his mouth to say something and the bell rang and we all left. I caught up with Natasha and hugged her.

"I don't know what I'd do without you."

"I don't know what I'd do without me, either," she said, batting her eyelashes. "That'll teach him to fool around with the dictionary. Tune in tomorrow for the difference between *disciple* and *disciplinarian*. Come on, it's time for Chemistry."

"I'm not doing Chem," I said. "I've got Biology."

"With who?"

"Carr."

"Carr? That dreamboat? '*Not doing Chem*,' she says." Natasha looked around the crowded hallway, narrating. Few kids looked up; everyone was used to Natasha going on about something, and we were all zombies this early in the morning, anyway. "'*Not doing Chem*,' when all the time she gets Biology with Carr. That's more Chem than I'll ever have. I've got that four-eyed man with the toupee. So when will I see you?"

I started to pull out my schedule to compare, but Natasha was suddenly swept away by a thick-necked rush of football players who apparently let nothing stand in their path on their quest for punctuality. For a minute it felt like a Hollywood prison camp movie where the husband and wife are dragged off to different trains, though I must admit Natasha didn't look too dismayed at being caught in the stampede. "Easy, boys!" I heard her call, and I looked down at my computerized card to see where to go next:

HOMEROOM: DUD
FIRST PERIOD: CALCULATED BAKING
SECOND PERIOD: POETIC HATS
THIRD PERIOD: ADAM ADAM ADAM ADAM
FOURTH PERIOD: FREE LUNCH
FIFTH PERIOD: APPLIED CERVIX
SIXTH PERIOD: ADVANCE TO RIO BY CAR
SEVENTH PERIOD: THE FRENCH SEVERED MILTON

Funny how one's eyes are bleary in the mornings:

HOMEROOM: LAWRENCE DODD
FIRST PERIOD: CALCULUS: MICHAEL BAKER
SECOND PERIOD: AMERICAN POETRY: HATTIE LEWIS
THIRD PERIOD: CHOIR: JOHN HAND
FOURTH PERIOD: LUNCH
FIFTH PERIOD: APPLIED CIVICS: GLADYS TALL
SIXTH PERIOD: ADVANCED BIO: JAMES CARR
SEVENTH PERIOD: FRENCH SEVEN: JOANNE MILTON

Doesn't look much more believable, does it? Perhaps it has been edited for your amusement and to protect the innocent, if any. This is the first year they've included first names on our schedules, and we will never let Lawrence forget it.

It looks like I'm alone in Math. None of my friends. Mr. Baker seems fine. We have to cover our books. Even Hattie Lewis had very little to say about American Poetry except that we have to cover our books which contain it. Hattie Lewis, who opened my eyes to books and the world, to whom I owe the very act of writing in a journal, had little to say except that we have to cover our books. It says something about school that the first thing our mentors tell us is to cover up tomes of knowledge with recycled paper bags. Or maybe it doesn't. I only had time for half a cup of coffee this morning, and the coffee available here where I am editing this is extremely bitter, like the author/editor herself.

At least in English I have friends – Kate Gordon, the Queen Bee, was in there, and so is Jennifer Rose Milton whose name is so beautiful I must always write it out, completely: Jennifer Rose Milton. Her mother is Joanne Milton, the beautiful French teacher who has written a cookbook of all the recipes contained in Proust. To give you an idea of how beautiful Jennifer Rose Milton is, she can call her mother *Maman* and no one minds. Gabriel was there, too, although he might have to transfer out to make his schedule work. Gabriel Gallon is the kindest boy in the world, and somehow the San Francisco Unified School District Computer System has figured that out and likes to torture him. Today he will attend three English classes and four gym classes, even though he's a senior and isn't supposed to have gym at all. Jennifer Rose Milton came in late and sat far away from me, but Kate sat right next to me and we exchanged heaven-help-us glances about book covering for a full forty minutes. As the bell rang we compared schedules and learned that we

16

have only English together. Jennifer Rose Milton glided toward us and hugged us all, Gabriel first, then Kate, then me. "I wish I could talk," she said, "but I must run. *Maman* says the first meeting of the Grand Opera Breakfast Club is tomorrow, so see you then if not before." She flew out, followed by Gabriel, who was hoping to catch our guidance counselor, an enormous Cuban woman who lives in an office with three electric fans and no overhead lighting. There are always suspicious-looking students glowering around her like bodyguards; going in to have forms signed is a little like discussing détente with a banana republic's dictator. "Viva la Revolution!" I shouted to him as he left, and half a dozen students looked at me quizzically. Kate threw her head back and laughed, though there's no way she could have gotten the joke; she has the other senior guidance counselor, a warm, friendly woman *sans* fans. Kate, though, will never admit to not getting the joke. It's as if we would depose her. We clasped hands – "Be strong!" she mock-whispered – and she had to go off. I wanted to hear firsthand about her conversation with Adam re those letters he had received from some breathless woman, but there wasn't time. Perhaps at Grand Opera Breakfast tomorrow.

What you'd like to hear about, of course, is the first face-to-face meeting with Adam. But as with the difference between authority and authoritarianism, it's hard to talk about something that barely exists. As my bleary-eyed first take at my schedule indicated, I knew I'd see him in choir – he's the student conductor, which isn't just something to write down on his college applications. It's that Johnny Hand is a dim lush who wanders in and out of choir rehearsals and occasionally performs meandering show tunes from his either long-dead or entirely fictitious nightclub act. Adam handles all the music and teaches it to us. So the first meeting of choir consisted of the one hundred or so members (ninety of whom are female) milling around the rehearsal hall while Adam sat in a folding chair, in conference with the other choir officers, trying to figure out what the hell to do. Johnny Hand was nowhere to be seen – he probably needed jump-starting somewhere. Adam saw me as I came in and gave me a half wave and rolled his eyes. I sat down and wondered whether the eye rolling meant he wished he could talk to me instead of talking to the chirpy president, vice president, secretary and treasurer, or that he can't believe I had the courage to catch his eye.

On the way out of choir, I passed the room where the band and orchestra rehearse. Rolling their eyes, Douglas Wilde, my ex, and his girlfriend Lily Chandly, strolled out carrying their instrument cases. He is a violinist, she a cellist so there's no bitterness here because she's much better for Douglas; I'm practically tone-deaf and anyway, I broke up with *him*. Douglas, as usual, was dressed to the hilt in an off-white linen suit, complete with pressed handkerchief and pocket watch. Dating him was a bit like being in an old movie. I hugged them both, each in turn. Douglas, the dear, didn't mind – it was, as they say in tabloids, an amicable parting – but Lily emitted such a glare that I was thankful that those were true instrument cases and not Mafioso euphemisms. Had I written to these people during the summer I wouldn't have to re-establish anything. Douglas had to rush off (after disentangling himself from Lily's smugly possessive good-bye kiss), but I stayed with her as she went to her locker. She handed over her computerized schedule card and I discovered that we were about to have lunch together.

"I think it's great that you two are still together," I said as we sat down at one of the appropriate benches in the courtyard. Like homing pigeons, all the right people were in all the right places after summer break.

"Yes, me too," Lily said, relaxing a little bit. I could see her remembering that she was my friend and not my rival. I spied Natasha and waved for her to come over; she saw me and walked across the courtyard, accompanied by – I swear I could hear it – the clatter of male jaws dropping to asphalt. She had taken off her black leather jacket as the day got hotter and was wearing a translucent tank top that made the following fashion statement: *Here are my nipples*. That may sound bitterly envious, but that's only because I am.

"Same shit, different year," she said by way of greeting. She grasped Lily's well-combed head and kissed both cheeks. "Tonight I get to make flash cards of the periodic chart. How's the scrumptious Jim Carr?"

"I haven't had him yet."

"Well, give yourself time," she said, taking out a blood-red metallic lunch box decorated with lacquered photographs of her idol, Marlene Dietrich. Where does she find these things? "It's only the first day. Oh, how was *choir*?"

Lily looked up from her apple. "What's in choir?"

"Flan's current flame," Natasha whispered.

Lily looked relieved and I was thankful that Natasha let her know that I wasn't after Douglas. "Who? Have you been dating someone this summer?"

"She spent all summer in Europe," Natasha said, opening her lunch box. Inside it were twelve large shrimp in a bag filled with ice, and a small container of cocktail sauce. "Not that anybody received as much as a postcard." Natasha and Lily turned to me and tut-tutted in unison. Why hadn't I sent postcards to them instead?

Lily took another bite of apple. "So if Flannery isn't seeing someone, how can she have a current flame?" Only Lily would want to get the terminology straight before finding out who the mystery man was. Is.

"The candle," Natasha said, shrimp between teeth, "is not yet burning at both ends. He doesn't know yet."

Lily nodded sagely. She was ready. "Who is he?"

I sighed. This part was always a little embarrassing. "Adam State."

"*Adam State*?" she screeched, and the apple dropped out of her hands and rolled into the middle of the courtyard. Everybody was quiet and stared at it. Natasha, of course, broke the silence.

"*To the fairest!*" she cried, and people laughed and went back to their lunches. Though I'm sure nobody but us understood the Homeric reference, everyone understood Natasha doing something crazy.

"Having a crush on Adam State is like having a crush on Moses," Lily said matter-of-factly. "He's too busy doing his own thing to notice you."

"In *The Ten Commandments* Moses had a lover," Natasha said, absently.

"*The Ten Commandments* is not a documentary, Natasha," Lily said, and looked me over like a talent scout examining a piece of meat. "Flannery, I wouldn't bet on his candle getting lit." She took her napkin from her lunch bag and began to clean her tortoiseshell glasses.

"I heard he just broke up with somebody," Natasha said, fluttering her hands in a gesture that indicated that she may have heard this from the wind.

I tried to sound worldly and confident. "He is the only appropriate person for me to like," I said, and Natasha and Lily exchanged a look. Natasha said nothing and

20

finished her shrimp, and Lily put her glasses back on. I watched her hands as they absent-mindedly practiced cello fingerings at her side. Lily will probably attend a conservatory next year. I think she lost some weight over the summer. What was that look about? Did someone have a crush on me? The sun glinted on the apple, but the gods didn't seem interested today. Maybe they had to cover their books. I'd better stop all this description now, because I'm in Civics and my teacher, Gladys Tall, who lives *up* to her name, is getting suspicious. I couldn't possibly be taking this many notes on her lecture, because the notes would have to look like this: *cover your book cover your book cover your book*

Wednesday, September 8th

Would that everything in life began with the Grand Opera Breakfast Club. For those who have opened the time capsule and found this journal as the sole chosen memento for this wondrous century, let me elucidate: The Grand Opera Breakfast Club is a precious stone that killed two birds that flew around the head of Joanne Milton, Roewer's best French teacher and mother of Jennifer Rose Milton. One bird was the fact that Jennifer Rose Milton's friends (that is Kate, Gabriel, Natasha, myself, etc.) always weaseled our way into French with Mrs. Milton (it's so strange to write that – to us she will always be *Millie*) and not entirely inadvertently turned it into what we called a *salon* but what the head of the department told Millie was *socializing*, even if it was in French. The other bird was in the form of our principal, an ex-football coach named Jean Bodin who is as large as a truck and half as smart. He was giving Millie a bad time for not sponsoring a club. Every faculty member was supposed to sponsor a club.

It was Jennifer Rose Milton, beautiful Jennifer Rose Milton, who had the idea. It was when *she* was going out with Douglas, and he was trying to woo her away from the wispy-voiced feminist songwriters she liked to put in her tape deck by steering her toward the classics. So, over dinner with *Maman*, Jennifer Rose Milton conceived of the Grand Opera Breakfast Club, an organization so pretentious that no one but our friends would join it, which would enable us to have a *salon* after all, except not in French, and would give Millie a club to sponsor. Once a week or so we'd meet before school in a classroom, listen to opera and eat breakfast. In her gratitude, Millie volunteered to buy the pastries.

This morning was *La Boheme*, and so was the opera, if you catch my meaning. Millie, Jennifer Rose Milton, Douglas, Kate, Gabriel, Natasha, and V——: I felt for the first time that I was amongst comrades and that we were all facing the new year together. Of course we couldn't meet two whole hours before classes began, so we only listened to the first act, with the artist/lovers meeting in their garret. We munched and listened. We got powdered sugar all over the libretto. Douglas, in a dark blue three-piece suit, tried to lecture us; we shushed him. Gradually the burnt play, the shirked rent, the pawned key all became background for our own small dramas.

"I can't believe all my babies are seniors," Millie said, adding accent marks to someone's homework with a leaky red pen. A single red drop stained her cheek like a bloody tear; I note this image now for a future poem.

"I can *certainly* believe it," Natasha said. She was looking in a small hand mirror and examining her lipstick for flaws — she might as well have been examining it for the crown jewels which were just as likely to be there. "Douglas, what were you saying Marcello had to do?"

"Not Marcello, *Schaunard*. He's telling the story right now," Douglas said, and his eyes lit up. I think one of the reasons it ended was that his eyes never lit up for me the way they did for classical music. I realize that in the long run I may not be as wonderful as a Brahms symphony but I think I'm good for a Haydn quintet. "He was hired to play for a duke, and –"

"*Lord*," Kate corrected, looking up from the libretto.

"Well, a *royal*, anyway. The lord told him he had to play the violin until his parrot died."

"I'm sorry," V__ said, fingering her pearls. The pearls were real; she wore *real* pearls to *high school*. "How and why did a starving musician have a pet parrot?"

"The *lord's* parrot," Douglas said. "Honestly, V__."

"*The Lord's Parrot*," I said, "will be the name of my first play."

"Your first play for whom?" Natasha asked, raising an eyebrow delicately highlighted with glitter. Maybe the crown jewels were to be found on her face, after all.

"Hush, you savages," Douglas said. "Anyway, Marcello has to play until the parrot dies."

"Well, my point, lost somewhere in all this, is that that's how I've been feeling. We've been at Roewer all this time, waiting for some goddamn parrot to die." Natasha took another doughnut. What I would do to be able to take another doughnut and still look as good as she does.

Douglas thought for a second. "Well, Marcello manages to bribe the maid into poisoning the parrot. Who could we bribe?"

"To kill whom?" Lily said, always demanding accuracy. It was still early, so none of her hip-length hair had strayed from her sculptured bun. "Who is the parrot in this situation?"

23

"*Bodin*," Millie said, muttering the name of our beloved principal under her breath, and then, suffering from a rare bout of professionalism, looked up from another scarred homework assignment, saying, "Who said that? I didn't say that."

"Killing Bodin would be extremely difficult," Natasha said. "Digging a grave that large would be six weeks' work."

"Is there some creative murder method in *La Boheme*?" Kate asked in a tone of voice meant to imply that she once knew the answer, but it had slipped her mind.

"Nobody gets killed, they just get sick," Douglas said, and drew out his pocket watch. "It's almost homeroom," he said.

"Then we'd much rather discuss something of infinitely more importance," Kate said, "like the first dinner party of the season."

"*That's* more like it," Gabriel said.

Kate pulled out a spiral notebook. "I was thinking this Saturday, if everyone's free." We all nodded; we'd postpone surgery for one of our dinner parties.

"Let's make a list," Lily said, licking jelly off her fingers.

"You and your *lists*," V___ said fondly, swatting at her. Lily kissed her on the cheek. "I can't have it at my house, even though I'd love to. My parents are entertaining."

"*Your* parents? *Entertaining*?" Kate asked in mock surprise. Her parents are *always* entertaining, though in person they are *never* entertaining, if you follow me. We've never had a dinner party at V___'s house, even though each time she says she'd love to.

"We'll have it at *my* house," Kate pronounced. "Now, a guest list."

24

"Well, everyone here," Lily said, counting us off on her fingers. "There's Flannery, Gabriel –"

"Yes, yes, yes," Kate said. "We don't have to list all of *us*. We're you know, the basics." She scribbled down our names on a piece of paper. "The Basic Eight."

"Are there only eight of us?" Jennifer Rose Milton asked. "We're such a menagerie it seems like more."

"Yep, just eight. The Basic Eight are as follows: Kate Gordon, Natasha Hyatt, Jennifer Rose Milton, Flannery Culp, Lily Chandly, V——, Douglas Wilde and Gabriel Gallon."

"Why are the men last?" V—— asked.

"If you have to ask . . ." Natasha said, rolling her eyes.

". . . you can't afford it," I finished, and Natasha smiled at me.

"Who else shall we invite besides, um, the Basic Eight?" Lily asked.

"How about Lara Trent?" Gabriel asked. "I've always thought she was nice."

"*Absolutely not*," Natasha Hyatt said. "Such a *drip*."

Jennifer Rose Milton put her hands on her hips. "She can't be that bad. Let's invite her. We'll give her a chance."

"*Absolutely not*," Natasha said. "She once told me I wasn't a good Christian."

We all threw up our hands and said "*No!*" in unison. One thing we don't tolerate is organized religion. Right-wing parent activists are going to love that sentence, but loath as I am to give any ammunition to those who are frothing at the mouth about our godless schools, it's true.

"How about Adam State?" Kate asked. She met my eyes quietly, and I appreciated her tact, which was a little out of character. Not that Kate is the sort to tease about our romantic inclinations, but she might at least raise her eyebrows. Just about everyone must have known about me and Adam, so just about everyone waited for me to answer.

"He seems a little conceited to me," Gabriel said. Don't smirk at me, reader; I said *just about* everyone, not *everyone*.

"And we *certainly* don't want any *egotism*," Natasha said. "*Heaven forfend*. We don't want to be friends with anyone who's at all self-important." Millie snorted in the corner at that.

"I think he's nice," I said, casually. I'm sorry, I didn't write that in a way that properly conveyed the mood. "I think he's nice," I said, CASUALLY.

"I do too," Lily said, loyally, and Kate wrote him down.

"How about Flora Habstat? She's my only friend in homeroom."

Kate narrowed her eyes and sighed. "It's always difficult to tell if someone's interesting in homeroom. The setting is so dull, how can anyone really shine?"

"Well, let's try her," Jennifer Rose Milton said, and Kate wrote her down.

Natasha pulled out her hand mirror again. "Can I just warn you guys about something? I've heard that Flora constantly quotes the *Guinness Book of World Records*."

"*What*?" V— said. "I know her, and I've never heard her do that."

"That's just what I've heard," Natasha said, airily. Kate and I exchanged a look. We were both wondering if we were missing some obscure joke.

"Who else?" Kate said. The bell rang.

Idea for a story: A man falls in love with a woman and writes her letter after letter. We never read the letters she writes to him. His love grows and grows through the letters. He can't stand it anymore. Then something drastic happens . . . but what?

O my boggled head, around which numbers spun all period. The second day of school and I'm already lost in Calc. I covered my book last night, just like everybody else, but after that I got lost. I looked around me – no friends in that class, none at all – and everyone was taking notes, nodding along with Baker and his spirals of chalk. My mind sputtered and began to sink. I clung to the life jacket of sketching out story outlines. I think when I reread my journal this year I'll always be able to tell when I was in Calc by the paragraphs of story entries.

For some reason we got out of Baker's class early. The bell system here is computerized, which means of course that it doesn't work; the bells ring, ignored, at random, as if a loud, unruly ice-cream man is wandering around Roewer High School. Baker let us out of class and the hallways were nearly deserted. I arrived early for Poetry, which was a gift. Hattie Lewis was there.

Hattie Lewis likes to tell her students stories from when she was young, but I can't quite believe those stories because it seems that she must have been born a wise old woman. Her classroom is her lair. It's industrial and ugly like everyone else's classrooms, but it has an aura of classiness and culture. For one thing, there aren't any faded travel posters or soft-focus photographs of sunsets with "Reach For Your Dreams" superimposed over them up on the walls, but the aura transcends the cheap Impressionist reproductions that have replaced them. It comes from *her*. She doesn't have to tell anybody not to chew gum; they just know it. She dresses more ridiculously than any other Roewer teacher (and the competition is stiff) – all crazy-quilted skirts and vests with embroidered flora – but no one laughs, even when she's not around. Her first name is Hattie, but no one has a mean nickname for her. Showing up early for her class and thus being alone with her felt like showing up early for Judgment Day and getting to hang out with the angels before the crowds arrive. (It sounds like I mean it felt like death. Calculus must still be crowding my brain.)

Our conversation was about the literary magazine, of which I am editor. She's the faculty sponsor. Our first meeting is tomorrow after school. I can't forget about it.

LIT MEETING TOMORROW!!!

I asked her what poets we'd be studying this year, and was embarrassed when she listed all these names I had never heard of. I mean, I recognize Robert Frost, and of course e. e. cummings, but I consider myself a poet and had never heard of these people. She must have seen my face as I struggled to hide my ignorance.

"Relax," she said. "You *will* be wise. You're young. You can't have everything right away." When something simple and true takes you by surprise, it hits you in the stomach. Before I could say anything people starting piling in. Hattie Lewis didn't skip a beat. She had us all sit down and she spent the rest of the period talking about Anne Bradstreet. I took notes; I had never heard of Anne Bradstreet.

Now I'm in choir, and even with Adam still gathered in a corner with the other officers, the calm of Hattie Lewis's words comforts me. I can't have everything right away. Plus, sometimes it's enough to watch him. Still no sign of Mr. Hand, the real choir teacher.

From a spiral-bound notebook passed between two desks in Gladys Tall's fifth-period Applied Civics class, taped into these typed pages:

Kate, what is Mrs. T talking about? I've been staring out the window.

Tell me about it. You were far, far away. I've had to roll my eyes at myself all period.

Sorry. I didn't get much sleep last night.

Flan, what did I tell you about whoring on school nights? You're always tired and grumpy the next day. I'm going to call your pimp and give him a piece of my mind. If he doesn't reschedule your hours you'll never get into a good college.

You *must* stop writing things like that to me. I don't think Mrs. Tall bought the fact that I found the concept of supply and demand humorous.

On a much more important note, I saw Adam today but I didn't invite him to the dinner party. I thought you might want to.

You know him better.

You want *to* know *him better.*

Still, I'm waiting for him to call *me*.

You need an excuse before you can call somebody. He doesn't have an excuse to call you. Anyway, somebody else is after him, so you better get moving. He said that somebody had written him love letters all summer.

The notebook wasn't passed anymore, despite there being a full fifteen minutes left of class.

Jim Carr has eyes like a hawk, so I can't write much in here, but I would like to note that for the seventh semester in a row – every semester I've been here – Mr. Carr has managed to find a curvaceous female education grad student to serve as his teaching assistant. Most teachers here don't have any teaching assistants at all, except for the occasional French friend of Millie's who needs work, but Carr manages to find a bevy of them. There are a lot of stupid biology jokes to be made here, but my beautiful expensive Italian leather-bound black journal is too nice for such cracks.

Home again, home again. I'm bored of my routine already, and it's the second day of school. Natasha picked me up from Bio – "Is that this year's model?" she asked, glaring at the assistant – and walked me to French, trying all the way to convince me that *I* should invite Adam to the party. Finally she said I could think it over tonight and that otherwise Kate'd do it tomorrow. My plan is that he'll call *me* tonight, and I, quasi-spontaneously, will invite him to the party. After I hang up the phone, I will go out to the garden and frolic with my pet unicorn, which just as surely exists as the rest of my scenario. Sigh. Gotta go read some Bradstreet. She's an early American poet; what do you mean you've never heard of her?

Thursday, September 9th
This morning when I went outside I found that the newsprint from the *Chronic Ill* (as it is called by a rather fuddy-duddy columnist) had spread from my fingertips

to the whole wide sky. I got off the bus and stared at the traffic, trying to think of a very good reason to cross it and walk up the three-block San Francisco hill to school, when V—— pulled up in her car and opened her door in one swift swoop. She said nothing, just beckoned, and I got in. Inside it was warm and V—— was playing the Brandenberg Concertos.

"Bless you!" I shouted. "Bless you!"

V—— merged. "I didn't sneeze," she said. "Although you are going to get a cold if you continue to insist on taking the bus each morning." Like many people of noble descent, V—— often assumed that everyone's habits were born of personal choice and not necessity; why people *chose* to live in war-ravaged countries was always beyond her.

"Hey, this is the faculty parking lot."

"I always park here. The student lot is simply too shabby."

"What about the parking guards?"

"Flannery, look at me. They're never sure if I'm a teacher or not." She was right. The tailored suit, along with the stockings and omnipresent pearls, brought her to that nebulous area between eighteen and twenty-eight. It was very handy when we went to nightclubs. We walked right past the parking guards, who were two huge black men. She even nodded to them, professionally.

When we reached the front doors we had to go our separate ways. "Lily and I are having coffee after school," V—— said, "and I'd be delighted if you would join us."

"Sorry," I said. "The *Myriad* meets today. Got to do the literary editor thing. Thanks for the ride."

"Anything," she said, reaching up and fixing my collar, "for one of the Basic Eight."

"Don't tell me that term has been canonized," I said. "I'm not sure I like it. It sounds too much like some mystical society, or like something concerned with a master race."

V—— thought for a second. "I – ," she said, and the bell rang. She dashed off, and that was the last of any discussion about the propriety of the term. But I've typed it into the record: it was never a concept with which I was comfortable. So all this talk that the Basic Eight was some unholy alliance, some secret society, should stop with this conversation. Whatever we were, we were bound together unofficially, casually; and I objected to it loudly from the start. Or would have, anyway; the truth of the matter is that I walked all the way to school, but that conversation happened *sometime*, surely; plus, I needed to fully introduce V—— and voice my objections to my reading public, to all wary parents and curious teenagers.

Idea for a story: A woman loves a man, but through some slip of the tongue everyone thinks it is the wrong man, including the wrong man himself, who begins to pursue her. When she finally makes the truth clear, all of society shuns her as a woman who leads men on. She dies alone. The story could be called "A Slip of the Tongue."

I didn't go to choir today. I just couldn't take it. Luckily, some people have lunch third period (yes, *lunch, third period*, at a time that's even a little early for *brunch*. It's sickening that all over America the promising young generation is made to eat at ten-thirty in the morning), so it didn't look like I was cutting class. Of course, I ran into Gabriel, who has the worst schedule on earth, world without end. He was sitting in the courtyard, staring at a sandwich so intently it looked like he was making some sort of political statement: black man, white bread.

"Hi," I said. "You're not seriously thinking of eating lunch at ten-thirty in the morning, are you?"

"Seriously is the only way I can think at ten-thirty in the morning," he said glumly. "The worst thing is that they *still* haven't worked out my schedule. I *still* have to go to gym four times a day. There I sit, a *senior* surrounded by trotting sophomores, baffling gym teachers."

"Quit bragging," I said. "It's not difficult to baffle gym teachers. Listen, will you take a walk with me? I can't face going to choir."

"Why?" he said. "Calculus I could understand, but *choir*? I thought nothing ever happened in choir."

"It doesn't," I said. "I'll tell you about it as we walk."

"To the lake?" he asked, rewrapping his sandwich.

"To the lake," I agreed. By the time this diary is found, the plates of the earth will probably have moved and covered up Lake Merced, a small body of bile across the street from Roewer surrounded by fairly pretty groves of trees amidst which you can find the occasionally intertwined pair.

I didn't even wait until we got there, though, to tell Gabriel everything. I told him I had an unrequited crush as soon as we reached the tennis courts at the edge of campus, which lay damp and empty and clogged with dull brown leaves. I told him that it wasn't just a crush but love as we jaywalked across the cracked asphalt that separated Roewer from Lake Merced. I told him it was Adam State when we reached the jogging path, littered with dogshit and somebody's dingy discarded sweatband.

33

"Adam State?" he said, doubtfully, as if I had misspoken.

"Why does everybody say it like that?" I said, stepping off the path, toward the trees.

"Because they're surprised," he said. "Douglas we expected. He's as pretentious as the rest of us. But *Adam State*? How did you even end up talking to him?"

"He was in *Arsenic and Old Lace* last year, remember? Adam and I both had small parts, so we ended up talking a lot. That's when I knew."

"I can't believe you're calling it *love* when you don't even have a relationship with him."

I can remember my speech word for word, even though I'm writing it after school as I wait for lit magazine people to show up, and yes, even one year later as I'm rewriting it. "Gabriel, there are two kinds of love. One kind is gradual, like what I had with Douglas. We were acquaintances, we were friends, we were more than friends, we were in love. It was steady, like warming soup. It's part of a process that people go through with everybody – like with me and you, for instance. We warmed through acquaintance to friend, and we won't warm any further. But the other kind is more like Cajun cooking. Like pan-blackening something." I knew this metaphor would connect with Gabriel because he cooks for all our dinner parties. "It just strikes you. It's just as delicious. It's just as real. In fact it's probably more real; it's an entrée rather than a soup. That's how I feel about Adam. It's a connection, a connection bigger and stronger, in many ways, than I ever had with Douglas. It's not all about the façades of shared interests or attitudes. It's something deeper."

"Then there's no need to despair," Gabriel said, looking elsewhere. It was almost as if he were talking to himself. "If it's something that goes beyond all façades, then it's out of your control. If it's meant to be, he'll respond. If not, then it wasn't meant to be. I know when *I'm* feeling something that strong, I just get paralyzed and don't know what to do. Maybe he's feeling the same way and doesn't know how to respond."

"Do you really think so?" I said, hugging him. I watched his hands flutter around for a minute before hugging me back.

"We're going to be late," Gabriel said, but when I told him it was my lunch period he agreed to stay by the lake. "I suppose I can cut my third English class of the day." We rounded a corner and there was Jennifer Rose Milton, sitting on the grass in the middle of a clearing. She jumped up.

"Hi guys," she said, looking behind us. "What are you doing here?"

"Having a conversation, Jenn," I said. I don't call her "Jennifer Rose Milton" out loud, of course. "What are *you* doing here? Alone?"

"Oh, you know," she said vaguely, gesturing toward the lake. "I'm just —"

Gabriel turned and gave me a *look*. "We'd better go," he said. "We'll be late."

"Right, OK," I said, and Jennifer Rose Milton smiled. We walked away and back toward school. "She must be meeting somebody," I said. "And it must be somebody special. She doesn't have lunch with me. She's cutting a class. Jenn *never* cuts class. Her grades are *perfect*. Let's go get coffee."

"You'll have to miss more than lunch," he warned.

I shrugged. "Civics, Bio. I'll be back in time for Millie. We can walk to the Mocha Monkey."

We walked to the Mocha Monkey. The Mocha Monkey is an embarrassing cafe, but it's the only one within walking distance of Roewer. We usually end up there after school dances; it's also one of the few cafes open late. It's embarrassing not only for its name but also for the monkey faces *embroidered* on each of the chairs. You can try to have a meaningful conversation, but all the while in the back of your head you know you're sitting on a monkey's face. I ordered a latte and Gabriel had tea, which was served in its own individual pot with a monkey's face painted on it. The two of us sat there for most of the afternoon, talking and laughing there in the monkey house.

Lit meeting went fine. Jennifer Rose Milton came, of course, and so did Natasha. And so did . . . drumroll please . . . none other than Rachel State, freshman sister of Adam, a waif of a girl swathed in black clothes and white makeup. Natasha nicknamed her The Frosh Goth on the way home, as we sat in her car listening to Darling Mud and trying to think of ways I can abuse my power as editor in chief to get to Adam through his gloomy sister. She invited me to spend the night (there was a Dietrich movie on TV she wanted me to watch with her), but I declined, not that I attended enough classes today to have much homework. But I wanted to read Bradstreet, and write some poetry of my own, and think about wise Gabriel's words about what was meant to be.

Friday September 10
While I sat around last night waiting for Adam to call, somebody must have sacrificed a lamb or something, because all of yesterday's gray was all burned off, and by the time I was riding the bus to school the sun was searing through the tinted windows like something that killed all the dinosaurs. I reached into my bag and immediately found my sunglasses in a rare case of

morning luck. I put them on and didn't talk to anyone. I looked for V___ when I got off the bus, hoping that V___'s gorgeous car could become a permanent morning motif, but as yesterday's ride was added, as you remember, one year later in rewrites, V___ of course was nowhere to be seen.

Halfway up the hill, however, Kate tapped me on the shoulder. "I've been calling out your name for an hour and a half," she said. "You walk extremely fast. *Quickly*, rather. Didn't you hear me?"

"Well, for most of an hour and a half ago I was home, across town, so no," I said.

Kate rolled her eyes. "Hey," she said, "did you invite Adam to our dinner party last night?"

"No," I said, "and I don't want to talk about it."

"OK," she said, lining up a new subject like the next bullet in the chamber. "I wish to attend an extremely modern event tonight, with you if you're free: the cinema."

"What's playing?"

"It's Benjamin Granaugh's new movie. *Henry IV*." Kate was the only one of us who could successfully pronounce *Granaugh* every time.

"Of course I'll go. Want to do dinner beforehand?"

"Sure. And speaking of dinner, do you want me to invite Adam for you? Not to discuss the undiscussable." But discussing it anyway.

"I guess you'd better. We shouldn't hold our breath waiting for me to make a move."

"Well, suit yourself." By now we were at the side entrance, which is closest to Kate's homeroom. The PTA had placed a welcoming sign there which said: "WELCOME! HOPE YOUR SUMMER PREPARED YOU FOR A YEAR WHERE YOU WILL BE PUSHED TO THE

LIMIT ACADEMICALLY, ATHLETICALLY AND SOCIALLY!" framed by smiling faces drawn in Magic Marker. I'm pretty sure it should be "a year *in which* you will be pushed." Kate leaned against the doorway and absentmindedly poked one of the faces in its eye. "It will be a shame, though, if Adam gets stolen by somebody who writes *love letters* to him over the summer. To introduce yourself like that over the summer, when nobody can do anything about it, is so tacky, don't you think?"

"Speaking of love lives," I said, plowing on, "do you know if Jenn is seeing anyone?"

"That's one of my missions for today," Kate announced. "Do you know that she cut class yesterday and went to the lake? Gabriel told me. If she was meeting somebody, it must be somebody *very interesting* if she doesn't want us to know."

"I was with Gabriel," I said, eager to be considered a primary player in all this intrigue. "She acted really flustered when Gabriel and I ran into her. She was definitely meeting *somebody*. I can't believe *you* don't know who it is yet. Are you losing your touch, Mata Hari?"

"*Certainly not*," Kate said, archly. "I just found out about this lake incident late last night. Give me time."

The bell rang. "Time is something I don't have," I said. "I've got to run to my date with Lawrence."

"*Who?*" she shrieked after me, but I didn't look back. You're always guaranteed more attention from Kate if you keep her on the edge of her seat.

Saturday September 11th

Waking up this morning felt like a logistical problem, but though I haven't solved it I have identified what the

38

problem is. I am large. No, Flannery, say it outright: I am *fat*. I forgot to pull my shades down last night so morning came on like gangbusters. The sun reminded me of that woman riding six white horses in "Comin' round the Mountain." Then I began to feel like the mountain. I moved one leg, then the other, to the floor. Gradually I became aware of how much room even half my body took up in this bed. It was startling: I remove half my body from the bed, and my bed stays full. Now either Archimedes was wrong and none of us really take up any space at all or I just hadn't noticed my full load lately. If only half of me fills the bed, I wondered to myself sleepily, is that because I have small legs, or is it for some other reason?

Small legs – fat chance. I walked into the bathroom and the scales simultaneously rose beneath my feet and fell from my eyes. I'm not going to write down the number here in this expensive Italian leather-bound journal, but rest assured, for those who crave statistics, that the sum of my parts is truly elephantine. All that bullshit I was crowing to Gabriel down by the lake – how there's no attraction between us – all that isn't rooted in some achieved platonic ideal, it's rooted in my own generous thighs. Nobody wants me because I'm large and ugly. I looked at myself in the mirror, naked, and assessed myself like the headmistress of a girls' finishing school. I'm large and ugly.

It's funny, you'd think that ugliness is pretty much innate and that there isn't anything you can do about it, but if you think about it logically that's not true. After all, I'm not just ugly; I'm also large. If I were smaller, there wouldn't just be less of the largeness, there'd be less of the ugliness, too. And if someone has less ugliness than they did before, one could just as well say they have more beauty. Kate called me to ask which Bradstreets we were supposed to read, and I ran my theory by her.

"Kate," I said, after reading her some titles and page numbers I had somehow managed to write down, "if one person were less ugly than another, we could also say they were *more beautiful*, right?"

"What are you talking about?" Kate said. "Does this have to do with Adam? He's coming tonight, you know."

"I know," I said glumly. There was no way I was going to be small and beautiful by tonight. "No, this doesn't have to do with Adam. I'm just asking, theoretically, if a person got less ugly could it be said that they got more beautiful?"

"Well," Kate said dryly. Kate was saying things dryly, I was saying them glumly. I think these adverbial embellishments make the conversation sound less stark. "This is just theoretical?"

"Right," I said. "Theoretical. You know, like any intellectual conversation."

"Well," Kate said, and this time she said it carefully. "Well," Kate said carefully, "I would have to disagree with your statement. Martin Luther King said that peace was not merely the absence of violence but the presence of a positive force, or something like that, and I think it's the same thing with beauty. I mean, you don't look at some vast and beautiful landscape and think, *There's nothing ugly here*."

Kate's well-meaning smoke screen hasn't foiled my unshakable logic, and I will extend it further. A less fat body makes a more beautiful person, so we need something that makes a less fat body, and of course we all know what makes a body less fat: less food. When I think of all the food I consumed just last night I am sick at my extravagance, and judging from my fat legs, my fat stomach, even my fat arms, this sort of extravagance goes on all the time. All that Thai food I ate last night for instance, that chicken dish and those greasy, greasy fried egg rolls, the grease of which luckily seems to have found its way to my hair instead of my body. The chocolate-covered mints at the movie. I will hereby dismiss, again, my justification that dieting is some tacky Middle American bourgeois pastime. It is very sensible, dieting. Simply eating less food and thus becoming more beautiful. To no other problem in life is there such an elegant solution. To start my diet I will not eat anything until the dinner party tonight, and then I will only eat sensibly, just salad perhaps. No longer will I allow myself to become as large as any of the obstacles that separate Adam and me from each other. To keep my mind off food I will do some schoolwork, thus also taking care of my other Cardinal Sin besides Gluttony: (Academic) Sloth. I will read Anne Bradstreet, another disciplined woman.

LATER

If there were any seeds of doubt in my mind as to whether I really loved Adam or just some image of Adam, they were all killed by the frost that was tonight's dinner party. No, wait, that sounds like it was some cold, deadly evening. I mean the opposite. I guess I mean that if the flower of my love for Adam was being stunted by any feelings of doubt, then tonight fully fertilized my seed and allowed it to grow. That works if you don't think about the fact that fertilizer is made of shit. I guess it's obvious I've had wine, but the evening was magical, magical, magical and I want to write it down before it evaporates into the night air like streams of sensual smoke.

Gabriel gave me a ride to Kate's, which meant we had to arrive early so Gabriel could start cooking. Gabriel is terribly, terribly fussy about his culinarities, and never lets us do anything, not even chop, so Kate and I sat at the kitchen table and speculated on possibilities concerning Jennifer Rose Milton's love life while Gabriel marinated some snapper and chopped red peppers with such ferocity that the off-white tiles of Kate's kitchen looked positively gory. Gabriel had a pure white apron over a very handsome coat and tie and kept smiling at me.

Natasha arrived, bearing cleavage and brie, and immediately fell into a squabble with Gabriel over how to bake it properly. Kate and I sat basking in the pretentiousness of it all.

"I have a full pound of celery to chop and it's already a quarter to seven," Gabriel said, wiping his hands on his apron. They left faint red handprints like the frantic last flailings of a victim. Who could have known?

"I'm telling you, Gabe," she said, incurring his least favorite of her nicknames for him; he preferred 'Riel pronounced "real" or Gall pronounced "gall." "A tablespoon of olive oil. It gives the whole thing some lubrication."

"To most areas where knowledge of lubrication is key, I yield to your expertise. But *olive oil* on *brie*? This isn't fucking mozzarella, Natasha!"

"Hey now!" I said. Gabriel seemed unusually tense, even for a new recipe. "Do I have to separate you two?" They continued to glare at each other and it struck me that maybe there was something going on that I didn't know about.

"For God's sake," Kate said, and flounced across the kitchen. She picked up the *Palatial Palate Cookbook* and thumbed through the index. The two litigants stood stock-still – Gabriel arms akimbo, Natasha clutching the brie like Hamlet holding the skull, waiting for Kate to render her decision. She played it to the hilt, flipped pages, flipped pages, flipped pages. Finally she spoke. "Ahem. I quote directly from Ms. Julia Mann in her section on brie baking: 'The addition of any oil to brie, or any other soft-ripening cheese, prior to baking, is redundant at best, disastrous at worst.'"

Gabriel tried not very hard to conceal a smug grin. Natasha glowered first at Gabriel, then Kate, then for no good reason, me. You could hear a pin drop.

And then a brie. It was wrapped in plastic, so there wasn't a mess, but the fall to the floor left the cheese looking wounded and misshapen. It was such a pathetic sight that I couldn't help but giggle, and in one of those magical tension-loosening moments that I believe float aimlessly around the planet, easing awkward situations worldwide, everyone broke out laughing. Gabriel put his arm around Natasha, and Natasha put her arm around Gabriel, and there we were, all laughing in a circle around a fallen brie, when Adam walked in.

The first thing I saw were his shoes, which were black and thick – the direct opposite of Adam, come to think of it. My eyes just went up his jeans, up the row of buttons on his Oxford, uneven like a lazy fence out in the country somewhere, up his freshly shaven chin to his smile to his bright green eyes, and I felt myself fall right into his pupils.

"The door was open," he said apologetically, peering over Natasha's shoulder at the fallen cheese.

"That's because we wanted you to come in," Kate said charmingly, standing up on tiptoe and kissing him on each cheek. Gabriel snorted and went back to the cutting board.

Natasha picked up the cheese with one hand and extended her other one to Adam. "Hello, Adam," she said demurely.

43

Kate returned the cookbook to the cupboard, clearing a path between Adam and Flannery. Their eyes met across the nearly empty room.

"Flannery," he said, and smiled.

"Flannery," he said, and smiled.

"FLANNERY," HE SAID, AND SMILED.

SMILED SMILED SMILED.

Ahem. Not only did he smile at me, he said my name, and there wasn't a question mark after it, as in "Your name is Flannery, am I right?" nor was it a simple, cold acknowledgment, as in, "I recognize you but I'd much rather talk to Natasha, who has cleavage." He smiled; I think, ladies and gentlemen of the jury, we can surmise he was glad to see me.

"Hi," I said. "I'm glad you could make it."

"Me too," he said. Our eyes met, and locked, and I know it's corny to say that but what the hell it's late at night, I'm a little tipsy and besides it's my own journal so who cares.

Kate coughed slightly and we came to. Adam blushed slightly, even; but his shirt was pure white, so it just made him glow even more. Don't think I don't realize the drippiness of this prose.

"Folks," he said – what a charming thing to say! "Folks!" "I know you asked me to bring wine, but I forgot to ask what we're having, so I didn't know whether to bring white or red."

Natasha looked stricken at the thought of no wine. "So you didn't bring any?"

Adam walked over and put a mock-comforting hand on her shoulder, then, electrically, on mine. "Don't worry, my angels," he said in a Prince Charming Voice, "I have a fake ID. I will run to a nearby liquor store and purchase wine for everyone. Just tell me of the entrée."

Gabriel turned from a skillet. "Snapper!" he said shortly, and turned back.

"You certainly are," Natasha said.

Kate stepped forward with a plate of chopped carrots, appeasing all with appetizers. "So, Adam, a couple bottles of white?"

"Sounds good. Can I kidnap one of you who knows about wine? If I go alone I'm bound to come back with lighter fluid."

"Well," Kate said, extending an arm out. I noticed she had done her nails for tonight. "Natasha needs to bake the brie, and Gabriel needs to cook, and the hostess certainly can't leave, so would you, Flannery?"

"Would I? Would I?" I said, and everybody laughed except Adam; it was a favorite joke of the Basic Eight God forgive me, but it's easier to write that nickname than list us all individually. It goes like this: A man loses his job, goes to a bar and gets drunk, and gets into a car accident while driving home. When he gets to the hospital he is told that his eye needs to be replaced with a prosthetic. His recent unemployed status fixed firmly in his mind, he prices several models: an amazingly lifelike and amazingly costly porcelain model, a reasonably lifelike and reasonably costly glass orb and finally the bottom of the line, which he chooses. It's made of wood.

He wakes up from surgery, looks in the mirror, and embarks on the life of a hermit for the next fifteen years. Heedless of the pleas of his friends, he refuses to socialize or even leave the house. Finally, a friend comes to see him, gets him tipsy and drags him to a discotheque. Our hero sits in a corner, hoping the dim ambience is hiding what looks like an ugly mahogany periscope dangling from his face. Then, across a crowded room – the camera swooping between extras – he spots a beautiful woman, sitting quietly alone, who stuns him from her feet to her – the camera sliding up her body – glabrous head! A bald woman! Someone who will understand his pain! Someone undoubtedly alone, because she, too, feels incapacitated by a medically induced deficiency on the head! Breathlessly, he rushes to her and shyly asks, "Would you care to dance?"

Her eyes light up. "Would I?" she repeats. "Would I?"

He turns and stalks away, but not before shouting, "Baldy! Baldy!"

Nothing made me happier than hearing Adam's laughter bounce off Kate's hill and up into the crisp night sky. "That's *wonderful*," he said. "*Wonderful*. So deliciously *evil*."

It was like I was already drunk by the time we arrived at the liquor store. Rows and rows of perfect green bottles shimmered around me like some perfect Egyptian reeds. From the corner of my eye the word "GIN" looked like the word "BEGIN." Even the poses of cigarette poster models didn't seem frozen but poised. Everyone was holding their breath (breaths? Who cares.), and for the first time I felt like they wouldn't be disappointed. It was like watching a movie and the two famous people first meet and you sit in the dark grinning because you know how it ends: They're going to fall in love.

We walked back, each with a bottle, and in the light of the street lamps our shadows looked almost identical. In the movies we would have kissed, but this being paper and not celluloid, we just talked. We discussed being back at school, how neither of us has done any work on college applications and whether Flora Habstat would really quote *The Guinness Book of World Records*.

When we got back the season had truly begun: Darling Mud on the stereo (loud music during cooking, quiet during dinner. Immutable.) and all the guests. V___ and Jennifer Rose Milton, with a slightly geeky-looking Flora Habstat in tow, were tied for most gorgeous, both in black silk pants to their embarrassment. Douglas, of course, was in linen, and, wincing at "on and on and on," was already flipping through records looking for dinner music. It's always his job, that and bringing flowers. Douglas is crazy about flowers. Natasha, who has gone out with him too, said that it felt like he was constantly giving her vaginas, but I felt nothing indecent; I just felt a little overwhelmed by all the xylem and phloem. But Douglas must have been pulling out all financial stops for Lily or something, because there was just a simple vase of daisies on the table. V___ begged Kate to let her polish something. V___ has some strange urges from being raised so rich and one of them is that she needs to have things polished before she can eat off of them. Kate scraped up some silver polish for her, and V___ spent the next fifteen minutes polishing some serving forks which were probably made of stainless steel but it made her happy. By the time we all sat down at the table the serving forks could have lit the room without the candles. Next to all the other tableware they looked like great shining daggers, fresh and ready to claim the life of someone close to us and throw the rest of us into turmoil and heartbreak. Not that Adam was killed with daggers, but it seemed like a good time to foreshadow.

Before we ate came the toasts. Kate, at the head of the table where she belonged and where she will always belong, clinked her glass. "Thank you for coming, ladies and gentlemen, to the first dinner party of the season."

"The season?" Flora Habstat said. "You guys really have a season? Like football?"

V__ looked at Flora in what is described in books as "archly." "*Not at all*," she said huffily, "like football."

"It's just an expression. Kate means the first of the school year," Jennifer Rose Milton explained hurriedly.

Kate sailed on like a queen. "I think we should all go around the table, each of us presenting a toast. I will go first." She cleared her throat and looked down as if collecting her thoughts, though I suspected she wrote the speech this afternoon. She raised her glass by the stem, as V__ had instructed us to do two years ago at our first dinner party. I cringe when I think it was just spaghetti with marinara and garlic bread. We all followed suit, and as my glass cooled my fingertips I felt connected to a long line of literary circles: Oscar Wilde and Dorothy Parker, and what's-her-name, Virginia Woolf, Byron and his friends, even Shakespeare and Company. I was acting in a tradition.

"To all of my guests, both frequent and infrequent," Kate said, bowing regally to Flora Habstat and Adam. "May we generally be happy, generally be witty, generally be honest, but above all always be interesting." We clinked and drank.

Gabriel, the next in clockwise order, was looking at Kate oddly. "And may we always be *friends*," he said. "That's my toast. Better friends than interesting."

"*Please*," Natasha said at my right, "better chicken than egg. Who cares?"

"Obviously *you* don't," Gabriel said. It grew deathly cold.

"I do believe I still smell that brie," Kate said, and we all laughed. Kate glowed at her *bon mot* briefly before nodding for Douglas to go next.

Douglas cleared his throat. "This may sound dire, but I would like to toast to the hope of making it

48

through this year. When my sister was a senior she never really told me what was going on, but she was really stressed and worried and cried a lot. I think that sort of stuff can really test friendships, and so I want to toast to being careful and trying to make it through." He raised his glass and we all slowly followed. Douglas always was a worrywart, but this seemed darker. Even the clinking of our glasses seemed to be at a lower pitch. For a second I almost ran to him and held him but then I didn't.

Lily looked like the burden was on her to lighten the tone, but snappy jokes aren't her style. She plans things out. She looked at her plate and then out at us. "Here's to rising above petty obstacles."

"*Must we*?" Kate asked. "What should we fight about, if not silly things like how to bake the brie? Must we reserve fighting for deep emotional conflicts?"

"I'm sorry. My toast was inaccurate." Lily narrowed her eyes. "Here's to letting our favorite superficial things, like baking brie, replace whatever other superficial things, like, say, college applications, may get in our way." With that, everyone drank; thinking about college applications tends to make us thirsty. "Amen!" cried Gabriel and Natasha in unison, and they looked at each other across the table, tried to scowl and finally grinned.

Flora Habstat was next and looked uncertain. She had been looking uncertain since we all sat down. Finally her eyes lit up hopefully and she raised her glass. "Here's to being pushed to the limit academically, athletically and socially!" The PTA slogan. At one of our dinner parties. The trouble with everyone trying not to laugh at once is that you can't look anywhere for fear of meeting someone's eyes. We all stared at different points in space in tableau, like a table full of mannequins.

49

Jennifer Rose Milton, at the opposite head of the table, tried to save the day. "I make the same toast as Flora, only more generalized." Whether she is more kind or more beautiful is completely up for grabs in my book. "May all the clichés people try to sell us about this time in our lives come true. I mean, it would be nice to be pushed to the limit academically, athletically and socially, wouldn't it? It would be nice to have the greatest time of our lives and to have our eyes shining with promise and all that, wouldn't it?"

We all nodded dumbly; if we had opened our mouths we still might have laughed at poor Flora.

Natasha was the only one who had the guts to push us to the limit socially by trying to break our pent-up laughter. "In that case," she said, her voice mock-softening, "I toast to world peace."

"You know," Flora Habstat said brightly, "I read in *The Guinness Book of World Records* that world peace is the most frequent toast at official functions."

We couldn't hold it. We all laughed loud and long, and luckily Flora Habstat looked confused rather than hurt so I think she didn't know what we were laughing at. "If it would be all right with our hostess," I said while everyone was still laughing, "I vote to dispense with the rest of the toasts. After world peace there's little else to toast."

Kate looked a little disappointed but didn't push it. "I suppose. Well, let's eat."

Gabriel went to get the plates that he had been keeping warm in the oven. V___ got up to help. Adam, at my left due to Kate's tactful place cards, turned to me gratefully. I could smell aftershave, just faintly. "How can I ever thank you for bailing me out of thinking of a clever toast?"

Sipping without nibbling made me bold. "Another bottle of wine via your fake ID?" I said. "Wine's scarce round these underage parts."

"Done," he said. "Though you'll have to come with me and give out advice. I'll call you."

"I'll call you." Just like that. One dinner party and I'm already miles ahead of all those soul-searching aerograms.

SUNDAY SEPTEMBER 12TH

Pardon the stains; I forgot to get a spoon so I had to stir the coffee with my finger. I'm on the living room couch, watching a televangelist with the sound turned down, one hand on the phone. It's almost eleven and I'm waiting for the check-in calls to begin. In order to draw up a comprehensive summary of the dinner party I will draw some topic headings and then write down quotes as each member calls.

THE PARTY IN GENERAL

Kate: *I think it went very, very well, don't you, Flan? I suppose we were all a bit rusty, but that's to be expected after a summer of entertaining ourselves.*

Jennifer Rose Milton: *Lovely.*

Natasha: *It killed me. It really killed me.*

Gabriel: *It was OK. I don't think I was in the mood for it.*

Douglas: (N.B. All quotes from Douglas are *via* Lily. Douglas had to leave early the next morning to visit his father and stepmother, who are in themselves the source behind the Grimm Brothers' step parent angst.) *He had a very nice time, particularly after an apparently horrific lesson at the Conservatory.*

Lily: *I had a very nice time, too. Why are you asking me these questions like you're writing down the answers?*

V___: *I wish I had arrived earlier so everything would have been polished. We could have had it at my house except my parents were entertaining.*

Adam:

THE VERDICT ON ADAM

Kate: *I'm all for it. I'll do anything I think of to help you. I remember how hard it was when Garth and I first started our relationship, so let me know what I can do.* (It was hard not to giggle. Kate loves to discuss relationships using everything she learned from her relationship with Garth, which was her only relationship and was one and a half weeks in duration.)

Jennifer Rose Milton: *He seems nice, but not really my type.* (She wouldn't elaborate on what was her type, or if she were in fact typing. A coy mistress, Ms. Milton.)

Natasha: *Certainly delicious-looking. That shirt begged for unbuttoning, but I don't think I could steal him away from you, dear. Whatever did you tell him on your wine walk that kept him so entranced all evening?*

Gabriel: *He seemed, well, acceptable, Flannery. I don't know. Don't ask me these things. I'm too, um, protective of you, I think.*

Douglas: *Douglas suspected that he studied under the Suzuki method, which he disapproves of, but that can't be helped.*

Lily: *Very charming, Flan, but I don't know what lurks underneath that charm.*

V___: *Snap him up, Flannery Culp! So polite! So well groomed! I didn't know they made them like that in public school anymore.*

Adam:

THE VERDICT ON FLORA HABSTAT

Kate: *Who? Oh, yes. Do you have to ask? She hasn't even called to thank me and it's nearly noon.*

Jennifer Rose Milton: *I think she was trying a little too hard, but she really is very nice, don't you think?*

Natasha: *Did I call it on* The Guinness Book *or what, Flan?*

Gabriel: *Well, I suppose she's very nice, but I think a little, how should I put it, non-exciting. A dud, frankly. I don't really mean that. I'm sure her friends like her very much.*

Douglas: *He didn't say anything about her.*

Lily: *I myself thought that she either had an incredibly subtle deadpan sense of humor and was laughing at us all night, or was very slow. It's sometimes so hard to tell.*

V___: *Well, she helped clear the table.*

Adam:

Adam:

Adam:

ADAM:

Vocabulary:

CONFIDANTE   UNREQUITED   EUPHEMISMS
EPIPHANY   ELEPHANTINE

Study Questions:

1. Did you understand the difference between authority and authoritarianism? Answer honestly.

2. V——, in reality, has more than one letter in her name. Why do you think Flannery calls her V—— in her journal? (Hint: V——'s family is extremely wealthy and could influence publishers to keep any of their relatives out of a book that could damage the family's reputation.)

3. The stories of great operas contain thwarted love, jealous anger and violent murder and are called great art. Yet others who demonstrate these things have been punished. Isn't this hypocritical? Discuss.

4. You have undoubtedly seen photographs of Flannery Culp in newspapers and magazines. Is she fat? Be honest.

Monday September 13
Sophomore year, Miss Mills, an English teacher rumored to be an ex-nun, taught us all about pathetic fallacy: If a

character in literature is feeling a particular emotion acutely, the inanimate surroundings – you know, weather, landscape, stuff like that – tend to accentuate that mood. Thus armed to work as a literary editor, I checked the weather when I stepped outside for the bus, knowing it would tell me how Friday's Calc test would turn out. The skies were gray, but it wasn't raining – I figured maybe C or C+. I began to trudge up the hill, only to speed my pace up to a bleary shuffle; Adam's tall thin shape was half a block ahead of me. I tried not to run so I wouldn't be too obvious: "Adam? (pant, pant) I didn't see you . . ."

"Adam?" I called out, ten paces behind him. Adam turned around and looked at me quizzically. It wasn't Adam; it was Frank Whitelaw. At that very moment the clouds broke.

Frank Whitelaw took a full three seconds to look up at the sky and then back at me. If it were anyone else it would be a masterpiece of deadpan timing; with Frank Whitelaw you knew that three seconds was top neural synapse speed. (I'm not sure if that biological term is correct because, as you know, I cut Biology all the time because I'm an academic flaky failure.) Frank Whitelaw was on the stage crew and I always suspected that some heavy prop had fallen on his head. Natasha's theory was heavy drug use, and Kate's had to do with his last name. She said anything that sounded so much like neo-Nazism was probably the result of in-breeding.

He opened his backpack and took out an umbrella. Held it up over the both of us. It was like being protected by a big, friendly ape. Outside the monsoon raged and dribbled. We struggled up the hill.

I was still dripping from the downpour of pathetic fallacy when I got my 13. At first I didn't know what it meant: a circled number 13 at the top of my paper. 13th place? There were about forty-five students in the class. Then slowly, the carbonation of truth burped up into the front of my brain: 13 out of 100. 13%. If there were a train wreck and only 13% of the passengers lived, it would be called a catastrophe. I glanced down the paper and saw the red checks that pointed out tiny bits of correctly attempted equations like survivors in the mud, thrashing around amidst the inked *X*'s of the bridge that, ill-conceived and badly constructed, had fallen at the first testing. Baker's explanations of "the more difficult problems" – meaning there were some that were actually supposed to be *easy* – blurred by me like ambulance chasers as I sat gaping at the wreckage. Did they have good English Literature programs at Community Junior College? There I would be, living at home while my friends wrote cheery letters from ivy-covered libraries filled with creaky first editions. *Dear Flannery, Having a wonderful time. You would really love it here. Too bad about that Calc test.*

Given that he didn't call yesterday and that he isn't even in my Calc class, there's no reason why I should have felt Adam's hand on my shoulder, strong and comforting, but I did. It was only when I turned around that I discovered it was Mr. Baker.

"Hey," he said gruffly. "Don't worry, it's only the first test." I looked around; sometime in my daze class had been let go. "You know, I don't think that it's that you didn't know the material. You just panicked. You know what you did wrong?" I let him answer his own question because the only answer I could think of was, "Think up short story ideas every day during class?"

"You didn't follow Baker's Rule," he said. What was he talking about? I looked down at my book; it was covered.

"You want to hear Baker's Rule?" he asked with what he must have thought was a winning smile. I'm sure I had on a losing frown, myself. I was too numb with failure to think of all these wordplays but I *could* have thought of them so I've written them in now.

"Baker's Rule is: do *something*. Never just stare at a problem that you think you can't solve. Do *something*. And this doesn't just apply to Calculus, believe me." He patted my head a little too hard. "OK, Flannery?"

"OK," I said. Thanks so much, Mr. Baker. I feel so much better now. *Do something*. Why waste his talents on Calculus when he could be such an effective presidential aide? Next period I have to go to choir to see a man who doesn't love me and if they get to the Cs, sing for him all by myself, and during lunch I have to track down Jim Carr and apologize for cutting Bio on Thursday otherwise he too will mortify me in front of the entire class. Hattie Lewis is now telling us that tomorrow we'll study "The Day of Doom." I want to tell her she's a day late.

Adam opened the door and called my name and I walked in and realized that it wasn't Adam who had opened the door, it was Johnny Hand, the drunken nightclub singer and alleged choir teacher. What a powerful word, *alleged*. What an important word it has become to me. He smiled at me a little unsteadily and walked out of the little room, leaving me alone with someone else. I was pretty sure it was Adam but I'd made that mistake too many times already.

As you've been noticing, I hope, today's journal entry keeps telling you that I think other people are Adam. I've put this in there not only to make you realize the full universality and ferocity of my love but to demonstrate the chaotic randomness of the entire crime, indeed the entire situation. In other words: Adam could have been anyone. Our bodies, our material "selves" are, ironically, immaterial.

But it *was* Adam. I was alone with Adam, in this stuffy little audition room. The situation felt clinical so I reacted accordingly. "Well, Dr. State," I said, "I've been having this pain in my neck for going on four years now, and I think it may be high school. Will you check it out?" I sat in a folding chair.

Adam looked up from his Musical Director Notes. "Are you trying to tell me you want to play doctor, Ms. Culp?"

"Please," I said, batting my eyelashes. "It's *Miss* Culp." We both laughed. I could scarcely believe how charming and flirtatious I was managing to be. Maybe I was channeling Natasha through some incident of black magic or something.

Yes, I *really* did say that. But I was *kidding*. I have *never been involved in black magic in any way, shape or form*. Please write your senator. More on this later.

"I was happy to see your name next on the list," Adam said. "If I heard one more tone-deaf alto I was going to lose my mind."

The spirit of Natasha was exorcised in one swift blow. "Um," I said. "Um." Not quite as witty and alluring. "Um, I'm a tone-deaf alto, myself."

Adam winced. "Oh," he said. "Well, I didn't mean – some of my best friends are tone-deaf altos. *Alti*, rather." He grinned sheepishly at me.

"Do I need to sing in front of you?"

"Are you really a tone-deaf alto?"

"I'm afraid so. Roewer doesn't think that running the literary magazine or being in plays fulfills the creative arts requirement, so I have to do something."

"All right," he agreed. "I'll put you down as an alto. You don't need to sing."

"Thanks." I got up to go. If he called me back, I decided, then he liked me.

"Don't go yet," he said, reviving my faith in a Divine Being. And no, Mrs. State, not Beelzebub. "Let's pretend I'm auditioning you. I need some kind of break from the parade of alleged singers. Just talk to me for a minute."

"OK." I sat back down in the folding chair. "What should we talk about?"

"Let's talk about that kooky dinner party. I had a great time. Do you guys do that often?"

Kooky? I could hear Kate screech in my head. "Well, that was the first one of the year, but yes, we do it a lot. Beats renting movies or something, don't you think so?"

"Definitely. I just hope I get invited back."

"Well, if you play your cards right . . ."

"Um, listen, I feel like I haven't been." He cleared his throat. "Playing my cards right. I'm sorry I haven't said anything about your letters."

I held my breath. Sometimes it's best to keep quiet – not very often, I don't think, but sometimes – and this was one of them. I cleared my throat and began. "Don't worry about it. They were probably impossible to answer – particularly the last postcard. I was, I don't know, caught up in Italy or something. There was no way you could have answered – particularly the last postcard. I'm sorry. Summer can be so strange. It removes all context or something. It's like being in a vacuum. I just wrote you, that's all, I've been trying to apologize for it for a while but I didn't. But I will now. Apologize, that is – particularly for the last postcard. I know that you haven't known what to make of the letters, and I'm grateful that you haven't told my friends that it's been me writing them, but you needn't worry about them – particularly the last postcard. I'll just pretend that I never wrote to you, and you can just

59

pretend that you never received them – particularly the last postcard. I mean, we can still be friends, or acquaintances, or whatever we are – dinner partners – but we can just pretend all that Chianti-laced wide-eyed correspondence never happened – particularly the last postcard." When I go to see a play and somebody makes a speech that lengthy, I'm embarrassed, and it's a play. People are *supposed* to be making speeches that lengthy in a *play*. This isn't a play.

"What postcard? I didn't get any postcard," he said. "I just got two letters, very nice letters, and I wanted to thank you for them."

"Oh," I said.

"Did you send me a postcard, too?" He stood up and walked over to me. In another world, I could have just leaned in and kissed him. Perhaps it would have made a difference. I could have moved fast. Instead I just thought fast.

"I don't know," I said. "I thought I did. But I wrote so many postcards."

"I didn't tell anybody you wrote them," he said, "because I thought that people would think they were love letters." He moved his hands slightly, palms up, in a gesture that meant I don't know what. "*I* thought maybe they were love letters."

Now it was his turn to kiss me, don't you think? "I thought that maybe they were love letters." Distantly, a sound of warm violins. He steps closer. Slight swelling (of the music, of course). And then a kiss. It didn't happen. I couldn't stand it. "I thought that maybe they were love letters," and then nothing.

"Maybe they were," I said, and I stood up myself and left the room. I wanted to slam the door, but it was one of those public-school doors that just wheeze closed. *Swish*.

The rest of the choir looked up at me for a second. "Next!" I called off-handedly, and strode out the door.

It is the moment that followed – the end of fourth period on Monday September 13th at Roewer High School – that the loudest birds of the gaggle of attending quacks have proclaimed to be the impetus for what has been called everything from "a series of unfortunate behaviors" (Dr. Eleanor Tert) to "the most bloodthirsty of teenage acts I have ever discussed on my program" ("Dr." Winnie Moprah, the degree is honorary from a school of dubious academic reputation). Tert's book *Crying Too Hard to Be Scared* says:

> It is impossible to overemphasize the importance of this psychosexual voyeuristic moment in Culp's adolescence. [What rubbish! Of course she could overemphasize the importance of it. What if she said: "This psychosexual voyeuristic moment in Culp's adolescence was responsible for world hunger"? That would be overemphasis, wouldn't it? That's what's wrong with the coverage of my story: not so much bias as *inaccuracy*.] Imagine Culp, in the aftermath of one of the first moments of sexual awakening in her argument with her eventual victim [again: *inaccuracy*. He was *not my victim*.], wandering in a sexualized daze to the office of a teacher whom she trusted, seeking advice and counseling [*inaccuracy, inaccuracy, inaccuracy*]. Yet when she walks in she finds her teacher betraying her trust, indeed the very trust of the teaching profession, locked in an embrace with a student [*inaccuracy*]. It was the ultimate betrayal for young Culp, and triggered a horrific, though slightly

delayed, response – much like Poe and his mother's death as discussed in my first chapter [horrific and not at all delayed amounts of *inaccuracy*].

And even putting aside facts for a minute, Dr. Tert's description has serious *semantic* problems. *Embrace* is too elegant a term for what Carr was doing. Just about the only accurate thing Eleanor said was that I walked down the hallway and into a classroom. Unlit Bunsen burners and half-dead tadpoles and faded color posters of the digestive system all greeted me, but Carr was nowhere to be seen. Off the main classroom was Carr's office, which we weren't supposed to go in because it contained dangerous chemicals. I heard a scuffling from it, like a rustling of paper. "Mr. Carr?" I called out, cautiously, and put my hand on the half-open door.

"I don't know," I heard someone say, softly.

"Mr. Carr?" I asked again, and pushed the door open all the way.

Mr. Carr was in one of those phony white lab coats that biology teachers wear in an apparent effort to look like they're in an aspirin commercial. At first it just looked like he was standing there, grinning at his desk, but when I followed his gaze I saw the teaching assistant half sprawled on the blotter, watching him warily. He leaned in and kissed her again. His hand was on her skirt, high up. She said, softly, "I don't know." It was not a coy "I don't know." It was a wary "I don't know." It was not "I don't know, why don't you choose the position?" It was "I don't know if I should be in this position." He leaned in and kissed her again. I didn't move. I was pretty sure that I wasn't supposed to be seeing this and I was pretty sure that it wasn't supposed to be happening at all. Talk about dangerous chemicals.

"Come on," he said, somewhere between seduction and irritation.

The teaching assistant's eyes were half closed, but she saw me anyway. "Ohmygod!" She sat up suddenly and bumped her head on a low-hanging shelf of petri dishes.

Mr. Carr whirled around and looked at me. His eyes were bright and scary. "What do you want?" he yelled. "What do you want?"

"I'm sorry I cut class Thursday," I said, backing out of the room.

"I'm in a meeting!" he yelled. "This is my office! You have no right to come in here!" He pounded the door as I scurried past the tadpoles, the posters. A chair clattered to the floor. "Get out!" I got out. In the hallway, some people had heard all the bellowing and were staring at me: a couple of guys were sitting on the floor, their backs against their lockers, open textbooks in their laps, a girl with dyed-black hair, a dallying janitor. I ran to the stairway and heard somebody running behind me, running after me. Carr kissing her wasn't scary. Carr yelling was scary, and now he was coming after me.

The girl with the dyed-black hair grabbed my arm as I hit the ground floor. "Leave me *alone*," I said, and then realized it was Natasha. I hugged her, hard. I could hear my own breathing, hard. The sound of that breathing is something I'll never forget.

"What the *fuck*?" she said, all snarling lipstick and fingernails. "What the *fuck* was he shouting at?"

"I went in to apologize for cutting class on Thursday," I said. I was still breathing. I sounded like an iron lung.

"Take your time," she said. "Here, sit down. You sound like an iron lung." We sat down on the second-to-last step. I rubbed at my face. Some people look good when they're crying, but I'm not one of them so I tried my hardest to stop. The sound of Carr shouting began to dim in my mind's ear, and instead I began to hear, over and over, the *plunk* of the teaching assistant's head against the petri shelf. I started to laugh.

Mind's ear? I don't know.

Natasha looked at me warily, the way you look at someone when they shake, then cry, then laugh. A shadow fell over us and we looked up and saw our vice principal, a fat black man who always wore plaid vests and expressions of self-righteousness. His name is Mr. Mokie – pronounced so as to rhyme with "okey dokey." He likes to tell people to think of him as a friend and not just a vice principal. Natasha eats those sort of people alive.

"No sitting in the stairways, girls," he said. "Fire marshal's rules."

"I *am* the fire marshal," Natasha snarled. "We're having a drill."

"Look," Mr. Mokie said. "I don't make the rules, girls. Think of me as a friend, not just a vice principal. After all, the final word in principal is *pal*. Now move along."

"Pals don't tell me to move along," Natasha said. "We're just going to sit here for a minute, OK? Let us break your stupid rules just once. We won't report you to *der Führer*."

Mr. Mokie wrinkled his brow. "I don't speak French," he said. "Anyway, they're not my rules. I don't want to give you detention, but I have to. My hands are tied."

"Nobody's making you," Natasha said.

"If you don't follow the rules, I have to do it. My hands are tied."

"*Don't give me any ideas!*" I screamed. I could hear the echo, bouncing way up the stairwell to the top floor and beyond, where God and the fire marshal live. It was a raw sound. Mr. Mokie scampered away, presumably to fetch some paperwork.

Natasha turned to me, clearly impressed. "Nice work. Pretty soon you're not going to need me around."

"Don't be ridiculous," I said.

We smiled at each other, friends. "So what happened?" she asked. "We fought for the conversation spot, we'd better have the conversation."

"I can't talk about it," I said. "Why don't you just read about it?" I reached in the bag and took out my journal. Her eyebrows shot up; I never let anybody even touch the journal. "Go ahead," I said. I flipped it open to the right page and handed it to her. She looked at me again and then just sat there. Read it, right up to the part where I handed her the journal. Oh, wait. That won't work. I can't have written it down yet. All this goddamn *clanging*.

The bell clanged – rang, rather. "I have to go to Civics," I said.

"We'll talk about this later," Natasha said, handing the journal back to me.

"Don't tell anybody about this!" I shouted, and she ran back up the stairs, a girl with dyed-black hair. I walked dumbly into Civics, slunk into a chair, and wrote everything down.

Jennifer Rose Milton whispered to me that *Maman* had had too much red wine with some dinner guests last night, so today in French Millie corrected papers behind sunglassed eyes while we split into groups and read dialogues out loud to one another. What did you put in the soup that night? Shallots and a little red wine. Red wine! Goodness! Wasn't that expensive to purchase? No, no, not if you go to that store on the corner of Lake and Forest. Lake and Forest? Sounds too pastoral for a modern girl like me! Ha ha ha ha ha! Did you get the shallots at the market? Yes, and I had to go to four stores before I found fresh vegetables. They are so rare in these (can't translate) French times. Did you see your teacher hitting on the teaching assistant? Yes, I did. Was she enjoying herself? No, she wasn't. I think my teacher was too slimy for a modern girl like her! Ha ha ha ha ha! What (can't translate) times we have here at Roewer!

Tuesday September 14th

LA BOHEME

Act Two: *A square in the Latin Quarter. On one side is the Café Momus. Mimi and Rodolfo move about within the crowd. Colline is nearby at a ragwoman's stand. Schaunard is buying a pipe and a trumpet. Marcello is pushed here and there by the throng. It is evening. Christmas Eve.*

Act Two: *A square of desks in the Roewer Quarter. On one side is the Café Millie, where Jennifer Rose Milton and her mother are in quiet exclusionary conversation. Douglas and Lily are nearby, staring into each other's eyes. So far away as to be scarcely visible, somebody feels like a ragwoman: Flannery. It is morning. Nowhere near Christmas break.*

It was a low turnout for Grand Opera Breakfast. Douglas, dressed rather informally in a coat and tie rather than a matching suit, talked to me once, to point out some irregularity in the time signature of the opening horn part, or some regularity, I don't remember. Lily smiled at me, then turned her head until she was smiling at Douglas. Jennifer Rose Milton looked up from *tete-a-tete* avec *Maman* as I walked in and gave a half wave before turning back. Everybody was paired up. Even the lovers in *La Boheme* hadn't run into any trouble yet, singing in the café like fools. I sat down at the table myself and munched too many doughnuts. Good plan, Flan; scarf down pastries and then *surely* you'll be noticed more. Though I guess I could attain some sideshow freak value . . .

The pastry calories must have worked – Jim Carr, for one, managed to spot me from a mile away. "In my office," he said briskly, propelling me by the elbow into that same room, the tadpoles, the Bunsen burners, everything. A few kids were in there for homeroom already, reading comic books – the kind of kids who show up early for homeroom and sit around and read comic books, waiting for their lives to start. I flexed my cell walls and stood firm. Those sort of kids make good witnesses. Whatever he had to say to me he could say here in the classroom and not alone in his sleazy office.

Little did I know. "She was always strange," kids like that would say, only a few months later. "I suspected from the outset." Hardly the stuff of good witnesses.

"In my office," he repeated as I stopped at the poster of the digestive system.

"Alone in your office?" I said loudly, and a couple of the kids looked up from the latest issue of *The Tarantula Team Adventure Series*. Jim Carr flushed slightly. Behind him, the small and large intestines seemed to curl forward as if to wrap themselves around his neck. His voice lowered accordingly to a strangled half whisper, when somebody wants to be quiet and yell at you at the same time. His eyes were scary again. Nobody was going to step into this conversation. Nobody was going to rescue me. The intestines were only a poster.

"I wanted to apologize for yelling at you yesterday," he said in what is called in books, low tones. "I shouldn't have talked to you that way." He folded his arms and waited for me to say something. "Well?"

I looked around nervously. The homeroomers were lost in their bustling metropolises again. They knew what to expect; the mutants would be routed. But what did Carr expect? "Your apology is accepted," I mumbled, and started toward the door.

He touched me again. He had me by the elbow again. "Well?" he said again.

I couldn't meet his eyes. "I don't know," I said.

"I expected an apology from you, for barging into my office like that," he said, and happily, that did it. He sounded so bureaucratic that he no longer sounded like a madman; he sounded like Mr. Mokie. Confrontations with bureaucratic idiots I could handle.

"In that case, I'm sorry I barged into your office like that. See you sixth period," I said, and then turned toward the door. Kids began to stream in and sit down.

"Wait!" he called, sensing his power over me was somehow ebbing despite his continued grasp on my elbow. "You are not to mention our encounter in my office to anyone. You haven't told anyone, have you?" Now *he* couldn't meet *my* eyes, but I looked straight at him. "Don't tell anyone, OK?" His desperation overrode his ability to produce a winning smile; he moved the corners of his mouth upward but all I saw were teeth.

"See you sixth period, Mr. Carr," I said, and left. The hallways were quiet; I was late for homeroom.

"You're late for homeroom!" Mr. Dodd called out as I entered.

Suddenly I was too weary to answer. "Sorry," I said, and sat down.

Natasha shook her head and walked out of her seat to come talk to me. "*Sorry*," she said, in a "we are not amused" voice, "was a sorry response to Dodd's dud."

I looked back at her. "I refuse to answer sentences containing an overabundance of alliteration," I said. "I just came from Carr's room."

"I meant to ask you about that," she said, and took out her all-important nail file again. "What happened?"

As I told her, she filed her nails harder and harder until I thought I'd see sparks. "That *shit*," she said, "Trying to make you feel bad for catching him with someone. We ought to *do* something."

She sounded like she was reciting Baker's Rule. "Do something," I said. "What can we do? She's not actually a student, so it's not like it's illegal or something, so we can't tell anybody."

"I already told Kate," she said. "Soon everyone will know."

"Jesus, Natasha," I said. "I'll get in trouble."

"For entering a teacher's office during lunch? I don't think so." She shook her head. Her hair moved like a shampoo commercial, if people in shampoo commercials dyed their hair black. "But maybe he will. It's certainly unethical if not illegal." She smirked at me. "Don't worry, we'll do something. Trust me."

The bell rang.

Wednesday September 15th

After school, Drama Club finally started: after drama, the drama. Ron Piper is an angel in a black turtleneck, though everybody looks like angels in black turtlenecks so maybe it's hard to tell. Ron Piper, our beloved drama teacher, even thinner and, incredibly enough, even more effeminate than I remember, bounced all around the stage, welcoming us to what he hoped would be a "brilliant theatrical year," coyly refusing to tell us what play we'd be putting on, and apologizing for not showing up last week. The most exciting announcement he had was – is this an act of cosmic synchronicity or what? – that eight free tickets to the San Francisco Theater production of *Hamlet* were in his possession, to be given to the eight people who could name the most plays by the Bard himself. Well, all eight of us weren't there – Lily is too immersed in classical music to venture out onto the stage, and V___'s bitchy mother says that the Roewer stage is too common for a oops I can't say her last name, but you get the idea. But the six of us who were there began screaming out the names of them, mercilessly drowning out the voices of the ten thousand shy freshman girls who show up for Drama Club every year, audition inaudibly and end up selling refreshments to parents at intermission. Why do *shy* people invariably show up for Drama, anyway? Do their shyness coaches make them go? One of them actually guessed *Cyrano de Bergerac*, if you can believe it. Yeah, honey, Shakespeare also wrote in French; he was Canadian, you know.

Am I a snob?

In either case I don't know why I'm blabbing on and on about petty details when you're waiting for the point of the story. I got one, Jennifer Rose Milton got one, Gabriel got one, Douglas, Natasha of course and Kate who named a bunch of historical plays I hadn't even heard of, and Flora Habstat got one (W. S. must be Most Famous Playwright in *The Guinness Book*) but I could tolerate her next to me in a dark theater and just when Ron was about to hand over the last ticket to one of the shy twerps and I was thinking that with my luck I'd end up sitting next to her answering her stupid whispered questions all night ("Why is Ophelia acting so weird?")

from the back of our cavernous auditorium came the booming shout, "*Cymbeline!*"

I don't have to tell you who it was, do I? You know that when a booming shout comes from nowhere, it's the romantic hero. He walked grandly down the center aisle as Ron, grinning (and I think I could detect a look in Monsieur Piper's eye that would confirm conservative school board members' suspicions about hiring people of Ron's, shall we say, *persuasion*; I wanted to hiss at him, Bette Davis-like, *He's mine, Ronny*), handed Adam the ticket. Adam had the ticket to ride, and if you think this baby don't care you probably don't know that it was Moliere who wrote *Cyrano*.

Adam took the ticket and told Ron he couldn't stay; he just wanted to make sure his name was on the Drama Club list. "Dentist," he said, pointing to his straight clean teeth, and when he saw me looking at him he winked at me.

I mean, OK, winking is a little, I don't know, horny-old-uncle, but Adam did it with just the right amount of self-consciousness, with a hint of rogue. *Panache* – it was very *Cyrano*. So much can be said, *erased* with a gesture like that. Well, not *erased*. The love wasn't erased, or even the ache, but its *context* changed. I didn't feel the despair, like my shoes were filled with rain and I just figured out that I had been waiting at the wrong bus stop for an hour and a half and that Adam didn't give a shit about me. Now the tension I felt about Adam was laced with expectation, rather than pain. Like Adam was biding his time, waiting to make his perfect entrance into my life, the way he strode into the auditorium at precisely the right moment and turned my dread of an evening with a Shyness Patient into something that could be called, with only minimal overinterpretation, *a date with Adam*. A *date* with the man

I love. *Cymbeline*. None of us had mentioned *Cymbeline*. Had it been the proper century I would have swooned. Did I say that already?

LATER
One last note: Because everyone else went on ahead, by the time I reached the bus stop, my head still in the clouds, the bus had come and taken all my friends away. Bored, hungry, I sat on the bench, and who should sit next to me but Carr's assistant. Talk about awkward. "Hi, what's up since my high school teacher made a pass at you?"

"Not much," she sighed. OK, really I just said "What's up?"; to say the rest would have pretty much been redundant. She looked tired and had folders and folders of papers with her. The Bio test, I realized. *My* test.

"I could save you some time," I said. "I'll just correct my own exam. Scout's honor."

She smiled, faintly. "Actually, yours is the only test that he's correcting. He wouldn't let me; he said it was a conflict of interest."

Talk about awkward – oh, we already *were* talking about awkward. I sat there opening and closing my mouth like a baby bird. I kept starting to say something. On my third try she interrupted me, although I don't know if you can call it interrupting if the other person hasn't said anything.

"He's a shit," she said. I don't think I'd ever heard anyone in the education profession say "shit" except Millie. The bus was nowhere in sight. I became a baby bird again.

"He's a shit," she said again. "A perverted shit. Everybody told me I shouldn't take the job. Everybody *told* me," she said, slapping her hand against the bus

72

map printed on the side of the stop, color-coded routes scrawling across the city like something in a biology book. "But I took it anyway. When I get home I feel so gross I don't even want to touch my own kid."

Her own *kid*. Jesus. The baby bird wants *more* food, *more* food. She looked at me and realized who I was. "I shouldn't be telling you this. I'm just *screwed*," she said. "I shouldn't be telling you this. I'm sorry. But at the end of the semester *he* writes me an evaluation, and if I get a bad one then it won't do me any good if I have a credential or not. No one will hire me. That's what he did to the TA he had last semester, though nobody told me *that*" – she poked my neighborhood – "until I'd already taken the job. I shouldn't be telling you this. But just remember" – she stood up; the bus was stopped, gurgling in front of us like a phlegmy infant –"he's a shit. Remember that. Aren't you getting on the bus?"

She looked at me over the pile of tests. Behind her, the bus driver, fat as hell, shot me an impatient look. "No," I said. I stood up and took a step into a large puddle of someone's discarded cola. Evil corporate chemical sweeteners seeped in and began to soak my sock. The bus doors closed and the infant pulled away, whining and coughing. I had just realized I needed to be waiting at the other bus stop.

Thursday September 16th
Carr didn't read it. He didn't fucking read it! I'm in Biology right now, and we all got our tests back, mine corrected by the teacher himself (how he must of strained himself, he who is used to his love slaves/assistants performing that task) because of, as I learned yesterday, a conflict of interest, aka Flan, caught him with his pants almost literally down, and he didn't even read it. I just

about fainted when I saw the A on top – no way did I get a smidgen of credit on that essay question, and that was one-fifth the grade – but he didn't read it. I mean he literally didn't read it. I turned to the page with the essay question on it and saw that I had actually written: "Biologically, these functions are important for the sustenance of a living system" and no one called me on it. What is it – an apology? A bribe? I'm flunking Math and applying to college and my love life is a roller coaster and that isn't enough – I need this bonus Moral Dilemma.

"Take the A," Natasha told me, taking a swig of her is-it-really-alcohol-or-just-water flask as she spun the steering wheel. Outside, pedestrians watched the car warily, like it might kill them. Sometimes accepting a ride home from Natasha is more stress than it's worth, although so is Advanced Biology and I show up every day. Darling Mud blared; I ought to contact them about being compensated for endorsement when this is published.

"You know, there is a strong possibility that you actually earned it," she said. "I'm going to run over this woman in the ugly hat."

"That hat is not worth prison," I said. (These parenthetical asides distract from the dialogue, I know, but can I just say: denim, plaid brim, bright yellow feathers.) "There's no way I earned it, Natasha. I calculated it right afterward. It was a B and then only if neatness didn't count for the sketches."

"I've seen your sketches," Natasha said. "With you it's not an issue of neatness but *semblance*. You can't *seriously* tell me that anyone would have pressed charges if I had destroyed that denim canary."

"It looked like it was in a kilt, no less. Probably a canary of Scottish royalty."

"And, as I recall," Natasha said airily, stopping in front of my house, "we learned last year in Shakespeare that when you kill Scottish royalty the whole thing becomes a mess."

"Yeah, yeah, yeah," I said. I got out of the car, sourly. Natasha hadn't made me feel much better. "When shall we two meet again?"

"Tomorrow, of course," she said, spitting gum out the open window. "Are you going to the dance tomorrow night?"

I hadn't thought much about it. "I hadn't thought much about it," I said, cleverly.

Natasha rolled her eyes. "Oh, well," she said, "I know that you want to give the matter your full attention before you decide. It's a *high school dance*, Flan. You know, most people aren't so spacey when they get an unexpected A during their most important semester for college."

"Natasha, he's a *shit*!" I said. "He makes me feel yucky. I feel like I can't touch anything because Carr slime is all over it." I thought about the teaching assistant not wanting to touch her kid.

"*Look at me*," Natasha said. I looked her right in the eyeliner. "Forget about Carr. You can't do a thing about it, and in the meantime he's giving you better grades than you deserve. If you had half a brain you'd play it up and you'd never have to study in that class again. *Look at me, Flan*. Now go inside and write in your journal and thicken up your skin a little bit. And don't forget, 'your life, your woe, your death: all embraced in dreams.'"

That did it. We cracked up, loud and loose. "That really was a dreadful poem," I admitted. "Of course, as editor I'm supposed to remain objective –"

"And confidential," Natasha said. "So you don't have to confirm what I already know: it was a Frosh Goth creation, was it not?"

"How did you know?"

"The little State girl blushed and blushed as we all ripped into it. Very satisfying, I must say. Usually you start off the first meeting with one of your own poems so it's actually pretty good."

"All right, enough flattery, I'm cheered up already," I said, and I was. I looked around, and in the foggy afternoon light my dull neighborhood looked cheerful – the lawns, the throwaway coupon books on everyone's porch, Natasha's gum on the street, moist as a kiss. It must have been pathetic fallacy again.

"That wasn't flattery," she said imperatively. "Flan, you're extremely talented."

"Yeah, yeah," I said, poking at the gum with my shoe. I realized it was probably water in the flask – nobody drank liquor while chewing peppermint gum at the same time.

"You *are*," she said, putting the car back in drive. In the back of my mind I said a silent prayer for those pedestrians who would be in Natasha's way. Especially the ones in ugly hats. "I just *know* that you're going to do something that will make the whole world sit up and take notice."

Friday September 17

Is this funny or am I just suffused with end-of-the-week giddiness? V__'s mother won't let her go to the dance because of some stupid (rich old family name) family commitment. Lily, Douglas, Natasha and I were sitting around at lunchtime making up catty nicknames for her. I can't repeat any of the suggestions of nicknames, because they all play off the Queen Mother's first and last names, both of which are of course secrets. But it makes no difference; suffice to say that the one that stuck we found hilariously funny. *Satan*. We laughed and laughed, there in the courtyard, Natasha with her bright red lipstick,

Douglas in another one of his linen suits, this one a sort of off-white, Lily with her tortoiseshell glasses and me looking surprisingly slim, I think, in these gray pants I used to have back then. We elaborated and laughed some more, imagining cute polished mother-of-pearl horns sticking out of her carefully shellacked bun, a pitchfork kept in the elephant-foot umbrella stand in V___'s hall. *Satan*. Of course later this nickname would get us into heaps of trouble, but that morning it was hilarious.

OH MY IT'S LATER
Tonight tonight tonight. Those were the words to that song and how true they are. Tonight tonight tonight. I had honestly forgotten over the summer the surreal, stupid but irresistible deadly charming intensity that is a Roewer dance. Was that a sentence? I'm checking . . . yes it was. Subject and verb both, and that's how I feel, too. Tonight, tonight, tonight I am both subject and verb. I can't seem to stop moving, and you'd think a bottle of cheap champagne is a depressant, right? But as you know, you gorgeous black leather notebook, I know shit about biology. Flan, begin at the beginning, it's a very good place to start, all those lessons about narrative structure are melting away under all this fizzy wine.

Two New Year's Eves ago (how's that for beginning at the beginning at the beginning) my parents had a party and it was no problem at all sneaking one of the five boxes of champagne up to my room during the hubbub, they were having me act as waitress all night anyway so I felt it was my due. It lives under the bed, where my parents never check (plus, the fact that my parents have disappeared this year means they never check anything). On special occasions I take out a bottle. I took one when I got home from boring boring school and called folks to see who wanted to meet early at the lake for cocktails before actually proceeding to the dance. I couldn't get ahold of Natasha, Jennifer Rose Milton said coyly that she already had plans but would see me at the dance (of course, I would find out exactly what sort of "plans" – narrative structure, Flan, narrative structure), and Gabriel was weird about it. He said he didn't want to get drunk with me. He said it just like that – at least I think he did. "I'll just see you there," he said glumly. What is *up* with that? Anyway, Kate was game, but by then there were too few people for me to call Lily and Douglas because I didn't want it to be one kissy couple and the two single girls, drinking out at the lake. I've seen that movie; they all end up revealing deadly secrets and killing one another. Anyway Lily and Douglas didn't even show up.

Well I showered and changed my clothes and took the bus down to the lake, clutching the champagne neck inside my backpack, feeling the delicious paranoia that only a minor clutching alcohol on public transportation can feel. Spun off the bus and sat on a log, watching the sun setting and a bunch of grimy freshman girls drinking something they'd snuck out of the house in a food storage container. They shrieked with laughter as they spilled whatever-it-was on their shirts; I remember thinking that Carr would smell the liquor on them and lead them, shaken but still tipsy-giggly, to the office to wait for their parents to pick them up. All right, I couldn't have been thinking about Carr before I found out he was chaperoning, but you probably didn't catch that, anyway.

"Happy New Year!" Kate cried out as I popped the cork. Kate was wearing an outfit consisting entirely of the color dark blue. She always wears outfits consisting entirely of the color dark blue, and always will wear outfits consisting entirely of the color dark blue, world without end. We gulped and giggled and talked about nothing, enjoying the Indian summer night but not the mosquitoes that flew in it. Just when the bottle was drained, what I thought was a large black backpack of one of the freshgirls looked up and it was no backpack but Rachel State, the Frosh Goth, Sister Of The Groom. She stared at me from eyes circled in what looked like coal. In fact, between her black lipstick and her black clothes and dyed black hair I would have to say her overall impression was distinctly mesquitelike. If you were bad all year and of the Christian faith, you could expect Rachel State in your stocking.

"Rachel!" I cried out, hoping I was impressing the hell out of her, "Come meet my friend Kate!"

She scowl-staggered over while her friends gaped. The bubbly must have mellowed Queen Bee Kate Gordon (did I just use the phrase *the bubbly*?!?), because she didn't cringe or mock or anything; she just said hello. How 'bout that.

"Rachel is Adam State's sister," I told Kate brightly.

"And you –," Rachel slurred, pointing a black nail-polished hand vaguely in my direction. "*You're* the one who wrote Adam love letters all summer."

If this were a movie – and don't tell me it's not melodramatic enough to be one – some great disaster would have struck right then, and we would have glossed over the mortifying moment by running to shelter, bailing out the boat, comforting the bereaved, calming the horses, anything, anything but standing there – with *Kate*, Queen Bee *Kate Gordon* no less, while the worst poet I've ever seen went and blabbed my only secret. But as it turned out, no tidal wave was needed; not that Lake Merced could have produced much of one.

"No, she's not," Kate said, without blinking. She wasn't covering up for me; she was genuinely, drunkenly, *stupid*, just for a moment. Tomorrow morning, I have to drag my hungover ass out of bed and spend all my money on novena candles. If ever the proof of a Benevolent Deity, this.

"Oh," said the Frosh Goth, closing her eyes to regain her balance. Her black lipstick was smeared like she had just eaten fudge. "Then you must be the one he really likes." She turned to her surprisingly nonblackened friends and explained, gesturing limply. "There are two girls, one who is chasing him, one who he wants to chase."

Fuck the novena candles, I'm sleeping late. "Come on," I said to Kate, trying to sound bored. "Enough hanging around Merced with the Frosh Faction."

We stumbled into the building that challenges us academically, athletically and socially, only to find that Carr was one of the evening's chaperones. Now *that's* a challenge. Carr took our tickets and glared at me. We entered our high school for the second time that day, now festooned with streamers. I could hear the bass lines of the music coming from the gym like an approaching army. Gabriel and Natasha bounded up, already dance-sweaty, and grabbed us. "It's on!" Natasha shouted, and I looked at her in her tight black jeans and sequined bustier with a big fake rhinestone *X* in the center of it and just didn't care anymore. We went into the gym and danced and shouted and danced. They were playing that song that goes "Tonight tonight tonight," it's still in my head. I love that song. Everything was great, all champagne blurry and the boys weren't looking at the bustier but at me (dream on, little Culp girl) when I stepped out into the hallway to get a drink of water and all of a sudden I was in The Chamber Of Horrors. I can only describe them by exhibits:

EXHIBIT ONE: JENNIFER ROSE MILTON LEANING AGAINST THE WALL AND MAKING OUT WITH FRANK WHITELAW! I don't know if I've recorded here in this journal the only conversation I've ever really had with Frank Whitelaw – he ran into me once maybe last week, when it was raining – but he is a slow man. I mean *stupid* slow, not like he moves slowly. In fact, given the location of his hands on Jennifer Rose Milton's gorgeous thin body, I would say that slow is most certainly *not* how Mr. Whitelaw moves. So *this* is who Jenn has been seeing.

EXHIBIT TWO: JIM CARR, BIOLOGY TEACHER, FLIRTING WITH SOPHOMORE CHEERLEADING CHICK, STROKING HER HAIR EVEN. Enough said, I trust. Not only that, they were blocking the drinking fountain. I turned and went down the hallway you're not supposed to go down during school dances because, I don't know, something horrible might happen to you, and like I was a character in one of those religious pamphlets they give out, something horrible did happen, right then, because there was

EXHIBIT THREE: DRUNK MARK WALLACE, leaning against some lockers with his bloodshot eyes and a sweat-stained T-shirt that read: "Black By Popular Demand." Just what I needed. Mark Wallace is perhaps the most obnoxious person at Roewer, and when drunk he's downright belligerent. Natasha had to crack a bottle of beer over his head at a cast party once – but that's another story. This story goes like this:

Once upon a time, in a hallway too far from supervision, the Big Bad Mark Wallace asked Flan what was up, and Flan said nothing much and the B. B. M. W. asked what her hurry was, and Flan stuttered something and then Mark told me I had nice tits. What do you say to that, exactly? So I said nothing, and turned around and that's when he reached over and grabbed one of them, trying to kiss me on the neck at the same time. I think that Mark hoped that my body would respond in ways that were beyond my control, and he was right: I threw up, all over his political statement. Then, while he gasped and gaped, I turned and ran. I turned the corner and ran the rest of the way down the hallway. I had almost reached the gym when I felt a tap on the shoulder. It was Carr; behind him, a cheerleader looked at me with the same smugness as the States.

"Culp," he said, licking his lips nervously, "you're not supposed to go down that hallway." He put his arm authoritatively on my shoulder; I think that's what did it.

"Carr," I said, "we all do things we're not supposed to. Now get your hand the fuck off my shoulder."

"OK, Flan, time to go home," Gabriel said, appearing from nowhere. He put an arm around me and I instantly broke down. I kept my head down so I couldn't see any more Horrors. People were probably laughing at me, pointing at me, but I didn't see them. I kept my head down and kept walking, a strategy that turned out to be handy later, on courthouse steps and the like.

"So," Gabriel said conversationally as he buckled me in and started the car. "Have a nice evening?" I laughed and he laughed and I told him about the only Exhibit I thought it was appropriate to talk about: Jennifer Rose Milton and Frank Whitelaw. He was impressed.

"Not bad work for a lush," he said.

"Hey," I said. "You'd be a lush too if you'd have joined me at the lake. What, did you have a better offer or something?" He looked so sad, so suddenly.

"I just –" he said, and I looked at him and saw that he was longing to say something. He had rolled down the window for me, and the night air chilled me. I waited, but he didn't say anything.

"You just what?" I said as he pulled onto my street. The air kept chilling me, and I kept waiting.

"I just –" he said, and stopped at my house. He sighed and then smiled emptily. "I'm just tired," he said, and let me out. I went inside and swallowed all the aspirin and water in sight. What was that all about? Well, it's too late to think anymore about that or anything else. It's too late to think about it. I keep dozing between sentences, but I'm going to stay awake and write a poem or die trying.

There's no poem here. Draw your own conclusions.

Saturday September 18th

Back here, in editing land, as I retype this journal and try to set everything right, I have drowning dreams. The gurgles I hear all night break through my only window, and dribble onto the floor. I wake up when the water level reaches the mattress and soaks it. By that time it's pouring down. It's hard for me to get out of bed because the itchy wool blanket is heavy and bloated in the torrent. The gurgling is everywhere. Water fills my hands, my mouth and my own screams add to the gurgles as I wake up, this time for real. Sometimes if I've been shouting this fat matron of a woman asks me if I'm OK. Now *there's* an essay question that nobody would give me an A on. *On which they'd give me an A.*

This morning the Satanic Minion of Hangover Hell must have had it in for me because the phone rang in the middle of a dream in which something terrible was chasing me. It was Kate, asking if I wanted to meet everyone for focaccia at The Curtain Rises, this upscale non-Italian Italian place across from the theater. *Hamlet*. I forgot about *Hamlet* just like we forgot all about *Cymbeline* last week. If we had remembered *Cymbeline* then I wouldn't be worried about *Hamlet*. He's going to be there. "Should we invite Adam for focaccia, too?" Kate asked, and I wish those science fiction phones had been invented so I could have reached into the screen and my hand could have come out in her bedroom and slapped her. She could barely keep her delight at my disastrous evening out of her voice. So many exciting things for you to spread around, Kate! How nice for you! I told Kate I'd invite him myself – let her choke on that, little gossipy twit – and took a shower. Do you think if I turned the shower on to its harshest frequency it could wear some of the flesh off me? I mean, if babbling brooks can do it to stone . . .

"You're being too harsh on her," Natasha said to me when I bitched about Kate. How's this for a friend: She had let herself into my house using the key that everyone knows we keep under the flowerpot (Attention burglars: it is there no more) and fixed poached eggs and coffee and Bloody Marys. She was slicing celery into suggestive stalks when I came down in sweats.

"I thought you might need some recuperation assistance," she said as I hugged her.

"Sometimes having you around is like hanging out with those gorgeous bitter single girlfriends of the heroine in romantic comedies."

Natasha bit the tip off one of the, um, stalks. "But baby," she said. "I'm the real thing. What happened last night? Each person I talked to only had a scrap of the story; it was like some Robert Louis Stevenson ripped-up treasure map thing."

I told her the whole Chamber Of Horrors, but the problem was I couldn't tell her everything because nobody but nobody knows that I'm the one who wrote Adam all those damn letters and that postcard that I would give my right arm to go back in time, beat up the Italian postal carrier and destroy. Natasha listened intently, sipping the Bloody Mary and the coffee alternately, and eventually I got around to Kate's phone call, and that's when she told me I was being too harsh on her. Thought I'd never return to that, did you? Remember, I was hungover then, but now, typing this, I'm stone sober. Remember what's real.

"Flan," Natasha said. "Kate's not *delighted* you had a terrible evening. But you must admit, telling Carr to get his hand the fuck off your shoulder is a pretty irresistible tidbit."

"How does she know about everything already?"

"How does she ever know? Don't worry about it."

"But she's going to tell everybody about Mark," I said.

"What if she does? Everybody knows Mark's a scumbag already," Natasha said. "You may recall a certain incident involving his skull and my beer bottle? Now calm down and eat your egg and we'll go catch a movie. There's a one-fifteen matinee of *Stage Fright*; if I drive quickly we can make it."

If she drove quickly indeed. "I don't think my stomach could take food right now," I said. The poached egg gaped at me like a ripe breast. I thought of my own sagging ones – not in the least bit nice; Mark must have been even drunker than me – and didn't dare put anything into my body that could turn into more body. What a perfect excuse a hangover is not to eat anything. I should drink more often.

"You have to give your stomach something else besides a Bloody Mary and a cup of coffee or you aren't going to last through the fall of Denmark," she said.

"I'll have focaccia. Oh, speaking of which, I told Kate I'd invite Adam tonight. I can't believe he's going to be there. How did that happen?"

"Who would think we would have forgotten *Cymbeline*?" Natasha said. "Whoever – or *wherever* – Cymbeline is. So call him."

"I don't have his number," I said.

"You most certainly do," Natasha said. She took the rest of her celery and poked my uneaten egg right in the nipple. "Who exactly do you think you're talking to? I'm sure that you looked it up months ago and wrote it down in that gorgeous black leather notebook thing. Where is it, anyway? It's never far from you."

"It's right here," I said. "I'm writing down this conversation."

Sorry. I just can't hear myself think around here with that damn *radio* down the hall. If you can believe it, they're playing the same song that I have in my head today: Tonight tonight tonight. How the present resonates with the past! How the Flan of yesterday and the Flan of today intermingle, like best friends, like confidantes!

I left a message on his machine and by then it was three o'clock, with no chance of catching the movie. Natasha said she'd go home to change and pick me up. "What are you going to wear?" I said, out of the sheer desire to keep her in my house. "You looked great in that sequined thing last night."

"*X* marks the spot," she said, tracing last night's rhinestones on her body like she hoped to die, sticking a needle in her eye. "You want to borrow it tonight?"

"There's no way I'd fit into that," I said.

"It's bigger than it looks," she said.

I crossed my arms in front of my stomach. "Thanks."

"Oh Flan," she said, "I didn't mean it like that. Come on. You know that. I just mean –"

"Forget it," I said. "I'll see you soon. I have to iron my muu-muu now."

"*Flan*," she said, putting on some really smashing sunglasses. "I came over and fixed you breakfast, listened to your woes. What more do you want from me?"

I felt dumb. "Your forgiveness," I said meekly, and she smiled and hugged me, patting me on the back like a weary mom. She waved and headed out the door. "And a ride!" I called out. In front of the house, the world still looked a little too bright, but I was going to survive. "I also need a ride!"

Natasha zoomed off, and I went upstairs, found my journal right next to my bed, and wrote this all down. I'll let you know what happens with the inscrutable man and the crazy woman who loves him and all the intrigue and deception and murder. *And* how the play turns out, ha ha ha.

Sunday September 19th

So I haven't been in Bean and Nothingness *five minutes* – I'm still savoring the first frothy sips of latte and haven't even opened the journal yet – when Flora Habstat walks in, sits at my table and talks at me for the rest of the day. A whole day, wasted. Not a word in edgewise, either to her or my journal, lying there neglected on my table as Flora went into a free-form monologue on applying for colleges, how tired she was of school, this new band Darling Mud – had I heard of them? – and assorted World Records. She literally talked to me for about an hour and a half, and when I said I had to go to a bookstore, she went with me and dragged behind me as I pretended to scan the shelves, babbling and babbling and babbling. By the time I took the bus home it was seven o'clock and time to do my homework before turning in. And after such a miserable evening last night, too: Douglas and Lily tense as hell over some offstage fight, a whiny, inappropriately plump Ophelia, Gabriel not showing and Kate, coyly and significantly, refusing to tell me why and a blunt and obvious fake plaster skull. Plus Flora sat between Adam and me and talked Records to him from curtain to curtain. Dammit, Flora, why do you always ruin everything?

A prophetic remark. I hope you picked up on that.

Vocabulary:

ALLEGED   PSYCHOSEXUAL   TÊTE-Á-TÊTE
PHOSPHOLIPIDS   DISTRAUGHT   BELLIGERENT
VENDETTA   PROPHETIC

Study Questions:

1. What would you do in Flan's shoes, if you received an A you didn't really deserve even though you were a really good student, but you just didn't care very much about biology, and if you got it as sort of an apology or a bribe from a sleazy biology teacher that you probably couldn't do anything about? Consider the issues before deciding, and remember that you can't really imagine what it would be like to be in the shoes of Flannery Culp because you're not her.

2. What functions do you think are biologically important for the sustenance of a living system?

3. What is the best experience you have had at a high school dance?

Monday September 20th

After such a refreshing weekend, I am looking forward to starting another week of being pushed to the limit academically, athletically and socially at Roewer High

School. Go team! The bus was forty-five minutes late this morning.

I'm sitting on the lumbering late bus, thinking about the way I'm going to start my Monday: by filling out an unexcused absence form for the cranky secretary. The last time the bus was late she actually told me, "Don't tell me the bus was late. That excuse won't work anymore today. About ten kids ahead of you said that *their* bus was late, too." I tried to explain that we all took the same bus, but there was no pulling the wool over *her* eyes. She wasn't born yesterday.

LATER

When I walked into the building I thought for a moment I had mistakenly come in on Sunday. It was time for homeroom to be over but no one was in the hallways. I ran into some grumpy gym teacher who barked "Go back to homeroom!" so I went to homeroom, opened the door and everyone was sitting silently at their desks. Dodd was standing formally at the front of the room with his hands behind his back like he was waiting for the firing squad. Written on the blackboard, underlined, was the phrase "MOMENT OF SILENCE." *No kidding*, I thought, and found my seat. Even Natasha looked respectful; that's when I *knew* something serious was up. It didn't seem right to ask during the MOMENT OF SILENCE, so I waited it out. Finally Dodd cleared his throat and everyone relaxed and talked quietly. "Now you know why you shouldn't be late," he said to me pointedly.

"What in the world?" I asked Natasha. She sighed and took my hand, and that's when I knew someone was dead. I feel really guilty when I write this, but it was something of an anticlimax when Natasha told me it was Mark Wallace. Of course, *anticlimax* is *not* the word for how Mark's death was rewritten later. Dr. Eleanor Tert, of course, was the biggest culprit. I quote extensively and without permission from her *Crying Too Hard to Be Scared*:

> The tragic death of Mark Wallace, one of the most visionary students I have ever had the privilege of analyzing, was key in Flannery's development of her apocalyptic anti-religious fervor. Seeing her ex-boyfriend punished so immediately with a vengeful lightning bolt in the form of an automobile accident undoubtedly added to Flannery's God-wish. Mark Wallace was killed by an act of God, she reasoned; therefore, anyone who ever did her wrong in her tumultuous love life was doomed to die, and maybe God needed a little help. Hence the ritualistic murder.

And from Peter Pusher's *What's The Matter with Kids Today?: Getting Back to Family Basics in a World Gone Wrong*:

> Flannery Culp saw in her high school's rather limp-wristed reaction to the inevitable result of juvenile delinquency, particularly among minorities, a chance to exploit the freeloading humanist environment to which her educational system had fallen. It should come as no surprise that a school whose honors poetry class studied "ignored geniuses" like Anne Bradstreet and Emily Dickinson but not Keats or Shelley would soft-pedal the moralistic side of the death of the Negro teen Mark Wallace, or that a teenager, being educated in a moral vacuum, would see these soft-pedaling

surroundings as the perfect environs to hide the almost-perfect crime. [Wake up, America!]

Inaccuracy, inaccuracy, inaccuracy. Oh, and please note: That last sentence isn't at the end of that particular paragraph, but is at the end of so many others in the book that I couldn't resist adding it. I can't even begin to address the *inaccuracy*, but suffice to say that the reason we weren't studying Keats or Shelley in my *AMERICAN* Poetry class should be self-evident, even to Mr. Pusher, and that one cry of "nice tits" – are you listening, incidentally flat-chested Dr. Tert? – does not an ex-boyfriend make. Not to mention that the good Dr. Tert did not "analyze" Mark until he was already dead.

Here is what actually happened, from Flannery Culp's *Journal of a Woman Wronged*:

> Sometime Friday night, Mark Wallace, a boy no one liked very much, neither for his generally nasty behavior nor his self-righteous up-from-slavery politics he used to justify it, after getting smashed and making a slimy pass at me, stole a car with some buddies and smashed it into a telephone pole while Roewer High School slept. When Mark Wallace woke up, his buddies had fled into the night and he was dead. When Roewer woke up, Mark Wallace was a noble young martyr, killed for being, as Principal Bodin said over the squawking PA, "in the wrong place at the wrong time."

Doesn't everyone die by being in the wrong place at the wrong time? Bodin droned on and on, praising Mark's mischievous sense of humor and his artistic skills. Last year he had spray-painted an unflattering portrait of Vice Principal Mokie, with a speech bubble containing his annoying motto – "the last word in principal is *pal*" – coming out of his crotch like some sort of auto-erotic ventriloquist's act, for which he had been suspended despite the fact that he claimed he was protesting Mokie's racism. Dodd walked around the room with a shellacked frown on his face, occasionally putting a gentle hand on people's hairdos. He started to do it to Natasha but she bared her teeth at him.

It was in choir that things got ridiculous. They stopped auditions so we could rehearse the special number for tomorrow's Memorial Assembly. Tipsy John Hand actually took the helm and went on and on about Mark, of course, telling some stories that must have been about somebody else, and finally passing out copies of the gospel song "Ride the Chariot," which Mr. Hand had heard was one of Mark's favorites. Uh-huh. I can't believe that tomorrow (actually, today – it's after midnight as I write this, sitting in my room with Darling Mud on low) I'm going to get up at an assembly and sing "I'm gonna ride the chariot in the morning, Lord," in memory of someone who died in a car accident. The only good thing about choir was that Adam, deposed from conducting by the boozy eulogist, was standing in front of me in the skimpy tenor section and I didn't have to face him.

Biology was a travesty – no surprise there, I guess, but Carr talked about being able to trace the end of a life to an ultimate cause.

"Mark died from a blow to the head, but that isn't scientifically complete," he said. He began to draw a car on the chalkboard, and everyone's eyes widened. "After all, any one of us can go up to a telephone pole and bang our heads on it." I sat and hoped for a demonstration, but no dice. "We'll get a sore head, maybe a lump, but we don't die." Carr stared at the car on the board like he had no idea what to do with it. "So obviously the speed of the car had something to do with it. Now, I haven't seen any official reports of the accident, but let's assume that he was going at around eighty miles per hour, or 'mph.'" He put it in quotes in that annoying gesture that makes each hand into a little bunny. Prosecutors use that gesture all the time. "So we could say that Mark died from going eighty mph, but even that is not scientifically complete. *Why* was he going eighty miles an hour? Everyone knows that eighty miles an hour is not a safe speed at which to travel. But his judgment was impaired – by alcohol." Suddenly tomorrow's assembly was looking quite tasteful. "Therefore, we can scientifically determine that the ultimate cause of Mark's death was alcohol, and I think there is a stronger moral lesson when we have a scientifically complete explanation than if we just were to say that Mark died due to a blow to the head."

"But that isn't scientifically complete," some student said. I slouched down lower in my desk. Great, after a tacky monologue now it's time for a tacky discussion. "*Why* did Mark have alcohol? He was at a chaperoned school dance, with adult supervision. Perhaps those adults failed because they were too busy *flirting with the goddamn cheerleaders!*"

"You may recall, Flannery," said Mr. Carr, "that as a chaperon I was busy chasing down other people who were breaking the rules, such as yourself."

Everybody was staring at me. One girl snapped her gum. "*I* happen to be a cheerleader," she said. "Do you have a problem with that?"

The teaching assistant poked her head out of the office, curious about the commotion. "There's something you should all know about the good Mr. Carr," I said, and the bell rang. Everyone scattered except me and Carr and the teaching assistant. We had a MOMENT OF SILENCE.

"I know you've been upset lately," Carr said, "but your behavior in class today was absolutely unacceptable."

"*My* behavior?" I said. I heard the fury in my voice, but I didn't quite feel it. It was like I could hear the real Flannery, telling me to calm down because this was a very important semester and if I blew up at Carr my chances of an A would be greatly reduced, and all the while this angry, violent Flannery went on and on. "*My* behavior? You're making passes at your assistant, you try to bribe me by giving me a good grade I don't deserve, and you let a student die because you're so busy making moves on –"

"I think you've said just about enough," Carr said in a deadly voice. "You're obviously very upset about the death of your boyfriend, so why don't you take it easy instead of taking it out on your teachers."

"My *boyfriend*?" I said. "You and Dr. Tert *both*!" I stalked out of the classroom and right to Bodin's door. The situation was obviously escalating, and I needed outside help. My temper was getting out of control, and Carr had dropped in my eyes from a slightly sleazy teacher to an absolute monster. I was going to tell all and let the chips fall where they may. In short, I was going to ask to transfer to a different Advanced Biology class.

Principal Jean Bodin's secretary is a perfectly nice woman, except for the fact that she has snakes for hair.

"*What*?" she snarled immediately when I entered the room.

"I need to see Mr. Bodin."

"*Principal* Bodin's schedule is full today."

94

"Well, I have an appointment to meet with him right now."

Suspiciously, she opened her appointment book. I could see that it was blank, had been blank forever, world without end. Who ever needs to see a high school principal? "And who are you?"

"Superintendent Culp," I said, drawing myself to my full height (not much). I forgot to say that it's always apparent that this secretary's stone-turning gaze had apparently been directed long ago at her own brain.

"Principal Bodin," she said into the phone, "Superintendent Culp is here to see you."

Jean Bodin, large as life and twice as fat, opened the door. "Superintendent Culp!" he boomed, like an aging sports hero. Then he saw I was just some kid. "You're just some kid," he said.

"Who needs a new biology teacher," I said.

"I'm busy," he said, raising his hands in an A-Student!-Usher-Her-Out-Immediately! gesture.

"Maybe you can find a few minutes before the superintendent shows up," I said, and Bodin sighed and led me in to the inner sanctum. Medusa scowled; she always hates it when Perseus shows up. Check it out, Peter Pusher! A limp-wristed humanist who knows the classics!

Principal Bodin sat in his big chair and put his hands in back of his head like he was about to do sit-ups, though given his size he's probably never done any of those in his life. As a footnote, he must have gone on some radical diet a few months ago – in the press conferences at which he spoke extensively about new measures the San Francisco Unified School District had taken "virtually to ensure that teen-to-teen murder would be kept at an all-time minimum," he looked positively slender. "What seems to be the problem?"

"Nothing *seems* to be the problem," I said, "There *is* a problem. The problem is that Mr. Carr and I are mutually incompatible. I need a new biology teacher. Give me Mrs. Kayak (even though she sleeps behind dark glasses during class at least once a week). Give me Mr. Hunter (even though he displays at best a passing knowledge of biology). Give me anybody. I can't stay in there any longer." I bit my lip, hoping it was trembling. I figured the Teary Approach was a good opening strategy. I could always go for the Unstable Approach if things got too rough. It was too bad it wasn't gym; all I'd have to do was look at my lap and begin a sentence and the Man In Charge would let me do anything I wanted.

"I can't help you," Bodin said. All three chins moved as he spoke. "As you know, all of our classes are filled to capacity. If I let *you* move" – he gestured in my direction, presumably to remind me who I was –"I'd have to let *everybody* move, and *then* where would we be? Everybody would be coming in every few minutes, claiming that they were *mutually incompatible.* Everybody would catch it. The school would be a mess."

"This isn't a *virus*," I said, apparently deciding to go for the Angry Approach instead.

"You're right," he said. "It's not a virus. And you know what? I don't think it's a *problem*, either. You know what it is?" He grinned beatifically, a Caucasian Buddha. "It's a *challenge*. Your biology class is tough? *Good.* It *should* be tough. You're here at Roewer to be pushed to the limit academically, athletically and whatever-the-other-one-is."

"Sexually," I offered.

"Yes. *No. Socially.*"

"It's the same thing."

Bodin looked at me like he just realized I hadn't brought him a birthday present like I said I would.

"Well," he said. "There's nothing I can do. It's a *challenge*, for *you* to work out."

"*Please*," I said quietly, trying to backpedal to Teary again.

"Medusa!" Bodin called. "Show this young lady out, please."

The titan still babbling behind him, Perseus stormed out of the cave without waiting to be shown out, casually swinging his sword and decapitating the Gorgon at the front desk, but as I walked farther and farther down the hallway I felt like less and less of a hero. After all, tomorrow I have to go in and see Carr again, and Bodin's secretary will probably grow another head like that other creature back in Greece.

Tuesday September 21st

"MARTIN, MALCOLM AND MARK," the banner read, stretched loosely across the top of the auditorium stage so the letters rippled and lurched, and to this annoying abundance of alliteration they forgot to add MORTIFICATION, so I kindly supplied plenty of that. Instead of blundering into Bodin's office yesterday, I should have hung out in the Visual Arts Center, because once I realized what they were drawing I could have stomped all over it, ripped up the butcher paper. Ripped up *all* the butcher paper. For after I participated in an off-key, half-learned version of what most definitely was *not* Mark Wallace's favorite song, conducted by Johnny Hand, the art classes presented a fidgety assembly with a triptych of hurriedly painted portraits, each about the size of – well, about the size of an enormous head painted on butcher paper.

Martin Luther King, Malcolm X and Mark Wallace. Two great civil rights figures and Mark "Nice Tits" Wallace.

Principal Bodin spoke, reprising word-for-word large sections of yesterday's intercom elegy for virtually the same audience, while local TV cameras took note. Later they used a shot of Bodin's speech during the umpteenth Basic Eight scoop – "death is no stranger to Roewer High School" – with Bodin and his chins clutching the podium against a background of the lower half of Mark's face.

Principal Bodin was finishing up by telling us to go to our classes, but never to forget Mark Wallace, when a bunch of Mark's friends stood up with their fists raised. One of them, speaking as "a representative of Mark Wallace, his friends and The People," which I thought was an interesting distinction, demanded that school be canceled for the day, raising his voice even louder as the television cameras swiveled to find him. He reminded Bodin that if a white student had died the school would definitely be closed. This turned out not to be true, but Bodin didn't argue the point. He agreed immediately, licking his lips and standing directly beneath the half-opened mouth of the middle head like Mr. X was about to eat him. Everyone cheered – which gave the whole proceedings an even more eerie feel – and we all left. I didn't have to catch anyone's eye to know that we'd all meet at the Mocha Monkey, and sure enough within twenty minutes Natasha, Gabriel, V___, Kate, Douglas and I were all sipping lattes and draping our coats on simian faces. V___, always having the upper hand in matters of pocket money, had bought a big plate of some luscious-looking biscotti, and I would like to proudly say that I only ate half of one. Natasha – you know, thin, beautiful Natasha – took three.

"What this gang needs," Natasha said, eating the third, "is another dinner party. *Are* we charming sophisticates or aren't we?"

"Oh," Kate said, clasping her hands together. "We *are*, we *are*!"

"Yes," V___ said, "with just the Basic Eight. No outsiders, particularly those who quote from any nationally syndicated collection of record setters."

"Friday night?" Douglas said. "I know Lily can make it then."

"Where *is* Lily?" Kate asked.

"She had to go home and practice," Douglas said, miming a cellist.

"She has to practice being home?" V___ asked.

Douglas tried to look offended but gave up and laughed. It's good to see him without Lily chaperoning.

"Friday it is." Kate said. "Where should we have it?"

"My parents are –"

"Let me guess," I said, and everybody chimed in. "*Entertaining*." The last of my steamed milk went down wrong.

"*My*, we are punchy today," Natasha said. "My house is out too."

"And mine," I said.

"You just said that," Douglas said. "Kate?"

"OK," she said. "But can we watch a movie afterward? I've been craving noir."

"*Well*, OK," Natasha said airily. "I *guess* I could sit through an old movie. *Maybe* – just *maybe*, mind you – one with Marlene Dietrich in it."

"OK, it's all set," Gabriel said, rubbing his hands together. "I'll cook. Something with peanuts, maybe." He leaned against V___ and gave her a kiss on the head. "Let's get away from all these monkeys. Flan, do you need a ride?"

"No, Natasha will take me," I said.

"That's nice of her," Natasha said dryly. "Let's go."

99

I heard a few bars of Darling Mud when Natasha turned on the motor, but she immediately ejected the tape. "I'm so *sick* of them," she said, and put in something with echoey guitars and a man singing earnestly about the pain in his heart. Very unlike her. "You know what?" she said, swigging from the flask and scowling impatiently at the car in front of us. "*Gabriel*, Flan. *Gabriel*. He is so fucking *chivalrous*. Go go go! The speed limit is just a rough *guideline*," she snarled. "He is so *fuck-ing chiv-al-rous*." Each syllable was punctuated by a blast of the horn. "Don't you think so?"

"I don't know what you're saying."

"It just *hit* me," she said, merging. "Asking you if you wanted a ride home. Listening to your love woes by the lake. Taking you home after the dance when you were such a mess, you know what I'm saying?"

"No," I said, and she looked at me, turned up the music and clamped her mouth shut all the way home. She opened the car door and looked at me like an overbearing mother, watching me disobey her. "No," she said, "you wouldn't." I got out, shut the door and looked at her.

"Come in and have some coffee," I said, but she was already halfway down the block. What the hell was *that*?

Wednesday September 22
God, I'm bored. Bored of high school, bored of my friends, bored of editing this goddamn journal. Nothing happened today, how's that for the prime period of my life? Nothing. I cut choir and hung out with Hattie Lewis, there, that's something. She was correcting papers, though, so she barely said a word. She got some red ink on her nose, is that what you want to read? Carr passed out fruit flies, what more do you want? We're going to breed them and

see the colors of the eyes of the next generation, how's that for riveting prose? Do you approve of that sort of education, schoolchildren watching bugs have sex, Peter Pusher? How's that for some psychological insight into a symbol for Youth Gone Amok, Dr. Tert? After school we played a game where we improvised scenes with Ron Piper – you remember him, folks, you witch-hunted him all November – changing the tone instantly by calling out a genre. "Gothic!" he called out and we were gothic; "Western!" he called out, and we were all western. What do *you* want, reader? How shall the rewrites go? You're paying taxes for my room and board, so I'll do anything you want. Isn't that what you wanted? Wake up, America!

Thursday September 23rd

Today's the day. This is the day that Flannery Culp commits the crime. I can almost feel the itch on your noggin as you scratch your head, reader. You didn't think it was this early, did you? You thought it was around Halloween. How confusing. Could it be that our narrator is unreliable? No such chance. Mind like a steel trap, I have. Lucky for me, because there's a Calculus test *tomorrow*, covering "what we've been doing," Baker said, glaring at me like I was an idiot when I asked. "What do you mean *we*?" I wanted to say, but there's no reason to fish for an F where you're pretty much guaranteed one by your own skills. Oh boy.

In other Glaring News, Adam has been glaring at me all period as I sit and write this. He *should* be glaring at the tenors, who can't get their parts right for the life of them. But as he drills them he keeps glaring at me. It makes my stomach do that snapped-elevator-cable thing. Everybody hates me. Maybe I'll get up the guts to talk to him next period; we haven't had a real conversation since we went and got wine, aside from me confessing my love during my alto audition. I lead a ridiculous life.

LATER

So after choir I waited for everyone to leave, until it was just Adam, sifting through sheet music on top of the piano, and me, and two hundred thousand folding chairs. He pretended not to notice me for a full minute, I could count on the official school clock clucking above us like some Authoritarian Hen. Where's Natasha when I need her? She'd know what to do. All I could think of was clearing my throat.

Adam looked up, sourly. "Hi," he said like he'd rather be sorting sheet music than even looking at me. "What's up?"

"No fair," I sighed, not looking at him. "That was my question."

"What do you mean?" he asked. He had a little pile of sheet music he was straightening, clunking it on the piano top like knuckles. It punctuated the buzzing in my head.

"I mean what's up?" I said, meeting his blank eyes. "You've been glaring at me all rehearsal."

"I'm just tired," he said, lying. "I meant to be glaring at the tenors."

"Oh," I said. The clock clucked. "You know, if something's bothering you, you can tell me."

"Well," he said. "I *am* sort of annoyed that you keep cutting choir."

"What? When?"

"Yesterday, for example."

"Well, *that*."

"You've cut a number of times."

"Well, it's nothing *personal*," I said. "I didn't realize it bothered you. I mean, you know how it is. Sometimes you have stuff to do."

"Forget it," he said, and grabbed his backpack. "I have to go."

"What's *wrong*?" I said, and heard with horror that I sounded like a whining girlfriend. "You glare at me today, you barely spoke to me Saturday night."

Adam put a hand on my furious shoulder. "I just need some room," he said, taking his hand away and running it through his (gorgeous!) hair. "I just need" – gesturing nowhere – "a little room." He left and I was alone with the folding chairs. I looked around the cavernous rehearsal hall and felt yet another stupid pun leap out of my throat like acid. "You don't need a little room!" I shouted at the gaping door. "You already have an *enormous* room! *Look* at this place!"

I stalked out the door and almost ran into him. Somehow I assumed he'd be long gone. He was watching me with typical boy detachment, like I was some toddler tantruming and that any moment he'd pick me up by my feet and take me to bed.

No chance of *that*, I suppose.

"*What*?" I said.

"I'm sorry," he said.

Pop! All the air left me. "Oh," I said. He didn't *look* very sorry, but what can you say when someone says they're sorry, particularly if they don't really have much to be sorry for. So I love him. So he doesn't know if he loves me yet. What can anyone do?

"Come on, let's talk," he said, gesturing toward a side door. A talk outside the side entrance was something; people either made out or broke up out there.

Both of us were sighing in unison when Adam opened the door and we stepped out into the little dismal postdoor area. Another PTA sign, half-ripped, was taped to a wall; apparently we were supposed to be pushed to the limit academically, athletically and so. A brimming trash can, cigarette butts and a small bench with Carr's teaching assistant sobbing on it. Oh.

Adam and I looked at each other and I felt our own small troubles wilt. Adam cleared his throat but she didn't hear, or didn't look up. "I'm going to –" I said to him, stepping toward her, and he nodded, turned around and went back into the building. When the door slammed shut she looked up, saw me and started crying harder. For some reason I froze for a few seconds and the world froze with me – I could even hear birds chirping like they do in suspenseful outdoor scenes in movies. Poised between comforting her and running back to find Adam, I didn't know what to do. I just stood there, and then I heard in my head the Voice of Calculus, Mr. Michael Baker. He was reciting his rule, Baker's Rule: do *something*. I guess somewhere in my head I was actually studying for the Calc test. Do *something*. So I did.

The door stuck for a second, so I had to pull it extra hard, and it made a wheezing noise that let me know I was supposed to be pushing. So I pushed in, and stalked down the hallway, around a corner, almost ran into Adam. Without thinking I just shot out my hand and pushed him aside; I heard him hit the lockers, hard. I kept walking. When I reached my biology classroom I peeked inside to see if Carr or some studying geeks were around; nobody was. That would probably mean the door was locked and that I'd have to pull it off its hinges.

No such luck. The door opened immediately, and the cabinet was unlocked, too. Using my whole arm I picked up all the test tubes like I was gathering daisies. Some of them dropped to the floor and shattered, but the other ones I did methodically: I put them on the desk, and one by one I uncorked each one and set all the fruit flies free. *Fly out the window,* I thought. *Sleep with anyone you want, red eyes, blue eyes; sleep with yaks if you so desire, fucking Drosophila!* I walked back out of the room and stepped into the hallway just as the bell rang. People washed over me, a tide of binders and fruit-flavored gum and snatches of gossip. I sat through Applied Civics like a zombie, and walked slowly to Advanced Biology like a conquering general on his way to see the city burning. I have to work on my grandiose walk; I was late.

"You guys have a free period," Carr was saying as I opened the door. "We were supposed to start work with the fruit flies today, but my teaching assistant let all the fruit flies escape. She's been fired. There'll probably be a new assistant next week."

Friday September 24th
What sort of loser cuts Calc to sit in the library? I'm sitting in the part where ivied-campus posters loom over you like those annoying suspicious teachers who prowl the aisles of the classroom during tests until you can't keep your eyes on your own paper, only on the annoying suspicious teachers telling you to keep your eyes on your own paper. The posters remind me why I'm here: I'm here at Roewer to get As, so I can go to college and read books in artfully lit libraries and peer into test tubes in well-equipped labs and read a little Thoreau on beautiful lawns and play Frisbee with people of different races. I need to forget about squinting at expensive black leather journals in awfully lit libraries and peering into test tubes of fruit flies (luckily, I *can* forget about that; the next shipment won't arrive for a few weeks) and reading a little Dickinson in potato chip-littered courtyards and playing mind games

with people who are for the most part of my race. I must concentrate on the future, on where I will be. I need to try to forget about Carr. I can't touch him. He's indestructible. I just need to hang on, and take plenty of notes and make it through this. I want to go to college; I don't want to end up some loser, living alone under a bridge or something.

Or a criminal. I don't want to end up a criminal.

My only lucky break in all of this is that I probably won't get busted for Drosophila Liberation, because Carr has already blamed the wrong person. So even if everyone *does* know (I could have sworn that Bio Room was empty, where were those geeks, hiding under the tables like it was an earthquake drill?) that it was me freeing the fruit flies, nothing will be put on my permanent record.

Get it down in ink, Flan: today is the day I start being Super Student. I will not allow myself to sink into the mire of the present, I must reach toward the future. Even now, editing, I feel that way. I can't sink into the mire of the present, but must reach back and back into the past, holding each day of last year up to the light, to illuminate the truth for all of you. Listen to me.

LATER
You know, despite all my world-weariness and cynicism, I think I've always believed that there is one person in the universe who you're truly meant for – *for whom you are truly meant* – and the fact that sometimes there are two or even more people on the earth you can fall in love with really bothers me. It suggests that if you work hard you can be meant for anyone. Maybe that's a more comforting notion. The champagne poured and poured into my mouth tonight, and I can see that it's pouring back out. Start over, sister.

Gabriel drove me straight to the grocery store from school, and straight from the grocery store to the dinner party so he could wash and dry all the mushrooms properly in time to eat. I forget what kind of mushrooms they were, but fancy ones. We went to Kate's house and I immediately felt underdressed, still wearing my school clothes and all. Gabriel had brought a shirt and tie in a bag, of course, but that had never occurred to me. So while Gabriel used his special mushroom brush, brought in the same bag as the shirt and tie, Kate found me a sweater big enough for me to fit into (yes, such sweaters do exist) in a lovely shade of – can we guess? – navy blue, and when I came back downstairs Douglas and Lily were already there and Natasha was just coming up the front steps. Darling Mud was on (loud music during cooking; quiet during dinner, immutable), and Gabriel had enlisted Kate as Shrimp Deveiner. I peeked in the kitchen, but Kate and Gabriel were in earnest conversation and looked up like I'd caught them with their hands in the cookie jar, so I scooted to the living room. Natasha had brought an artichoke-heart dip and some chopped red peppers and broccoli florets; I guess she was anxious to avoid the should-I-bake-the-cheese-or-not controversy of last weekend. Was it really last weekend? It feels like ages ago. Oh, it wasn't last weekend; it *was* ages ago. Douglas – stunning linen suit – and Lily were diving into it like they'd been doing something strenuous all afternoon. I don't want to think about it. Natasha looked up, suddenly, and strode to the stereo. "I'm getting very tired of Darling Mud." She took the tape out and stared at it like it tasted bad. Badly.

"Oh sure," Kate called from the kitchen. Ears like a bat, that girl has, the better to be Queen Bee. "You're sick of them and you haven't even taped them for me yet."

"I'll get to it," Natasha said, emptying her bag on the carpet. "Somewhere in this mess is the new Q.E.D. album."

"*Prattle and Hum*? You bought it?" Douglas asked.

"Since when has a classical snob like you heard of *Prattle and Hum*?" either Natasha or I said, I can't remember.

"Prattle and *what*?" V—— asked as she came up the stairs. "The door was open, Kate. I brought flowers because Douglas said he didn't have time." She had a bunch of lilies, one of which she had turned into a corsage.

"What have you been doing all afternoon, Douglas?" Natasha asked pointedly. She was on her knees, rifling through lipsticks, eyeliners, loose change and individually wrapped chocolates and condoms. Douglas turned red and coughed, but was saved from a reply when Natasha found the tape. "Here it is! And it's not *Prattle and Hum*; it's *Gurgle and Buzz*."

"What are we talking about?" V—— said. "And Kate, where is the silver polish?"

"You'd better hurry and polish everything," Lily said, handing Natasha a stray condom with a dry look. "Gabriel said that dinner must be at seven-thirty *sharp* or the rice won't be right."

"It's only five after," V—— said, consulting a gold watch. "And Jenn isn't even here yet. Is she the only one we're waiting for?"

"I think so." I started to count to seven on my fingers. "Me, Douglas, Lily, Gabriel, Kate, V—— and –"

"Flora Habstat?" Lily said.

"*No*," Natasha said, putting on the Q.E.D. tape, "*not Flora Habstat*."

"So *yes*, Jennifer Rose Milton will complete the Basic Eight."

"It's so nice," Kate said, emerging from the kitchen and wiping her hands on a Mona Lisa apron, "to *finally* have a dinner party that's just *us*. Give me a broccoli."

Frank Whitelaw appeared on the front steps just as the earnest voice of Q.E.D.'s singer appeared on the stereo. "I keep finding what I'm not looking for," he whined (the singer, not Frank) as he (Frank, not the singer) bounded up the stairs. We all stood there looking at him like he came out of a spaceship. We all would have stood there all night, stock-still, had Jennifer Rose Milton not come up behind him, apologizing for being late. For *being late*. She brings someone as dumb as a bag of hammers to one of *our* dinner parties and apologizes for being late.

"It's OK!" Gabriel called from the kitchen. He hadn't seen Frank Whitelaw yet. "The rice is taking longer than I thought." He strode into the living room. "In the meantime a little broccoli would be – Frank!" A beautiful recovery for our champ. "I didn't know you were coming! What a surprise!"

"Surprising indeed," Kate said. "You'd better polish another place setting, V——."

"I brought champagne," Frank said, like he'd been trained to say it and couldn't say anything else. He held up four bottles of champagne, two in each enormous hand. I caught myself thinking about the hand/genitalia ratio and just when I was about to gaze mid-khaki and hazard a guess I stopped myself and looked back at the bottles. Well, that was something; no one had come up with anything to drink yet, and I hadn't had time to stop at home and raid my New Year's stash.

"It's cold, even." Jennifer Rose Milton said winningly, like she could read our minds. We all waited for Kate to make up her mind.

"Very well then," she said, finally. "Let's pour."

Frank poured, and kept pouring, and Gabriel's rice was perfect, perfect, perfect. We chatted away, and Frank detracted surprisingly little, being as he didn't talk much; it was just like there was an enormous chunk of wood perched to Jennifer Rose Milton's left, occasionally kissing her. After dinner Kate put on a noir videotape while the shrimp pots soaked, but in our champagne haze we dozed through it, rousing only when Natasha turned off the movie and the static blared us awake.

"I will not have Marlene slept through," she announced. "It's time to go home."

"It wasn't even Marlene; it was Veronica Lake," Gabriel said grumpily. "You were obviously napping, too. Come on, I'll take you home, Flan."

I jumped up. Gabriel never has to clean, because he cooks, and I wouldn't either if he took me home. I kissed everyone good night (well, *nodded* at Frank) and stood at the top of the stairs as Gabriel found his school clothes, his whisk, his special pepper grinder and the mushroom brush and kissed everyone good night (well, *nodded* at Frank). Kate grasped his shoulder, looked at him significantly and gave him a brief thumbs-up; she must have really liked those shrimp. Outside the air was cold and Kate's sweater was thin, but Gabriel, chivalrous as ever, gave me his blazer and I walked to his car feeling the cool night air. From the hill where Kate's house is you can see a bright view of the city, and I leaned against his car and stared at the constellations of streetlights, winking at me like mischievous creatures of the night, while Gabriel tried to get into his automobile. The lock on the door always jams.

"Shit!" he said, and I was yanked out of my reverie. "Sorry," he said when I faced him.

"No problem," I said. "I could look at this night for hours."

"Well, hopefully it won't take that long," he said, pursing his lips. He looked nervous. "Do you have any plans tomorrow night?"

"Oh, you know, I'm the lead in that Broadway show, I should probably call the pope. The usual," I said. "Why?"

"Well, do you want to see that movie where Andrew MacDowell is the professor and falls in love with his student? It opened this week."

With a cameo by Jim Carr, probably, I thought, but out loud I said, "That sounds good. We should have planned this at the dinner table, though; they'll probably figure out something else as they scrub pots."

Gabriel tried the key again; no dice. He looked at me like I wasn't making it any easier. "I wanted to ask *you*," he said, and I got it.

"Oh, right, better to make plans without Mr. Whitelaw around," I said. "No reason to spend the *entire weekend* with him."

"No, I mean *just you*," he said, looking at the lock. He started to look at me but looked back at the lock. He looked at the lock. "I wanted to ask – *just you*." He looked at me and sort of rolled his eyes. He showed me the key he had been trying, moved down a notch on his key ring and showed me another, tried that one in the lock and opened the door effortlessly. "Just a movie," he said like he was apologizing.

"Just me," I said slowly, "and just a movie." The car door gaped open. It was the passenger side door. He was opening the car door for *me*.

"Right," he said, and looked out toward the city. "I mean, if you want. We could *all* go, too. It doesn't matter."

I got in the car and unlocked his side for him. He got in and started the car, gripping the steering wheel like it might spin out of his hands even though we weren't going anywhere. Like it might spin away. With champagne in my head I could say anything. With champagne in my head I could sit right next to Gabriel and think, *But what if Adam calls and asks me out tomorrow night?*

"Why don't you call me tomorrow," I said, and Gabriel looked at me like an enormous question mark. "When we have a newspaper in front of us, so we can see what time it starts. I have so much champagne in me I can't possibly schedule anything. How about you? Should you be driving?"

"I'm fine," he said, and in the dark his teeth smiled like what's-his-name's cat. He looked at me sheepishly and just about broke my heart. "I'm a little giddy," he said, "but I'm fine."

You know, despite all my world-weariness and cynicism, I think I've always believed that there is one person in the universe for whom you are truly meant – and the fact that sometimes there are two or even more people on the earth you can fall in love with really bothers me. It suggests that if you work hard you can be meant for anyone. *Maybe that's a more comforting notion,* I thought as I watched Gabriel drive, but inside I wasn't sure. I could deny Adam and make myself be meant for Gabriel, but what would that be? Would it be like studying hard and getting good grades, or would it be like sneaking into a room I had no business in and setting free little bugs that were never supposed to be free, never supposed to be flying unfettered in the air? I know, I know: *in which I had no business.*

Saturday September 25th

Douglas, the only man in my life who I thought *wasn't* doing strange things, knocked on my door at nine-thirty in the morning. The two of us looked at each other, me in my robe and damp hair and he in a brown heathered suit and a hat.

"Hi," he said. "How've you been?"

"You mean during the last nine hours since I've seen you? Oh, fine. You know. *Sleeping*. What are you talking about?"

"I thought that maybe it was a perfect day for walking across the Golden Gate Bridge."

I stood there thinking that perhaps I had stepped into a time warp. Walking across GGB had been my standard date with Douglas; all that was missing was the flowers. I had a brief ray of hope that what I thought had been last summer and this first month of school had in fact been a long, fevered dream, and that I was waking up and it was my junior year. I was still going out with Douglas, I hadn't done anything dumb like write letters all summer to some boy, I was going to sign up for Chemistry instead of Biology, I wasn't going to commit a murder fairly soon and my grades didn't count quite as much toward college. Douglas must have read my thoughts because he smiled and said, "Not like that, not like that, I figured you've had enough of *that* this weekend. You must not have had coffee yet."

"Yeah, well, it is before ten o'clock. Why did you come over so early?"

"I couldn't sleep. Plus I figured if I waited any longer some other member of the Basic Eight would scoop you up and put you through the third degree about Gabriel."

"And *you* wanted to do it first."

"No, I wanted to walk across the Golden Gate Bridge. We can talk about him or not. We can talk about *anything* or not. Now go get dressed and I'll make the coffee. Where do you keep the filters?" He was already in my kitchen, opening cupboards – but, typical male, the wrong ones of course. Not like he'd ever been in my house, making me coffee nineteen thousand times. I reached over his head and opened the right cupboard. For a moment my face, my mouth, was right near his neck, and I felt a flush go down my body, naked and still damp under the robe. I hadn't had anything close to a sexual moment with Douglas for quite a while. It was odd. He was looking at me like he was afraid I was going to hit him, and when I avoided his eyes and looked back at his neck I saw why. For a minute it looked like a birthmark, but I knew Douglas's neck. The purplish blotch on his neck wasn't a birthmark. I looked back at him and he looked terrified.

"Um, aren't you supposed to wear turtlenecks to cover those up?" I asked him. "Surely you own a turtleneck, Douglas."

"I don't, actually," he said. "Gave them away." His hand strayed to the mark and stayed there. I handed him the box of coffee filters and he looked at it for a second before taking his hand off his neck and taking it from me. I remembered suddenly that I had bought him a turtleneck, a nice one, black, last Christmas. I thought it was a good time for me to go upstairs and get dressed.

It was a perfect day for GGB walking. San Francisco tourists always attempt to pillage our city in short shirts and Bermuda shorts, and on foggy days like this they are soundly defeated. Today they could be found huddling in rental cars, clutching one another and grimacing for cameras, they were an innocuous presence; Flora Habstat would have written *The Guinness Book* to tell them no one asked us to take a family portrait with white sailboat dots and an island prison in the background. *Here we are on the Golden Gate Bridge,* those pictures seem to say, mom and dad smiling emptily with hands placed artificially on the shoulders of itchy, embarrassed teenagers. What Douglas had to say was less clear. He kept making small talk about nothing and nervously covered his neck when anyone else went by. Eventually we walked in silence, Douglas looking at the ground and me looking at him, running my hand along the fence they recently installed to give suicides an added challenge.

"So, how are things going with Lily?" I said.

He looked past me at the fence. "A lot of people must jump from here," he said. "I wonder why. I mean, I *know* why they want to end their lives, but why here?"

"So I'm hearing that things aren't so hot," I said, and he looked at me and smiled.

"Sorry," he said. "I guess I *am* a little gloomy today."

"The *weather* is a *little* gloomy today. You are *lots* gloomy. *Are* things with you and Lily all right?"

"They have their ups and downs," he said, gazing at the water. "You dated a classical musician so you know how it is. With two it's almost constant melodrama."

"You act like that's a bad thing," I said. "And how does Mr. Classical Musician know about the new Q.E.D. album?"

"I don't know," he said, and for the first time all day I really looked at him. His eyes looked so tired they were almost closed, and his whole face was wrinkled with worry like a prisoner, or a widow. He looked as if he might cry. Above him seagulls cried too. He looked up at them, down at the water, over at the traffic, not at me. "I don't know," he said again.

"*Hey,*" I said. "*Hey.* This is *me.* You know, *Flannery.* You can tell me *anything.* What's going on?"

"Nothing," he said reflexively, the way people do when you ask how are you and they say fine and then remember they have cancer. "I don't know."

"Are you bothered by what Gabriel is doing, you know, with me? Because, you know, *I* haven't even worked out what's going on with that –"

"No, no," he said impatiently. "I don't care about that. I mean, I *care* about what happens with you, of course, but –"

"Then is it things with you and Lily?"

"No, no, no –"

"Because, I mean, how bad could things be if you're bruising each other all night?"

"I didn't get this from her," he said, quickly, quietly, pointing at his neck. I felt a chill, and it wasn't the fog; I was properly dressed in a sweatshirt, remember?

"*What*?" I hissed. I looked around us hurriedly. Some lone brave tourists, shivering in shorts, were nearby; Lily was unlikely to have any connections with them but you couldn't be sure. "What are you saying? Are you dating somebody else?"

"Um –"

"*Douglas,*" I said, "are you seeing another woman?"

"No, no," he said, quickly. "I'm not – it's too complicated to go into right now, but –"

"*Douglas,*" I said, ducking my head to meet his eyes. "Lily's a friend of mine. *You're* a friend of mine. What's going on?"

"I don't want to – I *can't* talk about it now."

"Douglas, Lily isn't going to talk to those tourists. I can't promise that *I* won't tell anyone, but –"

"Just *please*, I need you to do something for me," he pleaded.

"What?" I asked, seeing just how frightened he looked. Whatever this was, it was bigger than Lily and me and the whole Basic Eight. "What?"

"I need to cover this up, of course, that's what," he said, pointing to his neck and looking around like a spy. "Do you have something, makeup or something? I can't let Lily see this! What would she think?"

"Probably what I'm thinking," I said. "I don't know, Douglas. I'm not going to help you cover up for something unless I know what it is."

"Look," he said, running his hand through his hair. "I'm not seeing another woman, OK? Is that what you want to hear? That isn't what's happening. But Lily will *think* that's what's happening, and I need you to cover up for me! Please!"

"Just buy a turtleneck," I said. "Don't get *me* involved in this, Douglas! Lily's my *friend*, and she's paranoid enough about the two of us without this."

"I *can't*," he said. "This thing will take a few days –"

"*Hickey*," I said. "*Love bite*. Just say what it is. You have a *hickey* that comes from someone who isn't –"

"It will take several days to wear off, and I can't wear turtlenecks for several days in a row. Everyone's used to seeing me in these suits! What will they think?" He was getting absolutely panicky.

"Well then, go buy some makeup."

"I can't do that," he said. "I can't do that, I can't do that, I can't do that, I can't do that –"

"Calm down, Douglas. *Jesus*."

"You've got to help me."

"I don't know."

Douglas's face grew angular, his eyes squinty. "Listen, Flannery," he said in a low voice. "No one's supposed to tell you this, but on Thursday Bodin called some of us into his office. Me, and V____, and Flora and I forget who else."

I blinked, trying to keep up with the changing subject. "What did our good principal want?"

"Well, he'd heard the rumor about you setting the fruit flies free, and he called in some friends of yours to sort of grill them."

"Flora's not a friend of mine."

"Yes, she *is*, Flan. But you're missing the point."

"Who else did he call in? Gabriel?"

"No."

"Natasha?"

"No, she wasn't there that day, remember? In fact, *you* weren't, either, which is what saved you. But you're missing the point."

"What do you mean, *I* wasn't?"

"Well, everybody knows you were there that day, but for some reason you were officially marked absent. Dodd must have spaced out –"

"Or got me and Natasha confused –"

"Whatever. But what that meant was you couldn't have done anything if you weren't there. But you're missing the point."

"Did you guys back up my story?"

"Yes. We told Bodin we'd heard the rumor, too, but that we didn't think there was any truth to it. Of course, we didn't say that you weren't there that day, because we didn't know, but Bodin seemed too dim to really catch that, plus Carr was chomping at the bit to fire that assistant –"

"Carr was there?"

"Yes. But you're missing the point."

"OK, OK," I said. "What *is* the point?"

"The point was, we backed you up even though we didn't know the story. All we heard was that you had done something kooky in a classroom, and knowing your love of *panache* we guessed it was probably true. But even though we were suspicious we backed you up, because we're your *friends*. We *trusted* you; we knew that even if you had done something wrong you had a good reason. And once Kate had the opportunity to fill us in it turns out you *did* have a good reason."

"So what does this have to do with you?"

"I'm telling you. Sometime you'll be filled in, and you'll know I have a good reason. But right now I need your help and you have to trust me." He actually started to cry, right there. Just a few tears, but that's a lot for a boy, even one who can tell Shostakovich from Tchaikovsky and wears linen suits to school. "Please."

So I helped him. But I didn't feel good about it. Something in the way he told me about the scene in Bodin's office made me feel obliged to help him. Like my friends, unbeknownst to me, had made a move, and I had to follow. They had upped the loyalty ante of the Basic Eight, and now I followed. OK, I didn't feel that way until later, but it *could* fit in this situation. It took forever – Douglas was really paranoid, so we had to drive to some desolate neighborhood, and I went in by myself and bought a bunch of different shades of base, and then back at my place, with the shades down, I tested them until I found the right one (surprisingly, a fairly dark one, considering how pale I consider Douglas to be) and blended his neck until the bruise faded. He made me promise to meet him early, before school every day, until it faded. We compromised, and he said he'd drive to my house to do it, and that he'd fill me in as soon as he possibly could. I can't even imagine.

Once he'd left, I cleaned up the coffee mugs, and noticed that Douglas had left his hat at my house. I took it upstairs and put it on a chair in my room, on top of Kate's blue sweater. I checked the answering machine, thinking there'd be a message from Gabriel, hoping there'd be one from Adam, but I had forgotten to leave it on.

It was getting on toward six o'clock. I considered calling other people, asking them what the plan was for tonight, but then I realized they'd probably planned something to leave Gabriel and me alone, so I just sat in the living room, listening to the Bach that Douglas put on and writing this all down. It's now ten o'clock – the latest showing of the movie was nine-thirty. So I think it's safe to say that I don't have a date with Gabriel this evening. Or Adam, for that matter, or even some coffee date with Natasha or someone. I'm alone. There's a poem in that, but I don't want to write it. I don't want to be someone who spends Saturday night alone at home, writing poems about being alone.

Vocabulary:

LIMP-WRISTED   ELOCUTION   DROSOPHILA*
GALLIVANTING

*May be difficult to find in some dictionaries.

Study Questions:

1. In this chapter, Flannery writes: "I lead a ridiculous life." Do you agree with her assessment? Why or why not? Do you lead a ridiculous life? Why or why not?

2. Is it rude to bring an uninvited guest to a dinner party? Should you be excused if it's your boyfriend? What if he's dumb?

3. Do you think Flannery did the right thing with Douglas at the Golden Gate Bridge? Do you think Douglas did the right thing with

Flannery at the Golden Gate Bridge? Do you think Bodin did the right thing with Douglas and the others in his office? Did Douglas and the others do the right thing with Bodin, and Flannery, in Bodin's office? Do you generally do the right thing? Questions like these will be repeated several times throughout this journal, but write down an answer each time, so it's fresh.

Monday September 27th

Super Student was almost late to homeroom today, because it took longer than I thought to blend Douglas's neck at my house. If you can believe it, I had to duck when we entered the student parking lot because Lily was right there and Douglas didn't want for her to see us together. I had to run down the hall to Dodd's room, wondering why. I mean, if he marked me absent *again* I could cause a little more havoc and not get caught. But not me, oh no. I'm Super Student, remember? Don't you remember on Friday, how I sat in the library and wrote out a pledge to be Super Student, *all the while missing my fucking Calc test*?

Well, don't feel bad, I didn't realize it either until I showed up late for Calculus and everybody was getting their tests back. Baker didn't even look at me until the bell rang and everybody left us alone.

"Are you going to try the I Have A Really Good Reason For This approach, or just skip directly to Have Mercy On Me Mr. Baker?" he asked, erasing the board.

I swallowed. "That would be the latter," I said.

He turned around. "You know, based on the score for your last test, you could form a cohesive argument that statistically you had a chance of a better score if you didn't show up, but even so I take it as a personal insult."

If there's one thing that drives me nuts it's when teachers take it as a personal insult when you screw up. I mean, I was already taking it as a personal insult to *myself*, getting an F on a Calc test and thus keeping my F average at an even keel and ending up living under a bridge, and now, Mr. Baker was insulted, too. Bring on the Fs, leave out the bonus guilt, thanks very much. "I didn't mean it as a personal insult," I said, standing up and getting my books together. "I was stressed out, I cut class, I forgot there was a test. I'm sorry. I'll send you a balloon-o-gram or something so you'll feel better about giving me an F."

"You know," he said, "your *attitude* isn't going to help you get anywhere, either."

How wrong he turned out to be. I looked at him, and realizing that Super Student or no, it wasn't a very good plan to alienate all of my teachers during the first semester of my senior year, I put my books back down. "I guess now wouldn't be the right time to ask you for a letter of recommendation." He and I looked sternly at each other, and then both shrugged, both smiled.

"Can I give you a makeup test?" he asked. I wanted to tell him I'd already had one this morning, with Douglas, but instead I just nodded. "Will you get an F on it anyway?" I nodded again.

"You know," he said, "one of my students in fourth-period class has been doing some tutoring. The two of you could meet, after school or something. I don't need to tell you that it's an important semester, Flannery."

"I know, I know. Who is this *wunderkind*?"

"Her name's Flora Habstat. Do you know her?"

I'm sorry, I'm too miserable to write down the rest of the conversation. I'm missing what Hattie Lewis is saying, anyway. We're starting Poe today. You know, ever since I heard Poe was manic-depressive, I'm thinking maybe I am too. Who knows? I mean, plenty of people purport to know, from Dr. Tert's (in)expert testimony to talk-show queen Winnie Moprah: "I'm guessing that Flannery Culp had lots of pain in her life." That's really what she said, "lots of pain," like I owned some undeveloped land somewhere, filled with prickly plants and broken glass. I'm guessing, Winnie, that you have lots of money in your life, but little else. Ah well, life goes on, I guess, as Hattie Lewis writes page numbers on the blackboard, and I look at Flora Habstat's phone number which Baker scribbled on paper for me. All these numbers, assigned to me: numbers on dockets, prison record numbers, legal fees, where I fit into national statistics on teenagers, murder, witchcraft.

LATER

Gabriel was waiting for me outside of choir. You'd think that *sweet* would be a land far, far away from *irritating*, but as it turns out they're right next door, and always having border disputes. Gabriel would do anything for me. Why don't I want him to?

"Hi," I said.

Gabriel looked at me for a moment before saying, "Hi. Can we talk?"

"Of course," I said, leading him out the side entrance where Adam had led me. The comparisons were driving me nuts. I opened the door and we walked out and sat on a bench just as someone was getting up from it. A woman in her twenties, grinding out her cigarette with her bright red shoe, too old to be a student and too young to be a teacher; what was *she* doing here? What was I?

"I just wanted to say," he said quickly, and my heart sank. He just wanted to say that he'd had too much to drink the other night, or that he's had second thoughts and realized I'm a fat lesbian, or something. "I just wanted to say that it's OK with me, I'm happy for you, and that I'm not angry at you, though I am a little angry at *him*, though just for Lily's sake, not for mine. I just think it was bad timing for me, that's all. That's all I wanted to say. That's all," he said, and actually stood up like there was nothing else to say.

"What are you talking about?" I said.

"I know about you and Douglas," he said. He smiled, weakly. "I think it's great that you guys are back together. You always made a great couple."

"We made a lousy couple," I said, "but that's not the point. We aren't back together. What are you talking about?"

"Didn't you guys have a date on Saturday?"

"Well, we walked across the bridge and talked. It wasn't a *date*."

"What did you talk about?"

"*Gabriel*!"

He shrugged sheepishly. "Sorry. I guess it was nothing."

"How did you even hear about it?"

"From Kate."

"And Douglas told Kate?" Douglas was getting odder by the moment.

"No. This will really sound like she's a spy, but it's true. Kate had some cousins in town, and they took some pictures Saturday afternoon at the bridge. They went to one of those one-hour development places and were showing them to Kate when she saw you and Douglas in the background."

"No way."

"It's true."

"Come *on*."

"*Really*."

"And so Kate called you right away, and you just decided to accept it as gospel, not even calling me?" I asked.

"Give me a break, Flan," he said gently. "I was feeling delicate enough, and everybody knows the bridge was you guys' big date thing."

I put a hand on his shoulder. He smiled like I knew he would, instantly and from the eyes. "And you were going to give me up without a fight," I said. "Shame on you."

He turned toward me. We looked at each other, mouth to mouth. "So what are you saying?" he said. I hesitated, and that's when the side door banged open and out came Adam, laughing with a couple of people I didn't know. I suddenly felt like I needed a little room, like Adam had said to me.

"I gotta go," I said. "I have Biology. I'll talk to you soon." I got up and brushed past Adam, who pretended like he was just noticing me. "Hey Flan," he said. I looked at him and wished I had been marked absent so I could throw him down a well. But *anyone* could have thought that, Dr. Tert; it's just in the context of my later actions that my wish becomes sinister.

I muttered all the way to Biology like a bag lady, and when I got there I had a small humiliating experience. I tried the door, found it locked and realized I was early. Sheepishly I realized why they were locking the doors, and as I backed up I ran into the science geeks who were sitting in the hallway, locked out of their study hall.

"Something you need to do in there?" one of them asked, and I did my best to maintain a dignified expression. Life goes on, I guess; when Biology finally began Carr introduced his new assistant. The woman grinding out her cigarette. Remember? With her bright red shoe.

Tuesday September 28th

Not one to wear much makeup, except during a brief period of unfortunate experiments with glitter eye shadow in seventh grade, I never got to experience the girls-in-front-of-the-bathroom-mirror-giggling-and-gossiping bonding that has been promised me on TV since I was very little, so having Douglas meet me every morning for Cover The Hickey is the closest thing. It gives me a sort of closure with him, too – first we were friends, then lovers (well, sort of – we never did much of *that*, Pusher), and now we meet every morning so I can help him hide his love bite from his love interest. Ah, the way of the world. Or *this* world, anyway; I don't suppose peasants in Zaire are discussing Oscar Wilde and applying the right shade of base. Or *are* there even peasants in Zaire? Zaire's in Africa, right? Just kidding, Peter Pusher, I just wanted to hear you gnash your teeth. I can hear it clearly, over the gurgling, even.

"Do you know what I've been thinking about?" Douglas asked me, craning his neck while I moved in for the kill. We were in my bathroom. If he had his eyes open, Douglas could have seen my bedroom in the reflection in the bathroom mirror, seen his hat perched on Kate's navy blue sweater. For some reason I haven't gotten around to returning either of those things yet. I don't know why. Douglas always keeps his eyes closed during this process, though.

"Telling me where you got this?" I asked, halfheartedly. There was no progress on that.

"No," he said. "Absinthe. Oscar Wilde had it sometimes."

"Oh yeah? Mrs. Lewis was telling us that Poe took it too. What about it?"

"Well, it might be fun to try some."

I looked at him. Drugs weren't usually something the Basic Eight did. Not out of any Puritan goody-goodiness, but because it just seems so *uncouth*. Marijuana conjures up unwashed longhaired men, LSD brings to mind a spirituality that we would consider immature even if it were genuine, and all those powdered things can't help but make me think of men with slicked-back hair, wearing silk suits of ghastly colors, with tall thin blondes on their arm, high and dumb. But absinthe? Writers, artists and thinkers, lounging around salons, their thinking growing ever lucid thanks to some magical potion – *that* was pure *us*. "You know," I said, "it might be. Where would we get some?"

"I don't have the faintest idea."

"Good," Lily said at lunchtime when I told her about it. Natasha and Lily and Douglas and I were in the courtyard, discussing the possibility. Natasha, of course, was up for it right away, but Lily looked at us over her tortoiseshell glasses like we had gone mad. Do you think that transition from home to courtyard was a smooth one? "That stuff is supposed to fry your brain."

"So's coffee," Natasha said carelessly. Today she was wearing, and getting away with, a cape. A *cape*. No one else could wear a *cape* to school; people would think they were pretending to be a wizard or something. But Natasha looked like a visiting countess, sexy and regal.

"It is *not*," Lily said. "Absinthe messes with the chemicals in your head. Chemicals I would presume to say most of us want to keep intact."

"Poe took it," I offered.

"And *he* was certainly a picture of perfect mental health," Lily said. How was I to know that Dr. Tert's book *Crying Too Hard to Be Scared* would contain chapters on both Poe and me, though never making the absinthe connection? Which is odd, considering that Winnie Moprah not only focused on it in the episode about the

Basic Eight but then had a separate show about absinthe abuse in teenagers, also starring Flora Habstat, once again talking about something she knew nothing about. What a bitch.

"You're no fun," Douglas said.

"Thanks a lot." Lily looked at him sharply.

"Come *on*," he said. "Flan's up for it. Don't you think it would be fun?"

"I feel like I'm in a bad TV movie about peer pressure," she said. "I have to go somewhere and practice."

"You have to practice going somewhere?" Douglas said, modifying V___'s mockery. Natasha and I couldn't help it; we laughed. She stood up and stalked off, or as close to stalking off as you can do while dragging a cello case along with you.

"It seems you guys are always bickering lately," Natasha said, stretching her legs out on the bench where Lily and her cello had sat.

Douglas sighed. "It's not her fault. It's mine. Hey, speaking of mine, do you have my hat, Flan? I think I left it at your house."

"No," I said, for no reason. "I mean, I'll look, but I don't think so." I don't know why I said that. Like a slowly dying engine, stuck underwater, my head gurgles along, waiting for all my sentences to end: the one that keeps me in high school, the one that keeps me in prison, and this one, which is a run-on. Actually, they're all run-ons. I'm babbling, aren't I?

LATER
Today is the day that my Advanced Bio report was due, and I think the fact that I've never mentioned it in this journal reflects my interest. Mine's on sunburn. Just

before class began, I went up to Carr's desk to add my report to the little pile of reports. Carr was standing at the sink, behind the new teaching assistant who was washing out test tubes with a miniature toilet scrubber. His hand was on her ass, but when he heard someone at his desk he took it away. Then he saw it was me, looked right at me and put his hand back on her ass. I didn't blink. I just stood there for a second and felt a chill like when you bite directly down on ice cream. Walking up to the bus stop, I saw the assistant sitting disconsolately at the bus stop again, alone. I just walked across the street and took the right bus. I'm on it now. Where is my life? Where is it interesting?

Wednesday September 29th

Natasha and I cut school all day today. Between Adam, Gabriel, Douglas and Carr there was scarcely an island in the Roewer Sea where this little castaway felt safe. And Natasha – well, Natasha wouldn't worry about such trivial, earthly matters as attendance. We drove out of there, stopping briefly at Well-Kept Grounds for a latte to go, and went to the beach. We bundled together on a big rock, me sipping latte and Natasha sipping from her flask, and talked of more important things than the school we were missing. Talked about, I don't know, books and love and what we were going to do after we left our hallowed halls. We made a date for Saturday night, just the two of us, seeing a revival of one of Natasha's favorite non-Marlene movies, *Way Down East*. We made a standing date for any Saturday night when we didn't have something absolutely fabulous to do – then the two of us would do something, just us. All we needed was each other, we decided. Flan and Natasha were all Flan and Natasha needed. Sure, the other Eight were wonderful people, but we, we were the stuff of kings. We hugged each other tight, and I suddenly pulled away and leaned out from her so I could see her face as she leaned her head back and took another sip, brushing her hair away from her face and wiping the dark lipstick off the neck of the flask when she was done. She caught me looking at her and rolled her eyes before putting the flask down on the rock and fluffing her hair with her hands, posing for my gaze in a mock pout. I love her. I miss her so much. I'm going to stop writing now.

Thursday September 30th

The transcripts I ordered from the Winnie Moprah Show finally arrived – both the one about the Basic Eight and the one on absinthe abuse. I snitched a crayon and am circling my favorite parts in a color V___ would have no trouble calling "flesh," a pallid, pinkish shade that reminds me of really old gum, stuck on the street and pounded flat and dull. Speaking of which, here's Winnie opening the show:

> I'm glad you could join us today. The number eight has had a variety of historical meanings, but never one as sinister as what it now means to all Americans: the Basic Eight, the notorious gang of teenagers [as those horrible school pictures of us are flashed on the screen.] To look at them now, they look like any American teenagers, maybe ones in your hometown at home. But these teenagers – [shaking her head like she can't believe it] children, actually – were on a rampage, a rampage of drugs, alcohol, substance abuse, Satanism and other alternative lifestyles, a rampage that went unnoticed by their parents and other school

authorities until it ended in the tragic murder of Adam State. [As a photo of Adam is shown, the camera slowly zooming into his smile until all that is on the screen are his large, cute teeth] Adam was one of the most popular boys at Roewer High School in San Francisco, and at the time of his murder he was on the cusp of a dazzling future: college, and then undoubtedly a brilliant and lucrative career, perhaps raising children of his own. But Adam State's dream is over, now. His life has been drastically cut short by the Basic Eight. Of course, the trial of Flannery Culp, ringleader of the Basic Eight, is still going on, so we cannot comment on her innocence or guilt, but here with us to discuss these murderous events are [as the camera panel-pans] Mrs. Stacy State, grieving mother of Adam and now president of the Adam State Memorial Anti-Satanic Teenage Murder Education and Prevention Council, the first national organization to have the courage to take on this tragic and complex issue; Peter Pusher, a nationally renowned expert on The Family, author of the book *What's the Matter with Kids Today?: Getting Back to Family Basics in a World Gone Wrong* and president of the Peter Pusher Think Tank on National Reform; Dr. Eleanor Tert, nationally renowned teenage therapist and author of *How Kids Tick (You Off)* and the forthcoming *Crying Too Hard to Be Scared*, a profile history of the psychological torment behind famous Americans from Edgar Allan Poe to Marilyn Monroe to Flannery Culp; Flora Habstat, the member of the Basic Eight who pulled the whistle, currently in recovery under the auspices of a twelve-step program; and Rinona Wide, the twice-award-nominated actress who will be playing Flannery Culp in the upcoming television movie *Basic Eight, Basic Hate: The Flannery Culp Story*. Thank you for joining us, everyone.

I've said it before and I'll say it again: *inaccuracy*. I have so much commentary I'd better properly notate them. The offensive phrases will be in quotations, followed by the line number on which they appear for handy reference, followed by the corrections from the person who gave Winnie Moprah a much-needed boost in ratings.

1. "The number eight has had a variety of historical meanings . . ." (lines 1–5) What is the dear (honorary) Dr. Moprah talking about? Perhaps she's thinking of the number of days in the week?

2. ". . . your hometown at home." (lines 6–7) What boggles the mind is that she doesn't say these things off the top of her head; her eyes clearly glide along cue cards just off-camera. So somebody drafted and wrote the phrase "your hometown at home" in big felt-tip letters, and nobody thought to think it was redundant.

3. ". . . other alternative lifestyles." (line 10) Notice how she just slipped in Douglas's homosexuality, as if that's an abomination, too, on the par with me beating Adam to death. (Gosh, the gurgling is loud all of a sudden.) The *nerve* she has, to make such judgments.

4. ". . . cusp of a dazzling future." (line 17) Grades weren't even turned in when he died.

5. ". . . president of the Adam State Memorial Anti-Satanic Teenage Murder Education and Prevention Council." (lines 25-26) Mrs. State is in fact Chairperson; the council has no presidency. I know this because the ASMASTMEAPC regularly and pointedly sends me their monthly newsletter. ("Authorities estimate there are more than five hundred Flannery Culps in America, running around completely unchecked." How difficult it must be for you citizens, not able to tell the Flannery Culp you know from the other unchecked 499.)

6. ". . . nationally renowned expert on The Family." (line 28-29) Mr. Pusher's renown, and indeed his expertise, is entirely the result of his almost-constant appearances on Winnie Moprah's show. That isn't fair.

7. ". . . nationally renowned teenage therapist." (lines 32-33) See note 6.

8. "Flora Habstat . . . member of the Basic Eight." (line 37) *Lies, lies, lies.* What a *bitch.*

LATER
I'm so burnt up by this that I can't even remember what happened at school today. It's not that I feel it personally, I'm just intellectually upset by the *inaccuracy.* Lily's note to me is not just insulting but *poorly devised.* I mean, just read it:

Flannery,
    I have to get some things off my chest that have really been bothering me. Maybe you'll think it's cowardly of me to write them down instead of talking to you in person, but I kept losing my

133

nerve. You have to admit, Flannery, sometimes you can really be a really intimidating person. I know that's not your fault, really, but I just wanted to tell you that, so you'd know why I'm writing this down instead of just talking to you.

You've probably guessed that I want to talk about Douglas. And before you jump to conclusions and think that I'm thinking that you and Douglas are back together, I'm not. Gabriel told me about you telling him about what Kate told him (Gabriel) about what her cousins told her about you and Douglas on the bridge, and I believe you. But it doesn't really matter that nothing went on, because it's irrelevant. What I'm trying to tell you is that when you spend time with Douglas alone it takes away from my relationship with him, even when nothing goes on. [This last sentence was crossed out, but only with a single line, so clearly I was supposed to read it without really being able to blame Lily for it.]

I'm not really trying to tell you that I don't want you to be friends with Douglas, but I think you haven't really been sensitive to how it makes me feel when the two of you spend so much time together. I think that my relationship with him is suffering because of whatever-it-is that he's sharing with you, even if it's just time.

We don't have to mention this again. I'd just prefer it if the two of you [this, too, was crossed out, but repeatedly; I had to hold it up to the light and make out the letters carefully, one by one.]

Lily

OK, now before I do the notation thing again, I'd like to advertise a little contest. Guess how many times the word *really* is used in the note. Go on; guess. *Eight*, that's how many, including the one that I wrote in brackets. Lily used the word *really eight* times in a one-page note. *Eight times*. Well, on to the notation:

1. "Flannery." (line 1) Not even a Dear. Suddenly I'm not dear to her. The whole thing makes me angry.

2. "I have to get some things off my chest . . ." (line 2)

Oh, what's the use. The whole letter just burns me up. But just one lucky event, and a small one. But crucial. Lily stared at me throughout Lit Mag meeting today, just looking at me and not talking, not even offering an opinion on the poem somebody wrote about a cat, for God's sake. Then she left, early and significantly, looking at me directly before she shut the door behind her. My small bit of luck was sitting at the end of the table, where Lily had been. I lifted it up, and below it was the note, written on a piece of binder paper in bright black ink and folded in half, lengthwise, with FLANNERY on it in big letters. I read the note straightaway, ignoring what was on top of it, and rushed right home on the bus. But I hadn't forgotten to slip them into my pocket.

Her tortoiseshell glasses, expensive and important, so much a part of Lily that it was unimaginable that she had actually forgotten to take them with her. They are emblematic of Lily – a sort of Lily Chandly talisman. Like Douglas's hat, or Kate's sweater in her trademark navy blue. I've moved these objects to a bare shelf in my closet, rather than on the chair in my room – can't have anybody spotting them. Later, of course, they were bagged and numbered and shown to a jury of my peers, visiting the museum of my life, peering through it, ignoring the PLEASE DO NOT TOUCH signs as easily as Mark Wallace did, just reaching out and groping me. They couldn't see Kate's brief, lazy imitation of the Headless Horseman as she eased into her sweater before heading outdoors, or the way Douglas's hat perched on his head, looking both dorky and sexy, or the way Lily would put her glasses on whenever she needed to think hard about something, as if the lenses clarified things both inside and out. They just saw these things on *display*, as *evidence*. They couldn't see the forest for the trees, or however that saying goes.

Friday October 1
Douglas came over in the morning today and rang the doorbell as I was drying my hair and humming "With You With You," by Q.E.D. I heard it on the radio this morning. We had a full minute of sonic miscommunication like a suspense movie. I thought I heard the doorbell, over the hair dryer, but when I turned it off I didn't hear anything. I turned it on again and swore I heard the doorbell. I turned it off again, etc., finally stomping downstairs and opening the door, knowing it would be Douglas.

"Go away," I said. "I'll take the bus to school."

"What?" he said nervously, clearly saying it for no reason. He was looking around him like an escaped convict. Not that I would know. "Can't we talk?"

"No," I said. "Talk to Lily."

"I can explain everything," he said.

"You couldn't possibly." I started to shut the door. The Q.E.D. song had put me in such a peaceful mood, and now this.

"I'm gay!" he cried. I took my hand off the door but didn't open it. Douglas's face was in the half-opened

136

door like something in a vise. His cheeks were splotched with red, suddenly, and beneath the brim of his hat I could see he was crying.

"What?" I said nervously, clearly saying it for no reason.

"I'm a homosexual," he said medically.

We looked at each other for a second, and something about the silence cracked us both up a little. The door swung slowly open on its own accord and as it did I saw more and more of Douglas. Then it was open all the way and Douglas stepped in, rumpled and out of breath like he'd been somewhere cramped. Like, um, a closet.

"Homosexual?" I said. "Isn't that what they do to milk?"

"I hope not," he said, and started to sob. He just put his head down on my shoulder, *plop*, while still standing a few steps from me. His shoulders shook. It felt so literal: "crying on my shoulder." I moved closer to him until we were actually embracing. I'd never heard anybody crying like that who wasn't a little kid, lost or bleeding.

"You know, you're right," I said. I was amazed to find myself crying too, but just a little bit. "They *steam* milk. Look, I'll show you." I strode to the kitchen and got out the coffee filters. In a flash I remembered the first time I saw the love bite, my mouth so near his neck as I reached over him for the same box of filters. It had felt, then, for a second, like we were about to kiss, and in another flash it hit me: Douglas and I used to kiss, all the time, and now he was gay. And, a third flash – the first two still lingering in my eyes like flashbulbs – I realized what the hickey meant. He had reassured me that he wasn't seeing another *woman*. I realized I was crumpling the box of filters into a ravaged building. I looked at it and felt like the storm had passed and I had come up from the storm cellar to see what had happened to the place where I lived.

I turned and looked at him. "*Really*?" I asked, and he nodded, wiping his eyes. He didn't sound like he was crying now, and his shoulders were still, but the tears still ran freely down his face. He sat down on the couch, and I stood up straight and made the coffee. I stared into space as I steamed the milk and it scalded and the smoke alarm went off, which was a relief, because Douglas had to run over and wave the smoke away from the screeching device with his hat, so we were in the same room again.

"I'll take mine black," he said. He opened the wrong cupboard, looking for mugs. My smile felt forced as I watched the smoky hiss of cold water hitting the scalded pot. I found the mugs; he poured the coffee. We sipped and said nothing.

"So is that where you got –" I said finally, touching my neck, and he nodded.

"Is it anyone I know?" I said, trying to keep from sounding gossipy.

Douglas snorted. He looked very tired. "It's no one *I* know," he said.

"Are you being careful?" I asked. "I don't mean to sound like your mother, but you know –"

"My chosen lifestyle is a risky one?" he asked lightly.

"I didn't mean it like *that*," I said. "I'm *sorry*, Douglas, it's just taking me a while to adjust. I just *heard* about this."

"You didn't guess? You couldn't tell?"

"I don't know," I said, looking at my friend Douglas, classical musician and actor, who dressed in linen suits, always brought flowers to dinner parties and cried during the sad parts of operas. When he and I had been going out, I'd had to spend a considerable amount of my time defending his sexuality to people at Roewer. Of course, *when he and I had been going out* would be the key part of that phrase. I don't go out with gay men, as a general policy.

"It's OK."

"Did you know then, and not tell me? Come to think of it, does Lily know now?"

"No one knows now," Douglas said. "I didn't even mean to tell you. It just slipped out. And I don't know how long *I've* known. I guess I don't have to tell you that I don't want anyone else to know."

"Not even *Lily*?" I said. "Let me tell you one thing about women, Douglas, not that you'll need to know, now. They generally assume that their boyfriends are heterosexual."

"Don't tell Lily!" he said. *Cried*, rather.

"I hadn't thought of telling her *myself*. But *you* should tell her."

"I can't," he said. "Not yet. And don't tell anyone else."

"I won't, I won't," I said, already imagining what Natasha would think of this. "I promise. But you've got to set things straight with Lily."

"So to speak," he said with the ghost of a smile.

"What? Oh. *Oh*. Right. Douglas, Lily's mad at me because she thinks, well I don't know what she thinks. Let me show you this note she wrote me." I bounded upstairs and got it from my room. As I picked it up I noticed my hands were shaking. *It's no big deal*, I found myself telling myself. *Lots of people are gay*.

I went downstairs and showed it to him. "Why did she number all the lines?" he asked as he read it.

"No, I did that."

He looked up. "Why did *you* number all the lines?"

"Never mind *that*. Read the note. You see how she purposely crossed out that part on lines 17 through 19, but left it for me to see?"

"Flan, give me a break. I'll tell her soon, I promise. Come on, I'll drive you to school."

"*Douglas!*"

"We're late already."

"I'm not going to school. Neither of us are. We're going to talk about this. Oh, wait, I *have* to go to school. I have to turn in my essay to Lewis or she'll kill me. Come on."

Douglas didn't speak to me the whole way there. Or *wouldn't*, rather. Douglas *wouldn't* speak to me the whole way there. I sat in the passenger seat, Lily's note still crumpled in my hands, and wished that I smoked so I could have a bitter cigarette at my fingertips, fuming along with me.

Douglas parked, and I swung my door open, almost knocking Gabriel down. I looked at him, one leg out of the car already, and felt the world grow pale like everybody got the flu at once.

"Hi," I said hoarsely, trying – unsuccessfully, I knew – to make my face look like he hadn't caught us at something. I heard Douglas get out of the car, behind me, and I waited for him to say anything. But he just walked away, and I was left shivering in the chilly morning.

"It's already homeroom," Gabriel said.

"I just know," I said, "that someday I will actually be present and accounted for."

"I was looking for Douglas," he said, gesturing helplessly. "I wanted to talk to Douglas."

I pointed to Douglas's departing figure. "Well, he's over there," I said.

140

"Are you two going out?" he asked me.

"Haven't we settled this?" I asked him.

"You know," Gabriel said, looking up at the cold air, "I wasn't surprised when I didn't see you this morning. If I were you I wouldn't come to school, either." Even from someone as sweet as Gabriel that sounded like a threat.

"Gabriel," I said, "please."

"What's going on?" Gabriel asked. "Flan, you're driving me crazy."

I looked at him, Gabriel, this person who for some reason was now dangling on a thread I was holding, and I could only think of one thing to do. Maybe somebody else would have done something else, but I was just me, a senior in high school trying to get into college, flunking Calc, trapped in a biology class with Jim Carr, suddenly the center of controversy among my friends who saw me as a confidante, an adulterer, a liar, a slut, a collaborator, an overweight slob and who knows what else, all except Gabriel, who stood there in the student parking lot seeing me as the person he loved, and it suddenly became so easy to see myself as someone who was in love with Gabriel, as he was in love with me, and I held my breath like you do when you're opening a suspiciously dated carton of milk and kissed him. It was a long kiss, the proper length of kiss, I told myself, for the beginning of a relationship. I felt Gabriel stiffen, react despite himself and finally surrender and kiss me back. I stepped backward and into the car door; it slammed shut and we both jumped and stopped kissing. We grinned at each other, his as wide as the Pacific and mine, I fear, as shallow as Lake Merced. Some *Gurgle and Buzz* song popped into my head, but just out of reach, scarcely audible.

"Are you sure this is OK?" he asked me, and my mind scurried out of the swampy lake back to Gabriel. He was cute. He cooked and would never treat me wrong. No one would be mad at me any more.

"Yes," I said, and he took my hand instantly and led me into the school building. The bell rang just as we walked in the door, and the hallway began to fill up. "I'll see you soon," I called to him over the roar of people my age who had a purpose, who knew where they were going and only had three minutes to get there. "I'll talk to you soon."

I opened the side entrance, and there was Adam.

"Flannery!" he said, smiling. "I've been looking for you!"

I tried to make my voice sound like his voice didn't make me weak in the knees. *You have a boyfriend,* I found myself telling myself, trying to picture Gabriel clearly in my mind. "What do you want?"

"What's wrong? You look a wreck."

"Thanks a lot," I said.

"Hey, I thought we were friends."

"And *I* thought you needed a little room," I said, feeling a little bored by all this until he suddenly took my hand. Suddenly I was warm, for the first time all morning since I got out of the shower. As warm as "With You With You." "What?" I squeaked. The way my life was going,   some great-uncle of Kate's was bird-watching, accidentally photographing me with Adam to show Gabriel, but fuck it. Let him. I'm over here next to the orioles, Uncle Bob!

"I wanted to ask you to dinner Saturday night," he said plainly. He was wearing a button-down shirt of pure white; did I mention that? He makes me into a walking cliché; did I mention that? Melting at his voice, swooning inside, the whole bit, a pure shot of desire.

"Really?" I started to say, but changed it, just in time. "Saturday?" I said. I started to shake my head, but from nowhere a sentence dropped into my head like a note in a bottle. *Gabriel wouldn't have to know.* "Yes."

"Really?" he said, and then frowned like he hadn't changed that in time. Adam was excited to ask me out. *Excited.* Maybe a little nervous. All he had needed was a little room; who didn't need that, once in a while? "Um, I'm busy all day Saturday, so I won't get ahold of you. Will you meet me in a cafe somewhere, let's say six-thirty?"

"Death Before Decaf?" I said. "That's close to where I live. We could just go back to my place and have sex." That last sentence I purposely crossed out before I said it, but left it for him to hear.

"Sounds great," he said, blinking. "Death Before Decaf, Saturday, six-thirty. See you then." He looked at me, and smiled widely like everything was easier than he thought. With a pang I remembered Gabriel, after the dinner party, showing me he had found the right key to his car door.

"I Keep Finding What I'm Not Looking For," *that's* the Q.E.D. song that had popped into my head after kissing Gabriel in the parking lot. But this time, it was a different one, the album's closer. "You're young and you're experienced," the opening vocals whisper while a guitar purrs gently. The first kiss was gentle, and I thought that was going to be all. "And I can taste it," the singer snarls, and the drums kick in, the full band in full force, the bass crackling like the feel of cold cement on your back as you lean against a building you hate, a building you've always hated, to kiss a man you love and have always loved. I don't know how the rest of the lyrics go – I haven't heard the song enough yet – except for the chorus: "Swept away by your ready desire/I surrender to your kiss of fire." That's the title of the song. When the kiss was over we looked at each other, out of breath, the silence around us expectant, just like it is when a great album is over. "Kiss Of Fire."

Saturday October 2

Well, life could be worse, I'm not trapped on ice floes or anything, not like the gin was even *cold*, I have to go throw up. Fuck him.

Ahem. It's later now, and although "sober" ain't the word for what I am it'll have to do; I'm not sitting on the cold tile of my bathroom floor with my cartoon-face night-light laughing at me anymore. He didn't show, that's why.

Back from another bout. I think the easiest way for my addled brain to chronicle this ignominious defeat is through a time line:

6:27 Flan leaves house to walk to Death Before Decaf, planning to arrive a few minutes late.

6:33 Arrives. A. S. has outfoxed her and Flan is forced to order a latte and sit waiting. Luckily she's brought *Salinger's Nine Stories*, which she's rereading for the umpteenth time. She figures that it's a good conversation starter, plus she can successfully pull off reading it carelessly, so when Adam comes she will be casual. In reality, her hands are sweating, and she keeps wiping them on napkins despite the self-righteous NAPKINS=TREES TAKE ONLY WHAT YOU NEED sign.

6:48 Orders another latte. Overcaffeinated and nervous, Flan suddenly realizes she's read the same sentence in "For Esme with Love and Squalor" sixteen times in a row.

7:00 This is the deadline. Finally, Flan overcomes her own willpower and does what she knows will do her no good: takes her black leather notebook out of her bag and checks what time Adam said he'd meet her. Yes, it is fucking six thirty, put your journal back in your bag and order another latte.

7:18 Catches herself praying.

7:22 Decides her hands are so shaky that she may drop the latte on the way back to her chair, so she doesn't order another one.

7:33 Flan doesn't know what to do. Saturday night stretches before her like unwanted limousine service, waiting for me to tell it where to go. I can't go home.

7:41 I was about to order some food. "Death Before Decaf offers a wide variety of low-fat salads" peeps another helpful sign, just when I was feeling fat enough, thank you, but about to collapse as a result of three lattes' worth of blank jittery energy poured hot into an empty stomach. I reread the mocha-stained menu, flipping it over halfheartedly to see if what I wanted was on the other side. No, he wasn't *there* either. Suddenly I couldn't see anything. Adam had put his hands over my eyes for me to guess.

"Guess who?" a decidedly female voice said, and in a flash I saw things as clearly as if I had invented them myself: Natasha, whom I had forgotten to call and cancel, had come to Death Before Decaf to grab a latte before meeting me for *Way Down East* as we had agreed the other day at the beach.

"Hey!" I said, twisting my voice like a wet towel, wringing it tight into surprised, enthusiastic tones. This takes practice but it works.

"What's wrong with you?" Natasha asked.

"Nothing."

She rolled her eyes, bored. "Well, I'm glad I found you. I got tickets already but we should zoom across the street, *dahling*. If we don't hurry we'll be sitting in the front row, and that's too close to the organ."

We scurried across. Just as the bored, multipierced usher was ripping my ticket in half, I looked back and saw Adam, rushing into the café, his clothes torn and bloody. He had clearly been in a car wreck. Just kidding.

The lights were dimming when we walked in, so we sat in the back row and put our feet up on the seats in front of us. I felt disoriented: *Who* was I with? *What* were we doing? My shaky stomach fluttered like that movie where she's pregnant with an alien. I don't know what it was – the opening shot of Lillian what's-her-name looking wan and helpless or the shimmering reverberations of the corny but sad organ chords – but as soon as *Way Down East* started I began to cry. I was being quiet, I think, but my shoulders shook Natasha's leopard skin coat from the back of her chair. She heard the fake-bone buttons clatter on the floor; she took her eyes from the screen and watched me with the same rapt, detached attention. She reached down into the pocket of her fallen coat. I thought she was going for tissues, but I should have known. Lit by the yellowish glow of the old movie, she handed me the flask, which was polished to such a shine that I saw the reflection of the movie clearly in it. Lillian, as an abandoned woman, was learning that she was pregnant.

The gin wasn't even cold. It was just straight, warm gin, and to say that it burned my throat wouldn't begin to describe what it felt like. I read *Julius Caesar* sophomore year and was remembering Mrs. Brutus's suicide via hot coals down the throat. Now, thanks to method acting I could play Portia to the hilt. I took another swig and by that time I couldn't tell whether I was still crying, or some gin had leaked out and was dripping off my face like tears. You don't have to be an A student in Advanced Bio like me (ha!) to know that empty stomach+three lattes+swigs of straight warm gin=one drunk girl by the time our heroine was clinging to ice floes, rushing down a river. I kept swigging; next thing I knew Natasha was putting her arms underneath my armpits to help me out of my ratty plush seat. I tried to stand up by myself outside the theater and slid down the wall to the floor. The usher was looking at me curiously; it occurred to me that he probably worked for Kate. I opened my mouth to tell Natasha this and to my horror found myself crying again. Natasha was sitting on her knees looking at me like a gargoyle, except she was gorgeous.

"Jesus, girl," I said. I mean *she* said. I'm going to go wash my face again.

"Jesus Christ, girl," she said. "How much did you drink?"

Wiping my face with my fist and feeling grubby, I looked at her and turned the flask upside down. The last trickle fell onto the grimy floor. I leaned my head back against the theater display case, inside of which was a poster advertising what was coming up, and felt the cold wash of shame fall over me like thick netting.

"What happened to you?" Natasha asked, and I told her. I told her everything – kissing Gabriel, kissing Adam, Adam standing me up, and everything that had happened to Lillian. Halfway through that last part I realized she had been there for the movie.

"Yeah, yeah, I was there for the movie," she said, standing up and pulling me up, too. The whole street glimmered loudly at me like a snow globe. San Francisco fog was rolling in, canned ambience for my own dense gloom.

"Now look at me, Flan," Natasha said. She ran a hurried hand through her perfect hair, haloed in the streetlights. She took the flask firmly and screwed the cap on tight. "You were *screwed over* tonight. What are you going to do about it?"

"Are you mad at me?" I asked her, my lip quivering. "Why aren't you mad at me? *You* were the one who got screwed over. I stood you up for our movie date, and I didn't even call –"

"Don't worry about that," she said, holding up her hand. She reached down and picked up my forgotten bag, draped it over my shoulder like a bandage. "I'm always here, whenever you want me, you know that. I can take care of myself. It's *you* you should worry about. What are you going to do? You have to do *something*."

"You sound like Mr. Baker."

"What?"

"That's Baker's Rule: do *something*."

"Well, he's right."

"I don't know."

"Of course you don't," she said, sighing. "Well, I have to go. I have somebody to meet." She raised her eyebrows, just slightly. Glamorous. "I'll call you in the morning, Flan. Or maybe I'll just come over. You might not want to hear the phone. Don't forget aspirin, Flan."

"You know," I said, jumping trains as only a caffeinated drunk can do, "I always secretly thought you only had water in that flask."

She smiled. The fog was rolling in thicker, thicker. "Sometimes it is, Flan. The secret is to keep everyone on their toes. Everybody's got to keep guessing or you have nothing left. You shouldn't have written him those letters, Flan." She saluted me – her nails catching the lights of the theater – and walked off into the fog. It was rolling in thicker, and thicker; soon planes wouldn't be able to land and I'd be stuck here for good. There was no trace of Natasha, which left me feeling empty and alone, like I'd been stood up for a date and just gotten drunk, by myself, in the back of a revival movie theater six blocks from my home. Like this was my Saturday night. Disgusted, I found my car keys and shakily drove home.

Oh, shut up, Peter. I didn't drive home; I'd *walked*, remember. I even gave you a clue in the previous paragraph: "six blocks from my home." But you didn't listen. What's the use of even writing this all out if you're not going to fucking listen?

Vocabulary:

GNASH INEXPLICABLE SUBJUNCTIVE DEFIANT
EXORBITANT INVULNERABLE EXPECTANT IGNOMINIOUS

Study Questions:

1. Discuss the advantages and disadvantages of the I Have A Really Good Reason For This approach versus the Have Mercy on Me Mr. Baker approach. Which would you have used in Flannery's situation?

2. Lily uses the word really eight times in a simple one-page note. Study your own writing and find a word you use too often. Look it up in a thesaurus and come up with at least eight good synonyms.

3. Flannery writes: "Well, life could be worse, I'm not trapped on ice floes or anything." Which do you think is worse: being trapped on ice floes or being stood up by a man you love?

4. Everybody keeps getting mad at Flannery, but it's not her fault. Discuss.

Monday October 4th

I'm glad you could join us today. Absinthe has had a variety of historical meanings, but never one as sinister as what it now means to all Americans: the Basic Eight, whose notorious deeds were spurred on by their abuse of this innocent-looking liquid. Here with us to discuss American absinthe abuse are [as the camera panel-pans] Mrs. Ann Rule, grieving mother of an absinthe abuser and the founder of the American Association Against Alarming Absinthe Abuse, the first national organization to have the courage to take on this tragic and complex issue; Peter Pusher, a nationally renowned expert on The Family, author of the book *What's the Matter with Kids Today?: Getting Back to Family Basics in a World Gone Wrong* and president of the Peter Pusher Think Tank on National Reform; Dr. Eleanor Tert, nationally renowned teenage therapist and author of *How Kids Tick (You Off)* and the forthcoming *Crying Too Hard to Be Scared,* a profile history of the psychological torment behind famous Americans from Edgar Allan Poe to Marilyn Monroe to Flannery Culp; Flora Habstat, the member of the Basic Eight who pulled – *blew* – the whistle, currently in recovery under the auspices of a twelve-step program; and Felicia Vane, a teenager who claims she only uses absinthe socially. Thank you for joining us, everyone.

When my doorbell rang this morning it didn't surprise me; I felt like the Egyptians must have when the rivers had already turned to blood and the cattle had all died: *Ho hum, locusts. Guess Ahmed wins the plague pool.* When I opened the door Douglas was standing there looking both sheepish and dashing in an off-white linen suit.

"Oh, Douglas, you didn't get another one, did you?" I said. "I just can't be late to homeroom anymore. This is an important semester, and some of us don't have the classical-musician thing to put on our college applications."

Douglas put a finger to his lips and smiled like an elf.

With his other hand he held up a small bottle of greenish liquid, superimposing it over his face so he looked like a leprechaun.

"You found some!" I said. "Wherever did you find some?"

"Oh, let's just say I managed to procure some in my travels in the underground," he said.

I stood aside to let him in. "That's right," I said. "I forgot you live among the depraved now."

"I have *always* lived among the depraved," he said. "Are you sure you want to be seen with me?" He was twisting his voice like a wet towel, wringing it tight into casual tones. This takes practice, but it works on most people. I can spot it a mile away, though. It's in the eyes. Douglas was scared.

"Don't be silly," I said. "Come on in before you're spotted with a controlled substance."

"I told Lily," he said, suddenly and too loudly. He finally took the bottle of absinthe down from his face. Now he just looked like a person.

"Come on in," I said again, and he came on in and I hugged him. I felt his arms, warm through the linen. Suddenly there was a reason to leave the house and see other humans, because some of them were *good*.

"I'm proud of you," I said.

He stood there and gestured emptily, five times. "I'm proud of me, too," he said, rolling his eyes.

"How did she take it?"

"Well, you know Lily. She had to think about it. She told me she wanted to think about it for a few days." He shrugged.

"Oh, Douglas," I said.

"Everything's messed up," he said. "I messed everything up."

Dr. Tert: We've found that a general feeling of helplessness often leads to experimentation with substances.

"Everything might be messed up," I said, "but *you* didn't do it."

"It doesn't matter," he said, looking at the carpet.

"I have to get to homeroom," I said. "Are you going to give me a ride?"

"Proudly," he said, suddenly grinning. "I mean, who cares if we're seen together in the student parking lot, once it's known that I, um, don't worship at your church?"

"Don't shop at my store," I offered. Suddenly it was easy.

"Don't eat at your salad bar."

"Don't play my board game."

"Haven't mastered your instrument," he said, and we drove to school shrieking with laughter like happy-go-lucky teenagers on a joyride.

Felicia Vane: It's a joyride. I can quit whenever I want to, but I don't want to. It makes me feel – happy-go-lucky.

Mrs. Rule: That's sad.

Peter Pusher: That's not sad. That's pathetic!

Winnie: Dr. Tert?

Dr. Tert: Well, I think we should try and be fair. It's both sad and pathetic.

152

"So, when do you think we should do this?" Douglas the Leprechaun said. You know, leprechauns are neither sad nor pathetic. Think about that, honored guests and experts. Airline passengers, bookstore browsers. True-crime freaks.

I took the bottle from him and regarded it. The greenish liquid inside was iridescent and a little thick. I looked through it at everything: dear, brave Douglas; the dreary student parking lot; the fogged-in Lake Merced; the lanky, awkward figure of my Applied Economics teacher Gladys Tall carrying an overhead projector to the side entrance, the cord trailing behind her like something umbilical. Everything looked magical through this green liquid. It looked like a pastoral place, a better place.

Mrs. Rule: Of course, many teens use absinthe for escape. They see a drug-induced haze as a means of getting away from the pressures of everyday life.

Peter Pusher: What pressures do kids have nowadays? Which channel to watch? They don't have any *real* pressures. You're just making excuses for them.

"Friday night?" I said. "That feels really far away, but we don't want to do drugs on a school night. Plus, all eight of us probably won't be free until the weekend." How's that for self-responsibility, Peter? Incidentally, nice toupee you've got there.

"Maybe you and I should do a trial run," Douglas said. He looked shyly at me and I realized suddenly that at least for now I was his only friend. "You know, try it ourselves before springing it on everyone."

"Good idea," I said. For the first time the prickly sensation of possibly doing something very stupid began its caterpillar walk down my spine. It was not an unpleasant feeling. "Tomorrow, after school?" I asked. "We could go to my house."

"Great," he said, and gave me a kiss on the cheek. I must have jumped, because then he jumped and looked at me like I was going to swat him across the nose with a newspaper.

"Don't worry," I said. "Everything's going to be OK."

The first thing I saw when I entered my beloved high school was Kate, leaning against her locker and talking with Adam. Could I have just one easy day, here? Could I just get home one day and have nothing to write in this journal? And it's *Monday*. What sort of cosmic deal do I have to make?

Peter Pusher: If kids got back to the Lord, they'd find that all of these so-called pressures would go up in smoke. And I'm not talking about the smoke of absinthe!

"Hey, kids," I said, and I heard my voice sound perfectly unconcerned. I even caught myself looking over the tops of their heads so they'd suspect there was someone more interesting in the background. "What's up?"

They were friendly, unruffled. Both of them. *Adam*.

"Same shit, different day," Kate said, rolling her eyes heavenward. Adam smiled thinly at me and shoved his hands in my pockets. I mean, *his* pockets. There, did you hear it? Gurgling, clear as – oh, of course you can't hear it. Maybe when this book is put on tape for carpooling commuters who can't read without getting carsick they can add the gurgling, thick and loud.

"How was your weekend?" Kate asked. There was no guile in her voice or in her eyes, but you can't see it in the face of the good Dr. Moprah, either.

"Oh, you know," I said. "The sun came up; the sun came down. I think I had too much fun Saturday night."

"*Fun* is an interesting choice of word," Kate said. "I heard you and Natasha were out of control."

That damn *usher*. I tried to clear my head rather than strangle my friend. "Speaking of which," I said, "we need to meet vis-à-vis our upcoming activity on Friday night."

"We certainly do," Kate said, pretending to know what the hell I was talking about.

"You don't know what I'm talking about," I said, "but you will soon. Lunch, maybe?"

"We don't have lunch at the same time," she said, smiling. Her eyes met Adam's for a second. "What's the big secret?"

"Sorry," I said, stage-glancing hurriedly at Adam, "members only."

I should have known better than to attempt this game with Kate, so early in the morning. She could match me stroke for stroke. "Oh," she said, in a resigned, indulgent voice. "Adam, would you excuse us?"

"Actually, I need to talk to Flan, too," Adam said. His hands were still in his pockets and he was still looking at Kate. They looked at each other like two people pausing before an open door, negotiating who was going to enter first, not caring much.

"I'll catch you later," Kate said. "I need to copy over this French homework anyway or Millie will eat me for lunch." She waved at us and walked lazily off. Adam turned and considered me, like a waiter on break. Would he do me the favor of refilling my water glass?

"I have nothing to say to you," I said. Paradoxical but true, like just about everything in this journal.

"Well, I have something to say to you," he said. "I'm sorry."

"That'd be a lot more convincing if you weren't lounging around against lockers," I said. "Like, for instance, if you were saying it to me on the phone. *Yesterday*."

"I had to spend all day with my family yesterday," he said.

"And the day before that?"

"What?"

"You know, Saturday? Six-thirty? Death Before Decaf before dinner?"

"You have to turn everything into a joke, don't you?" he said.

"What happened?" I said. I felt my whole body lean forward, like those bean sprouts we all had to plant in first grade, winding their way around construction-paper barriers with your names scrawled across them in primitive printing, reaching for the sun. I was trying to be furious at him, but all my fury was shunted by the photosynthesis of love. "Photosynthesis of Love," nice title, that. Keep it.

Adam looked down at the ground and kicked Roewer's floor with his foot. He suddenly had the dejectedness of Douglas and I wondered briefly if everyone I kissed was turning gay.

"I just" – he made some sweep with his arm – "I just have a lot going on right now. I'm sorry. I just have all this . . . *stuff* to deal with."

Understanding sunk in me like a stone in water, settling me, making me heavier. He had a lot going on. "Hey, that's OK," I said. "I just wondered where you were, that's all. It's a rough year."

156

He looked up. "That's it exactly," he said like I discovered penicillin. "It's a rough year. I guess I'm sort of a mess."

"Well, unfortunately, my life is perfect right now, so I can't relate at all," I said, and he smiled and put his hand on my shoulder, warming me through. I stood on tiptoe to kiss him, but he didn't stop smiling. It was just one flat kiss against his cute grin, but it was enough. No kiss of fire, but it was enough. "Call me soon," I said, and he nodded. The bell rang and I scooted off to homeroom, but even over the rush of all the other latecomers I heard him sigh with what I thought, back then, a naive little high school student, was fondness and not relief.

Dr. Tert: Flannery Culp wanted her life to be a bed of roses.

Winnie: Don't we *all* want our lives to be beds of roses?

Dr. Tert: Yes, but Flannery didn't know how to stop and smell the roses that were in her bed.

Peter Pusher: What I think was wrong with Flannery Culp – what I think is wrong with all delinquent teenagers Flannery's age – is that there is anything – or *anybody* – in her bed at all.

Thunderous applause.

Tuesday October 5th
V___ picked me up from the bus stop this morning, just as I was considering skipping another day. "Thanks," I said, and V___ gave me a kiss on the cheek as she pulled out. I

put V___'s elegant little purse and silk scarf on my lap so I wouldn't squash them flat when I sat down. "Good morning."

"Good morning to you," V___ said primly. "I can't finish the croissant on the dashboard. It's yours if you like." I peeked in the paper bag: almond, my favorite. I looked down at my enormous jeans.

"No thanks," I said, "I'm stuffed." I'm still hungry as I'm writing this down in Calc. I should have eaten that croissant.

Q.E.D.'s *Gurgle and Buzz* album, a record I really like, was playing quietly as V___ headed toward the faculty lot as usual. "I wanted to ask you something," she said, motioning to the nervous freshmen who were craning their necks to see if they could walk safely in front of the car or if V___ was going to run them over.

"Ask away," I said.

"Well, I have something of an unrequited crush on my hands, and I thought you might have some advice for me."

"Who's the crush on?"

She looked down at her parking brake, putting it in place and keeping her hand on it. "Steve Nervo."

"Really?" I squeaked. Steve Nervo is this gorgeous leather-jacketed guitarist who has a permanent hold on Most Popular every year. The stuff written about him in the first-floor girls' bathroom stalls would make Peter Pusher's hairpiece stand on end. I'd always assumed V___, elegant V___ who wears real pearls to school, was above having a crush on the boy everybody has a crush on. *On whom everybody has a crush.*

"I can't see it," I said. "I picture you with some well-dressed gentleman."

"Like Douglas?" she said.

"*No*," I said. "Definitely *not* like Douglas."

She looked at me curiously. "Why'd you say it like that?"

"Um, nothing," I said. "Actually, thinking about it for a second, it could work. The gritty rock star putting the nice girl from the nice family on the back of his motorcycle and riding away."

"Well, not on a *motorcycle*," she said with a look of distaste.

"And would Satan approve?" No, no, Mrs. State, we called V___'s mother Satan, remember?

"Well, probably not, but it doesn't matter, because it's not going to happen. That's why I thought you might have some advice for me." She opened the door of the car and put one perfectly toned leg out gingerly onto the asphalt.

"What do you mean?"

"*You* know," she said, taking her elegant little purse from me and glancing behind her at the backseat, looking for something. "You have an unrequited crush and I thought you might, I don't know, have little exercises that you do or something, to get your mind off it. Did you see a scarf lying around here?"

"I'll have you know," I said stiffly, "that my love life is anything but unrequited. I had a date with Adam this week-end."

"You *did*?" she said. "Well, that *is* exciting. I can't believe I didn't hear about this. How did it go?"

"Fine, fine," I said quickly. Oh, Lord, strike me down now. "I don't really want to talk about it, I'm afraid I'll jinx it. Don't tell anyone, OK?"

"Of course not, of course not," V___ said vaguely, and too quickly. Shit. "Did you see a scarf when you sat down? Real silk? I forget the label."

"No," I said, opening my door and getting out of the car. "You know, I think I'll eat that croissant after all."

"*Bon appétit*," she said. "Maybe I put it in the trunk? Who knows? I'm so spacey this morning. Hold on a second. That's *great* about your date, Flan. Oh, but won't Gabriel mind? Where *is* that scarf?" V___ flitted around, finally getting out of the car and going to the trunk. I grabbed the croissant bag and shut my door. The trunk sprung open but there was no scarf inside, of course.

"I could have *sworn* I had it this morning," V___ said. "I always wear it with this outfit. It *brightens* it. Has it just fallen off the earth, or what?"

"This is a big trunk," I heard myself saying, suddenly. "I bet you could fit a whole person in here, if you scrunched him in."

V___ looked at me blankly. "I have to go," she said. "I'll see you later." In a whiff of some expensive floral perfume I was left alone with my pastry. Now, as Baker babbles about some difficult problem – "Do *something*," he's saying, as if it's always that easy – I'm regretting eating that pastry. My legs seem to have bloated even since this morning, even considering the bulge of wadded-up silk in my right-hand pocket.

LADDER

If you think about it, *later* and *ladder* are really the same word because time is straight up and down, like a ladder. I mean, *ladder*. Douglas is sitting on the couch, and you probably won't believe this but I'm realizing that even from here on the floor, lying on my stomach, I can see his fibers. I mean, his *suit's*. Plus I can see the fibers of the upholstery, merging with the fibers of his suit. It's all held together by fibers, I'm realizing. In fact, if you think about it, strands are fibers too, like DNA strands. I guess

Jim Carr has taught me something. Actually, he's taught me a lot. I guess that's why he's a teacher. Douglas's eyes keep getting wider and wider, which is a little freaky. What time is it? Time is like a ladder, oops wrote that already. It's just that this leprechaun juice is making me feel time so acutely, curling around me like a smooth snake, squeezing out my breath before I know it. Or like a silk scarf, ha ha.

Wednesday October 6th

Ron Piper announced the play today, finally. We were all lounging in the auditorium, making our seats squeak and talking about nothing, when Ron Piper walked to center stage and clapped for our attention.

"Shouldn't that go the *other* way?" Kate asked, and Ron smiled and rolled his eyes at us.

"If I waited for *you* to clap for me . . ." he said, and everyone laughed. He put his hands on his skinny hips as he began his speech, and for the first time I realized that Douglas is really thin, too; is that some genetic thing? Maybe I'll ask Douglas. Oh, God, that's so tacky: *Maybe I'll ask Douglas, my gay friend.* If Douglas died in a car accident they'd probably put up a mural triptych of him with, I don't know, Oscar Wilde and Plato. Was Plato the gay Greek?

"In the years past," Ron said, "we've been doing drawing-room comedies and standard mysteries, and those always worked well. *Very* well, in fact. I think you all have really grown as actors." Here I looked down at the auditorium floor, modestly eyeing the ancient gum. I had played the murderess in last year's mystery, hiding my evil with such skill that the audience always gasped when Kate stumbled upon the crucial clue that incriminated me. "I think you're ready for something more *important*. You might be intimidated by this choice, but if you let me work with you" – this is a phrase he always used – "I know we can do it. Some of you *won't* be intimidated, I know" – here Kate looked *pseudo*-modestly at the floor – "because some of you have been *itching* to do something like this."

"I wish he'd just announce it," Douglas whispered.

"Give him a break," Natasha said, leaning way back in her chair, her perfect hair spreading out in a perfect fan. "He's a high school drama teacher. This is as thrilling as it gets for him."

"That's not nice," I whispered. "I think he's great. Besides Millie, he's our only ally in this loony bin."

"So, without further ado, I will announce our play for this year's fall season. People have been begging me for Shakespeare forever now, and I'm happy to announce that the Roewer Drama Club's fall production will be William Shakespeare's *Othello*."

I thought everybody would clap, or at least *ooh* and *ahh*, but you could have heard a pin drop – providing it didn't land on any of the wads of gum. I didn't understand why. *Othello* sounded good to me, and I wondered who it didn't sound good to. *To whom it didn't sound good.*

I scanned the faces of the Eight who were around: Natasha, Douglas, Kate, V___, Jennifer Rose Milton who was wrapped around Frank Whitelaw and why-is-she-in-our-lives-if-no-one-likes-her Flora Habstat, but they were all looking at me. Or *behind* me, as I turned around and saw Gabriel, who was looking like he'd swallowed something the wrong way. I realized suddenly why it was so quiet: everyone knew that Gabriel and I had kissed but that I hadn't actually talked to him since Friday. Kate had probably told him everything, and even though I have no idea how much Natasha told Kate – you can never tell, with Natasha – everybody probably knew *some* version of the story. But why were they suddenly concerned with this drama, in the middle of Drama? Didn't anyone care about the drama of a black man's jealousy for his white girlfriend?

Oh. That's when I realized why they were looking at him. Gabriel is the only black guy within five miles of Drama Club, and Othello is the only black guy within five miles of Shakespeare. Well, that isn't true – I think there's some African prince in what's-it, the anti-Semitic one, but *still*. It's a little weird to announce a play with a black man in the lead role when there's only one black man who's going to play it.

If Ron was aware of the tension he didn't show it. He said there'd be auditions next week, even keeping a straight face when he said that anyone could try out for any part. He ended the meeting, and the auditorium cleared in seconds, leaving me and Gabriel and all that ancient gum.

"So," Gabriel said, his voice trailing off into nowhere. "Flannery." His tone suddenly flashed me back to fourth grade, staring at my little empty school desk as Mrs. Collins, an evil woman with an immense nose, said the same thing. "Flannery." It was my turn for my class presentation, and I was staring at the space on my desk where my diorama was supposed to be. Instead it was at home. I knew I was going to die.

"I don't know if I have anything else to say to you," he said.

Directly above my head, on the auditorium ceiling bleached from unchecked leaks, a lightbulb burned out with a crackle. "Well, I have something to say," I said. "I'm sorry."

Gabriel blinked, his eyelids moving through all that ice. "That would be a lot more convincing if you weren't

163

saying it when I finally caught you alone," he said. "Like if you were saying it to me on the phone. Like if you'd *called* me."

"I've had a hectic few days," I said.

"And before that?"

"What?"

"You know," he said. "All weekend? Like maybe we could have seen each other?"

"You have to turn everything into a joke, don't you?" I found myself saying, for no reason. I was thinking dimly how I'd break ice, in real life. By throwing rocks at it until it cracked.

"What?" he said. "What's happening, Flan? I can't go on like this. You're making me wish I'd never brought this whole thing up."

I looked down at the ground and kicked the gummy floor with my foot. "I just" – I made some sweep with my arm – "I just have a lot going on right now. I'm sorry. I just have all this stuff . . . to deal with."

My rock made a perfect arc, and worked. I felt understanding sink in him like a stone in water. I had a lot going on. "Hey, that's OK," he said. "I just wondered where you were, that's all. It's a rough year."

I looked up at him and saw his hands move, just slightly, like he had a minor tic or wanted to touch me. "That's it exactly," I said like he'd discovered penicillin. "It's a rough year. I guess I'm sort of a mess."

"Well, unfortunately, my life is perfect right now, so I can't relate at all," he said, and I smiled and put my hand on his shoulder. I could give him that. He leaned in and kissed me and it was enough. It was no kiss of fire – I couldn't give him *that*, not anymore – but I could give him that. It was enough. He smiled at me. "Call me soon," he said, and I nodded. He walked off and I was alone, looking at a bare stage and stepping in gum.

Maybe It's Friday October 8th

I have no idea what time it is, but all I'd have to do is check the almanac, because it's exactly sunrise. My handwriting is getting neater and neater as the gray sky gets lighter and lighter. Even howmanywhatever hours later, the light looks greenish. Everything is magnanimously beautiful. I mean *magnificently*.

The reason my handwriting is so messy is not only because I've stayed up all night etc. but because the texture of this cement is making the paper uneven. I'm in the parking lot of the Rivertown Mall with Gabriel and Natasha, lying on my stomach on one of those big cement planters they have there, with some halfhearted ice plant and lots of candy wrappers in it. The first rays of the sun are shining on them and I can just barely read their ingredients. That's why I'm writing so big, so I can tell what I'm saying. IT'S BEEN A MAGICAL EVENING.

Day 'n Nite Foto is the only place we can think of where you can get your pictures developed in one hour and that's open at this one. Otherwise, I swear, we would not be giving our hard-earned money (sweaty quarters, dollar bills crimped into dead origami) to an establishment that not only misspells both *night* and *photo* but uses that most ugly of contractions, the telltale '*n*.

While emptying my pockets to pay for the developing, I almost dumped Jennifer Rose Milton's earring and Gabriel's pocketknife, both of which I managed to procure during the evening's blurriness. Gabriel is walking up and down the parking lot right now, retracing his steps and looking for it, but last I checked, Jennifer Rose Milton hasn't even noticed that one of her perfect ears is missing one of her perfect earrings. Kate's sweater, Douglas's hat, Lily's glasses, V___'s scarf, Jennifer Rose Milton's earrings, Gabriel's knife, all I need is something from Natasha. Natasha has a small portable radio perched next to her flask, over on the next island, and is smoking a cigarette and doing lazy ballroom dancing steps. Either the radio or the flask would do, but I don't have to do anything this morning. I can just bask in the glow of this magical evening. I'm hanging out at dawn with Gabriel and Natasha, waiting to see what develops. (Metaphor.)

It made the most sense for us to have it at my house – everyone else's parents would have been breathing down our necks – so we just went there directly after school. It had been so hot all day that just about everyone took showers and changed into borrowed clothes, which made it weird: all these people wandering around my house wearing my clothes like folks auditioning to play me in the movie.

V___, of course, looked positively unruffled after the long hot day and was in the kitchen slicing everything into perfect patterns, and Gabriel had found some old fancy champagne glasses from some parental function during my childhood and was putting on a stark white apron so he wouldn't get mussed while he washed them out, and Lily came down, looking better in my black top than I do and wearing her new glasses, Jennifer Rose Milton was on the phone to Millie saying she'd spend the night here and simultaneously shouting up the stairs that her turn at the shower was next, and Douglas came down with his hair soaking wet and uncombed, wearing the only thing of mine he could fit into – an X-tra large tour shirt of the Sartres, who were this band we were all into last year for about ten minutes. I had forgotten all about that shirt; it was so big I couldn't wear it even as a nightshirt so I kept it up on the top shelf of my closet. *The top shelf of my closet*, that made me think. I bounded up the stairs as I heard a familiar guitar riff down in the living room. Somebody had found the Sartres album and was playing their one hit, "Go Back to Bed."

When I opened the door of my room both Kate and Jennifer Rose Milton shrieked impulsively. They were both dressed in towel-togas, Kate having just showered and Jenn apparently about to. They were both standing on tiptoe in my closet, peering at the top shelf, but I think I caught them in time.

"You scared us!" Kate said wildly, stalking to the other end of the room and sitting quickly on the bed. Jennifer Rose Milton was looking at me curiously.

"What were you guys looking for?"

Kate whirled around to face me but I saw Jennifer shake her head, just slightly. "Something to wear," Kate said instantly, and I was filled with relief. I think I could have easily explained away my little collection but I didn't want to, and plus I'd have to give everything back and start over. "Did you ever give me back that sweater I lent you at the last dinner party?" Kate asked. "You could just give me that back now."

"I'm pretty sure I did," I said, opening a dresser drawer. Downstairs I could hear people singing along with the Sartres. "If I didn't it would be in here. But you don't want to wear a sweater, anyway. It's too hot. Here, take this."

"But this is your favorite shirt. You don't loan anybody this shirt."

Natasha stuck her head in the door and raised her eyebrows and her glass of champagne at me. "What are you doing in Flan's closet?" she asked Jenn, who was on her tiptoes again.

"Look what I found," she said and my heart stopped. "A camera!" She held up my cheap camera, which I hadn't used since Italy. "It even has film. Can we use it?"

"Of course," I said.

"This will be *great*," Kate said.

"What I think will be *great*" – Natasha imitated Kate's voice with a snarl – "is when people will learn to stop peeking in each other's closets!"

"I –" Kate started but Natasha was gone; I heard her laughing downstairs already. The music got turned up. Jennifer Rose Milton handed me the camera and her towel slipped a little bit. What I'd do to have breasts like that. Kate put her head in my shirt like an ostrich in the sand, and I went downstairs. Any uneasiness was instantly dispelled; Natasha and Douglas had found last year's yearbook and were cackling over this ugly picture of Mr. Dodd with a sombrero over his head for the Festival Internationale. Gabriel put a piece of bread with tomato and feta in my mouth and I nearly swooned it was so good. He looked so sweet grinning at me like that that I took a picture and everybody got into picture taking. Half the roll was gone by the time Jennifer Rose Milton came downstairs in a pale red dress I can't fit into anymore because I'm such a tub. "Tub," it says "tub." You can't read it because the cement I'm writing on is sort of bumpy. I noticed she hadn't bothered to put her earrings back on; she must have left them on my dresser or something.

We tossed the camera to one another and we'd each snap one and toss it to the next person, taking pictures of practically the same moment from totally different angles, never holding the camera longer than a few seconds like it was some enormous game of paparazzi hot potato. Finally I corraled everyone onto the couch for the photograph.

Take it out now; hopefully the publishers have complied with my wish to have a copy in each book. How odd that you can look at it now, when I'm sitting around watching the sun come up, waiting to see what the photograph looks like. Although in my mind's eye I can see it quite clearly: Kate, leaning on an armrest rather than sitting on the couch like a normal human being, placing herself above us and looking a little smug. V___ right next to her, fingering her pearls, looking better than everyone else with her perfect makeup, better than Natasha even, and that's saying a lot. Lily and Douglas, snug on the couch, Lily between Douglas and me. As usual. Douglas was talking to Gabriel about something and didn't want to stop his train of thought just for a stupid picture so he'll probably have an impatient look on his face. Plus it'll be weird to see a picture of him when he's not wearing a suit. Gabriel, his black hands stark against the white apron, squished into the end of the couch and looking uncomfortable. Beautiful, beautiful Jennifer Rose Milton standing at the couch in a pose that would look too formalized for anyone else who wasn't as beautiful, and stretched out luxuriously beneath us all, Natasha, one long finger between her lips and batting her eyes at me. I can't wait to see it.

There in the picture, I miss you all so much.

We ate thick squares of imported chocolate with whole hazelnuts in them, and licked our fingers afterward. Gabriel licked mine until Natasha made a gagging noise and he stopped. Meanwhile, Douglas was opening and shutting cupboards, his face flushed from champagne and expectation. Somebody finally switched off the Sartres and put on some melodramatic string quartets, Lily probably. I rose unsteadily from the floor where I had been leaning against Gabriel and letting him give me little neck kisses while we all chattered away, but by the time I reached Douglas he had found all the necessary equipment: a small pasta strainer, a box of sugar cubes, a steel bowl and a dainty little saucer.

"This isn't the way we did it before," I said.

"I heard about another way," Douglas said. "A better way. In fact, we took *way* too much last time. We could have seriously fucked ourselves up. This time we ingest a tiny amount, and it tastes better, too." He put everything on a tray, along with the leprechaun bottle, and walked grandly back into the living room.

Winnie: Often, teenagers start on the path of absinthe addiction when they try it at a party. In a party setting, particularly with a strong peer group, it's practically impossible to resist.

Peter Pusher: Nonsense, it's very possible to resist. I think it's wonderful that little Flora here resisted.

Flora Habstat: I didn't resist.

Peter Pusher: Oh. But if you had –

"And now the moment you've all been waiting for," Douglas announced, and waited for everyone to remove the stray pieces of feta and bread crumbs so he could put the tray down on the coffee table.

"What's all this paraphernalia?" Lily asked.

"Yeah, I thought you guys just drank little shots." Kate picked up the saucer like she was shopping for antiques and suspected this one was fake.

"As it turned out, those little shots almost killed us," I said.

"Really?" V___ said. "And now you want us all to try it?"

170

"Oh, I *love* this," Lily said.

"Come on," Natasha said carelessly. "We're young."

"Precisely my point," Lily said. Gabriel wanted to say something but just looked at me instead. "I think I'll hold off on this absinthe thing until I'm ninety-five, so if I *die* –"

"Nobody's going to *die*," Douglas said. Natasha snapped a picture of him, just as he said that. "Flan's exaggerating, as usual. I've just since heard that it's not exactly the recommended amount. But the way we're doing it now, it's perfectly safe."

What it felt like then. What it feels like now, in the parking lot. This self-conscious carelessness of being a senior. Maybe, generations ago, young people rebelled out of some clear motive, but now, we *know* we're rebelling. Between teen movies and sex-ed textbooks we're so ready for our rebellious phase we can't help but feel it's safe, contained. It will turn out all right, despite the risk, snug in the shell of rebellion narrative. Rebellion narrative, does that make sense? It was appropriate to do it, so we did it.

"How many of us are there?" Douglas asked, counting out sugar cubes.

"Yes, let's see . . ." Kate theatrically wrinkled her brow. "What's our nickname again? The Basic Four?"

"Oh," I said. "It's such a relief to just have *us* here. Just us at a dinner party." I stretched out my legs and found Natasha's stretched out legs. We intertwined like kelp.

"It really is," Lily said seriously.

"Just *us*," I said, "without, oh, I don't know –"

"Lara Trent," Douglas said.

"Or Adam," Gabriel said, and everyone giggled. Kate mock-glared at him, briefly.

"Or Flora Habstat," Natasha said. "Or Jim Carr."

"Or Frank Whitelaw," Jennifer Rose Milton blurted out. Everybody looked at her. It was suddenly quiet, except for the string quartet.

"*Really*?" Kate asked.

"We're having a little tiff," JRM said primly. She looked into her champagne glass like she had dropped something into it. "I don't really want to talk about it."

"Then you *shouldn't*," V___ said, smoothing Jenn's hair.

Douglas took a fork and chimed it on his champagne glass. "Suppertime!" he said, and poured the absinthe onto the sugar cubes, where it turned them the color of fancy mints. Douglas caught Lily's eye and moved his eyebrows, just slightly; she went over to the stereo for perfect drug music. All *that* and they still communicate like lovers. Douglas gingerly took each sugar cube and put it on the little saucer. The last one plopped down just as the harpsichord started. Some classical music – Bach, I'm pretty sure. We all giggled like schoolchildren as we passed around the cubes, each taking one. When V___ said, "Take the first one you touch," everyone laughed too loudly. Then we all lounged back and let it take effect.

In some ways it reminds me of the sunrise itself. One minute it's dark. Then you perceive a vague light in a scarcely delineated direction, and before you know it the whole world is rippling with light, and soon it's blazing and you can see everything. The harpsichord was playing one of those fugue things, which usually sounds a little to me like somebody playing any note they want to but this time around I could not only hear each voice and each melody but I could expand on it: Kate's brash laughter working in counterpoint to the left hand (right hand? left

172

hand, I think) of the harpsichordist, and then Lily was reading something out loud from Hattie's class, Poe I think, but then we all got distracted by the food and just ate and ate and ate – I have this vision of V___ standing in front of the open refrigerator door bathed in the light like she was being abducted by aliens, reaching in with both hands and putting everything edible onto the counter: cold pasta, and lemons, spicy mustard spread on crackers, an old jar of maraschino cherries, and pickles, and suddenly Douglas was holding one of the pickles and explaining to all of us the right way to hold it in our mouths and everyone laughing so loud and blushing so red it was like being in the middle of an enormous gardenia. Suddenly we were noticing that the Bach CD was skipping all over the place, showering us with little harpsichord shards that hit me like hail before turning off and replacing itself with cha-cha music, with Natasha leading an enormous conga line up the stairs, all around the bedrooms with everybody taking a turn stepping into the bathtub for a special solo dance – Gabriel's stiff and awkward, Douglas's surprisingly lithe, Lily's wild and hulalike, Natasha's insanely sensual, Jennifer Rose Milton's spectacularly elegant, V___ doing a mock minuet with her palms outstretched like something painted on the walls of the pyramids, with Kate just putting her hands on her head like antlers and saying "I'm a moose! I'm a moose!" and then we were all saying it, skipping downstairs saying "I'm a moose!" which made me wonder what time it was so I looked at the digital clock in the kitchen but I pressed the reset button by mistake and spent what felt like the rest of the weekend watching the bright red numbers go zipping by. People were taking turns blowing bubbles out of a plastic bear so bright blue it felt like a postcard sky of a national park. V___ was suddenly asleep and snoring with her mouth open. Kate was wrapping herself in the living room curtains and murmuring that she was a beige mummy. Douglas was looking at some coffee table book of Michelangelo's David. Lily was in the downstairs bathroom, looking in the mirror and whispering her name over and over while Jennifer Rose Milton sat on the toilet, nodding in agreement and eating peanut butter out of the jar with her fingers and perfect nails and maybe one hundred bracelets and I thought about grabbing one but I remembered the earrings upstairs so I took Gabriel up to my room and we kissed and kissed. I tried to take all the chocolate off of his tongue until I remembered it wasn't a strawberry and Gabriel cupped one of my breasts, over my shirt, and suddenly began to cry. Natasha poked her head up and rolled her eyes at me. She had been underneath the bed and looked like a dust bunny herself. The three of us giggled and I quietly put Gabriel's pocketknife and Jennifer Rose Milton's earring in my pocket. From nowhere we were seized with the idea that we were detectives and needed to solve the mystery of why everybody was asleep downstairs, even Jennifer Rose Milton with one hand still in the peanut butter and the other one half in her mouth. I took the magnifying glass from the unabridged dictionary and we giggled and looked for clues on everybody's face and I opened one of Kate's eyes and saw it staring back at me like a wet marble. Gabriel was afraid we would accidentally burn somebody with it even though the sun wasn't up yet and that's when we had the idea to go develop the photographs and see the sunrise in the mall.

Gabriel has brought back the photographs, developed and in envelopes. In part of some glorious cycle of synchronicity, every roll you develop at Day 'n Nite Foto gets you a new free roll of film, like throwing one rock into the river and stepping on it before looking around for the next roll. Or something, but you know what I mean. Now that I know this, Day 'n Nite Foto will always be my photo developing place, despite its grammatical problemics, unless it changes its name to Day 'n Nite Foto Shoppe, in which case I'd have to boycott because every word of the store name would be misspelled. Oh, *Day*. But still. Natasha and Gabriel and I giggled through the pictures: mostly blurry and at odd angles because we'd been tipsily tossing the camera, but then there was the one: Kate, leaning on an armrest rather than sitting on the couch like a normal human being, placing herself above us and looking a little smug. V___ right next to her, fingering her pearls, looking better than everyone else with her perfect makeup, better than Natasha even, and that's saying a lot. Lily and Douglas, snug on the couch, Lily between Douglas and me. As usual. Douglas was talking to Gabriel about something and didn't want to stop his train of thought just for a stupid picture so he has an impatient look on his face. Plus it's weird to see a picture of him when he's not wearing a suit. Gabriel, his black hands stark against the white apron, squished into the end of the couch and looking uncomfortable. Beautiful, beautiful Jennifer Rose Milton standing at the couch in a pose that would look too formalized for anyone else who wasn't as beautiful, and stretched out luxuriously beneath us all, Natasha, one long finger between her lips and batting her eyes at me. And me, of course. I'm there too, looking right at the camera. We all hushed when we got to it. We looked at it for a minute, and then Gabriel put his hand on my bare neck and I grabbed all the pictures and stuffed them in the envelope. We walked home in silence, feeling grittier and grittier with each step. As soon as I opened the door and saw everybody still sprawled all over the living room, all my plans for making them coffee went out the window. Forget my friends and forget breakfast, I wanted all these people the fuck out of my house.

Vocabulary:

LEPRECHAUN DEPRAVED DRUG-INDUCED PHOTOSYNTHESIS

Study Questions:

1. Calculate the minimum dimensions required to fit an entire person in the trunk of an automobile, if you scrunch him.

2. Do you think that high school actors are ready for something as important as a production of Shakespeare's Othello? Keep in mind that most of the cast of Roewer's production of Othello were honors students.

3. Who took that group photograph at the absinthe party? And I know what you're thinking.

Monday October 11th Columbus Day

Somewhere in the aftermath of those darn sugar cubes not only the rest of Saturday but Sunday have fallen somewhere, irretrievable. Like Jenn's earring – she called me yesterday because she lost one in the fracas. I think I probably stayed in my room, because last night I discovered I was hungry, went downstairs and realized the house hadn't been cleaned up. The bowl of drained absinthe was still underneath the strainer and soiled napkins lay everywhere. A big champagne-glass ring was right on David's groin. By the time I cleaned up and found something to eat (and there wasn't much – we had pretty much cleaned out the pantry) I wanted to go back to bed. I woke up this morning, took a shower, got dressed and then realized there wasn't any school today because just about five hundred years ago somebody got the continents mixed up, gave everybody smallpox and then got called a genius. So now I'm in Death Before Decaf with a latte and an allegedly fresh muffin, trying to start a lazy day at seven-thirty. I can't decide whether to read my Poe assignment or my Whitman assignment first, so I'm flipping the muffin paper in lieu of a coin. It falls like a dead bird. Heigh ho, heigh ho, it's off to Poe I go.

Tuesday October 12th

SCENE: The hallway outside the auditorium, directly following *Othello* auditions. At rise, KATE is at her locker, putting away some books and talking with V___ and FLAN.

Kate, Flan and V___ (mocking auditionees in hysterical unison): *"That I did love the Boor to live with him!"*

Kate (as they all laugh): *That would be Moor, little girl.*

Flan (mock-innocently): *Oh, I get it. I love him the more.*

Adam (appearing from nowhere as he always does): *Talking about me again?*

Flan (blinking, blankly): *Maybe.*

V___: *Oh. Um, excuse us, Adam. We need to –*

Kate: – *wash our hair*. Hairs.

Flan: *Hair*.

Exeunt KATE, V___.

Adam: *Hi*.

Flan: *Hi. You looked really good up onstage.*

(FLAN waits for lightning to strike her down.)

Flan: *I mean –*

Adam: *Thanks*.

Flan: *You know what I mean.*

Adam (looking into her eyes): *I think I always do.*

Chorus: *Is this man charming like a host or like a snake?*
      Is he for real or is he fake?
      Flan does not know what to make of it,
      If Adam is full of love or full of shit.

Flan: *Yeah, well.*

Adam: *When are we going to have that coffee?*

Flan: *I think I know better than to meet you at Death Before Decaf.*

Adam: *That isn't fair.*

Flan: *You're right.* (She sighs; ADAM leans in close.) *I don't know better. Give me a call.*

Adam (touching her cheek): *I will.*

Gabriel (appearing from nowhere): *Hello.*

Chorus: *Fuck.*

Kate (Offstage, from down the hall): *Adam, are you still giving me a ride?*

Adam: *Um.*

Kate: *Adam?*

Adam (calling out): *Yes* (spreads his hands out, emptily, and leaves).

Gabriel looked at me like he just couldn't believe it. "I just can't believe it," he said.

"Let's not talk about anything here," I said.

I craved a latte but I ordered a monkey-shaped pot of tea for Gabriel and me to share. I thought he'd like that, and I was right: he smiled faintly. We sat down underneath a sculpture of a monkey, hanging precariously on the wall. It reminded me of a joke that used to crack me up in third grade: *Why did the monkey fall out of the tree? Because it was dead.*

"Listen," Gabriel said, and then looked at his tea for so long I caught myself trying to listen to it. Given the seashell-ocean thing, if you put your ear to a teacup, what do you hear – the source of the tea or the source of the cup? "Listen," he said, and I looked back up at his face. His eyes were red.

"Listen," he said, and then looked down again.

"I'm listening, I'm listening," I said, and we both smiled.

"I just need to know what's going on. After this weekend, I felt sure we were together, and that made me so happy." He swallowed. "But then when I see you talking to Adam I wonder what is up. If you just want to be friends, I can live with that. I love you too much to have you not be in my life. But I just can't stand this roller-coaster thing. We spent all that time alone, just watching the sunrise, and I was just so happy, but then I see you making a date with Adam."

"I wasn't *making a date with him*," I said. I wanted to add, "And we weren't *alone* all that time; Natasha was with us. And we were on drugs. And stop telling me that you love me so much, it makes me want to die."

"Well, he said he'd call you, and he was –" He started to mime Adam putting his hand on my face, but he couldn't continue. He didn't need to; I still felt it there myself.

"Gabriel," I said quietly. "The *Othello* auditions are over. I was just talking to him."

He blinked, sipped. "I guess I'm just still in character," he said. Feeling like a marionette I reached across the table and took his hand. Gabriel smiled small. "Maybe it's just going to take a while before this all feels natural."

"I think so," I said.

"Because you make me so happy –"

The monkey fell.

Chorus: *The boy has also fallen for our Flan.*
She has no course in life; she has no plan.

180

It's senior year; her grades should be sky-high:
She's flaking, flunking Calc. We cannot lie.
The boy she loves is playing with her mind
Her love for G. is of a different kind.
Flan can't bring herself to tell this dear, dear friend
Their ill-conceived romance forsooth must end.
She's gaining weight; soon all will call her Fatty.
In her mind are words from teacher Hattie:
"Relax," she said, "You're young. You will be wise."
But now it's not in sight. Tears fill her eyes.
But for Flan, her strife has only just begun
She kills the boy October thirty-one.

Wednesday October 13th

For most of this entry there's a soundtrack: can you hear it? It's actually nonspecific but of a particular type: any theme to any spy movie you can dream up. You know, the espionagy twang of guitars, an agitated bass line, sinewy sax, washed-up semistars singing of martinis and car chases, and usually, inexplicably, love. Got it in your head? Then we can continue.

Most of these photographs no longer belong to me. They were sold to tabloids to defray legal expenses. Whatever I paid to have them developed at Day 'n Nite Foto paid off considering that groveling "investigative journalists" paid up to eight hundred bucks a pop. Just how investigative is it to call an alleged felon's lawyer and negotiate for snapshots?

EXPOSURE ONE: A happy couple making out on the bus. I hate them. Why does it always work out for people who wear ugly clothes? I hate them so much when I got it developed I wrote I HATE YOU all over them in big red felt-pen letters.

EXPOSURE TWO: Kate and Natasha at the bus stop, waiting for me. Kate doesn't see me yet – that's how I could snap the picture – she's standing there with her arms crossed, pursing her lips. She's obviously cold. Behind her is Natasha, who is looking right at the camera and rolling her eyes at me. And no wonder, considering the conversation Kate and I had as we trudged to Roewer.

"Flannery," she said grandly as I disengaged myself from public transportation. It was like she'd been trying to catch my eye for some time and I had finally come over to give her a refill. Natasha, still behind Kate's back, mouthed it right back at me: "Flannery."

"Kate," I said, and meant it.

"I always feel a little bit like a deranged stalker waiting for someone on the bus like this," she said, "but sometimes you want to talk to someone, and you don't see them one day at school, and then all of a sudden the week's almost over."

"This small talk makes it sound like I'm about to get fired," I said.

"Don't be silly," Kate said. "I just wanted to talk to you."

"Well," I said, shrugging and rolling my eyes. It was so reassuring of Kate to tell me I wasn't fired. "You'd better get to it. Before you know it the week'll be over."

Natasha snorted. We walked silently for a few seconds while Kate stared off at Roewer looming over the horizon, collecting herself. She sighed and began.

"Flannery, I just wanted to know where you stand with Adam. Now that you're together with Gabriel, you obviously aren't actively pursuing him, so technically it's an irrelevant question, but –"

"Inquiring minds want to know?" I finished for her, echoing a TV ad for a tabloid newspaper whose articles on us were particularly offensive. *Now that I'm together with Gabriel.* Suddenly it was canonized, like "Basic Eight." First I kiss him in private, then at a party, and all of a sudden I'm together with Gabriel.

"No." Kate took a navy-blue handkerchief out of the pocket of her navy-blue blazer. "I don't just want to know for gossipy reasons." Kate never does. She always has a philanthropic reason for needing to know some piece of information.

"You never do," I said. "You always have a very good reason for wanting to know everyone's business."

It's always even odds whether Kate's going to take offense to something like that. She looked at me for a moment, wavering, and then, even though she was smiling, said tensely, "You obviously haven't had your coffee yet. Or *enough* coffee." Behind her back Natasha held up her flask and wiggled it at me, but Kate must have caught it in her peripheral vision because she turned to Natasha and gave her a curious, withering look. "We'll talk later, Flan."

"No," I said. "I've had enough, um, *coffee*. Tell me what you have to say, Kate."

"It's just that I'm finding – I have found –"

"The Holy Grail," Natasha said.

Kate didn't even acknowledge the wisecrack. "I think we've all really been getting to know Adam, and, I don't know, *liking* him. I think we'd all like to like him *better*."

"What?"

"*Know* him better. We'd all like to *know* him better. And I think – I'm not just speaking for myself – we all feel a little tentative about that, because we don't know how you feel."

"I'm fine, thanks."

Kate granted me a gratuitous smile. "I mean that we'd like him in our circle. What do you think?"

"You make it sound like a cult," I said. I know; I know: ironic.

"I just wanted to know if you're OK by that."

"Of course I'm OK *with* that," I said. "I have to go."

We were at Roewer. "Of course," Kate said, carefully. "I have to go, too. See you later?"

"It's a safe assumption."

EXPOSURE THREE: A good one, and I'm not alone in my opinion; *America Unveiled* paid two hundred bucks for this one: Kate walking through Roewer's side entrance with a puzzled frown. Behind her is the "PUSHED TO THE LIMIT ACADEMICALLY, ATHLETICALLY AND SOCIALLY" sign, tattered to photogenic disarray, like something kids *just don't care about* anymore.

EXPOSURE FOUR: Michael Baker at the blackboard. I forgot to mention we had another test yesterday which I flunked. Here he is seen writing his Rule on the board and underlining it. Do *something*.

EXPOSURE FIVE: After Poetry I managed to take this one of Hattie Lewis at her desk, with Jennifer Rose Milton and Gabriel looking on as she explains something from a book. Flora Habstat wandered into the background of this one, dammit, though because of all her spotlight hogging – "The Whistle Blower," indeed – it meant this one fetched four hundred bucks, or about an hour of lawyer time.

EXPOSURE SIX: An attempt to capture Adam on his way to choir. However, Vice Principal Mokie blundered into the viewfinder and covered it.

EXPOSURE SEVEN: Guitar: twang-a-twang-a-*twang*. Successful attempt to capture Adam on his way to choir. Raising his eyebrows and smiling at something a perky second soprano is telling him while wiping his brow with a navy-blue handkerchief. Smiling at her like he never smiles at me. Her name is Shannon and she wears sweater-vests with flowers on them. You can stare and stare at a photograph and sometimes never see what's right under your nose. Or what isn't, like for instance its monetary value. Fifty bucks.

EXPOSURE EIGHT: Gabriel, framed by the door of the choir room. He's waiting for me. He's holding a rose. He's sorry he was so jealous yesterday. Two hundred bucks.

EXPOSURE NINE: Lily and Natasha in the courtyard at lunch, peering over their economics textbook, covering up some diagram and laughing themselves silly as they try to recite it. There's a test next period, and they're going to flunk. In the lower right-hand corner, hanging over the edge of an overstuffed garbage can, Flan's lunch bag. Inside it (invisible), a discarded red rose. Two hundred.

EXPOSURE TEN: Jim Carr's hand on the chest of the grimacing teaching assistant, a little blurry because I had to lean through the office door, snap it and lean back before anybody saw. I bet this one could have fetched tons of money if it weren't for what happened to Mr. Carr. One thousand, two thousand – who knows? I've never blackmailed someone. I know, you're thinking, *big deal*, but it matters to me, OK?

EXPOSURE ELEVEN: The whole gang sitting around in Millie's class, before Millie's class started: Douglas, Kate, Lily, V——, Natasha, Jennifer Rose Milton, Gabriel, and, dammit, *Flora Habstat*, who once again wandered into the background. This is the picture that fetched eight hundred bucks but launched the media's thousand ships. This is what crystallized the myth that Flora was one of us. She was not one of us. No one was one of us until we all agreed about him or her, and I didn't agree: Q.E.D. The original Latin phrase, that is, not the band.

EXPOSURE TWELVE: The same shot as eleven, except extremely gurgly. Blurry, I mean, *blurry*. I got distracted.

EXPOSURE THIRTEEN: The same shot as twelve, except not blurry, but everybody's looking at the camera.

"What are you doing?" Kate asked. The needle screeches off the soundtrack.

"Nothing," I said, ineffectually. "Just taking a picture."

"I hate candid photographs," V—— said, taking out her compact and looking in the mirror.

"I wanted nonposed pictures of you guys," I said, wondering how that sounded.

"Whatever for?" Jennifer Rose Milton said.

"I have no idea," I said, and everybody laughed.

Gabriel came over and gave me a peck on the cheek. "Where's the rose?"

"You'll never believe this," I said, "but it literally fell apart right in my hands during Bio. All the petals came off and fell all over the place. I felt like the Evil Queen or something."

"*When* did you feel this way?" Kate asked. Jennifer Rose Milton and V—— bit back smiles. Gabriel glared at them.

"Hey," I said, "what are we doing this weekend?"

"Well," Kate said, "Friday's the dance, but Saturday, nothing. Have a plan?"

"I was thinking we haven't had a Sculpture Garden party yet this year."

"That's right!" V___ exclaimed. "And it's already *October*. What were we thinking?"

"Let's do it Saturday," Kate said. "Who else besides the Basic Eight?"

"What's the Sculpture Garden?" Flora said.

"It's a sculpture garden," Natasha replied with elaborate patience.

"It's in the Hall of Fine Arts," Jennifer Rose Milton put in hurriedly.

"*Outside* it, really," Lily said.

"We go there, bring food and music –"

"But isn't that illegal? The Hall of Fine Arts isn't open at night." Flora was puckered with concern, literally *puckered* like some overripe fruit.

"*Please*," Kate said. "It's not like we'd ever get arrested there." Note the foreshadowing.

"Hey," I said. "Speaking of illegal, we still have plenty of absinthe left. The effect in the Sculpture Garden might be –"

Everybody but Natasha and Douglas shook their heads in Puritan unison. "I don't know, Flan," V___ said. "That stuff addled my brain. I don't think I should take it again before finals." Douglas, Natasha and I made quiet eye contact.

"OK," I said.

"OK, OK," Millie said, clapping her hands. "I guess we should give the taxpayers their money's worth and teach you monkeys something."

EXPOSURE FOURTEEN: The cast list for the Roewer High School Production of Othello, tersely posted at the Stage Door:

Role	Explanation of Role*	Person Who Got the Part
Othello	Jealous, deadly black guy	Gabriel Gallon
Desdemona	Beautiful innocent victim	Jennifer Rose Milton**
Iago	The villain	Adam State
Emilia	His wife	Flannery Culp***
Cassio	O's right-hand man, framed as an adulterer	Douglas Wilde
Roderigo	Iago's sucker	Frank Whitelaw****
Duke	Um, the Duke	Flora Habstat*****
Brabantio	D's moody dad	Steve Nervo******
Montano	Governor of Cyprus	Rachel State*******
Bianca	A courtesan	Kate Gordon********
Officers, Clowns, Musicians, etc.		people we don't care about

* These explanations provided for ignorant readers who only read glitzy true-crime books instead of anything of substance.

** Kate will draw blood.

*** Oh my God I get to play his wife.

**** An idiot played by an idiot. Ron Piper is a genius.

***** Bitch. Not only do I have to spend time rehearsing with Flora Habstat, but she's playing a male character. Ron Piper is an idiot.

****** V___ is probably kicking herself that she didn't try out for the play. Reading lines for weeks next to one's love interest is a sure way to – calm down, Flan, don't get ahead of yourself.

******* Rarely does a Dark Horse sneak into the cast like this. And in the case of the Frosh Goth, I do mean a dark horse; she's probably the only cast member who will have to remove makeup before going onstage.
******** *Kate will draw blood.*

Ironically [here Winnie executes a perfectly designed bitter smile], the members of the Basic Eight were rehearsing for a performance of William Shakespeare's brilliant tragedy Othello. But they ended up performing their own tragedy: the tragedy of murder.

THE REST OF THE ROLL: Overexposed. (Like the photographer herself.)

Thursday October 14th

Reread *Othello* last night. Adam's going to kill me. Oh the irony, but fuck *Othello* and fuck tragedy and fuck irony even, while I sit around being so clever the real evil is underneath my nose, *way* underneath my nose, like around my – what did dear departed civil rights leader Mark Wallace call them? – *nice tits*.

At this point in my journal you'd find me saying, "Back up, Flan. Start at the beginning, Flan." Well, all the Honors English narrative structure shit ain't getting me nowhere, friends and neighbors. I'll start wherever I want to. It's not like anybody's going to read this. (Fuck irony. *Fuck* it.)

It's not like I was already stressed out – I mean it's not like I *wasn't* already stressed out. *Fuck* it, I can't add up all the double negatives what I mean is that I was already stressed out. After staring at all those gorgeous photographs of Adam I psyched myself into talking to him about our coffee date before Choir today. Adam had a cold and was blowing his nose with a navy-blue handkerchief when I approached him. Before I could help myself I touched his neck, and he smiled until the handkerchief came off his face. Then he frowned distractedly like I'd woken him up. I said I wanted to talk to him but he said he had to talk to the choir president, how about after rehearsal. I said sure but before the last note we sang was through ringing in the rafters (OK, I'm upset, my imagery is a little stilted) Adam was *out* the door, leaving me alone. Gabriel was waiting for me with another rose. I let him kiss me. At lunch, Lily and I talked about oh who cares what we talked about, who *cares*, the point is that when I got to Advanced Bio the new teaching assistant had quit and Carr wanted to see me in his office after class and why can't I just say it? Carr's breath on me.

The way his eyes changed when he shut the door of his office and I was alone with him was like watching something shed off its larval form. "You've made me lose my assistant," he said, reaching over and holding my arm, just above the elbow. It felt like a bear trap, one of those things you'd chew your own arm off to get out of. *Of which to get out. Fuck* it. "I've never lost an assistant before. And you know the only variable? The only possible cause? *You.*" He was a lunatic. "I've never lost an assistant before, and I've never had *you* in the classroom before. Therefore –" he said.

Irony, I thought, could work here. "This doesn't sound like the Scientific Method," I said, babbling toward the door. He leaned in and kissed me. It felt like bile, like some horrible sea cucumber, his tongue. In a perfect world I would have thrown up, right into his mouth. This wasn't a perfect world. This was fucking Advanced Bio at Roewer

High School, sixth period. I was going to be late to French, because Jim Carr was Frenching me. *Fuck the irony*, Flan. I broke away from him and reached behind me for the doorknob. I turned it; it hurt my wrist. Locked. Carr gave a little snort of laughter and then took me by the shoulders like he was going to shake me, but threw me down on his desk instead. *Threw me down.* I don't think I've ever really been *thrown down* like that. I still have a bruise. A stack of binders fell to the floor and a forgotten cup of coffee turned over and drooled onto the blotter. That's where I was looking, that's what I was doing, watching the desk. That's what I was doing. What Carr was doing was reaching an arm under my shirt and up my back like snakes. He was trying to unclasp my bra but he couldn't do it. Come to think of it, of *course* he couldn't do it; it's hard enough for boys to do that when the girl is *willing*. I was thinking all these crazy thoughts and more. Giving up on the clasp he just reached under my bra and tweaked my nipple like he was looking for something good on the radio. I screamed and he pulled his hand away from my breast and slapped me, hard, against the face. He moved between my legs – God, when had I opened them? Did he think I had opened them for *him*? Right against my crotch I felt him and in a perfect world I would have thrown up again. This wasn't a perfect world, though; this was Advanced Biology, and I could feel the oh-just-say-it *cock* of my Advanced Bio teacher up against me. He rubbed against me like friction. I guess it *was* friction. I don't know, fuck it. Fuck irony. Which is pretty much what *he* was doing.

For a minute I thought somebody had burst in: Natasha, or Millie, maybe, wondering why I was late. She was hysterical, tears were just *gushing* down their faces, hot and streaming. "Just stop it! Just stop it!" Carr pushed harder on me, and faster and I'd had enough boyfriends to know what this meant. "Just stop it!" somebody kept screaming and crying and then all of a sudden the desk shook a shelf off the wall. Beakers shattered everywhere and then it was quiet. "Just stop it!" they screamed again, and I don't have to tell you who it was, do I? The door was locked, and it wasn't Carr, OK? Carr was looking at me, panting and pointing at me, looking around at all the tinkling glass. "You broke *millions of dollars of equipment!*" he shouted. "You're in *so much trouble!*"

"*Let me out!*" she screamed. "*Let me out let me out let me out let me out!*" The lead singer says the exact same thing in the middle of a Q.E.D. song. I stood up. My half-unclasped bra was piercing my back and it hurt like hell, *like hell.* Carr opened the door in one swift move. It didn't look locked; maybe he could say that, later: that it wasn't locked. I stood up and my hands were shaking against my legs, which felt so *fat.* I'd never felt fatter. No one would think that Carr would do this to someone so *ugly.* I saw a splotch of wet stain on his pants as I backed through the door. In a perfect world I would have thrown up on him right then, but it wasn't a perfect world. Instead I threw up in the middle of French and Millie let us out early to drive me home. She didn't say anything the whole way there and I sat upright in my seat, afraid to lean back because I still hadn't adjusted my bra and it still hurt like hell, I already said that. I was crying the whole time and I think I still am.

It was Natasha who took off my shirt and unclasped my bra. It had broken my skin and she took a cotton ball and poured a little of her flask on it. "You have a little red dot, that's all," Natasha said. Our eyes met in the mirror on my closet door. I was lying down in my bed and she was applying a cotton ball, I already wrote that.

She looked like a masseuse, standing over me like that with my shirt off. "Just a little red dot. It's very Hindu, which I understand is *in* this year." When I saw myself smiling at her in the mirror I suddenly felt my life back within my grasp, like your foot brushing the bottom of the pool when you're small and you realize you're back, safe in the shallow area.

My eyes, chlorinated, refilled. "Watch it –" Natasha warned. "Put a shirt on and come downstairs and let's have some tea."

"I'm not sure we have any," I said, putting on a shirt. "There's milk though, and water."

"Water," she said. "Yummy. Anything else?"

"The rest of the absinthe."

"I think your brain is addled enough," she said, tossling my hair. We sat on the couch and I stared into space while Natasha got us water. "Watch it –" she said again when she handed it to me, and I followed her gaze and saw my hands were shaking. She put down both glasses on the coffee table and gave me a big long hug. I was out of tears, apparently, but shook like one of those animals they keep outside supermarkets. Put the quarter in and centrifuge your kid. I felt centrifuged.

"My back hurts," I said, finally.

"It'll be OK," she said. "It's just a little cut. The real question is –" She took a sip of water. "The real question is, did it damage your spine?"

"What do you mean?"

"What are you going to do?" Her eyebrows were raised, casually, but the eyes were sharp.

"Um."

"Because you're going to do *something*. Or I am." She stretched her legs out and kicked off her shoes.

"I don't think there's anything to be done," I said.

"Baker's Rule," she said sharply.

"I just don't think –"

"*Baker's Rule*," she snarled. "*Baker's Rule. Baker's Rule. Baker's Rule.* Do *something*."

"What could I –"

"Do *something*!" She stood up and pointed at me. "Do *something*! If you don't do *something* –"

"*Please*!" I yelled. "*Please*! Don't shout at me!"

Everything stopped for a second. I felt the quiet of being alone in the house.

"Sorry," Natasha said. I held my hand out to her and she took it, and sat down. "I guess I'm just –" She gestured nowhere.

"Tomorrow I'll tell the principal," I said.

"Bodin?"

I couldn't picture talking to Bodin. "Maybe Mokie." We both smiled like they do in books, what's it called: *mirthlessly*.

"You need something stronger than water if this is all you can think of." She pulled out her flask and waved it toward my water but my stomach turned and I shooed it away.

"I can't think of anything," I said, but it sounded too casual so I said it again. "I can't think of anything."

"Look, if you complain to the principal nothing will happen. Remember when you tried to get transferred out of his class? You had to fight Medusa just to get in to see him."

"They wouldn't believe me anyway," I said. "The door wasn't locked. I could have left at any time."

"That's *bullshit*," she said.

"Plus, look at me." I looked down at my own body. "I'm *fat*."

"You are not *fat*."

"Whatever. I'm *large*, I'm *fat*, it doesn't matter. I'm *ugly*. Carr wouldn't have picked me. I mean, they wouldn't believe that. I'm ugly –" Natasha yanked me to my feet and dragged me into the bathroom. "*What?*" I said. "*What?*" I was terrified; I still wasn't ready for people to make sudden movements around me. "*What?*"

"Look in the mirror," she said, and slammed the bathroom door shut. There was a full-length mirror on the back of it, but a light blue towel was blocking the view. Natasha grabbed the towel and threw it to the floor. "*Look in the fucking mirror, Flan!*"

"*Don't yell at me!*"

"I am *so* sick of this," she said. She grabbed my head and turned it to the mirror. "Look in the goddamn mirror *right now*," she said, "and tell me what you see. You're *fat*, are you? Show me where! *Look in the mirror!*"

I blinked and then looked in the mirror, down to my feet and back up again. I stuck my tongue out at my reflection but Natasha grabbed my head again. I looked in the mirror.

"Are you fat?" I shook my head. A little figment in my head just melted away. I looked fine. My eyes were splotchy from crying and I was wearing an ugly shirt, but what the hell I was just lying around the house with Natasha and besides, I'd had a shitty day. So I wasn't a perfect toothpick. So I was bigger than Natasha. At least I was –

"I'm thinner than *Kate*, anyway," I said, and Natasha threw her head back and laughed loud. Cackled. I laughed too. Tears rolled down my face, and I laughed, right to the mirror. I laughed so hard I started heaving and had to lean against the sink. The air was getting thin. Natasha opened the door of the bathroom – my reflection, alone amidst porcelain and towels, swung toward me for a second only to bang against the wall. Leaning on her, I went up the stairs and got right into bed. I wanted to keep my clothes on. I kept my eyes open for a while and Natasha was watching me. She watched me until I closed my eyes, and kept watching me then, because I woke up twice more during the night and she was there, watching me, though in the morning she was gone.

Friday October 15th

It's incredible how many crucial details I forget to warn my readers about: I mean, today is Festival Internationale and what with being assaulted and everything I forgot to let you know. Today is Festival Internationale. "That roughly translates to International Festival," Lawrence Dodd was saying as I came into homeroom. Nobody cared that I was late; everybody was running around doing last-minute things. We'd had to have an adjunct Grand Opera Breakfast Club meeting to help Millie prepare everything for crepes. I had sweet, sweet batter in my hair.

All the different languages were already setting up their booths after homeroom; the Chinese classes seemed to be going all out this year, lanterns, paper dragons, blah blah blah. During Poetry I concentrated on Whitman, rereading each line as Hattie led discussions. I kept catching my hands trembling, and after class Hattie asked if I wanted to talk. "The last thing I want to do is talk," I said. Hattie always refused to talk to the press afterward, and for that I love her, even though she also refused to talk to me.

I was of course dreading seeing Adam, so I was straggling to choir looking for an excuse not to go when I literally ran into Millie, who needed people to chop fruit for the fruit fillings. I didn't want to think about anything.

I rolled up my sleeves and got to work and told Millie that I was feeling much better, thank you. I pity the cutting board, I chopped so hard. Soon all the fruit was done but signs needed hanging, menus needed to be written in large felt-tipped letters. I kept giving myself Robinson Crusoe pep talks: If you concentrate on getting your work done you don't have time to look up and realize you're alone on a desert island. When I did look up Jim Carr was in front of me.

"Hello there," he said. Festival Internationale was in full effect; like always, afternoon classes had sort of drizzled out and everyone was wandering around eating cuisine *internationale*. Salsa music blared on the intercom. My *pal* Mokie was wolfing down shish kebab. In a few minutes some gym teachers were going to do some mortifying belly dancing. Why wasn't there anyone there to help me? "Flannery?" he asked.

"Just tell me what kind of fruit you want," I said, surprised at the fury in my voice. Too bad it wasn't the best thing to say furiously; Carr just smirked.

"Whatever's good," he said, smiling at the crepe chefs standing behind me. In a low voice he said, "Have you told anybody about yesterday?"

"Leave me alone," I stammered. It seems I wasted all my fury on the fruit sentence. I looked at my trembling hands; I had clenched one so tightly I was leaving little half-moons of fingernails in my palm. "Just leave me alone."

"Are you bothering my kid?" Millie asked jokingly, putting an arm around me and wagging a finger at Carr.

"Never," he said, and leaned in and tapped a finger on my nose. Millie laughed and turned back around.

"I'm putting extra whipped cream on yours, Jim!" she called to him.

"You know," he said quietly, looking elsewhere. He seemed preoccupied. "Nobody would believe you."

"Jim!" Natasha called out. She was wearing a skin-tight top made of a sort of chain mail, with each piece being a different flag. Where does she find these things? "Jim," she said. "*Flan!*" I watched Jim peer at her chest as she leaned over and gave me a kiss on each cheek, pausing between them to give me a direct but unreadable look in the eye.

"Well, how are you?" he said, and she stood on tiptoe to give *him* two kisses.

"I'm feeling *internationale!*" she sang out, stepping back and twirling around to show off her top. "Are you chaperoning the dance tonight? Because I was hoping you'd give me a dance. Last time it was all *business*, Jim." She battered her eyelashes. Before he could reply she went right on. "Have you tried any of the food yet? It's so *good!*" Her voice was so high she sounded on the verge of hysteria.

"I was just about to try a crepe," he said, looking at me.

"Oh, those old things!" she said.

"Which you're supposed to be helping make," I said pointedly.

She dismissed us both with a little wave and then took Jim's arm. "You have to come try these Mexican fruit drinks the Spanish class is making. Aqua fresca. There's a kiwi-flavored one that tastes *so strange*. Let's go get one, Jim."

"Jim?" he said, raising his eyebrows. He was . . . dazzled that Natasha was paying him so much attention.

"Everybody's friends for the Festival Internationale, aren't they?" she said, and led him off.

I finally exhaled. Unclenched my scared hand. I had

been standing there with a ladle full of peaches in midair and was way behind on filling crepes.

"Flan?" Kate said for the third time. She was with Adam and snapping her fingers in my face like a hypnotist.

"Sorry," I said. "Just, um, dreaming of world peace." Adam had his mouth full and was wiping salsa off his chin with a navy-blue handkerchief.

"I'm sure we'll achieve it through Festival Internationale," she said, rolling her eyes. "At least we get out of class, huh? Listen, would you mind taking my turn at crepe making? I promised Ron I'd help with stage crew stuff."

"No problem," I said. She and Adam shared a brief glance.

"And I wanted to tell you that it's all set for the Sculpture Garden on Saturday night."

"Kate's told me all about it," said Adam, finally swallowing his bite.

"Yeah," I said, trying to find Natasha and Carr in the crowd. "It'll be great. Won't I see you guys at the dance, though?"

"Of course," Kate said. "We'll be there. I just wanted to tell you."

"Well, thanks," I said.

"Gotta run."

"Me too." Adam wouldn't look at me.

They were off and I was behind on fruit filling again. The courtyard was getting very crowded. The salsa music was off and something Arabic was on. Did we even have Arabic classes?

I was amusing myself watching the Frosh Goth spill chow mein on her black sweater when Natasha and Carr returned. Carr was looking oddly at his bright green drink.

"This is *very* strong," Carr said uncertainly.

"Well, finish it off so you can try the strawberry," Natasha said, sipping hers.

"What is this sudden interest in Mexican fruit drinks?" I said, eyeing her. She shook her head at me, barely. I put strawberries in a crepe and passed it down to Flora Habstat, who was doing the folding.

"I don't think I can finish this," he said, grimacing.

"Chicken," Natasha said quietly, and downed hers in one gulp. "I'll just go find myself a suitable drinking partner."

Carr took the bait. He smirked at her for a second and drank it all, choking on the last bit. "What is *in* this?"

"An aphrodisiac," she said. "Now go get me a strawberry one. I have to say something to Flan. Girl talk."

"OK," he said. He winked at her and turned around, almost running into Principal Bodin in a sombrero. When he was gone Natasha turned off her smile and stuck her tongue out.

"Asshole," she said.

"What is going on?" I said.

She smiled at me. "I have a present for you," she said, and took out a small paper bag. I reached for it, but she held it out of reach. "Not here. Come with me to the lake," she said.

"But Carr's coming back."

"Oh, no," she said, mock frightened. "Come *on*, Flan. Have I ever steered you wrong?"

"Don't start," I said, and turned to Flora Habstat. "Flora," I said, oozing sweetness, "could you take over for me for a few minutes? I, um, promised Ron I'd help with stage crew stuff."

"But I have to *fold*," she whined. She was wearing an ugly beret.

200

"Just do it," Natasha said, and took my arm. We scurried out of the courtyard and out a side entrance where Jennifer Rose Milton and Frank Whitelaw were making up/out. "Excuse me, kids," Natasha said grandly, and didn't speak again until we reached the lake and were sitting on a log.

"Here," she said, and handed me the bag.

"What's going on?" I said. I opened it; inside was a small reusable plastic bottle. It looked like one of the many small reusable plastic bottles that are stuffed into my kitchen cupboards at home.

"Thanks," I said. "I can see why you didn't want anybody else to see me getting this. They might get jealous."

"You're not getting it," she said. She was looking over at the lake like a victorious general observing a burning city.

I opened the bottle and looked inside. It was empty, but damp; light green droplets glistened here and there. It smelled like something I couldn't place. Iced tea. No. Brandy. No.

"What –"

"You know," she said, "that kiwi drink didn't taste so odd to me."

"You didn't," I said. My stomach fluttered.

"I most certainly did," she said, drawing herself to her full sitting height. "I thought of it last night while you were sleeping. It took me a while to find where you'd put the rest of it."

"Douglas said that much absinthe could – well, it could –"

"Yeah, I know," she said carelessly. "I mean, I figure Douglas doesn't really know shit about it. But so what. Whatever happens, it's a ride he won't forget."

I swallowed. "Natasha –"

"I don't think you should keep your present," she said. "I just wanted to show it to you, really." She took it from me and stood up. She walked right up to the water like she was going to cross it like a messiah. I followed her.

"Good-bye to you," she said simply, and threw it far. For a minute it just sat there – it was plastic – but then it filled with water and sank like a stone. My stomach sank, too.

"Well?" she said.

"This is – this is the biggest thing that anyone's ever done for me." She smiled and gave me a kiss on the cheek. We stared at the spot in the water like a moment in a movie.

We got back just in time. The food was running out and the belly dancers were in full bloom on a makeshift stage. Everybody was cheering and egging them on when the crowd suddenly parted, right in the middle like a bad haircut. Carr. He was waving his arms around, helicopterlike. The canned belly dance music screeched off and the gym teachers stood stock-still with their arms and finger cymbals up in the air. He was yelling something but I couldn't hear it over the crowd. People were laughing, thinking it was some joke *internationale* until they saw his face. I saw his face too, when he turned around with his hands on his head like he was doing sit-ups. He was flushed bright red and his eyes were bugging out; he had a large bleeding scratch on his face. Maybe he had bumped against something sharp, or maybe he had done it himself. Maybe it was self-inflicted. "Eyes!" he was screaming. "Eyes! Lies! Flies!" He lurched toward the edge of the courtyard and everybody scurried out of the way. Bodin was watching, pale beneath his sombrero, and Mokie kept stepping forward and back like that commercial where they make a cat dance by looping the film. "Flies!" he said. "Flies! Flies! Flies!" He was now pretty close to me and Natasha, close enough that I could see his eyes rolling around like small trapped animals and white specks of foam coming out of his mouth. "Flies!" he said, and fell flat on the ground. His legs were kicking. It was probably self-inflicted. Other people were screaming now, and Mokie had broken his paralysis and was at Carr's side trying to pick him up with one hand. His other hand was clutching a forgotten paper plate of taco salad. "Flies!" Carr said, and then just started raw, loud screaming. His face got redder and redder, like lobsters in boiling water, and then even redder. Mokie looked at the plate, dropped it and put both his arms under Carr's, but slipped on the taco salad and fell on the ground. "Flies!" Carr was on top of him wiggling like a big spider. Two of the belly dancers jumped down from the stage and were running over and everybody was screaming. It was just awful.

I looked at Natasha; she glanced at the spectacle in front of us like it was a movie she'd already seen, and then looked up at the sun, squinting. "This will be a Festival Internationale we won't soon forget," she said, and reached into her bag. She pulled out her sunglasses and put them on.

"Flies!" Carr was screaming again.

"Drosophila," Natasha said quietly to me, and I smiled and took her hand. Self-inflicted. Almost definitely.

Surprisingly, considering all *that*, it was one of the best dances ever tonight. I know it's a little anticlimactic to say that, but I do want to record everything of interest. Natasha and I shared another New Year's bottle of champagne back at my house, and she lent me the great international chain mail flag top. I half expected the dance to be canceled when we showed up at Roewer, but I guess they'd already booked the DJ and everything so they just went ahead with it. The music was great and the weather stayed warm so they had it in the courtyard. *Everybody* was there and there didn't seem to be any weirdness or anything; we were just all dancing and having a great time. I danced hard, hard, hard, mostly just with Natasha – I just couldn't get very boy-crazy tonight, I don't know why. Several times I found myself dancing in the spot where Carr had fallen and tried to move away from it, but you know how it's hard to really move anywhere on a crowded dance floor so I kept finding myself drifting back to it and eventually I just gave up. They played that "Tonight Tonight Tonight" song and for some reason that united all of us, the Basic Eight. We got in a big circle and sang all the words out. *Loud.* Gabriel and I danced into the middle of the circle and everybody cheered. I kissed him until I got out of breath while everyone whooped around us. I guess I was lying about that boy-crazy thing. The only bad side was, and I didn't notice it until I got home and flopped on my bed to write this all down, I think one of the metal flags must have rubbed against the scab on my back and reopened it. The scab from my bra clasp. I thought I was just sweating – I wanted to get all this down even before I showered – but it was blood that was running down my back. It bled a lot. When I went to the bathroom and looked at it in the mirror it was spread out like one of those aerial shots of volcanoes. Luckily I was pretty sober by that time otherwise it would have been really scary to look at. I wonder what Carr saw, besides, obviously, flies.

I wiped most of the blood off with tissues and now I'm going to shower and that'll probably clear the last of it off me. The only thing is, I see some of it dribbled onto the bedspread. I'm just too tired to deal with it tonight so I've probably ruined it. That stuff's supposed to be impossible to get out.

Saturday October 16th
Ring. Ring.

"Flan, it's Douglas."

"Hey, Douglas," I said. "Enjoy the dance?"

"Not as much as *some people* did," he said archly.

A bubble of imagery popped at the surface of my head: "With You With You" by Q.E.D. Everybody slow-dancing. Natasha and I swirling amidst the couples doing our best faux-ballet moves. Gabriel sitting on a bench, watching me with a faint, forced smile, and me pretending to be drunker than I was and avoiding his eyes because it's a slow dance and I should be dancing with my – *write* it, Flan! – boyfriend. Dancing around the couples like Cupid's little helpers or something: Jennifer Rose Milton and Frank Whitelaw. Rachel State and some boy with a postapocalyptic haircut. Kate and Adam, but not really a couple, just dancing together; Adam looks drunk. And V__ and Steve Nervo. V__ and *Steve Nervo*. "Wow," I said.

"Jealous?" he asked. I could hear his grin, even over the gloomy Russian classical music he was playing. "Getting into character already?"

"I'm not playing Iago," I said.

"But you're married to him. You're married to *Adam*," he teased.

"Stop. I'm over Adam."

"Yeah, right."

"Douglas, I'm with Gabriel now."

"Who exactly do you think you're talking to?"

"No, it's *true*," I said.

"Look, let's not even discuss it," he said. "I stopped being seriously interested in your love life as soon as I stopped being a part of it."

Another bubble hit me. "Speaking of love lives," I said. "Did I or did I not see you at the dance talking earnestly with some boy all night?"

"Well, not *all* night," he said. "I danced some. Remember 'Tonight Tonight Tonight'?"

"So, is he your boyfriend now?"

"*Flan*," he said. "It doesn't work that way."

"Oh yes, I forgot you people have a totally different lifestyle."

"*Flan* −"

"No, no, it's fine. As long as you don't try to push your agenda on *me* −"

Douglas laughed. "Shut *up*. I just mean, things are still weird with Lily, and this guy − I don't know −"

"What do you mean, things are still weird with Lily? You guys seem pretty comfortable."

"For public appearances, yes." He sounded like a press agent. "But she's still really upset. I still get the occasional teary midnight phone call."

"At least she's still talking to you."

"I think that about everybody."

"Douglas," I said sternly. "I can't take this much self-pity in the morning. Not *other people's* self-pity, anyway."

He chuckled. Douglas certainly was in a good mood this morning. Maybe after the dance − out of the gutter, mind! "Well, I'll change the subject from sex to drugs. Nobody else seemed game, but I'm totally up for an absinthe reprise tonight before the Sculpture Garden if you want."

"There isn't any more left."

"What do you mean? There was plenty after the party."

"Natasha and I took some last night."

"Without me?"

"It was a spur-of-the-moment thing."

"Well, there must be *some* left. If you'd taken it all, you would have pulled a Jim Carr."

I swallowed. "Yeah, what was up with that?"

"Millie said it looked like a stroke to her. Although he seemed perfectly healthy. So how about it?"

"What?"

"*Absinthe*, Flan. It's eating your brain already."

"Yeah," I said, seizing an opportunity. "I'd better not do it tonight."

"Well, can I stop by and get it, then? I think I can convince Kate and – I think I can convince Kate to take some with me. Are you going to be home later?"

"Douglas, there isn't any left."

"What did you do, sell it?"

"Um – I spilled it. I dropped the bottle down by the lake."

"Really?"

"Yes."

"What really happened, Flan?"

"I dropped the bottle down by the lake."

"Who exactly do you think you're talking to?"

You're beginning to see, I bet, exactly why I didn't hold up under cross-examination. "Remember when you said that if I took the rest of the absinthe I'd end up pulling a Jim Carr?"

"Yeah."

I took a breath. "Do you remember how Jim Carr had been treating me?"

Douglas laughed nervously. "Stop freaking me out, Flan. It sounds like –"

"I did."

A few bars of gloomy Russian classical music – probably Shostakovich, knowing Douglas. "Flan, I'm just going to say what I'm thinking out loud, just so – I don't know. Just *because*."

"OK."

"You're telling me that you gave Jim Carr a possibly toxic overdose of absinthe."

"Well, it wasn't *me*," I said. "Well, it sort of was. No."

"But Jim Carr *got* a possibly toxic overdose of absinthe."

"Yes."

A few more bars. Maybe Tchaikovsky?

"Because he was an asshole."

"*Douglas* –"

"I'm just trying to get it straight."

"There's more to it than that."

"I should hope so."

I don't know why I said it. "Hope springs eternal."

"*What*?"

"Nothing. Douglas, I want to tell you, but –"

"Look," he said. "Why don't you talk to *all* of us about it? Tonight, at the Sculpture Garden. Would that make you feel better?"

"Oh, God, Douglas. The object is for *no one* to know, not for –"

"Flan, come on. You *need* us. We can *help* you. I mean, this is *serious shit*, Flan."

"I know."

"So tonight, OK?"

My stomach sank, sank, sank. "I don't know."

"*Flan* –"

"All right, all right, all right. Tonight, tonight, tonight."

"You're singing my favorite song," he said.

I heard my own shuddering sigh. "*Stop*," I said. I felt like the camera was pulling up and away, through the roof of the house until I was a tiny speck on a sofa on a screen.

"I love you," Douglas said, over the telephone.

"Oh," I said. I sounded like a little mouse. I hung up and took the phone off the hook. I lay there for a while. I took another shower. I wrote this all down. I'm going to lie here for a while now.

LATER

I had to take the *bus* to the Sculpture Garden, because I didn't want to call Gabriel and Natasha wasn't going. "I was never planning on going," she said. "I have a date."

"But they want to talk to us about Carr."

"I can't believe you *told* them, Flan. That's so *stupid*."

"I didn't tell anybody. They just sort of guessed."

"Well, it doesn't matter. We don't have to answer to them or anybody else."

"Natasha, they want to help us."

"We don't need any help. Flan, I'll tell you a secret: you and I, we're better than them. Better than all of them. At least," she said, and I heard her take another flask sip, "*I* am. And you *will* be, if you stick with *me* and quit running to them for help in things we don't need any help in. Call me tomorrow." The phone clattered down. She and I are better than them – that's like meta-snobbery. So in either case I was alone for The Big Talk.

Kate spotted me and walked over to give me a big hug. I hadn't felt particularly in need of one, so I had to stand there as she kept hugging me. "We'll do all we can," she said. "Really, Flan." Her eyes were alight. She had been waiting for this moment her entire life: the hive had finally been called into action, and the Queen Bee was there to lead the troops.

"Thanks," I said. "Natasha couldn't be here."

"Yeah," Kate said. "She told me she had a date."

"That's what she told *me*, too."

Kate looked over my face like she was looking for flaws. "Well, come have some food." She turned and led me to the lions; I checked her out. I was definitely thinner. Silver lining and all that.

Everybody said "hi" to me, and Gabriel, Jennifer Rose Milton, Douglas and God-help-me Flora Habstat gave me big hugs like we were at a wake. I couldn't believe Flora Habstat was there. I was going to have to talk to *Flora Habstat* about all this. And *Adam*. Adam, V__ and Lily didn't get up and hug me, for which I was both grateful and disconcerted. It made the proceedings feel less like a wake but more like an interrogation.

We all stood there for a minute like more statues, the huggers standing up and the nonhuggers sitting down, with the criminal in the middle. Finally it was Adam, bless him, who brought us all back to life.

"Flan, you need some wine. We *all* need some wine. Sit down, everybody." Everybody laughed nervously and sat down on the wool blanket. Douglas pressed "play" and a string quartet began to do so. A plastic goblet with red wine in it was thrust into one hand; in the other I found a cocktail napkin, a piece of French bread, a chunk of brie and a leaf, in that order.

Everyone waited. "Well?" Lily finally said, rather sternly.

Douglas looked at her. "Let's wait until after we've had some supper, at least. To us, and our friendship," he said, lifting his glass. We all drank obediently and began to pass plates around.

"So, V__," I said, "I thought I might see Brabantio tonight."

"Who?"

"Steve Nervo."

"He couldn't make it," V—— said quickly.

"And Frank?" I said, turning to Jennifer Rose Milton.

"We thought that just, well, you know, just us should be here tonight," Jenn said. *Jennifer Rose Milton* said.

I looked at Kate, then at Flora Habstat, then at Adam, then back at Kate and said, "Oh." I quickly made my voice more pleasant. "I mean, I'm sorry I had to break up all these new couples."

Kate smiled, put down her wineglass and leaned back and kissed Adam. "Not *all* of them," she said.

I sat there and waited for another horror movie to begin. Maybe in this one the sculptures would come alive and eat people.

Peter Pusher: All these horror movies on TV – it's no wonder kids are so violent today.

Winnie Moprah: Of course, some TV is very instructive and illuminating.

Peter Pusher: Oh, of course it is, Winnie. I'm not talking about shows like yours. I'm talking about shows about murder and violence. Incidentally, thank you for allowing me to participate in your very instructive and illuminating program.

Dr. Eleanor Tert: Me too, Winnie. However, I must take issue with Peter. I believe that in the case of Flannery Culp, it was not the media which was responsible for her murderous behavior. Rather, it was –

Don't you love that? "*Rather*, it was" – who is she, British royalty?

> Dr. Eleanor Tert: Ahem. Rather, it was certain psychosexual factors. Approximately two weeks before the killings, for instance, she learned suddenly that Adam State had entered into a relationship with her close friend Kate Gordon. When she learned the news, she took it very hard.

> Flora Habstat: Actually, she took it very well.

> Dr. Eleanor Tert: Perhaps to the untrained eye.

Or perhaps to someone who was actually there, Dr. Twit. I swallowed.

"We didn't know how to tell you," Adam said.

"Yeah, I tried to tell you the other day. Before school, remember? When I met you at the bus?"

"I remember," I managed to say. I looked around and realized, unbelievably, that I hadn't said enough. Everybody was waiting for more. I took a sip of wine and wished Natasha was here. *She'd* have something to say, all right. "I'm sorry," I said. "I'm just surprised. I think it's great."

"You're really OK with it?" Kate asked.

"Of course," I said, looking around at everyone I was supposed to say I'm really OK with it in front of. I saw Gabriel, who I'd forgotten completely about; he was watching me with a look of such longing I couldn't do anything else but lean back and kiss *him*. I was some pawn, sacrificing itself to block the opposing queen. I wish I knew chess better to make that metaphor really resonate. "Of course I'm OK with it," I said, still facing

Gabriel. His smile was as wide as wide can be. "It's not like people have to apply for a permit from me before they can go out. I'm very happy for you guys." I heard my voice, so false it was all the statues could do to keep themselves from rolling their eyes. I felt my own eyes roll, stretch and break. I was crying, crying, crying. Even in my whirlpool of despair I had the smarts to hug Gabriel so he wouldn't think I was crying over Adam. I could almost feel Natasha shaking her head at me. *Nice going, Flan. "I'm very happy for you guys" and burst into tears.* "I'm sorry," I said. "I've had a rough couple of days."

Jennifer Rose Milton touched my arm. "You want to tell us about it?" she said, and I did. That is, I didn't *want to*, no, but I did.

I did.

"*Jesus!*" Lily said. She was covering her mouth with her hands but I still heard it.

"Come on," Douglas said like he didn't believe it for a minute. "Any one of us would have done the same thing."

Now Lily was looking at *him* in horror. "Are you kidding?"

"This is pretty drastic, Flan," Jennifer Rose Milton said.

"No wonder you were so kooky at the dance," V____ said. I was still leaning against Gabriel but he had gone all stiff. Not like *that*.

"I can't believe you did that," Lily said.

"Well, *I* didn't, not really," I pointed out.

"But you had a hand in it," Kate said.

"Not really."

"Well," Adam said, "you could have *stopped* Natasha, right?"

I poured myself more wine, then saw just about everyone's glasses were empty, so I began to pour everyone more wine like a charming hostess. Lily looked carefully at her cup and didn't drink from it.

"I don't know," I said, "I guess. I mean, I guess I could have run back from the lake and told Carr that he was poisoned and if he had believed me maybe they could have, I don't know, pumped his stomach in time and then I'd be in Juvenile Hall right now. Are you going to tell me that's what I should have done?"

"No," Jennifer Rose Milton said.

"No, no," Lily said, shaking her head, "but go back a little further, Flan. You should have told somebody right after – well, right after Carr – you know."

"I know. But who would I tell? No one would have believed me."

"I would have believed you," Douglas said quietly.

"Me too," Flora Habstat piped up. I wish she would have piped down.

"Flan, *any* of us would have believed you," Lily said.

"Look, I *know* you guys would have believed me. But who are we?" I looked around. "We're *kids*, OK? Smart kids, maybe, but *kids*. We wouldn't have been any more believable *en masse* and we would have been right back where we started, with no one believing us."

"So you decided to poison him," Lily said, looking at me and gulping down wine.

"It just happened," I said.

"*It just happened*?!?" Lily said, turning to Douglas. "And *you're* standing by her?"

"I didn't know what else to do," I said. To my mortification I was crying again.

"You could have gone to my mother," Jennifer Rose Milton said.

"*I didn't know what else to do!*" I stood up, but didn't know where to go from there. Everybody was craning their necks to watch me like they'd arrived late for the movie and had to sit in the front row. "If you had *seen* what he was like —" I looked around the Sculpture Garden. It was getting cold outside, but in my head all the memories and wine were seething hot. I needed Natasha.

"I'm behind you," Kate said suddenly. She disengaged herself from Adam and stood up. "I'm not saying what you did was the smartest thing in the world, but you know that already. But who knows what any of us would do in your situation."

Jennifer Rose Milton seemed to be thinking this all out. "That's true," she said.

Gabriel stood up, and put his arm on me like he was measuring the distance between us. It wasn't too far. "Me too," he said, and then Douglas stood up, and Adam, and then it was like that thing that happens after concerts: you're not impressed enough to give a standing ovation, but everybody else is and soon you have to stand up too, if only to see what's going on. From a distance, with everybody standing in a circle around a picnic blanket, it must have looked like some ancient ritual: I Was A Teenage Stonehenge.

"I think we can all sit down now," Kate said. "We look like some sort of ritualistic cult. Let's pour some more wine and figure out what we should do."

"I don't really know what we *can* do," Douglas said. "Jenn, I'm assuming that you'll hear about Carr's condition pretty regularly."

"We probably all will," she said.

"Is there any chance he'll regain consciousness?" Adam asked.

I swallowed. "He's unconscious?"

"Mostly," Jennifer Rose Milton said, avoiding my eyes.

"Well," Douglas said, "depending on how much absinthe he actually swallowed –"

"Come *on*," I said. "You have no idea if he'll wake up. Not *really*."

Everybody looked at me. "All right," Douglas said. "I don't. I was just trying to be helpful."

"You know, Flan –" Lily started, but Adam interrupted her.

"I don't think it matters if he does wake up," Adam said. "I mean, correct me if I'm wrong, but the way you told it to us, Flan, even *if* he's able to speak –"

"He's not able to speak?" I said.

"Not most of the time," Jennifer Rose Milton said.

"He won't know who did this to him. I mean, with all the wacky food *internationale*, he won't even know that *anyone* actually *did something* to him. It'll look like an accident."

"Nobody gets that many chemicals by accident," Lily said.

"Plus," V___ said, "Carr would be able to think of someone who *wanted* him poisoned."

"But what's he going to do?" Adam asked. "Go to Bodin and say, 'I think Flan did it, because I – well, never mind what I did'"?

"You're right," Kate said, putting her arm around him.

"Carr could think of *something* –" Lily started, but Adam interrupted her again.

"The main thing we've got to do," he said, "is not tell anybody about the absinthe party. If by chance they trace it to absinthe and rumor gets around that we've had that stuff, we're up shit creek."

"*You* haven't had it. *You* weren't at the absinthe party. Why are *you* suddenly in charge, Adam? What are you doing here, anyway?" I was in the middle of realizing that it was me who was talking when Lily stood up.

"I don't think you're in a position to be anything but *very, very nice* to all of us," she said.

"And besides" – I turned around and Kate was looking at me with haughty, haughty eyes – "Adam is most certainly one of us."

I was cornered. The night air blew through me and I realized I needed them; they didn't need me. I held out my hand for Natasha to grab, but she wasn't there; Gabriel held my hand instead. "I'm sorry," I said to Adam. "It's just been a rough couple of days."

Adam smiled and shrugged. "I can imagine," he said. "I mean *absinthe*, Flan. Who the hell gets killed by absinthe? Anybody could shoot someone, but *absinthe*? That has –"

"*Panache*?" I suggested.

"Well, *something*," he said. "I mean, getting killed by absinthe is something for the record books."

"Actually," Flora said, and I can't write any more.

Sunday October 17th

And that it was *right in front of my face*. The *whole time*. Look at this, from **Monday October 4th** no less, almost two weeks ago. No, don't try to tell me you'll look it up yourself. You're not reading this that carefully. You can't fool me. Just look:

> The first thing I saw when I entered my beloved high school was Kate, leaning against her locker and talking with Adam.

There it was, right in front of my face: "Kate, leaning against her locker and *talking with Adam!*" And what did I do? Did I tell them they simply had to try a fabulous fruit drink? No, I just went up and talked to them. I never would have *suspected* that they would have done something so low. And Friday night:

> "Kate and Adam, but not really a couple, just dancing together; Adam looks drunk."

But when I saw them yesterday, did I even suspect? NO! Instead I *apologized* for breaking up all these new couples:

> "I'm sorry I had to break up all these new couples."
> Kate smiled, put down her wineglass, and leaned back and kissed Adam. "Not *all* of them," she said.

I hate that: "'Not *all* of them,' she said." So *fucking* smug. I should have *known*, all along. It wasn't like all this dancing together and talking while leaning against lockers should have clued me in; there was a *fucking clue.* A clue, dangling in front of my face, like a flag. Here it is on Wednesday. Follow it as it changes hands, like some secret item passed between spies:

> Kate took a navy blue handkerchief out of the pocket of her navy-blue blazer.

And then:

> EXPOSURE SEVEN: Guitar: twang-a-twang-a-*twang*. Successful attempt to capture Adam on his way to choir. Raising his eyebrows and smiling at something a perky second soprano is telling him while wiping his brow with a navy-blue handkerchief.

But that wasn't enough; it was practically rubbed in my face and I missed it. Thursday:

Adam had a cold and was blowing his nose with a navy-blue handkerchief when I approached him. Before I could help myself I touched his neck, and he smiled until the handkerchief came off his face. Then he frowned distractedly like I'd woken him up.

Friday:

Adam had his mouth full and was wiping salsa off his chin with a navy-blue handkerchief.

The *handkerchief*, the fucking *handkerchief*, there it is, laughing at me. She gave him her *handkerchief*. And who knows what he gave her. Adam, I love you so – Adam and Kate, I hate you both. I have taken Kate's navy-blue sweater down from the secret shelf and I am staring at it, finding myself howling out loud, alone in my room.
THE HANDKERCHIEF!!!!!!!!!!!!!!!!

Vocabulary:

FORSOOTH   PRECARIOUSLY   PHILANTHROPIC
COURTESAN   CENTRIFUGED   SELF-INFLICTED
ANTICLIMACTIC UNTHRILLED

Study Questions:

1. When you drive by somebody's house late at night, what are some clues that would tell you if the person is home or not?

2. List the pros and cons of having a Festival Internationale in your high school. Do you think there's enough supervision at events like this? They should be safe for students and teachers, or it's not really fun.

3. Do you think Mr. Carr did the right thing with Flannery? Do you think Flannery did the right with Mr. Carr? Do you think Natasha did the right thing with Mr. Carr? Do you think Natasha did the right thing with Flannery? Do you think Flannery did the right thing with Natasha? Do you think Adam did the right thing with Flannery? Do you think Adam did the right thing with Kate? Do you think the Basic Eight did the right thing with Flannery? Do you think Mrs. State did the right thing with Flannery? Do you generally do the right thing? Questions like these will be repeated several times throughout this journal, but write down an answer each time, so it's fresh.

4. Did you spot the handkerchief earlier? If not, why not? If so, then what did you do about it? Nothing, right? God I hate you.

Monday October 18th

I should have read the script more carefully. I was unprepared. Was everyone watching me, or are Kate and Adam so involved they're ignorant of what they've done to me? Fat chance. Particularly Kate: *fat chance*. Ron gave a long speech about jealousy and love and when I heard Kate giggle at some little joke I wanted to die. "*She's a courtesan, she's a courtesan*," I kept repeating to myself while Ron went on and on: "You guys I'm sure have complicated love lives, but you must begin to enlarge your own scenarios in your mind, until they reach epic, tragic proportions."

"Oh, they *do*, Ron, they *do*," Kate said, and I wanted to slap her. Everyone giggled and I forced myself to roll my eyes at Gabriel. He grinned and puckered his lips at me, quietly. Help me.

Anyway, I thought it would get better once we actually started reading the script, particularly when Ron had the central characters sit in an inner circle of folding chairs so Kate had to sit on the outskirts. He put me next to Adam and far away from Gabriel; even the Fates know how it should work out. And then it happened, Act III, scene 3:

Iago: *How now? What do you here alone?*

Emilia: *Do not you chide; I have a thing for you.*

Iago: *A thing for me? It is a common thing* –

Emilia: *Ha?*

Iago: *To have a foolish wife.*

Emilia: *O, is that all? What will you give me now for that same handkerchief?*

Iago: *What handkerchief?*

I just sat there, saying my lines on cue, doing everything that was expected of me in the script, and what happens to me, in the last scene? Well, I hate to give away the end of this tragedy, but Adam stabs me. When the curtain falls, Adam has been revealed as the villain, but that's something the audience knew all along. Kate's still a courtesan. But me, innocent until the end and full of good intentions, me, I'm dead.

Tuesday October 19th

Homeroom started with a blast from the past on the intercom: "Flannery Culp, please report to the principal's office." In second grade, Sara Crain and I had stood in the girls' bathroom, shrieking with laughter as we discovered that paper towels, soaked at the sink and wadded into balls, will stick to the ceiling like moist stalactites. We had checked to see if the coast was clear as we left, sneaking back to handball and thinking we were safe. We hadn't counted on the resonance of second-grade laughter in the bathroom. Apparently one of the balls had eventually slipped onto Mrs. Parrot's unforgiving head. "Flannery Culp and Sara Crain, please report to the principal's office." This time around, Sara's name wasn't called, of course; she died in a fourth-grade car accident. I'd refused to leave my room for three days when I found out. We'd had a club whose membership was limited to us and some stuffed animals. You know how it goes.

Medusa showed me in without saying a word. Bodin was at his desk holding this plastic inflatable globe he has, about the size of a cantaloupe. He likes to toss it into a small basket and headboard he has on his wall, which I guess is supposed to be inspirational or something but instead looks terribly destructive.

"Hello," I said, and he looked at me but said nothing, just sat there twirling the globe. Jean Bodin is a big gross man.

"Small world, huh?" he finally said, holding up the cantaloupe of continents. I winced, like you probably did when you read "cantaloupe of continents."

"Yes it is," I said blankly, looking at it. "It *is* a small world."

He put it down on his desk. "Sit down," he said, and I sat down and he looked at me and said nothing again.

"What seems to be the problem, Officer?"

"The problem," he says, "is that we have a biology teacher in serious condition. *Your* biology teacher."

I remembered what he'd said to me the last time we'd had a conversation about my biology teacher. "That's not a *problem*," I said, "it's a *challenge*."

He smiled thinly. "Rightly so." *Rightly so*? "But Mr. Carr is in very serious condition. Do you know *how* serious?"

"Well," I said carefully, "I was at the festival –"

"Festival Internationale."

"Right. Festival Internationale. So I saw him when it happened."

His eyes were quick. "When *what* happened?"

"Well the thing. Whatever it was. The, um" – what had Jennifer Rose Milton said? – "the *stroke*."

"It wasn't a stroke," Bodin said. He picked up the globe again.

"What was it?"

"An overdose of drugs."

"What?"

"They're not sure what, but it's an overdose of drugs. I'm only telling you this because there's going to be an official announcement about it at an assembly tomorrow. An *all-school* assembly."

"Oh." He was only telling me this because everybody was going to know tomorrow?

"So that's my problem. My *challenge*," he said, smiling at me. He leaned back in his chair and tried for a basket. The globe bounced off the rim and landed on the floor near my chair. "But what I'm asking you is, what do you know about it?"

I looked down at the world. A rusty thumbtack was next to it, vicious side up. "What?" I said.

"You heard me," Principal Bodin said.

"What are you accusing me of?"

"Nobody's accusing you of anything," he said. "It's just that I have a biology teacher who will be out of commission at least for the rest of the semester – you have a substitute teacher coming in tomorrow, by the way, and I want you and your classmates to be on your absolute best behavior, so spread the word – I have a biology teacher who will be out of commission at least for the rest of the semester, and it's a biology teacher who you were in conflict with."

"With whom I was in conflict."

He looked at me for a second. "With whom I was in conflict," he said. "Now, there were some people who thought you were responsible for the little fruit fly prank last month. Remember that?"

"Yes."

"Yes what?"

What did he want? "Yes, Principal Bodin."

"Yes, Principal Bodin, what?"

"Yes, Principal Bodin, I remember. I mean, I remember that people thought I did that, but it turned out to be the student teacher." I thought of her, fired, raising kids, all she needed was some more shit thrown at her. But it was my skin or hers. He just kept looking at me. "It was the *student teacher*, remember?"

"Yes," he said. "I remember. But no one really knows, do they?"

"Look," I said. I stood up.

"Sit down."

"Look," I said. I sat down. "Look. I'm sorry about Carr, OK? But if he was taking drugs, it's not my problem."

"I didn't say he was taking drugs," he said. "I said there was an overdose of drugs involved. He could have been taking them, or they could have been *given to him*." He leaned back in his chair and regarded me.

I didn't say anything.

"All I'm asking is if you know anything about it," he said. "I know that you and Mr. Carr had your difficulties together, and you and your group of friends – well, you're sort of *fast*." He coughed into his hand.

"You mean *quick*," I said. "Me and my friends are intelligent, intellectual people. But you wouldn't know what that meant, would you? Oh, forget it. Just leave me alone." I stood up and turned to leave.

"Look, young lady," he stood up and walked over to me. He took my arm. "We aren't done here yet."

"*Don't touch me! Don't touch me*!" I screamed. He took another step toward me and tripped on the globe which rolled onto the thumbtack. The world popped. He looked down at his feet and I turned to go. When I was halfway out the door I felt his hand on my arm again. "*Don't fucking touch me*!" I screamed, there in the waiting area, and he let go like I was just out of the oven. Let his fear of sexual harassment lawsuits keep him off me. Even Medusa was gaping, and when I turned around and saw the other people in the waiting room, they were gaping too. Well, mostly. Jennifer Rose Milton and Lily Chandly and V___ and Douglas and *Adam*, they were all gaping. Gabriel had his hand over his face so I couldn't see his expression and Kate was looking both incredulous and mildly triumphant, like she'd known everything I was going to do, all along.

Of course, with all my friends waiting to be interrogated I found I had no one to turn to so I was alone in the hallway, upset, panting.

"Sounds like you did OK," said a sudden, dry voice, and I turned around. Natasha was there, with her hair in two long braids like a milkmaid. I've never been happier to see anyone. I hugged her, hard and long, and when I was done I stepped back and then just hugged her again.

"Where have you *been*?" I said.

"Sorry," she said. "I just lay low for a couple of days."

"I was *worried*," I said. "You could have been lying in a ditch OD'ing or something."

"There aren't any drugs around," Natasha said. "Carr's taken them all. What a drug hog."

I looked around to see if anyone was listening, but Roewerites are so used to Natasha that they walked by like she was my invisible friend. "We shouldn't talk about it," I said. "I think Bodin might be onto us."

"How did it go in there? I only heard the ending," she said.

"I don't know," I said, and then realized who it was that got me in this mess. "Just be grateful I didn't turn you in."

"Like anyone would believe you," she said, and her eyes sharpened at me. "I did it for *you*, Flan. How can you even think of turning me in? Plus, I've never even *had* Carr." She rolled her eyes. "You know what I mean. That's why it's perfect that I did it instead of you. No one can imagine it being me."

"Well, Bodin's imagining *something*," I said. "The whole gang is in there now. I'm surprised they didn't call you in."

"I'm officially absent today," she said.

"How are you ever going to get into college?"

"I have better things to worry about this week," she said. She sounded like she'd never worried about anything in her entire life. "Like how my new hairdo will go over."

"It's certainly – different," I said. "Very Norwegian."

"That's the look I'm going for," she said. "Like Heidi gone mad. Was Heidi Norwegian?"

I was suddenly, looking at her smiling at me, moved to tears. "If you want her to be," I said quietly. "Anything you want, Natasha."

She smiled and kissed my cheek. "Anyway, it was a little milkmaid hairdo like this that convinced Flora it

226

was OK to cut school today. She's waiting for us by the lake. We're going to lunch and a movie."

"No way," I said. "She's all I need today."

"What you need today is Flora not talking to Jean Bodin. The others we can count on, but Flora could blow the whistle any time. She's terribly frightened, Flan."

"*She's* frightened."

"Yes," she said, and looked at me. "When I heard Medusa call our names to go see Bodin – was that a second-grade deja vu trip or *what*? – I knew we had to enact Baker's Rule again. So I found Flora before she got to homeroom and convinced her to cut with us. Hopefully Bodin will forget all about talking to her."

"Since when did *she* suddenly become one of us?" I said. "She's not my *friend*, for God's sake, she's – I don't know, she's –"

"Someone who we have to make sure won't squeal," Natasha said. We had reached the side entrance. "Now, take a little sip from Mama's flask, dear, and put on a good face. Lunch and a movie."

I took a sip; this time it was water. "It's not even ten yet," I said. "A little early for lunch."

"So we'll buy shoes or something," Natasha said. "Sky's the limit."

I looked up and saw she was right. We were crossing the street to the lake and above me the sky was enormous and bright, like a bunch of presents you haven't unwrapped yet and you just *know* are going to be great. Bright bright blue with bright bright clouds streaked across it, it was a truly glorious sky. Birds were chirping, if you can believe it. Flora was there waiting and when she waved and smiled the scene was so perfect even she looked good.

The bubble only burst when the three of us stood at the side of the lake watching some ducks fight over something. Whatever it was – food, or maybe another duck – it suddenly sank deep and fast, and the other ducks were first confused, then bored and sheepish. They gave a few more halfhearted pecks at one another and then just began gazing into the water like always. I could almost feel myself falling. I could almost see what it would be like to be staring up at the surface of the water, with the ducks silhouetted against the sunlight streaming in. I realized no one would rescue me if I started sinking. Everyone would just gaze into the water like always, waiting for whatever was next. I felt smaller and smaller, and then I saw something eerie. I don't know if it was the angle of the water or the sun's rays creating some sort of a blind spot or whatever – I've cut too many science classes in my day to know – but when I looked down at our reflections in the water there were only two figures standing there. I quickly looked around me, but Natasha and Flora were both still right there on land, but in the water there were only two people. Because the water was still rippling from whatever had sunk, I couldn't tell who was missing in the reflection, but somebody wasn't there. Somebody was missing, Flora or Natasha maybe, or maybe me.

Wednesday October 20th
Lawrence Dodd was suitably somber this morning, considering he was wearing a tie with hula dancers on it, when he announced that we should all proceed "directly and quietly" from homeroom to a memorial assembly for Jim Carr. It seemed a little premature to me to have a memorial assembly for someone who wasn't dead, but when I got there it was much worse.

Jean Bodin got up and began talking into the microphone, but we had to wait a good thirty seconds

228

before the whine of feedback had run its full course. He looked around, wincing, and continued. That's right, he *continued* even though no one had heard the first thirty seconds. Natasha, sitting next to me, got out her flask. Kate, on the other side, got out a book.

"I'm sure even those of you who didn't see it happen are shocked," he said. "But Vice Principal Mokie can confirm it." Vice Principal Mokie stood up from the front row and waved inexplicably. The principal and the vice principal looked at each other for a moment, and then both of them coughed in perfect unison. "Well, without further ado –" Bodin said, and out of nowhere an impeccably dressed woman came out from behind the auditorium curtain and approached the microphone. Bodin gave a little bow – a little *bow*, what was going on? – and she began to talk. And talk. As follows:

Hello, children. I'm here to talk to you today about a story. *My* story.

"Hello, children," Natasha said to me, waving and making a goofy face. I snorted and got glared at by some fat Latin teacher.

"Is it grammatically right to say, 'I'm here to talk to you about a story'?" Kate whispered to me.

"Grammatically *correct*," I corrected her. It got quiet, and when I looked around me everybody was staring at us. I wondered why, until I looked at the stage and saw that woman staring at us hardest of all. Staring at *me*. That's how it felt, later: metaphorically. I thought I was just hanging out with my friends but it turned out everyone was staring at us, and that woman – can you guess who it was? – was staring the hardest. Staring at *me*. I stared right back at her and smiled; the best defense is a good offense or vice versa or however that goes. She looked down, looked up and started again. She had the ugliest hairdo you can imagine. Go ahead, imagine one – that's what it looked like.

Hello, children. I'm here to talk to you today about a story. *My* story. When I was your age, I thought I was on top of the world. I had participated in some beauty contests, and although I hadn't won any trophies, I was offered a job as a female flight attendant after graduation. I didn't have to go to college! I was on top of the world.

"She's really speaking to me," Natasha murmured.
"What?" Kate whispered in mock horror. "No trophies? Were those judges blind?"

Before too long I was promoted to first class. It was hard but rewarding work. On one flight, though, I was really exhausted. I could barely get on with my work.

"Executives must have gone pillow-less," Natasha said, and took a sip.

One of my fellow flight attendants noticed how low I was, and gave me something he said would perk me up. He was right: it was cocaine. I had heard a few bad things about cocaine, sure, but my fellow flight attendant told me it was perfectly safe. It felt great. I felt like I was flying.

"You were flying," Kate and Natasha and I said in unison.

Of course, before too long I was taking cocaine regularly, just to perk me up, I thought. I was in deep denial, and I'm not talking about a river in Egypt. I said I'm not talking about a river in Egypt. Well, you probably haven't learned about it yet, but the Nile is a river in Egypt, and when I said "denial" it sounded like – well, never mind. Sometimes I'd get too wired to work and would help myself to the complimentary champagne to calm me down, so I became an alcoholic as well. My alcoholism enabled me to continue my cocaine addiction, and vice versa. Do you understand that expression? I mean my alcoholism enabled me to continue my cocaine addiction, and my cocaine addiction enabled me to continue my alcoholism. I was under a lot of pressure –

"Cabin pressure," Natasha muttered. I can't resist adding these jokes.

– to perform well in my job, and ironically – that means, well, tinged with irony – my drug and alcohol problem prevented me from doing so. The method I was choosing to deescalate my pressures was escalating them instead, which is always what happens in addictive situations. I know that now. Now, I'm a survivor. That's why I'm here to talk to you today. One of your teachers received an overdose of drugs. Whether he took them on purpose or was given them doesn't matter in the slightest. What is important is that drugs have entered this world of Roewer High School as phony solutions to the pressures you face. That's what I'm here to tell you! Drugs are not the solution! I am the solution! Listen to me! My name is Eleanor Tert and I am here to help you all!

Thursday October 21st

Ten days. It seems like a good idea to add a sort of countdown to the proceedings here. Normally I wouldn't do anything so crass – I'm a writer, so I value narrative structure above all else – but I think the murder is something of a surprise.

I'm in homeroom now, and Bodin is over the loudspeaker with an update on Carr's condition, which remains unconscious. An enviable condition on boring days like this one. He told us that Carr is on the seventh floor of the Rebecca Boone Memorial Hospital if we wanted to send cards or flowers. Cards or flowers to an unconscious person?

There was a television show on when I was little, the premise of which was as follows: It is the future. We live in a space station on the moon. One day a comet breaks the presumed-permanent contact between the moon and the Earth and the moon breaks out of orbit. We are totally screwed and must spend several network seasons trying to get home. Strangely enough, I was experiencing a first-episode feeling as I left school, right in the middle of lunch: the sun hitting my bare arms as I opened the door like a singeing comet, the Roewer gravity clinging to me like some drippy friend, some love interest in an episode who doesn't bring in the ratings and so is never heard from again, like, I don't know, Gabriel, say.

The bus driver gave me a why-the-hell-aren't-you-at-school look and I gave him a shut-up-you're-a-bus-driver-so-bus-drive look right back. The suspicion that the idea I had was a bad one began to gurgle inside my head as I watched the sights go by: Chinese restaurants, video stores, doughnut shops, a hospital, shit. Had to walk three blocks the way I had just come, bought overpriced flowers in the lobby and before I knew it I was asking a bitter-looking seventh-floor nurse what room he was in.

This is one of those scenes that is going to be dreadfully overplayed in *Basic Eight, Basic Hate*, I'm afraid. Can't you just see it? Carr in a gossamer bed, with some romanticized token hospital equipment near him – maybe a little gauzy bag of IV equipment or a screen with green heartbeat lasers moving across it like ocean waves. The camera moves around me as I speak, occasionally focusing on Carr's unseeing eyes, provided by contact lenses so the hunky actor can blink unnoticed behind fake plastic comatoseness. "I'm so sorry," she weeps, tears perfect like crystal. Nothing red or splotchy. "I'm getting therapy now from Dr. Eleanor Tert, so with the help I need, and with your forgiveness, I can go on with my life." More after this.

The real hospital room wasn't blinding white but an irritating shade of pink that made everyone's clothing look awful. Apparently someone had dropped a box of plastic tubing on Carr and it had slithered into any available orifice in an effort to hide. His face looked like something that under no circumstances whatsoever you should eat. Yellow bruises splotched him like cheap discolored blush, and little larvae of what I knew was dried blood lurked around his nose, though it looked more like those plastic scars gross fourteen-year-old boys buy for Halloween. There were a few bunches of wan flowers and some cards propped open on a table that could swivel into position over Carr's bed, if he ever woke up, if he ever ate. I could see the insides of the cards, some of them signed by thirty or forty people. Whole classrooms were grieving for the person who lay there, I guess. There was nobody in the room.

The urge to leave school and come here was so impulsive I expected some emotional supernova when I finally saw him, but I just stood there thinking about nothing – thinking about fourteen-year-old boys' Halloween costumes, for God's sake. I looked over at Carr expecting some rush, but he just looked like a lump of nothing. There was nowhere to put the flowers, so I filled the little pink trash can with water from the empty clean bathroom – shower but no shower curtain – and stuck my cheap carnations in it. There was no room for them on the swivel table so I put them on the floor where they really looked like trash. Carr's eyes were closed. Outside somebody was paging a doctor over and over, and the squeaky wheels of something were making their rounds. Maybe the lunch cart, or maybe somebody in pain on a gurney. I was so seized with self-consciousness I felt like I had to say something, but neither triumph nor remorse washed through me. My hand itched.

"You deserve it," I said, finally, but I didn't think that either.

Friday October 22nd

If Adam had only nine days to live, how would he live his life differently? Believe it or not, Hattie Lewis is making us do dictionary exercises because somebody didn't know what *corpulent* meant. (Of course I do.) It's amazing how one person's mistake can wreck it for everyone. But the point is, I have tons of time to write down Adam's activities for the day. Of course, it's only second period, but he started early.

"I don't understand why we're doing this," Natasha said grumpily. We were rattling along two cars behind Adam. I had bribed Natasha into following Adam with a double latte plus a blueberry muffin with a crunchy glazed sugar topping that I could never eat if I wanted to keep fitting into my jeans. "I've never driven this slowly before in my entire life. Even this crunchy sugar topping isn't worth *this*."

I nibbled my thumb, my only breakfast this morning. Ahead of us, Adam was taking advantage of some red-light time to stare in the sideview mirror and brush his hair back from his head. His other hand was dangling loosely out the window, so limp it might have been severed, his skin beautiful even against the smoke of exhaust streaming from the bus ahead of us. We weren't driving to school. We were getting closer and closer to Kate's house, but I wasn't quite ready to accept *that*. He could have been going anywhere. Anywhere near Kate's house.

"Don't be ridiculous," Natasha said, gunning the motor. The car sounded strained from being kept at such a low speed. "He's going to pick Kate up. Why is this so surprising to you?"

Adam's fingers were tapping in time to something I couldn't hear. "I love him, I just love him, I can't help it," I said.

"You know, love means a lot of things," she said. "The first definition is 'intense affection,' followed by 'a feeling of attraction resulting from sexual desire,' 'enthusiasm or fondness,' and then there's 'a beloved person.' But the last one is important, too. Last but not least. 'A score of zero.'" Sorry. Every so often I'm opening the dictionary and pretending to be working on these stupid exercises.

Kate's street, Kate's block, Kate's house. "Pull over behind the parked car," I said.

"Oh Jesus," Natasha said, but she did it. "I need a drink. Open the glove compartment."

"You drink too much," I said, handing her the flask.

"You follow boys too much," she said. "Flan, what do you want from him?"

"I want him to be my *boyfriend*!" I shouted and then realized immediately how ridiculous that sounded. Because – listen to me, Eleanor, Peter, Moprah – it was more than that. All the words in this dictionary couldn't describe what it was. Large.

"I don't suppose it's at all relevant to point out you *have* a boyfriend," Natasha said.

Kate's stairs, Kate's door, Kate. Natasha and I ducked down low and Natasha took another swig. I was afraid to peer out and watch them so we just waited until we heard his car start.

"I can't believe it," I said, looking after them.

"I can't believe it either," Natasha murmured, but she was looking at me. "This boy is *bewitching* you, Flan. Why are we following him? You were always a maiden never bold, of spirit so still and quiet that your motion blushed at herself. And yet in spite of your nature, of years, of country, of credit, everything, you fell in love with such a jerk! Look at him! Your judgment is maimed, imperfect! Why would you fall for him? I mean, Douglas turned out to be a – well, you know how Douglas turned out – but he has always been *kind*." She practically spat out the word. "And now you have another kind boy, a *nice* boy, who would do anything in the world for you, and who do you follow in a car? Somebody who screwed you over, who will probably screw *Kate* over, and are you angry about this? Are you going to heed your fucking Calc teacher just once in your life and *do something*? What has he *done* to you, Flan? I vouch again that with some mixtures pow'rful o'er the blood or with some dram, conjured to this effect, he has wrought upon you!"

236

"What the hell's a dram?"

"Look it up," she snapped, and pulled out from the curb.

"Don't drive so fast," I said, "or they'll see us."

"You're acting like a nut," she said, swerving and sipping. I watched her throat swallow it; she looked so *alive*, like I could just reach out and touch her neck, her hair.

"I can't believe you're calling *me* a nut," I said. "Have you forgotten who the famed Roewer Absinthe Poisoner is?"

She grinned, finally relaxing, and turned to me as she ran a stop sign. "Poison*ess*," she said.

"Poisonous is right." Our wit will preserve us all. "You're missing the student lot."

"No, no," she said, lurching into it just in time. "Do you think I could get away with parking in the faculty lot, like V___ does?"

"Oh yeah," I said. "I think it's your shrunken head earrings that make you look most like a –"

Oh.

"What?" she said, and followed my eyes. Kate and Adam were kissing, quietly. It was the *quietly* that got to me, I think. If they'd been passionate about it – tearing their clothes off and rebuttoning them incorrectly – they'd have been lustfully reckless. But they were kissing in short bursts, little pats like kisses from birds. Kissing quietly, softly, like they were in love. I was crying and crying.

"Oh my dear Flan," Natasha said quietly, tossing her head back and finishing the flask off. She licked her lips and then wiped them on her hand, her dark lipstick staining her wrist like a suicide. "What has he done to you. What has he done to you."

"I don't know," I blubbered.

She sighed, equal parts exasperation and love. "Don't worry," she said. "I'll take care of everything."

"What?"

"I said I'll take care of everything."

"Natasha, *no*," I said.

"What, am I setting a bad example for the other children?" she said, smiling sharply.

"*No*," I said.

"No, I'm not a bad example, or *no*, I shouldn't take care of things?"

"*No*," I said. Let it be known, I said no. Nine days.

Vocabulary:

RESONANCE	INTERROGATED	SOMBER
DEPROGRAMMED	SUCCUMBED	SINGEING*
COMATOSENESS	DRAM	

* Not "singing."

Study Questions:

1. Did your opinion of Eleanor Tert change when you learned that she's a recovering cocaine-addicted stewardess? (If you already knew this due to her numerous television and radio appearances, not to mention her books, pretend you just learned it.)

2. Has your opinion of Flannery Culp changed over the course of this book? What changes your opinion of people, and what should be done about that? Consider that Eleanor Tert is now enormously successful and Flan is – well, you know where she is.

3. The Rebecca Boone Memorial Hospital is named after Rebecca Boone, pioneerswoman and wife of Daniel Boone. Though the

238

Boone family is now regarded as a pillar of early American history with their exploration of the frontier and their support during the Revolutionary War, the Boone family was twice forced off their land due to legal loopholes against which Daniel had a philosophical and moral objection. Despite these attempts by the legal system to destroy these people, however, Americans eventually learned the truth, and the Boones have now had their reputations overturned to the point that Rebecca Boone has a hospital named after her. Can you think of anyone else who is being treated unfairly by the legal profession? Can you help spread the truth about her, perhaps give her name to a new library, or bookstore?

4. Do you think friends should do things for one another, or people should do things for themselves? Consider the consequences of doing things – at least certain things – before answering.

Monday October 25th
Six.

"Homeroom has been extended today so all of you have the chance to complete this voluntary survey. Dr. Eleanor Tert, who all of you saw speak last Wednesday at the all-school assembly, has provided for us an all-school survey to help us. Recent events at Roewer High School have revealed problems which are facing virtually all adolescents in our country today, and Dr. Tert will be conducting a study here at the school through informal interviews of select students and faculty as well as these completely voluntary all-school surveys. You have twenty-five minutes to fill them out. Please don't forget to put your name in the upper right-hand corner. Anonymity is guaranteed."

1. PLEASE CIRCLE ALL THAT APPLY (male, female).

Well, both "male" and "female" apply. Just one of them applies to me. I circled "female."

2. PLEASE CIRCLE ALL THAT APPLY (Freshman, Sophomore, Junior, Senior).

I circled "Senior."

3. PLEASE CIRCLE THE SENTENCE THAT BEST DESCRIBES YOUR FAMILY:

    a. My family is perfect.
    b. My family has few problems.
    c. My family has problems but is mostly OK.
    d. My family has many problems.
    e. My family has lots and lots of problems.
    f. Orphaned.

Orphaned? I looked over, but Natasha was still hunched over her desk.

4. PLEASE CIRCLE THE SENTENCE THAT BEST DESCRIBES YOUR SEXUAL ACTIVITY:

    a. I have had no sexual contact with the opposite sex (i.e., virgin).
    b. I have had little sexual contact with the opposite sex (i.e., kissing).
    c. I have had some sexual contact with the opposite sex (i.e., petting).
    d. I have had sexual intercourse with only one person.
    e. I have had sexual intercourse with more than one person.
    f. Homosexual.

Douglas must be living in hell. I circled "d," for Douglas.

5. PLEASE CIRCLE THE SENTENCE THAT BEST DESCRIBES

YOUR USE OF ALCOHOL:

   a. I have never had any alcohol (i.e., virgin).
   b. I sometimes have one beer or one glass of wine.
   c. I sometimes have several drinks but do not get drunk.
   d. I drink fairly often but don't get drunk often.
   e. I drink and get drunk almost all the time.
   f. Twelve-step program (good for you!).

I leaned over and tried to see if Natasha had circled
"e," but I still couldn't catch her eye. I circled "d,"
crossed it out and circled "c," crossed "c" out, and tried
to recircle "d."

6. PLEASE CIRCLE THE SENTENCE THAT BEST DESCRIBES
YOUR USE OF ILLICIT DRUGS:

   a. I have never used illicit drugs.
   b. I have tried drugs once or twice.
   c. I rarely use drugs.
   d. I use drugs fairly often and am addicted to one drug.
   e. I use drugs fairly often and am addicted to all of them.
   f. Twelve-step program (good for you!).

c.

7. PLEASE CIRCLE THE DRUGS YOU HAVE EXPERIMENTED
WITH:

   a. Marijuana.
   b. Cocaine.
   c. Heroin.
   d. LSD.
   e. Mushrooms.
   f. Angel dust.
   g. Uppers or downers.

h. Trickettes.

i. Fingerbars.

j. Euphoria.

k. Moonbeams.

l. Tears of Love.

m. "Singing Pills."

n. Snopes.

o. Other. (If so, list them.)

With which you have experimented. Needless to say, I didn't put down absinthe in case the folks at Rebecca Boone had found something. I wonder if Natasha did.

8. PLEASE CIRCLE THE SENTENCE WHICH BEST DESCRIBES YOUR RELATIONSHIP WITH GOD:

a. I have strong beliefs in God in accordance with a commonly accepted religion and follow these beliefs always.

b. I have strong beliefs in God in accordance with a commonly accepted religion but do not always follow these beliefs.

c. I have some beliefs in God in accordance with a commonly accepted religion and follow them sometimes.

d. I have some beliefs in God, but they are my own and not in accordance with a commonly accepted religion.

e. Other. (If so, list them.)

f. Atheist.

9. PLEASE CIRCLE THE SENTENCE WHICH BEST DESCRIBES YOUR RELATIONSHIP WITH SATAN:

a. I fear Satan according to my commonly accepted religion.

b. I am occasionally tempted by Satan.

c. I do not believe in Satan at all.

d. I occasionally serve Satan.

e. Other. (If so, list them.)

f. Satanist.

Look, we didn't know. You have the advantage. You *know* it's six days. All *we* knew was that it was October 25th, senior year, time to really get going on college applications, this last Roewer year stretched out in front of us like a dying whale on a dirty beach. It smelled. Small children were poking at it. Authorities and scientists would arrive soon to chop it into pieces, but we didn't know that, so all of us, *all of us* checked "e." On the horizontal horizon bare before us we wrote variations of the same joke: "Satan is the mother of a friend of mine." "I know Satan's daughter personally." And the chiller. The one highlighted by a thin band of light, so when the entire page was shown on TV the innocent bystanders would know where to look. Often it was credited to me – a possibility that was too delicious for everyone to ignore. "Had I known the warning signs, I could have stopped them. My son would be sitting next to me today on your show, Winnie." As if you'd even be on the show if he hadn't been beaten to death in Satan's lovely garden in the first place. As if your appearance on the show means anything, Eleanor Tert's book means anything, as if it means anything that no matter what we wrote on an all-school survey, that it means anything to look at question 9 and see written there, in casual inside-joke ballpoint ink, "I am the spawn of Satan."

Tuesday October 26th
Five days. If you were counting on your fingers you'd be down to your last hand. Do a little preview with me, starting with your pinkie: Five, four, three, two, one. Then nothing. Then he's dead.

When I woke up this morning I was already on the

bus; don't know how I managed that. I was staring out the window for a few minutes before I noticed that Lily was sitting next to me.

"Oh, hi. Sorry. I'm so spacey this morning, I don't even know how I ended up on this bus."

"It's OK. Hey, have you heard the big weekend plan that will save us from this week's horror?"

"No," I said.

"Well, believe it or not, V___'s parents are leaving for *five days*. Sunday we're going to have a garden party, well into the evening."

"Sunday?"

"Yeah, and we thought we could all call in sick Monday morning, just lounge around Satan's Palace."

"Are you sure I'm invited?" I said. "Nobody mentioned anything to me."

"V___ just found out last night. She said your line was busy."

"Natasha and I were just gossiping. You should have had the operator break into the line for an event like this." I had in fact been arguing with Natasha over what she was going to do to Adam, if she should do anything, whether I should do anything, whether I was an idiot. Nothing was resolved, in case you're curious.

"Well, of course you're invited. *Everybody's* invited, although the morning-after thing will be just *us*."

"Sounds absolutely wonderful," I said. It did. Go on, take a minute to count down to Sunday. Count on one hand.

Wednesday October 27th
Four days.

This morning the Spawn of Satan was waiting for me just outside the faculty parking lot, near the side entrance. She was sitting on a bench, fiddling with her pearls and *smoking*. V___, *smoking*. Unbelievable.

"Hello, Flan," she said, biting her lip. She stood up suddenly, like she'd just heard a loud noise. The smoke wisped into the fog so for a minute it looked like the whole San Francisco sky came from V___'s menthol.

"Hi," I said uncertainly. Then, more certainly, "You're smoking."

"Am I?" she said. "I hadn't checked." A reference to a joke of ours: Do you smoke after sex? I don't know, I never check. Weren't we witty? All those one-liners crumpling like paper. She raised the cigarette to her lips again but she couldn't puff. It – *she* – was trembling.

"What's wrong?" I said.

She blinked. The cigarette dropped. "What?"

I crushed it out with my foot. "Tell me what's wrong."

She blinked again and suddenly was crying, just outside the faculty parking lot, near the side entrance to Roewer High School. Shakily she took a tissue out of her pocket, but instead of wiping her eyes she uncrumpled it and gave it to me to read.

V___,

It just isn't working out between us. Please don't call me. It's over. I will always remember you,

Steve Nervo

"Oh dear," I said, and then reconstructed it: "Oh, dear, my dear." Hugged her. "What an idiot."

"*I'm* the idiot," she said, breaking away from me and slapping her own chest like an Indian brave. "*Me.* I can't believe I fell for him."

"Everybody in Roewer has fallen for him, remember?

He's Steve Nervo. His name is all over the bathroom walls, for God's sake."

She cried harder. "Oh, dear, sshh," I said. I hugged her again, patting her stiff, ironed back.

"Why did he do it? I can't even call him and find out! How could he be so mean?"

In my own delicate state I knew I wouldn't be able to handle this alone, and as though I'd wished for her, Natasha materialized out of the fog.

"Because he's a shit," she said, munching an apple. "Who are we talking about?"

I gave her the crumpled piece of paper. She read it quickly, snorted and recrumpled it, throwing it to the ground near V____'s half-finished cigarette. She finished her apple as V____ kept crying and threw the core to the ground. I looked down at our feet: V____'s in expensive, tasteful dark blue pumps. Natasha was wearing bright silver hiking boots. I was wearing something somewhere in between. Natasha's foot began to tap impatiently; V____'s feet wandered all over as she blew her nose and got herself together.

"Let's go buy some shoes," Natasha said decisively.

"What?" V____ said. "I have to –"

"Shoes," Natasha said, cheerfully and firmly. "The better to kick some butt with, dear."

V____ smiled slowly and we all walked to the Malleria. By the time the pencil-thin fluttering salesman found something suitable for Natasha we were all shrieking with laughter and piles and piles of shoe boxes were surrounding us, like coffins for babies, like some infant morgue had suffered an earthquake and the three of us, tipsy from Natasha's flask, were picking through the rubble trying to figure out which dead person belonged to whom. V____ found a pair of white shoes – "too bad it's after Labor Day, but I can wait," she said primly – with little pearl buttons, and I found some sinister-looking black tennis shoes, the soles of which turned out to rub off everywhere in a very incriminating way. Natasha found these ghastly bright orange fake fur things with high, thin heels like spider legs. V__ insisted on paying for all the shoes, like Natasha and I had made some huge sacrifice in cutting school to shop.

Over a midmorning snack at the Worldwide Food Court (V__ had a quesadilla; I had egg rolls; Natasha had a quesadilla and egg rolls) we ironed out plans for Sunday's garden party. We'd come over Saturday afternoon to cook a bunch of stuff; it would chill until Sunday. Cold salads because we'd all been eating too much lately, although I was still thinner than Kate. V__ had a tentative guest list, and with great ceremony we crossed Steve Nervo's name off; Natasha had the idea that if we invited each and every member of the cast except Steve it would insult him further, so we added everyone's name, from The Frosh Goth to Sweater-Vest Shannon (who's in charge of props) to Ron Piper himself. Natasha said she was sure he'd be cool about the drinking. V__ was still slightly tipsy and so told me that Douglas had asked her to invite this superskinny boy from her math class named Bob. After much debate Flora Habstat did not get crossed off the list. Fictional characters next: both the Daisys, Buchanan and Miller, were welcome; Gatsby himself was not. Ophelia but not Hamlet. Both Oberon and Titania if they promised to be nice. Phoebe but not Holden. Pearl but not Hester. Desdemona but not Othello. I had to get to rehearsal.

By the time I walked back to Roewer I scarcely had time to stash my new shoes in my locker and head to the auditorium. We were running through the last two acts.

We weren't doing the beginning part. We were doing the part where it all comes unwound. The part of the plot where all the elements have been clearly established, and put in the right place. The part where you just sit and watch everything happen, where everything goes wrong and there's nothing you can do about it but wait for everybody to die.

Thursday October 28th

Three days, one for each of my eyes. Two outer, one inner. Just kidding. You really thought I believed that mumbo jumbo for a minute, huh? Be honest. That's one thing I've learned: be honest; always be honest.

"Honestly?" Natasha said, recapping the flask. From the smell of her breath it definitely wasn't water this time. "Heavens no, I'm not going to speak to you honestly. I'm *never* going to speak to you honestly. Where did you even *get* that idea, anyway? I've never spoken to you honestly and I don't plan to start. Get honesty from, I don't know, *Flora Habstat*." She spun the car through a right turn that would have killed us all had we been minor characters.

"But are you going to do something, or not?"

"That's the question *you* should be asking," she said, blowing a kiss at herself in the rearview mirror and turning up the stereo. She was playing me her favorite new band, Tin Can. They were loud and electronic, like the noises you might imagine happening inside a computer. Tin Can's singer sounded like he was singing through a tin can. "Baker's not even *my* Math teacher. I have Deschillo, and he never has *anything* interesting to say, and what does *yours* do? Gives you *the key*! You have *the key* to everything, to *everything*, *Flan*, and you ask me if *I'm* going to do something. Baker's Rule, Flan: *do something*. And you have to ask *me*?"

"Natasha," I said. "*Natasha!* You're scaring me."

She stopped the car suddenly, in the middle of the street. Luckily, there was no one behind us. She stopped yelling and looked at me; everything was quiet except for the traffic and Tin Can, who were shouting either "My heart" or "My art." "I'm not trying to *scare* you," Natasha said. "I'm trying to *help* you, dammit. That's what I'm here for. Adam is messing with your brain, and you have to do something *back* to him, just like Carr messed with your brain, and –"

"Carr didn't mess with my *brain*," I said, "he –"

"*Whatever*."

"What about Gabriel?"

"Save Gabriel. You can be with Gabriel when you get Adam off your back."

"He's not on my back. That's the prob –"

"*The problem is that you're not doing anything!*" she said. "*Do something! Do something! Come on!*"

"All right, all right, I hear you," Jennifer Rose Milton said, opening the back door and getting in. Where had she come from? "Thanks for the ride, even if it's only a couple of blocks." She smiled, and we could see she'd been crying. "Millie's taking a mental health day, but I had to come in. Bio test. Don't you hate those? Well, of course you do, Flan. Do you have a tissue or something?"

"What happened to you?"

Jennifer Rose Milton sighed. "Oh, you know. Just a little morning cry."

"What are you talking about?"

"Kate didn't tell you?"

We shook our heads in unison.

She swallowed and tried to smile again. "I guess I

can't rely on Kate to disseminate information so quickly. Frank and I – well, Frank dumped me last night." She burst into tears again. Behind us, someone honked and Natasha started moving again. "*He* dumped *me*! He just said 'It just isn't working out between us.' Can you believe it?"

"No," I said. "I've never heard him say a sentence that long. You must be very proud."

"Oh, Flan," she said, laughing, crying. "He *was* an idiot, wasn't he?"

"Well, he dumped you," Natasha said. "Give him *some* credit."

Jenn swatted her just as she parked. She blew her nose with a long shudder, loud and wet as the gurgling in my head. "I should have taken a mental health day, Bio test or no."

Natasha smiled thinly. "Jenn, I'm going to leave you in the Hands Of Flan. I gotta go."

Suddenly V—— was knocking on the car window. I opened the door and saw she was crying, too, again. "Oh, Flan," she said. "He's such a rat. A rat and a *liar*. Oh –"

"Now I *really* gotta go," Natasha said, getting out of the car. She walked six steps, turned back and got the flask, and waved it at us, looking at me sharply. "See you guys later."

I sat there for a second, but neither V—— nor Jennifer Rose Milton could reach me to their satisfaction, so I got out of Natasha's car and leaned against it while they both cried.

"He's seeing someone *else*," V—— said. "This little thin *freshman*! She's joined his band now, on *tambourine*! I can't believe it! '*Just isn't working out between us*' indeed!"

"I'm sorry," I said.

"I'm sorry too," Jennifer Rose Milton said, and burst out crying again and then V___ burst out crying and then both of them were crying on my shoulder – one on each shoulder, I mean. "I don't know what to *do*," one of them said, I couldn't tell which. Do *something*, I wanted to tell them, but it isn't always that easy. Sometimes you don't just know what to do, and with that bland cliché I will close this journal and end the entry for Adam's third-to-last day.

Friday October 29th

Two days. Kate filled me in at lunch.

"Did you hear the latest about Frank?"

"Yeah, Jenn told me yesterday," I said. "What a creep."

"No, no," Kate said. Her eyes lit up; she was pleased as punch I hadn't heard the latest. "He's seeing someone else."

"What? I thought things between them –"

"*Just weren't working out*,'" we said in unison.

"Yeah," she said. "I know. He's such a rat. It's Nancy Butler, of all people, remember, Mark Wallace's old girlfriend?"

"No," I said. "Nancy Butler wasn't going out with Mark. I believe she was going out with Martin Luther King."

"Well," she said, "someone in the triptych, anyway. But now she's hot and heavy with Frank. Jenn went ballistic when I told her."

"*You* told her?" I said.

Kate straightened up defensively. "Well, *somebody* was going to tell her. I thought that I should do it, you know, as a friend. You know, three couples within the Basic Eight have called it quits lately. You and Gabriel and me and Adam are the only happy couples left."

"Yeah, well," I said, trying to find something to say.

Kate crumpled up the bag of chips. "I'm just glad that I don't have to worry about –"

"Can I talk to you?" Adam said, looking at both of us. Just at that moment some stereo on the other side of the courtyard started playing the Tin Can album, like he'd brought his own soundtrack.

"Do you mean me?" I asked.

"Yes," he said, and we walked to a quiet corner. "I'll just come to the point. I made a big mistake, Flan. It's you, it's always been you."

"Well," I said. "There's not much we can do about it now, is there?"

"Don't be ridiculous," he said. "It will be difficult, but we can do it. We have to seize the day, Flan. Our love won't wait. Is your unicorn parked outside?"

"Yeah right. Yeah right. Yeah right," spat the chorus of the Tin Can song. Adam wrinkled his nose in irritation.

"No," he said, tiredly. "I don't mean *you*. I mean *Kate*. Can I talk to you, Kate?"

"Sure," she said, extending her hand to him so he'd help her up. He paused for a moment and took it, and Kate looked up at him and saw that something was wrong. "What's up?"

"I want to talk to you," he said again. I watched them walk to a quiet corner. The Tin Can song was getting turned up louder, louder, louder – no, it was Natasha walking toward me with her portable stereo.

"Howdy!" she crowed, blocking my view of Kate and Adam.

"Yes, yes," I said. "I'm trying to see."

"See what?" she said.

"I'm trying to find out," I said pointedly. "Sit down, Natasha."

She sat down. "What are we looking at?"

252

"Adam wanted to talk to Kate."

"I bet he did."

"No, no, it looks serious," I said. "Will you turn down that Tin Can?"

"It's Tin *Pan*, not Tin Can," she said, but she turned it down, whatever it was. Tin Pan sounded like they were using tin pans for drums, and the singer was still saying, "*Yeah right. Yeah right. Yeah right.*"

"'You bite, you bite, you bite,'" Natasha corrected me. "It's about vampires, I think." Adam was walking away from the quiet corner with an uncomfortable look on his face like he had to pee. Shannon, sweater-vested as usual, stood up from one of the Sophomore Benches and called out his name but Adam kept walking. "What's going on?" Natasha said, as Kate looked after him. She looked at him, she looked at me and then, standing there alone in the quiet corner, took out a navy-blue handkerchief.

LATER

"Are we even going to have the garden party now?" Gabriel asked me as he drove me home from a dismal dinner with all the dumpees: V___, Jennifer Rose Milton and my personal favorite, Kate Gordon. "It doesn't seem like we have much to celebrate."

"We've got to have it," I said. "An opportunity like this doesn't come very often. V___'s parents away? The Basic Eight let loose in that glorious house and garden?"

"People are upset," he said to me, looking confused. "Tonight was a bummer. We don't want to have a party that feels like a funeral."

"Sunday is *two whole days away*," I said. "I bet by then Kate will be saying, 'Adam who?' She's a big girl. She'll be over it in a jiffy."

"Right," he said, smiling. "That would explain why

253

she hardly ever mentions Garth."

"We're not going to cancel the party," I said.

"We could take off school Monday anyway," he said. "You and me. Lounge around the house all day." His eyes were on the road so he couldn't read my expression, but there was nothing I could do about him taking my hand.

"What's with everybody?" he said, suddenly quiet and tense. We were stopped at my house, and Gabriel was getting out of the car so he could come around and let *me* out. "What's with people, Flan? One minute we were all happy here, and now everybody's breaking up with everybody else." He shut his own door and I had a blessed moment of silence as he walked in front of the car to open my door. If I had been behind the wheel I could have just eased the car out of park, right when he was in front. He would have been pinned. *Speaking of breaking up*, I wanted to say, but no way was I going to start that sentence to his face, his eager and fragile face, expectant and so young, and cute. "I'm glad we're not going through that," he said. "No, no" – as I started to speak – "I'm not saying we'll be together forever or anything, I just mean that I really care about you, and I want to tell you not to worry. I'm not just going to walk up to you someday and say it just isn't working out. I've waited a long time for this, and I'm committed to staying and working out whatever we'll need to work out."

"Gabriel –"

He helped me out of the car; the chilly air closed in like a bite. "No, no," he said again. "I don't mean there is anything to work out right now. Don't look so worried." God help me he touched me on the chin like an uncle. "I just mean I'm here for you."

"I know, Gabriel," I said, and swallowed. The taste of

the hamburger I had for dinner – *fuck* calories – was still on my tongue and in my throat. As it turned out it was the last hamburger I ever ate. There was something about the way Adam died that changed me. When you watch somebody die like that there comes a point when they stop looking like a person. The act of killing someone, after all, even if you're just beating them with a blunt object over and over, is in effect squeezing the life out of a person, by which I mean: blood. Lots more blood than one would think, as it turned out. I mean, when it's pouring out of a body it looks like more than could ever fit in a normal-sized high school boy. Maybe a little taller than normal, actually. The blood covers so much of the personality: the clothes are soaked through, and the face is covered in it, so even if the mouth weren't split open and the nose weren't squished in like a red garden slug, it wouldn't look like a normal face. Adam kept trying to cover his face, but he was long past protecting himself, thrashing around in blood like a toy hopelessly smashed, engine whirring briefly before dying down. The blood covers the hands, the fingerprints even. (Note: I was wrong about that.) All the personality is drowned in it, like the actual taste of fries when Natasha puts as much ketchup as she likes on them. When the head caves in slightly like a deflating ball, when the arm, pinned beneath your foot, stops moving with a purpose and just starts flailing around like some separate creature trying to escape, it stops looking like a person. I mean, look at what I just wrote: *it*. *It* isn't a person. Somewhere in the momentum the whole deal stops feeling like one person affecting another, because the victim gets less and less human. First the mallet causes bruises, then bleeding and then smashing. When you can see past the pouring blood into torn muscle and cracked bone, it doesn't look like a person anymore. What it starts looking like is, meat. By that time it's too late to stop what you're doing, so you have to just bear down and finish it, like doing anything squeamish, cleaning fish or skinning chicken. Nobody likes doing those things but you have to do them, and if you're feeling gross about it you should just stop thinking about it as a cute little chicken or a happy fish swimming in the ocean or a classmate or anything, and just think about it as meat. No matter what they say – and at that point you can barely make out what they're saying anyway, so why listen to it? – it's just meat, that's all. A piece of meat with distinct dimensions, a definite size and volume. There's only so much blood it can hold, and when just about all of it is out you're done and you don't have to worry. The last lung may fill with blood, and collapse like a sinking balloon, making a gurgling noise that sticks in your head like the catchiest song you ever heard, gurgling there behind your eyes long after you're bored of Darling Mud or Q.E.D. or Tin Can or Pan or whoever they are, just gurgling away, even in your dreams and when you wake up, and the thrashing may continue longer than you thought – I mean, it takes a bit of time for the nerves to realize there's really not much brain left to send a message to – *to which to send a message* – but the personality is gone, the human part. It's just meat. The only trouble is, after something like that has happened to you, you don't want any meat. Real meat that is, like a hamburger. So I haven't touched red meat since the garden party. Or really, since tonight. The taste of my last hamburger lingering in the dark with Gabriel – a sensation to be remembered, locked in memory and noted in my journal as clearly as everything else.

"I could come in," he said.

"Well," I said, "I've been in these clothes all day. They

feel gross; I want to get out of them."

He raised one eyebrow, just slightly. Oh God. "I could come in."

For the first time since the school year began I wanted to have my parents be home, cute white American parents who wouldn't let my boyfriend – my *black* boyfriend, mind you – come in late at night under any circumstances. Because this way I had no excuse. What could I possibly say – "*It just isn't working out between us?*" He coughed slightly, and I thought for a minute I'd said it. "I told my parents I might stay at Douglas's," he said. "They're not expecting me back until morning. I could even stay over."

"Oh," I said.

"If that's OK," he said, smiling like of course it was.

"Oh?" I said, cinching my voice into at least a semiseductive tone. I had opened my door but hadn't stepped into the dark yet.

"So," he said, leaning over to catch my eye and taking a hesitant step forward. "If it's OK."

"Well," I said.

"Don't worry," he said, leaning in close and kissing my neck like a butterfly or maybe a flapping moth, hitting the same damn lightbulb over and over. "Don't worry about anything," he said. He must have felt how tense my body was, misread it entirely and completely. Oh, Gabriel. "Don't worry, I'm not going anywhere," he said, clinching it. We stepped into the dark together. My hand reached toward the wall to find the light switch but found Gabriel's hand instead. He gently helped me find the way to his shirt. "I'll hold you, all night," he said, wrapping me in python arms. The door slammed shut. In a movie it would cut to morning, but those of us living it have to go through all of it, minute by minute by minute like a school schedule or a well-kept diary or a thousand other things I can't even think of.

Saturday October 30th

One. When I woke up this morning Gabriel still had his arms around me like a straitjacket, not that I'd know. With difficulty I lifted his arm from around me and took a shower. When I got back I thought maybe he'd be gone, or at least up and about, but he was still fast asleep. I sat on the bed and watched him, trying to conjure up some sort of fond feelings, but instead it just felt like watching a movie you've already seen and didn't actually like that much. Who knows why you don't switch it off?

When I got up to change my clothes Gabriel's hand was suddenly on my leg. I turned and his eyes were wide open; happiness was making him bold as a drunk. His smile was so desperate I put my fingers to it to blot it out. He kissed and kissed my fingers. What I really wanted was coffee but I lay back down on the bed and we fooled around.

Then he wanted to cook me omelettes, but I made him go home instead. "Change your clothes and I'll change my clothes and pick me up and we'll go to V___'s and make salads. It's already eleven-thirty, plus we don't have any eggs. Come *on*, Gabriel."

"OK," he said. "I just don't want to be away from you."

"Stop, you're making me swoon," I said blankly. "Get in the car."

He blinked and decided I was kidding. "OK, OK." He got in the car, and I hurried to the kitchen to throw all the eggs down the disposal in case he caught me later. I didn't need to change my clothes, so I figured I had time to stop by Adam's house. Plenty of cars were parked on his street on a Saturday morning, so remaining inconspicuous was an easy caper.

The sky-blue flicker of a television was winking behind the States' lovely white curtains. Adam, on his last full day of life, was watching cartoons. I mean, there's no way to know for sure, I guess, but it wasn't his parents, and it wasn't The Frosh Goth. She's probably so excited to be invited to the Big Party tomorrow she has all two hundred of her black dresses out and is sitting in her slip, debating the merits of each one.

I thought maybe we'd find V___ in black shrouds or something, but when Gabriel and I walked into the kitchen she was actually laughing at something Kate was saying.

"The door was open," I said.

"No problem," V___ said. "If I devein another shrimp I'm going to go out of my gourd."

"Too late," Kate said, and they both giggled. I noticed two glasses, half-full of champagne; no wonder.

"No wonder," I said, pointing to the glasses. "Any left?"

Kate and V___ laughed again. "Lots," V___ said. "Satan bought crates and crates at some discount place. You want orange juice in it, or just straight?"

"Just straight?" Douglas said, coming in with Lily and what looked like a bag of two thousand limes. "In that case I'd better leave."

Kate and V___ laughed and V___ poured everyone champagne. The kitchen got busy. Somebody put on the old Darling Mud album and we sang along in between blasts of the blender. Lily was hand-whipping cream and Gabriel was doing something with mangoes in a small saucepan when Jennifer Rose Milton and Flora Habstat arrived, and for some reason even Flora's chatter about a record-breaking storm happening across the country wasn't as annoying as usual, or maybe it was the champagne. Natasha didn't show.

"Who thought that the Basic Eight would ever be socializing in *this house*?" Lily asked.

"Well," V___ said sheepishly, "usually my parents are –"

"Let me guess," Gabriel said, wrinkling his brow and turning down the heat under the mangoes. "Entertaining?"

We all laughed, and Douglas came back in the room to ask V___ if he should bring flowers tomorrow or if one needed flowers for a garden party. We all nixed flowers and dumped what we'd been chopping into bright silver bowls for Gabriel's use. Gabriel said he needed one more purple onion chopped so, being the girlfriend, I volunteered while everyone else beat eggs and eggs for some meringue thing that Jennifer Rose Milton insisted she knew how to make. Halfway through the onion my eyes were watering too hard to finish, so I asked V___ if there was anything nonkitchen to do and she said I could go out and help Kate move the lawn furniture. When I went out there I was surprised that the light was already into deep afternoon, and Kate wasn't moving anything but sitting on the steps with an empty champagne glass crying her eyes out.

"Oh," I said. I felt like one of those mute victims in monster movies, leaving the safety of her own home to help the scientists. They take her deep into the forest and show her footprints, claw marks, a shattered window in a wrecked cabin. She nods. Yes, the monster's been here. I'd know his wreckage anywhere. When Kate turned around the heartbreak of Adam's rejection was streaked across her face. It was like she'd borrowed my clothes. I sat down next to her on the steps. From here we could see the garden, mocking our messy lives with its perfect design, its flawless execution.

"Hey," I said. "Don't take it so hard. It *is* a lovely

garden. A lot of people are moved by horticulture, Kate."

She tried to smile but just cried harder. Grateful that I had been chopping onions and thus had every reason to have red, bleary eyes, I patted her shoulder until she was just hiccuping. "How could he?" she finally said. "How could he?"

"I don't know," I said. "He's –"

"Oh, God," she said. "At least with Garth, I knew what was going on, you know? I didn't want to face it, but really, I saw it coming. But this was from the blue. He just walked into the courtyard – remember? – asked to talk to me, and all of a sudden it *just wasn't working out.*" She started to cry again. A perfect white bird swooped out of nowhere and landed on the croquet set to peer at us. I could see each mallet gleaming at me, sturdy, able to withstand anything you could do with it. Maybe in some other language, some bird tongue, Kate crying meant something else, something better. Write a poem about this. Write a poem about everything.

"Let's get out of here," I said, grabbing Kate by the hand. "You and me, we'll grab some food or something."

"Yeah," Kate said, looking at her empty glass. "Or something." We went back to Kate's house and made a big Freshman Cocktail – poured an inch off each of Mom and Dad's bottles into a large plastic container, something we hadn't done in years. We stopped at a little corner store and bought two pints of fancy ice cream and some bags of cookies and chips, left the car at my place and went up to Twin Peaks, a big beautiful tourist view of the city rife with couples making out in cars on Friday and Saturday nights. It's great to go up there on foggy nights because it's the ultimate irony: a beautiful view you can't see. Kate and I drank to that, the square mouth of the plastic container spilling liquor on our shirts. We were freezing – it's part of the tradition of drinking on Twin Peaks that you forget to bring the blanket *again* – and there was way too much schnapps in the Cocktail but we kept drinking anyway. Kate talked and talked, and as it got darker and darker her navy-blue sweatshirt faded to black and I could just see her white face and hands hovering around.

"You're better off without him," I said. "We all are. He'll never come to one of our dinner parties again."

"And there's no worse punishment!" she cried. Some of her hair dangled in the Cocktail. "That's all we are, Flan, a bunch of dinner parties! A bunch of hostesses!"

"With the mostesses," I added. "Give me some Cocktail."

"Try these cookies. Too much cream filling, but – he's such an asshole, Flan."

"You're better off without him," I said for the millionth time. "Better off without Adam."

"Better off without Adam, Adam, Adam –" she sang to the tune of something. She was sniffling but I didn't know if she was crying or not, didn't know if I was.

"We're all better off without Adam. We would have been better off without the *original* Adam. Who needs him? Just a couple of Eves in the garden would have been OK."

"Yeah," Kate agreed, wiping her mouth with her sleeve. "If you and I had been in the garden, Flan, we would have left the fucking apple the hell alone!"

She and I cackled; behind us, some car was playing smarmy love ballads. "Better off without Adam," I said. "Better off without all the Adams."

Peter Pusher: That's nonsense. If there were only Eves in the garden the entire human race would have died out, and then where would you be?

262

"Oh, shut up!" I said fiercely, and stared out into the billowing fog. What with all the schnapps it was just *racing* up the hill like wild horses. I felt my eyes get wider and wider, and fill up.

"Just not working out," Kate was muttering, lying on her back. "Where the fuck is Orion's belt?"

"Around his ankles," I said. Not bad, considering how drunk. We were. "You know, Kate, it's really true how better off you are. And you *know* how I feel about him, how we *both* feel about him –"

"Yeah," she said, suddenly sitting up and suddenly angry. "I know *all about* how you feel about him. Buying me ice cream and cookies doesn't make it all better, Flan."

"What?"

"Oh, come off it," she spat. "I know it, you know it, everybody knows it. You've been in love with Adam since God knows when. For better or for worse Gabriel doesn't know, or won't admit he knows or whatever the hell, who knows with Gabriel. But Adam didn't like *you*," she said, throwing the plastic container far, far away. I had a brief memory of the absinthe container, sinking into Lake Merced. "Adam chose *me*. Or *did*, anyway." She was crying again. "I can't believe it," she said.

"I'm sorry," I said. My head throbbed with ice cream and liquor. "You know how I feel."

"Well," she said, with a nasty smile, "don't get any ideas. Don't think that *you* can have him now, because you know what? Somebody else beat us both to him."

I swallowed, tasted something sharp. "What?" I said. "What?"

"*What? What?*" she mimicked. "He told me it wasn't working out, Flan, but you know me. I found out there was somebody else. We should have moved *early*, darling. Remember, I don't know if you knew this, but somebody was writing him some kind of" – she yawned and took another cookie – "some kind of love letters? All summer? Well, *that's* who he wants. Adam loves the love letter girl" – she was starting to cry again – "and not me."

I threw up.

Sunday October 31st

Today's the day! I can't wait. The biggest event of the year. A day to be remembered – a famous day. We're going to be having so much fun, people are just going to *die*.

Of course I didn't say any of that; when last we saw me I was throwing up, remember? I woke up feeling like a yak was sitting on me. It turned out to be Natasha.

"Today's the day!" she said, straddling me like a rider, or a rapist. She had opened the shades so the irksome blaze of dawn was upon me like too much salad dressing.

"Get me some water," I said.

"I can't wait!" she said. "The biggest event of the year. A day to be remembered, a –"

"Famous day, yes," I said. Natasha was grabbing both my arms so I couldn't cover my eyes. "If you get me a glass of water I'll give you fifty bucks."

"We're going to have so much fun –"

"One hundred dollars, Natasha. *Two* hundred."

She laughed and got off me, ran to the bathroom. She came back with a glass of water that she –

"No!"

– poured on my head.

"I hate you," I said, dripping. "What happened to the good old days when you would be making me Bloody Marys and such?"

"No time," she said. "I'm too excited. You can't hate me. What should I wear?"

I stood up, wiped my face off. She was already going through my closet. "You think *you* are going to find something to wear in *my* closet?"

"I want to wear something *regular*," she said. "But, you know, sarcastic regular. Ironic. You know, for Halloween."

"Thanks a lot," I said.

"But I have *your* outfit," she said, holding up a shopping bag. "I'll be dressed like you, and you'll be dressed like me. Get it? We'll be like what's-it, like those twins who advertise chewing gum on TV."

I rubbed my eyes and walked to the bathroom. "Except those twins look exactly alike and we will look totally different."

She stuck her face in the door as I tried to shut it. "*Ironic*," she said. "Sarcastic twins. It'll be great. It's supposed to be *Halloween*, remember? But it's not a costume party, so these are sarcastic costumes. *Irony*. You know, I think I'll make us Bloody Marys after all. Come downstairs after your shower."

My body looked thinner in the shower, *leaner*. I looked in the mirror as I stepped out of the shower and blinked as I found myself not just unashamed but even a little proud, slightly strutty to stand naked for a few moments in front of a mirror. Then I put on sweats; I didn't even want to look at what Natasha thought I would wear until the worst of my hangover had passed.

The problem: no tomato juice. Natasha's solution: substitute spaghetti sauce from a jar. The result: Bloody Marinaras. She put a few strands of uncooked spaghetti as garnish instead of a celery stalk; I swear this girl's IQ is funneled into all the wrong places.

"You don't really expect me to drink this stuff, do you?" I said. She pointed to her half-empty glass with her swizzle noodle. I saw she'd chewed off the ends of the spaghetti.

"It's good, really," she said, lying.

"Watching you have some is enough for me. I'm going to make coffee."

"So, how was Heartbreak Hotel last night?" Natasha asked. "Kate told me you guys exorcised some demons."

"Leave it to Kate to gossip about *herself*," I said, looking for the damn filters. How my head throbs. I put my head down on the counter until the coffee was ready. After three cups I was ready for toast, and to fill Natasha in on Twin Peaks.

"I scarcely remember how we got home," I said. "I mean, I know I was in a cab, but I don't know if Kate was with me. I think I left the cookies in the car and the plastic container on the hill."

"*Peak*," Natasha corrected. "Quite an evening, Flan, particularly for you. Between the two of us we are leaving quite a trail of illegal plastic storage containers."

"Natasha, you're missing the point. Adam wants *me*."

"No he doesn't," Natasha said. "He wants whatever mooning chick wrote him love letters. Now let's go try on party outfits. Something tells me this night is going to be big."

I ached to tell her, but that mooning chick stopped me. "Natasha, if it turns out Adam does want me, what should I do?"

She was halfway up the stairs already. "Date him for three weeks, make him buy you stuff, dump him and tell everybody he's gay," she said. "Also, cut off his –"

"I'm serious," I said.

"So am I," she said automatically, and then said, "You can't be serious, Flan."

"I'm serious," I said again. I felt like maybe I would only say "I'm serious" over and over again, for the rest of my life. A sentence.

"Go upstairs and put on that dress," she said in a terrible voice. We looked at each other for a second and then she said it again. "Go upstairs and put on that dress. The sweetest boy in the world is in your hand like a small animal, like something you've rescued. Gabriel has given you his fucking heart, Flan, and what do you want? This *idiot* who is messing everything up! Charming his way into dinner parties and breaking the heart of somebody who, I agree, Flan, is sometimes a bitch but is *our friend nevertheless*! I've watched you whimper over him all year and it's only *October*! It's just fucking *Adam State*, Flan! Remember *Adam State*? For three years he just puttered alongside us like a tugboat and it was just *Adam State*, like *Frank Whitelaw* or *Steve Nervo* or fucking *Flora Habstat*, dammit. *Then*, all of a sudden, the moon hits your eye like a big pizza pie and you're mooning over *Adam State*. And I think, *OK*, this is a fine premise for the start of senior year: Flan chases boy, it could be any boy, it doesn't matter. It's just something to do – it's just the *plot*, Flan. So by all means flirt with him, invite him places and talk about him *all the livelong day*, but what happens?" Her shoulders sputtered up in a loud shrug. "What's the punch line, Flan? He doesn't like you. That's all. He *just doesn't like you*. He *doesn't like you*, he *doesn't like you*, he *doesn't like you*. And – and this should have been *good news* – he turns out to be evil. Says he'll call, doesn't call. Makes a date, stands you up. Capital *E*, capital *V*, *ill*. Evil, Flan!"

She started back up the stairs again but turned back, tossed her hair. "But *no*, apparently this is bad news, you

267

want the evil man all to yourself, and when he goes out with Kate – just to drive us both nuts – you *buckle*! You could have bawled out Kate, you could have bawled out Adam, you could have chained them up in a deserted shack and left them to die – but what do you do? *Buckle, buckle, buckle*! Kate, who's supposed to be your friend, takes Adam from under your nose – and what do you do? *Buckle*! Were you ever the least bit interested in Gabriel? I don't mean, do you think he's nice, I mean, the *least bit interested*? But you *buckle* and before you know it you have a boyfriend you *don't like* and you *don't* have a boyfriend you ought *not* to like! Then he dumps *Kate* and even *that* doesn't stiffen your fucking resolve, Flan! Evil, evil, evil, and all you can ask me is 'What if he wants me *now*? What if he wants me *tonight*?'" Her voice had its practiced snarl, a genuine, rehearsed sharpness like all the best speeches, throughout history. "Friends, Romans, countrymen, Flan, he's E-Vil and for once in your life I'm not going to do it for you. No secret absinthe potions tonight, darling! I'm going to go your own way – *my* own way, I mean – and I'm not going to look back and see what you're doing, but I hope for *once* you're fucking paying attention in Calc because you ought to do *something*, do *something*, do *something*!" Her eyes blazed with, I don't know, heartfelt theatrics and sexy fury. I had seen her bawl people out but never me. Not even our fights in the car had been like *this*. I was frightened.

"But what should I do?"

"You should *go upstairs and put on that dress*!" she said, frustrated. She ran a hand through her carefully disheveled hair, all the misplaced strands graceful as swans' necks. "And hurry up, because we have to stop at Basic Bakery and pick up baguettes."

She gave me a small smile and we both went upstairs to change and once we were inside the room *everything* changed. I don't know what it was, weird strangeness when you're talking and taking off your clothes and abruptly the nakedness just hits you. If it had been a movie the soundtrack music would have either suddenly stopped or suddenly started and there'd be a two-minute sequence with two teenage girls, changing their clothes back to back and stealing glimpses of each other. On the way out of the movie theater, people would say "Remember that part in the bedroom? What was *that*?"

It first hit me as I pulled off my sweats and realized suddenly I was naked except for my socks, and turned to grin sheepishly at Natasha, holding up one foot to show her. Except when I turned around she was already looking at me curiously like I had just emerged from a cocoon, with quiet wonder and expectation. I shrugged at her quickly but the spell didn't break and then I looked back at her, down her neck and saw that she was naked except for these cotton white underpants I wouldn't have expected of her. One hand was on her hip, below the underwear; she had obviously just realized she didn't need to take them off in order to change into some of my clothes. I started to smile at her, but she wasn't looking at me; she was looking at *me*. Behind her was the shopping bag with her dress in it and I stepped toward her feeling like a predator. She stiffened like something dangerous was getting closer to her skin, arching her neck, wary and still watching me. Watching my whole body. I could feel her gaze everywhere. I stepped so close that her breasts almost brushed against mine, and leaned over to get the shopping bag while she watched me the whole time, tense and expressionless. I stepped back and she walked toward me, tangolike. We moved like this, locked in each other's eyes, back to my dresser and finally she opened a drawer and had to look in it to find clothes. We exhaled and breathed.

Inside the bag was a fake silk black dress, shiny and cheap like a fake kimono. I had never seen anything like it – it was as though the concept of a dress had been explained to somebody who had never seen one and based on this explanation made a reasonable facsimile. It had thick red streaks on it, elegant and gory. It felt wonderful but I wasn't sure how it looked; the mirror was blocked by Natasha's body so all I could see was her flesh. Her underpants had fallen a little low, still half-off, and her pubic hair was peeking out like an escaping spider. What was happening? I moved nearer, feeling the dress move around me, feeling liquid and naughty. Natasha straightened up suddenly and put on a plain white T-shirt with a tiny stenciled flower at the center of the neck and then looked at me as I felt the sudden true flush of desire. Keep that line for a poem. She watched me and then looked at her own hand as she hitched her underwear back up. The spider scuttled underneath. Her breasts were as clear underneath my shirt as they were naked, clearer even. She kept her hand on her hip for a second, her fingers lingering on the cheap white cotton I couldn't believe she owned. She knew I was watching her, I realized, and looked at myself in the mirror. I was amazed how much like Natasha the dress made me look. No, wait: I was amazed that the dress made me look so much like Natasha. The sharp neck of the dress made my features look more clearly drawn, like Natasha's did, and the red streaks of the dress made a thin thread between appeal and violence. The scarlet hugged my body like snakes, accented curves I couldn't see in myself but always saw in Natasha, curving like beckoning fingers, like parentheses around remarks only funny to me, remarks only I could hear.

Natasha put on my blue jeans and looked inadequate. Even her perfect hair and the sneer of her lipstick couldn't balance out the bland costume. She looked like me, I bet: slightly slouched, a little off-center, ineffectual and something you wouldn't notice, not unless it was right in front of you. But I looked great. It was exciting to feel like her, and I felt a little smug that she'd be overshadowed tonight. She couldn't perform as well in that costume. But I looked great. This was going to be a day to be remembered – a famous day.

When she was looking elsewhere I reached up to the top of my shelf and grabbed a talisman that would complete my Natasha imitation. *Transformation*, I mean. I reached up to the top shelf of the closet: Douglas's hat, Jenn's earring, Lily's glasses – where was it? There it was: the nail file, with the two claw hands at either end. I slipped it into the dress's one pocket and turned around just as Natasha turned around, like a reflection in the surface of a lake. She smiled and handed me the flask.

We got the baguettes at Basic Bakery where the showy ovens shone red and hot on us like a pit of fire. We had to park two blocks away, there were so many cars, and making out in one of them were Frank Whitelaw and the girl on stage crew who curses like a sailor and can always fix the light board, fooling around. *Hello.* Frank "it just isn't working between us" Whitelaw, making it work with somebody else. Natasha and I had downed her whole flask on the way here, so we were already loud and obnoxious, weighted down with sheaves of loaves. When we came upon them I lifted my leg and kicked the window of the car, leaving a high-heeled footprint. Then we ran, looking back to see Frank and what's-her-name peering out the window. Her shirt was unbuttoned and it wasn't even seven-thirty yet.

The same Tin Can album was on in the house that had been on in the car. Lots of people were there already, but everyone was running around so it was hard to tell. V___ was on her knees in the front hall scrubbing something out of the carpet. Her face was red and tense but she was glad we had the baguettes. "In the kitchen," she said, gesturing off somewhere. We walked by a small bathroom decorated in wallpaper patterned to look like bookshelves and with a large framed portrait of Jennifer Rose Milton in it. Why would V___'s parents – wait a second. I gave Natasha the rest of the baguettes – she looked like one of those peasant women loaded with sticks – and doubled back to the bathroom. It was of course the real thing, not a portrait, crying already. It wasn't even seven-thirty yet.

"Oh, Flan," she said, and I shut the door behind us. The books loomed in close; the flask's gin was roaring up strong in my ears like a hair dryer. Jennifer Rose Milton had on a basic black dress and was holding one of those masks on a stick, but all that was shattered by her inelegant, coughy crying. "He's seeing somebody else," she said, leaning against the sink. The faucets were little golden swans which spat water when you turned them on, so I did. I hugged her, ducking down so her tears wouldn't land on my dress because I didn't know what it was made of and it might stain. "He's seeing somebody else," she said again, a little crossly as if I hadn't said the right thing and I realized that I hadn't said anything at all.

"There, there," I decided on.

"He said that things just weren't working out," she said, drooling, "but Cheryl just told me –"

"Who's Cheryl?"

"That *fat* girl," she spat, "who got drunk at Lily's cast party last year and threw up all over the yellow rug."

"Her name is Cheryl?"

"Yeees," she wailed, grabbing a tissue. The swans kept spitting. "She told me that Frank is seeing *Nancy Butler*. Can you believe it? Nancy Butler?"

I remembered Kate in the courtyard with me the other day, gathering her rosebuds while she could or however that goes. "I thought Kate already told you that."

"I didn't believe her," she said, sniffling. "I thought she was lying. I thought she was wrong. And she's *here*, of all the nerve. She's at the party, and she wasn't even *invited*."

"Jenn, of course Kate was invited."

"Not Kate, *Cheryl*. I mean, not Kate, *Nancy Butler*. She keeps wandering around asking where Frank is."

"Well," I said, "Frank is outside making out with somebody else in his car."

"Really?" she said, blowing her nose and looking at herself in the mirror. "You're just making that up," she decided, "to make me feel better."

"I wouldn't do that," I said, and I probably wouldn't. The books on the wallpaper had no discernible spines, like the people in the room. "He's outside now, in his car. Go see if you want."

"He doesn't even *have* a car," Jennifer Rose Milton said.

"Well, then it's *her* car."

"Whose?"

"I don't know her name. She's the one on stage crew who can always fix the light board and swears like –"

"That's Cheryl."

"This girl isn't fat," I said.

"The girl who can always fix the light board is Cheryl," she said emphatically.

"Well, then Cheryl isn't fat."

"But she is. People call her Fat Cheryl."

We both sputtered and laughed, loud. It bounced off the swans, the books, the smudgy mirror, the clock. It wasn't even eight yet and I was already laughing with somebody alone in the bathroom.

"How drunk *are* you?" I asked.

"Fat Cheryl," she repeated, and we both laughed again, loud. "Not as drunk as I would like to be," she said. She sat down on the closed toilet and put her feet up on the towel rack, smudging tiny matching towels I bet you weren't supposed to use if you lived here. "He's an awful person," she said meditatively. She stood her mask up on the towel rack and made it do a little puppet dance. We giggled and Adam opened the door.

"Has anybody seen Flan?" he said. He was wearing a tie and clutching a drink. Then he shut the door.

I blinked; Jennifer Rose Milton dropped the mask. I looked in the mirror and for a minute it looked like Natasha was facing me – I saw his mistake. "No, wait," I said, standing up. When had I sat down? "Wait," I said again. Jennifer Rose Milton turned off the swans and I opened the door and looked down the hallway. In one direction, nobody. In the other direction, a flashbulb.

"*Shit!*"

"Sorry, Kate," Flora Habstat giggled, and bounced down the hallway with her camera. "I'm taking pictures!" she crowed, and rounded the bend.

"I'm not Kate," I said, and this seemed important all of a sudden. "Jenn, I'm not Kate."

"You got that right," she said sloppily. She was pulling her hair back sharply and gazing at the mirror. She looked, suddenly, oddly like Lily. I rubbed my eyes and the real Lily almost stepped on me as she walked down the hallway.

"Flannery!" she said, and hugged me. Her smile was way too wide, and the music was suddenly turned *up* a notch. She pulled me out of the bathroom and down the hall; when I looked back Jennifer Rose Milton looked like decoration again.

"What we need," she said, pointing at me, "is food. I mean *a drink*."

The kitchen was wrecked. V___'s family had those copper pots hanging from a rack around the stove like torture devices, and somebody had pulled the rack out – or *half-out*, really, because it was hanging precariously from the ceiling with bits of plaster showering down like fairy dust. The pots had fallen long ago; they looked like dented relics on the kitchen floor. Gabriel was standing blankly in the middle of it looking like an astronaut who'd missed the last shuttle back to the mother ship. He had a clearly forgotten chef's hat lopsided on his head and was staring in awe at a mountain of pots and pans that were piled in the sink so that the sink itself seemed irretrievable and the entire counter – the whole side of the kitchen – appeared to be made of pots. Everywhere, something was dripping so the whole kitchen was making one big gurgling sound that echoed in my head. The kitchen table was stuffed with bottles of alcohol, full and empty; a punch bowl with sherbet and plastic cups floating in it. Empty beer bottles lined up like choirboys. Lots and lots of plastic cups, mostly overturned; a big bowl of melting ice. One tall cup was lazily drooling something bright red and syrupy onto the white carpet.

"Wow," I heard myself say. Gabriel turned around suddenly and gave me a big hug, his body sliding against my slippery dress.

"Where have you been?" he said.

275

"Sorry," I said. What time was the party supposed to start? It wasn't even eight yet. "How's the shindig?"

"This is the best party!" he sang out, waving one arm in the air. I followed the other one to a large glass of punch. Oh. Was *everybody* drunk?

"Is *everybody* drunk?" I asked, but the room started spinning just as I caught the self-righteousness in my own voice. "Including me," I added sheepishly, and when I closed my eyes I could hear Lily and Douglas laughing. Lily and *Gabriel*. I reached out an arm to steady myself and knocked over a small pile of logs, but when I opened my eyes I saw they were the baguettes. Gabriel handed me a glass of punch. "I brought these baguettes," I said, as I took a sip.

The punch was strong as death. One sip and the room spun again; I felt those three pieces of toast make a vague threat. Gabriel had his tongue in my mouth when a little skinny guy walked in.

"Is there any more Douglas?" he said.

"What?" Lily said.

"Punch?" he said.

Gabriel smiled. "Flannery, this is Rob," he said, putting his arm around the skinny guy.

"*Bob*," Rob corrected. *Bob.*

Gabriel leaned in to whisper to me. "Rob is the guy that Douglas, you know –"

"Wanted to invite?" I said.

Gabriel laughed. "Bob, do you want any punch?"

"*Rob*," Rob said.

What?

"Just kidding," Bob said. We all laughed, except Lily who hugged me suddenly and started to cry. I tried to keep her away from the dress but no dice. Gabriel was explaining something in detail to Bob, who sat down in a chair and was staring into space and nodding soberly.

"What's wrong?" I said to Lily, finally. How long had she been crying?

"Come outside," Lily said. We walked through another blaring hallway where Rachel State was performing a sweeping arm gesture to three other freshman girls, who were watching intently and trying to copy it.

"You're not doing it right," I said to them, and Rachel gave me a look of disgust. She was wearing a black leotard and looked like a mime. What was I talking about? "You're not doing it right, either," I said to her.

Rachel shrugged, and reached down to the carpet to pick up her bottle of beer. The music was turned up *another* notch. "*You* show them," she said.

"Come *on*, Flan," Lily said. I couldn't believe she was *still* crying. Behind me I heard Gabriel and Bob singing something, or maybe it was Twin Can. I blinked; Rachel and Co. were still staring at me.

"What do you guys *want*?" I asked them, taking another sip of – hold on! – the punch.

"Forget her," one of them said to Rachel. "She's drunk."

"Yeah, forget all about me!" I said to them. "Forget I ever existed!" What was I talking about?

"*Natasha!*" Lily whined. "*I'm upset!*"

Rachel and the girls giggled and squeezed past us into the living room. I wasn't ready to enter the living room yet. Where I wanted to go was –

"Let's go *outside*, Natasha!" Lily said. Then she blinked and looked at me. "Flan," she said, and burst into tears. Didn't this already happen? She led me to a glass sliding door and slid it open; I watched my reflection travel with it. We stepped outside. The air was cool and stingy. We sat on the stairs where I had comforted Kate just a few days ago. *Yesterday*. The garden was black except for some white ghost of a figure flitting around and some half-visible lawn chairs and croquet mallets – the red mallet in particular was in plain view. Lily was crying. Down a few steps, Nancy Butler was throwing up and it wasn't even eight-thirty yet. I put my arm around Lily and realized I was holding a baguette.

"There, there," I said, and started to giggle because Lily's shoulders were shaking and making the baguette wiggle in a jerking motion that looked like nothing but masturbation.

"Don't you laugh at me, Flan," she said, but started laughing herself. "Look at V——."

It was the white figure, V——, running around on the lawn picking things up, I couldn't tell what. She looked like a little bunny.

"What are you doing, Little Bunny?" I called, with both hands cupped around my mouth, so the baguette jerked around my lips like – well, like some other sex act. I took another sip of punch except the cup was empty. Somebody else's cup was sitting within arm's reach, though, so I switched them. No one ever knew that. "V——, what are you doing?"

"It's not V——," Lily said. "It's Kate."

"I'm not Kate," I remembered, and told Lily. "I'm not Kate."

"Of course you're not," she said. "You're Natasha. *Flan*. Kate's over there." She pointed at the white figure, who walked toward us and turned out to be V——, after all.

"I can't find the rest of the croquet set," she said crossly. "I'm missing balls."

"You don't say," Douglas said archly behind us, and Lily burst into tears. It was getting a little old, this bursting.

278

"What's wrong?" I asked. Douglas sat down next to me and Lily cried harder.

"She's still upset about us," Douglas said.

"But we broke up a long time ago," I said.

"Not *us*," he said, waving his wrist between us, "*us*." He waved his wrist between him and Lily.

"You've got to stop all that limp-wristed action," I giggled, leaning against him. He scowled, smiled, sipped punch from an empty cup.

"Where'd my cup go?"

"Forget about the cup," V___ said. "I can't find half the croquet balls, or the red mallet."

"The red mallet is right there," I said, pointing to it. Nancy Butler stood up and staggered back up the stairs wiping her mouth. When she slid open the door I distinctly heard Adam calling, "Flan?"

"I'm out here," I called, but somebody turned the music up and Nancy Butler shut the door. I stood up, felt the wind around my ears.

"Don't stand up, you're giving me a stiff neck," V___ said, sitting down. The four of us sat on the steps: V___, Lily, Douglas and me. I think that's right. The steps buzzed as the Thin Sham album beat the house into submission.

"This is a splendid party," I said, suddenly and politely to V___.

"Satan is going to kill me," she said.

"Take your soul for all eternity," Douglas said solemnly. We all giggled; Lily – you'll never guess what – burst into tears.

"Douglas, just tell me, once and for all, is it my fault?" Lily asked.

"Of course not," Douglas said. "It's not a *fault*, Lily. It's just –"

"It's his mom's fault," V___ said. "She's so bossy."

Somebody shrieked with laughter, sounded like Natasha.

"What are you laughing at?" Douglas said.

I kept laughing. "You have to admit, Douglas," I said, "she is *very bossy*."

"But that doesn't –" Douglas sputtered.

"I think it's my fault," Lily said quietly.

"Oh, come on," V___ said. "It does too, Douglas. If your mom had been normal – give me some of that bread, Flan – you'd still be going out with Lily."

"Going out with Lily is a sign of normalness?" I asked.

"No, no," V___ said. "Good bread."

"Basic Bakery."

"Well, thanks for bringing it, even if it was late. But I just mean that Douglas's bossy mother –"

"She's not bossy," Douglas said. "Where's Bob?"

"Oh, forget it," V___ said, pouting. "Come help me pick up croquet stuff, Flan."

"I'll go," Douglas said. He stood up and put a hand to his head.

I finished off my punch; it burned down my throat like lava. Lily leaned against me and I felt in her sobbing head the weight of the world.

"It was my fault," she said.

"There, there," I remembered. Was Jenn still in the bathroom?

"Just tell me, Natasha," Lily said. She broke away from me to look me straight in the eye. "Be honest with me."

"I will," I said, and waited for her question. Distantly, I could hear V___ and Douglas laughing on the black lawn, over the backbeat and the lead singer's devilish whine. The question didn't come.

"Just tell me, tell me," Lily said, raising her voice. She put her hands to her head like she didn't want to hear it. "I want to hear it, straight from you. Just tell me – I'm *fat*, aren't I?"

I looked at her thin frame, her wide eyes, and felt like I'd been punched in the stomach. The song ended and for a second there was just the chilly air and V___'s raw distant laughter, before another one began. "No," I whispered to her, but she probably didn't hear me over Bin Bang and the wind and her own heaving breathing. "No," I said. "Oh, Lily."

"He *said* so!" she yelled. The wind rose and drew her hair back sharply like an old movie star. "He *told me*, one time when we were fighting! He said *fat bitch!*"

"Douglas?" I said incredulously. In my head was how fragile he looked when he knocked on my door, all those hickey mornings. *Fat bitch?*

"Yes," she said, losing steam and blinking at me like I might hit her.

"He called you –"

"A *fat bitch*," she wailed, and sat down again, revealing Douglas coming up the stairs, looking wary and guilty. V___ was close behind, waving a croquet ball triumphantly; she'd still missed the red mallet.

"Hi," Douglas said. Lily looked at the ground.

"A fat bitch?" I asked, raising my eyebrows.

"We were fighting," he said. "I don't think I said that."

"A *fat*? *Bitch*?"

"I don't know," he said.

"Flan?" Adam called behind me, and still looking at Douglas I stood up and backed up the stairs into his arms. He held me warm and tight and we backed into the house while Douglas and Lily looked at each other and

V___ looked at the croquet ball like a gypsy fortune-teller. He shut the door.

Amazingly the hallway was empty. Adam's face was flushed and smiling, beautiful. His tie was askew, his teeth dazzling. I felt breathless, still revved up from anger and angst and gin, and my heart beat faster and faster like it does in love songs.

"I've been looking for you," he said, and gently took my hand. The music didn't seem so loud; it was like we were together in a magic phone booth, impenetrable and alone. Like wires were connecting us to an enormous universal network, like we were ringing.

"Hey," another call came in. Gabriel and Kate. Gabriel leaned in and actually *licked* my neck; I reached up and took the chef's hat off his head to at least erase *some* of the ridiculousness. "I've been looking for you," he murmured into me. Kate glared at Adam, then hooked her arm into mine as Gabriel kissed me again.

"More punch?" Gabriel said.

"Please," I said. "When did you get here, Kate?"

"I've *been* here," she said. "Where have *you* been?" She was looking at Adam like a ferret.

"Outside," I said. "Helping V___ find her croquet set and watching Nancy Butler throw up."

There was nothing like the thought of Nancy Butler vomiting, I guess, to break the ice. Everybody laughed.

"I'm going to go dance," Adam said, looking at me and – I wrote it so I'm typing it – getting me hot.

"I need some air," Kate said, and slid open the door. Douglas and Lily were screaming at each other. V___ walked in with her hands to her ears.

"Don't go out there," she said to Kate. "Come into the kitchen and help me clean up." Her dress dripped down her like melted wax. Gabriel rubbed up against me. "I can't find the rest of the croquet set, but fuck it."

Kate laughed louder than she wanted to, looking hurriedly at Adam out of the corner of her eye so he'd be sure and see what a great time she was having. "I think that will be easier tomorrow, when it's light outside," she said, and V⸺ nodded wisely.

"Also," V⸺ said brightly, "I'm missing an earring." I blinked and Kate was touching her bare lobe. *Kate* had said it.

Adam touched my shoulder and when I looked at him he was going the other way, down the hallway toward the music.

Gabriel, me and whoever else was there looked at one another. "More punch," we said in unison, and straggled down the hall.

The kitchen looked even worse this time around. The ceiling rack was hanging lower, more precariously, and somebody had tipped or thrown some of the pots off the counter onto the floor. Jennifer Rose Milton was sitting on the floor clutching an enormous bottle of vodka, nearly empty, crying hollow and hitting the bottle with a tiny clenched fist. Something about it looked ritualistic, like some corny Navajo ceremony in a voodoo movie. I raised my empty punch glass to her and she stuck her tongue out, then cried harder.

"Jesus, Jenn," Gabriel said, hurrying to her and trying to tug her up by one floppy arm. People were sitting on the floor crying and it wasn't even nine yet.

"I'm not getting up from this floor," Jennifer Rose Milton said, "until he says he's sorry."

"Sorry," Gabriel said.

"Not *you*," she said. "*Frank*. I'm not getting up until Frank says he's sorry."

"My parents will come home in a couple of days," V___ said seriously, measuring out punch. "You have to leave by then."

I laughed, then Gabriel did. Kate bit her lip and turned to me.

"What?" she said.

I wasn't sure. "I don't know," I said.

She blinked, staggered, held onto the table. V___ handed her a glass of punch and she sipped it, then grinned at me, with a drop of punch hanging on the end of her nose like a tiny red pearl. The moment was over, whatever it was. Then there was punch under *my* nose, and I grabbed it and drank.

Even stronger, now. It was like being bitten by a scarlet scorpion. Static energy grabbed my eyes and pulled my whole face inside out. It was so strong I squinted. The lights got turned *up*, more neon and white than ever. The music got weird in my ears for a second, bending like sirens do when cops drive by: first higher than normal; then, briefly, normal; then slowly sinking low. The world felt bright pink – I stretched my arms out wide and watched them slowly follow my instructions like reluctant Cub Scouts. What was I thinking? Where was I going? Then the liquor hit my stomach and I felt everything the scorpion had to offer: sting, spindly legs, poison, death. Outside lightning struck. I closed my eyes and with perfect clarity saw a parade of everyday objects: a spoon, a hamburger, a disembodied hand and Natasha's smirking face.

"Are you OK?" Gabriel asked me. I opened my eyes and saw his kind face, haloed by all the plaster dust and the broken rack, swinging slightly.

"Hello," I said, and he smiled.

"Are you OK?" he asked again.

"This punch is really strong," I said.

"Adam's a dick," Kate muttered. "What are all these baguettes doing here?"

"It's not even nine yet," I said. "You know who I haven't seen?"

"Trick-or-Treaters?" V___ said. "I'm surprised too. I mean, this party must be loud, but it can't be scaring *everybody* off. I bought a whole bowl of miniature Big Bars to give them."

"Miniature Big Bars?" Kate asked, and started to laugh. Too bad she'd just sipped; she coughed and spat punch on top of a stack of dirty steel bowls. The spat-up punch glimmered briefly, then just dripped and ran.

"Who haven't you seen?" Jenn asked. I wouldn't have thought she could follow along.

"Natasha," I said.

"You *are* Natasha," Jenn said dismissively. She took a sip from the vodka bottle and wiped her mouth on her hand, lipsticking the back of her hand.

"Pay no attention to her," Kate said. "She's drunk." I thought she was talking to me but when I turned to her she was facing Jennifer Rose Milton. Somehow V___ was sprawled on the ground and somehow I was sprawled next to her and somehow we were alone except for Jenn who was still hitting the bottle, in more ways than one.

V___ was out of punch and sipping rum from the bottle, coughing it up slightly each time she swallowed. I was doing the same thing. If we sat up we could swallow without coughing, but we couldn't sit up, so that was that. "If that rack falls," she giggled, "I am in *so* much trouble."

"You're already in so much trouble," I said, swigging. "Look at all those pots, V___." Jenn started to cry again.

"But that rack is the straw that will break the camel's back," V___ said. "I should really make another batch of punch."

"But I just made the kids lunch and I'm so *damn tired*," I said, from nowhere. What was I talking about? "We are never going to get this mess cleaned up tomorrow, V___."

"We might," she said, holding up an arm so she could read her watch. "It's not even nine-thirty yet."

Suddenly Adam was towering over us like a giant flamingo. "What are you guys up to?" he said.

"I can see right up your nose," V___ said confidently. Jenn giggled but kept crying.

"We're looking at the constellations," I said, inspired. "Come sit with us."

"Yeah, what do you think that looks like?" V___ said, pointing to the swinging rack.

"Move over," Adam said. He was really lying down next to me. My whole body buzzed like a microwave, except that microwaves don't buzz and my body doesn't plug in and make baked potatoes in ten minutes. What was I talking about?

"I would say that looks like a disaster," Adam said.

V___ giggled and sat up. "Come on, Jenn," she said. "Let's go try on my mommy's makeup."

"I'm not moving," Jennifer Rose Milton said firmly.

"I think we should leave Kate and Adam alone," V___ said, trying to grab Jenn's arms.

"I'm not moving."

"*Get the hell out of here*," Adam said tersely. Somehow we were lying down in a doorway, our heads on stained carpet and our legs on sticky floor. Somehow we were alone. Somehow the music was still loud and still that band, whatever-the-hell-it's-called; the beat was making the rack swing like a pendulum. Somehow Adam and I were talking about something: theater, I think. The line between audience and actor. I felt something warm on my neck, thrilling me. I kept talking about whether Halloween was a form of theater, if parties were a form of theater, if Adam kissing me meant I should get up and leave but it felt so nice, kissing me over and over on the same spot on my neck. It burned delicious like being branded, but as he ran his hand down my dress it turned out I wasn't a cow at all. That's what turned me on, as much as him kissing me: feeling my own body, thin and gorgeous against him like a celebrity. *Thin*, even. It was probably Natasha's dress that made me feel this way, but so many people thought I was Natasha it didn't matter. My body was thin against him as his hand moved on my skin under the dress, my own ready body. I couldn't stand it and opened my eyes; the rack was swinging above us like a grandfather clock and one warm finger curled inside me. I tasted my own rum-punch breath as I gasped out loud. He took my hand gently like we were walking on the beach in a billboard but led it to his pants, his own straining skin. His hand on my hand on him, rubbing, and my own dress lifting up along my hips. His damp finger excited me, then went deeper and I felt him moan against that same spot on my neck. My head was on the white carpet, probably ruined forever – Satan was going to kill V___ – but when my hips heaved, I felt under them, with the dress pulled up, the cold truth of expensive linoleum. Which is when Steve Nervo walked in and Adam pulled his finger out of me so quickly I felt a nail, sharp like a splinter. I exhaled; Adam sighed and shivered. I tugged my dress down and Adam and I pretended that we were just lying on the floor together in a doorway, looking at constellations or something.

"Hey," Adam said weakly in a hoarse voice. I held my hand up to that same spot on my neck to cover it. Where was Douglas when I really needed him?

Steve Nervo was nodding sagely, the lights's reflection on his black leather jacket wavering as the rack swung above his head like a circling vulture. He was drunk, I realized suddenly, so was I.

"Hey Adam, hey Natasha," he said, and leaned against the counter unsteadily. From behind him emerged a tiny little girl, leprechaun-thin and makeup-heavy. Who was she? She took his hand, oh –

"You must be that tambourine player everyone's talked about," I said, sitting up, thinking better of it and lying down again. I brushed up against the baguette that I couldn't seem to leave behind.

"Who?" Adam asked.

I gestured toward her, but she had already turned her back and was making out with Steve Nervo. Lip-locked, they were edging closer and closer to a precarious mountain of pots. "She's the one Steve dumped V__ for. She's joined Steve's band, on *tambourine*." I heard myself cackling uglily. "We're all very proud of her. *Wait a minute*," I said. "You're not invited to this party, Steve."

Steve stopped for a second and wiped his mouth. "It's a cast party," he said, and the girl looked at me smugly. I saw, suddenly, V__'s fragile face at the Malleria Worldwide Food Court. He was evil. We had crossed Steve Nervo's name off the guest list with much ceremony. I used the baguette like a crutch to help me stand up. Steve and Tambourine were kissing again.

"Hey," I said, and if I were rewriting this journal rather than merely occasionally editing it I would say: "in a drunken snarl." "Hey," I said, *in a drunken snarl*. "You were not invited to this party."

"Shut up," the girl said, and I hit her with the baguette, straight across the face. Unfortunately I kept swinging and the air was filled with the cacophony of falling pots.

"You *bitch*," the girl said, clutching her reddening cheek. Her eyes, and her eye shadow, blazed. I felt all-powerful in the red streak dress. I hit her again with the baguette.

"You *fat bitch*," Steve Nervo said, and lunged at me. I stepped back and tripped on Adam's legs, falling heavily on top of him. Only in a life going as horribly wrong as my own would Kate and V___ walk in at this time.

V___ started crying but suddenly just turned it off. Her face turned to rum-punch rage. "Get out of my house!" she screamed to Steve, who started to laugh.

"Oooh, I'm scared," he said in a high-pitched voice, and Ms. Tambourine laughed and kissed his neck and V___ stepped forward and in one swift arm motion swept the rest of the pots clattering to the floor. My head pounded and I felt a sharp pain in my thigh; Natasha's nail file was clawing my leg through the pocket.

"Get out of my house!" V___ said, breathing hard. Steve blinked and looked at her; the loud pots had startled the laughter out of him. Even the girl looked wary. "*Get out of my house fucking unthrilled man from hell!*" Bob and Douglas were standing in the doorway and began applauding and cheering; I saw that Douglas was holding a rum bottle. Rachel State and some other people I didn't know appeared in the other doorway, and with much applause Steve Nervo and his percussionist left V___'s Halloween garden party. The drunk crowds dispersed as drunk crowds do and it was just V___, crying again and picking up pots, and Kate and me and Adam and awkward.

"Now," Kate said, squinting, "may I ask."

"I don't have to answer to you," Adam said, instantly and harshly. He brushed his pants off like he'd just buried his mother. "Why can't you get it, Kate? It's over between us. *Jesus*."

"I can't believe this." Kate put her hands on her hips and threw back her hair. There was a blinding flash of light; Flora Habstat had taken another photo and whooped off.

"I can't believe this *either*," V___ said in a long high wail. She was holding up two broken pieces of a glass casserole dish like cymbals in the symphony.

"Look –" Kate said, and grabbed Adam by the shoulder. "Look –" Her voice was toggling somewhere between steadfast fury and embarrassing, whiny desperation. "Look –"

He looked at his shoulder like there was a dead mouse on it. It skittered off – it wasn't dead. Like my love for him.

She blinked; I felt shame in my stomach. "Look –"

"Just *shut up!*" he said. "You –"

"*Fat bitch?*" I finished for him. I raised the baguette up high –

Sorry, not yet.

– but he was smirking offstage. Kate was left looking at me with her hands open in a needy shrug. I looked right into her teary gaze and realized I'd just called her a fat bitch. The music pounded.

"I didn't –" I said to her, but she was already crying, shaking. Shaking. I went to hug her and she shook me off, shoved me right to the wall, wailing primal and loud. V___ dropped the casserole dish and put her hands to her head.

"How *could you!*" Kate screamed. "*How could you how could you how could you –*"

"It wasn't –"

With a squawk the music was off and a great roar rose from the living room. Kate and I looked at each other, and I felt, gloriously, the prospect of missing hot gossip rise up in her head and quench her fury, at least distract it. We both raced to the living room.

I realized I hadn't been there yet, for the whole party, and like a resort in off-season, this probably wasn't the best time. An enormous wooden table which had held the food had been turned on its side like people were making a fort. Plates and dips and who knows what else were ground into the carpet and Gabriel was kneeling on the ground picking up shards of something and dropping them into the gentle cup of his hand. Some blob of creamy something – salmon mousse, I think, it was sort of skin-toned – was perched on his face like he was about to apply whiteface. Douglas and Bob were sitting on the floor with a bottle between them; Douglas looked happy and Bob looked green. There were at least eighteen people in the room I didn't know, or knew barely – I think the sophomore with curly red hair was Debbie something or other – Frank Whitelaw was standing in the middle of the room like a wobbly Maypole, looking warily at a small whirlpool of bright cloth and arms next to him. Nancy Butler and Cheryl and Jennifer Rose Milton – *Jennifer Rose Milton* – were in a full-out knock-down drag-out fight in V___'s living room.

I caught a glimpse at Kate's face. *Jenn Milton. Fistfight.* V___'s living room. She was – *rapt.* Delighted almost to the point of sobriety.

Cheryl appeared to be winning – if in fact Cheryl was the one who could always fix the light board and cursed like a –

"Fucking cunt!"

Cheryl appeared to be winning, pulling Jenn to the ground by her hair and punching – actually *punching*, I don't think I had ever seen an actual *punch* in real life until jail – Nancy Butler right in the mouth. Nancy was screaming, but Jenn looked intense, like she was taking a final.

"Somebody turn the hose on them!" Douglas shouted, and everyone laughed. *Douglas* said that? I looked again; it was Bob. Something Nancy was wearing in her hair suddenly sprang out like a flying squirrel and hit Lily in the face just as she entered the room.

"*Natasha!*" she wailed and ran to me, sobbing into my waist. I took her cup of punch and downed it – felt the red roar of alcohol fill the void where the music had been. Her sobs shook my stomach like a bad meal. I was going to throw up soon. For the first time in my life I felt literally *blasted* – each cell electrically humming like the white heat of rocket ignition. I'd never been drunker. Blinking, I looked around the room and suddenly Adam's face was huge in front of me like I had arrived late for the movie and had to sit in the front row. He shone so bright I had to shield my eyes; he reached out and touched that spot on my neck. Lily slid down my body to the floor like a leaky balloon of drunk sobbing mess. "I'll be upstairs," Adam whispered to me, breathing. "If you want."

If I *want* – he was gone.

"*What did he say? What did he say?*" Kate screamed at me, so loud that several people looked over from the fight.

I took her hand, she slapped it away, I took her hand, she shook it off but I had learned, and held on. "He said he was sorry," I said.

"Natasha –" she said, and swallowed. "*Flan –*"

"He said he was sorry," I said again, forcing my voice into quiet resignation. How soon would Kate be distracted, so I could slip upstairs? I felt his finger inside me. I hadn't had the breathless sex gasping of fooling around on some parent's bed at a party since Jim Hadley, after that mystery play we did where I got killed in the second act. "He was sorry, and I'm sorry, too." Preapologizing. I looked at Gabriel, who was staring at his handful of shards with drunken Zen concentration. I'm sorry, everybody. Have to follow my heart.

Kate was looking at me, deciding whether she'd gamble on belief or not, when the whole living room shouted. We hadn't been paying attention to the fight, so I don't know how it happened, but Jenn grabbed Cheryl's leg and she fell to the ground. Jenn stood up and Nancy fell down, and then with horrid accuracy, Jennifer Rose Milton kicked Cheryl, then Nancy, each in the face, one with each foot. The girls screamed and held their mouths; in perfect sync blood ran between the fingers of their hands like choreographed scarlet floods. Jenn stepped back, clearly the winner. Even Bob clapped. Frank was looking at her in slow horror-anger.

"What did you *do*?" he asked.

Jennifer Rose Milton blinked for a minute like she too was just realizing that prim Jenn-Jenn, daughter of the coolest French teacher in the world, gorgeous and thin and gentle and thin, had just kicked two women in the face like one of those dizzying arcade games. But then she toughened right up.

"How *dare* you," Frank snarled. "It's *over* between us, Jenn, can't you face that?"

"Fuck you," she said calmly. "Get out of this house. You weren't invited to this party anyway."

"You *fat bitch*!" he said, and the party gasped like a Greek chorus.

"Get out!" she said. Cheryl was trying to stand up, bleeding on the rug. I realized I was still holding the baguette, though it was half-eaten and doubled over like a dying flower. I guess the Basic Bakery doesn't design its loaves to withstand battle.

"*No*," Frank said, and took a step toward Jenn. Nancy tried to stand up and Cheryl slapped her down. Jenn blinked and looked scared; Frank was dumb but tall and had stage crew arms. The party was getting more and more ugly. Behind me I could hear somebody throwing up.

Douglas stood up. "Frank –" *Bam*, Douglas was down. Below me, Lily screamed. Slapstick violence, that's what comes from watching too much TV. Gabriel was watching Frank closely but wasn't going to do anything. Nobody was going to do anything. Mr. Baker, no one listens to you. We are a nation of children letting horrible things happen, and flunking Calc. Frank raised a hand. It felt so literal: Frank *raising a hand* to her. She screamed and – although you'd think there was enough drama 'round these parts without a drama *teacher* – that's when Ron Piper entered the room.

Never had teacher supervision been so appreciated. He looked around the room, took in the overturned table, all the liquor, Rachel State slouched in a corner with her eyes closed and her mouth open. "Oh," he said. He was in a black turtleneck and had on a purple beaded mask I think we used for that French play we did sophomore year. "Hello, everybody," he said.

"*Ron!*" V___ said, from nowhere. Her hand went up to straighten her hair; Satan was doing something right. "I thought you would *never* come."

"It looks like this party is, well, a little –"

"*Nonsense*," she crowed. "Just a little charades getting out of hand. Some people were just leaving," she said, smiling directly at Nancy Butler who was already yanking her coat out from under the table, "but the party is still in full swing. Come in, come in. Love your mask. Is that from that French thing we did –"

"What's going on?" Ron said simply, not amused. Cheryl was wiping blood off her mouth with a little cocktail napkin already dripping mustard. "Is everyone OK?"

Not that there would have been an opportune time, but that's when Lily threw up, a tidy little pile on the floor. Even V____'s smile faltered and everyone waited while the room spun around my head again like one of those propeller beanies. It was a toss-up what Ron would do; he was a cool teacher, but he was a *teacher*. Millie would have burned us alive. Or, come to think of it, she may have merely stood there in shock after seeing her daughter kick two other girls in the face like some television ninja. With Ron, though, who would know?

Incidentally, Ron, if you are reading this, I'm so sorry that everybody burned down your house and stuff.

Ron looked at Lily on the floor and then knelt down to help her up. He didn't know her very well – she was never in the plays, but sometimes did makeup – but he took out a purple handkerchief and wiped her mouth. She leaned on him and wailed, her face bright red like a baby with that sickness thing that makes you cry all the time. Cholera?

"Oh dear," V____ tried. "Lily hasn't looked well all evening. A touch of the flu, I'm afraid."

"I wasn't born yesterday, V____," Ron said. "None of you guys are of age. I just thought this was going to be a garden party. All of you, Douglas, Bob" – how did he know Bob? Or do gay people just sort of *sense* one another? – "V____, Kate, Natasha."

"Flannery," I said.

"*All* of you should be ashamed of yourselves."

"We are," Nancy Butler said quickly. She had her purse and Frank had his car keys out; some people move like lightning when they're busted. "Good-bye."

Ron uprighted a chair and put Lily in it. "Now, I think –"

Flora Habstat ran in. She had a shower curtain draped over her like a cape. "Ta da!" she sang, and snapped several pictures all in succession: the corner of the room where Rachel was sitting, Douglas and Bob helping Gabriel pick up potato chips and Ron leaning over Lily and glaring at her. Flash, flash, flash. By the third flash Ron's face looked more careful, wary even. You could read it like a journal; he was slowly figuring out he had to save himself first. It wasn't a good idea for a teacher to be at this party. "You know," he said, but Flora cut him off with another "Ta da!" and ran out of the room shrieking. Flora was really coming into her own tonight.

"You know," Ron said again but I was already halfway out the room. I climbed the stairs two by two, Kate's face clearly in my mind: looking at Ron, a little scared, staring at Lily in pure gossipy satisfaction. She'd forgotten about me for the moment. I could slip away. My whole body flushed redder and warmer with each step, so that by the time I reached the top of the opulent staircase I was quite literally trembling with desire. That's the only way to put it. Look back through this book, reader. Hold your place with your finger and shut it; then reopen it and let your fingers fall to rest on the first day, another holiday: Labor Day. All this time I've been in labor, and it was all coming to fruition here on Halloween. It wasn't the right thing to do, but dammit, it was senior year. Soon I'd be off to college and adulthood. I'd never have this kind of freedom again. "I'll be upstairs," he'd said, "if you want," and I did want. "I'll *do* something, I'll *do* something," I kept saying to myself, flinging open the wrong doors: linen closets, a bare bathroom with mirrored cabinets gaping open. I'll do something, five stage crew people sitting in a circle smoking pot. I'll do something, I'll do something, I'll do something. This must be the right door. I pulled it open toward me, it banged my hip and the claw-hand nail file poked into my leg again. The room was dark but the door let light in, and for a minute it was something unimaginable, absurd: a sheet flapping in the breeze. *Never in a million years*, I thought, *does Satan string her laundry up in a spare bedroom*, before I realized it was the back of some girl, sliding up and down on top of Adam.

My last mouthful of punch spat out my mouth, jumping onto the carpet and shining there like a baby oyster. The girl turned around, but it was too dark to see. Had there been some other flight of stairs, some back way? Had Kate beaten me to it again?

"Kate?" I asked, and I heard Adam laugh, drunk and loud. I felt a chill come from under the ground, through the foundation of the house, up through the damp basement where Satan keeps her wine, through the door frame I was leaning on, to my gripping fingertips and with an easy rush through my whole body, stock-cold. I felt like a blue corpse, denied resurrection at the last cruel moment. What did the world want from me? *"Kate!"* I screamed, and then I felt Kate's hand on my shoulder. She was standing behind me. Our eyes met and I felt high school sisterhood, strong as oak, giving my shaking chilly body some sustenance. She reached past me and pulled the door open farther. In the stripe of light was all the evidence that ever should have been considered in this dire case, in these unfortunate circumstances, in this crime for our times: Adam's jeans, lying spent like shed skin. Some girl's shoe, a bra. Adam's button-down shirt, unbuttoned, the tie unraveled but still tunneled through

the collar. The torn square of a condom package, blank in the dark like a sugar cube stomped flat. And hurriedly discarded, gory with stretched-out buttonholes and ugly horizontal stripes: *a sweater-vest*. A sweater-vest. I must have made some noise in my throat because Shannon, still astride my victim, turned around like a predator was nearby. I felt my fingernails sink into the baguette, crumbs slipping into my fingernails brittle as balsa.

A long wild wail rose up. It sounded like the calls of mourning animals on public television, when one of their own goes down. When Mrs. State cried on television, the stoic Mr. State putting one quiet arm on her shoulder, the sound was theatrical, self-conscious. This was *real* grief, the real thing. When I turned around Kate's face was fire-engine red and her throat was way past crying. Her hands were clasped around her ears almost tenderly, sheltering them like orphans from the terrible sound. Shannon took one hand from her breasts and covered her mouth in horror, leaving her chest bare and vulnerable. The geometric beam of the open door into the room made me feel like I had X-ray vision; I swear that I could see her veins, her blood, red and alive, her whole breast cleaved like a melon under my exact medical gaze. I could see where it would hurt her most, little Shannon covering her mouth in horror.

The man under her shifted; Shannon fell mercilessly off him, *plonk*. Her hand uncovered her mouth and I saw that she was covering *laughter*. It wasn't horror at all, not yet. What more had I guessed wrong? I mean: *incorrectly*?

Adam was standing up, covering himself with a comforter swimming with some polite print. I think this was a guest room. The comforter spread below him like a thick ugly skirt, muttering against the carpet as he dragged it with him. His face was flushed, and in the sharp light from the corridor I could see drops of sweat on his bare chest, magnetic even now. He was grinning but his eyes were clear and angry as empty bottles. I could see, written all over his face, the straining dissatisfaction of interrupted sex. It's a look of craftiness, underneath anything they're saying about respect or fun or hang-ups or whatever else they can devise. Beneath that surface they're figuring out if the coast is clear so they can stop all this talk and just *get laid*.

Self-righteous indignation wouldn't have been the path I'd have chosen, but then again I didn't have a straining damp erection hidden behind clumps of bedding. "Shut the door!" he said, trying to sound merely embarrassed but looking at Kate and me like Federal Protection was our last hope. "Will you *shut the door*?" Obviously a rhetorical question; he was already shutting it himself. His rumpled head was in front of me for a moment. I raised the baguette –

Surely you didn't believe *that*, even for a moment. What did I just say: "I guess the Basic Bakery doesn't design its loaves to withstand battle." We only had a glimmer of his – what did I write? – rumpled head before the door slammed shut.

I looked at Kate again; her eyes were widening and white milky drool was dribbling down her chin. *"Adam!"* she screamed, and threw herself over me to try to pound on the door. Amazingly, I caught both her arms, one in each hand, and backed her away from the door like some wooden folk dance. *"Adam!"* she screamed again, and I looked back at the unapologetic door. Was he at it again, just thrusting away with all this raw noise outside the bedroom?

Kate sobbed against me all the way down the stairs, and when I reached the bottom I saw Ron Piper, one hand on the front door and watching me closely. I tried to smile weakly at him, so it would look like things were in control, just one of Kate's tantrums, you know, but when my lips curled up I tasted salt on them and knew I must look almost as bad as her. Ron gave a half-shrug at me and opened the door; cool air gaped out.

"Ron –" I said.

"I shouldn't be here," Ron said apologetically. "I mean, you kids can do what you want, I guess. I've never been to one of your cast parties, but I never knew it – well, I shouldn't be here. Don't worry, I won't say anything, but I'm not going to stay, either," he said. He was nervous. "Don't worry," he said, smiling razor-thin. Not nervous; *scared*. "I'm leaving." He could have thrown *everybody* out. He was a teacher. I slumped down and Kate fell to the floor.

The front door shut heavily, in exact sync with the music blaring back on again, only this time it was Darling Mud, "on and on and on." Kate was still wailing, maybe; it was hard to tell over the lead guitar. Her feet were kicking at the ground erratically and weakly in a halfhearted fit. I closed my eyes and leaned against the door frame of a bathroom, but the sound all went underwater and I couldn't see anything and I thought I would drown in the blurry roar, gelatinously thick and dark blue as Kate's stolen sweater. I heard something gurgling behind me. I turned and looked into the bathroom; skinny little Bob was vomiting into the sink. It was dripping everywhere, and Bob's throat was making horrible sounds; he reached out a hand to steady himself and smeared vomit on the bookshelf wallpaper. I followed some leaping cosmetics to Lily, leaning against the bathtub with a bathroom drawer she had obviously torn out from under the sink. She was swearing at Bob and throwing the contents of the drawer at his head, never hitting him. A shampoo bottle broke against the toilet, and my stomach reeled at the sight of the slow slither of the golden gel, down the porcelain to Lily's bleeding knee.

I lurched back into the kitchen, with the rack still swinging from the ceiling like a drunken ape. Rachel State was passed out in the corner, and her two drunk cohorts were trying to stand her up, one grabbing each arm. For no reason I whacked one of them on the back of the leg with the baguette; her knees buckled and Rachel's arm went down. Pain for the whole fucking family, I don't care. The whole liquor table was moving slowly like a fetid pond; everything, *everything* had spilled. The roar of water was competing with the music; I looked back at the brimming sink and saw that the faucet was on, the water puddling into all the fallen pots. Soon it would overflow.

Another bathroom, another vomiter; I walked by just listening to the straining stomach, the desperate throat, the limp mouth. In the living room the table had been uprighted but there was still food all over chairs and sofas and *walls*. There were still maybe thirty people in the living room and it wasn't even whatever-the-hell time it was; in one stained and soaking love seat Jennifer Rose Milton was dark with scorn, yelling at Gabriel who looked small and scared. "Ugh!" Jenn spat, a little roar of frustration. She was telling him something he wouldn't believe. Gabriel saw me and lit up like Christmas except I'm Jewish and don't celebrate Christmas. To me it's just somebody's birthday.

I muttered something at him, and he reached out his arm for me for reassurance. Jenn slapped his arm down and he glared at her and lifted it back up.

"I love you –" he said, and when I opened my eyes all his hands were reaching toward me, blurring like a school of squid, a calamari embrace. I covered my mouth in horror and found that I was laughing. "Flan –" he called, but I couldn't hear him because somebody had turned the music up, on and on and on. Across the room two people I didn't know were getting into another fight and I felt the whole house rising up in desperation, like a bubble straining to pop, to break away from that little plastic wand you blow them out of. *Out of which you blow them*, I corrected myself, as one of them slapped the other one in a blast of white light. Flora Habstat was on the floor, taking pictures of the fight from below and cackling shrilly, cracking my ears open. The room was hot and loud. Jenn was yelling at Gabriel again. "Douglas," somebody said, but it was Douglas and he was looking at me. "Kate's looking for you. *Natasha*."

"What?" I said, stepping up to him. "What?" His eyes goggled; his head bobbed. "*What*? Kate's looking for me? Natasha's looking for me? Kate's looking for – *I'm* looking for Natasha? What?"

"Gabriel's mad at you," he said, and then fell immediately to his knees like he was proposing. A streak of something was on his forehead. "Did Ron leave?" he asked, and I looked at his face, a large question mark. He was trying to think of the right thing to say, straining for it like it was up on a cupboard, out of reach. Put there for his protection, like poison for a child who *wanted* poison nonetheless. He was crying. "Flan –" he said, and the music was turned up one more notch, loud enough so that people could scream above it and never be heard.

Outside it was so dark I stepped into the blackness out of sheer faith and promptly stumbled over V____, sitting on the stairs. The air was stark cold, like, I'm running out of metaphors, ice. I sat down next to her, the air rustling my dress. V___ was crying.

"Natasha," she said, "he wasn't *invited*. He wasn't *invited*." She looked up and then covered her mouth in what had better have been horror. "I'm sorry," she said. "You're *Flannery*."

It was an insult; it was *true*, but it sounded like an insult, like V___ never would have told me these things, only the person who really wore the dress. "*What*?" I said. It was an accusation. "Oh, Flan," she said. She looked at me and wiped her eyes so hard I thought they'd come off, or at least be a different color when they emerged. "What's happened?" It was too dark to tell. "What's happening to *all of us*?" She swallowed and found a thin layer of control. "Wow," she said. "I sure am drunk, aren't I?" She tried smiling – classic overconfidence. The ice broke and, crying, she fell in. I patted her absently, but my whole body had been leadening since I'd sat down. I needed to lean against something, so I scooted along the stair, away from V___, until I was at the end and able to lean against a wrought-iron banister, with prickly shrub arms poking at me like the nail file, still clawing away in my pocket. Safe in shrub shade, I was invisible and cold but had a perfect view of the glass door, now sliding open as V___ sobbed. As it opened I could hear Jenn yelling, Flora laughing and Kate's raw wail starting up again, but it was Adam who emerged from the crazy house. His shirt was half tucked in and half tucked out. Somebody behind him was reaching their bare white arm out like something trying to sneak across the highway.

"*Adam!*" the arm cried, and I saw it was Shannon, still without the sweater-vest which was probably still crumpled at the scene of the crime. At the side of her face, presented to me in the glaring leak of living-room light, was a small scab, open and bleeding thinly down her face. From a fingernail, maybe.

Adam didn't see me. He bounded unsteadily down the stairs to V___ and put a hand on her shoulder both to rouse her and to steady himself. She woke up. "I'm leaving," he said pleasantly. "I wanted you to know, and thank you for a – thank you for the party."

Incredibly, V___ found her hostess persona, stumbling around her blasted mind. "Thank you for coming," she said, wiping her hands on her legs. "I'm glad you had a nice time. Let me show you out."

"*Adam!*" Shannon said again, but her own thin arm was sliding the door shut. With a click the party was muted.

"No, that's OK," Adam said easily, gesturing out to the garden. "I've found that I can get all the way home and never set foot on a sidewalk, just sneak through everyone's gardens. It's just six blocks. I'll go this way. The perfect way to end a garden party."

V___ was half thawed by the charm of the State. "Oh," she said. "How, um, nice. Are you sure?"

He kissed the top of her head, primly, like any guest. "Positive."

"Watch for that big black dog two yards over," she said.

He chuckled and stepped down one stair. "We have an understanding," he said. "Two of a kind, as it were."

V___ snorted indelicately and rolled her head back; her pearl necklace broke suddenly and all the pearls rolled down the stairs cooing like freed birds. V___ blinked at them; I can't even *imagine* what a drunken sight that was, in the full light of the house; all the pearls bouncing down stairs, family heirlooms lost forever in the Halloween dark. V___'s eyes got wider and wider and I left her poor brain debating between tears and sleep before she finally leaned back, right there on the sharp steps, opened her mouth and left the party.

I shook my head to clear it – *ha*! my head responded – and saw Adam's fading shirt, bobbing up and down as he walked through the garden. The sight mocked me, like in movies when the smug arsonist walks unnoticed through the billowing smoke, or the robber steps neatly into the getaway car while bungling police look up and down the street, never noticing the culprit. Adam was walking away from a house racked with all he had wrought, flitting darkly through the air as indifferent to accountability as a swarm of locusts. Somebody should *do* something; why wasn't anybody *doing* anything? Where was Natasha when everybody, *everybody* needed her? My eye fell to a pearl, spinning below me to some mad physic dance, its radius and behavior completely indecipherable to anybody who didn't have the formula.

Calculus. Baker's Rule. If Natasha wasn't here, if V___ was going to snore on the steps like a drugged-out watchdog, if no one anywhere was going to punish the guilty, *I* could do something. I could act for myself, push myself to the limit academically, athletically and socially.

I stood up and walked out there. I was trying to use the baguette as sort of a walking stick as I stumbled on bumps in the wet grass, but the bread was bent and damp and snapped right in two after only a few steps. I reached out for something else and found it: the red croquet mallet, just occurring there on the ground like some easy device, some plot element stashed there for the big moment. And this was it.

Although I was sure we were invisible from the house, the light of the party traveled farther than I'd thought, and after taking a minute to get used to the new dim I could see him clearly, walking steadily toward the tall trees and humming. Humming, even, he was so carefree, I couldn't believe it, although I must have been making some kind of noise too, because he turned around and craned his neck to figure out who I was.

"Who's there?" he said like a security guard. "Kate?" Then, more warily, "Natasha?"

I just walked toward him. It didn't matter who I was.

"Oh," he said, losing interest. "It's you, Flannery. What do you want?"

"Nothing," I said, "from *you*."

"Oh, *right*," he said, sarcastic in that loud tacky way everybody else stopped doing in sixth grade. The rum punch was getting geometrically sharp in my head, its corners piercing my head in distinct places, like ice crystallizing.

"Adam –" I said.

"Right," he said. "That's my name. Good *night*, Flan. Go back to the party." He started to turn around again but I grabbed his arm. He jerked it off and looked at me in scorn. "Don't *touch* me," he said. "Good *night*."

"*How could you*?" I said. "*How could you*? Did you see what you *did*?"

"Look," he said impatiently, "I'm *sorry*." He shrugged and smiled a small smile, sharp around the edges like my headache. "You probably won't believe this, but I thought it was *you* at first there upstairs, but, you know" – he started to laugh, then coughed. "Everybody makes mistakes. Now, if you'll excuse me –"

"I'm not talking about what you did to *me*!" I said. I don't know why I lied to him like that. "I mean how could you do that to *Kate*!"

"To *Kate*?" he said, laughing again, louder. *Whooping*.

306

"That's a good one, Flan. What I did to *Kate*? Why, I seem to recall that *you* were more than perfectly willing to do it with *me*!"

"*That's not true,*" I said. My head roared, sheer lioness rage. "*That's not true.*"

"Oh, it isn't?" Adam asked, wide-eyed. "Then why did you come upstairs in the first place? Fresh air?"

"Shut up."

"Look, you know it's true. We were *both* screwing Kate over, *both* of us. Not to mention *Gabriel*," he said. "At least Kate and I had broken up. You and *Gabriel* –"

"*Shut up!*"

He laughed, leaning back with his hands on his hips, presenting himself clearly in the half-light. He was drunk and I was going to kill him. We had reached the trees. Adam swayed unevenly, his face alternately flickering from the shade to the distant light of the party: dark, light, dark, light, a slow strobe. "Just face it, Flan. You're as bad as me. '*How could you?*'" he said, imitating me in a high screechy voice I'd heard coming from myself so many times, always hoping no one else had noticed. "'*How could you?*' How could *you* say that, Flan, considering what you're doing to Gabriel?"

"Shut up about Gabriel," I said. "He's *twice* the person you or Shannon or any of you will ever be! *Three* times!"

"Why is that?" Adam said. I saw his eyes roll at me for what would be the last time. "Because *Gabriel* is part of the precious Basic Eight?"

"*Shut up!*"

But he was on a roll. "Who will be invited to the next dinner party?" he asked in my voice. "Well, the *Basic Eight* of course –"

"*Shut up!*"

"But will we invite *Adam*? Is Adam *one of us*? Oh, I don't know."

"That's right," I spat, "you *don't* know. You'll *never* know. You're not going to be invited to the *corner store* with any of us –"

"*What punishment!*" He laughed. "I won't survive! What will you do to me next, hit me with that baguette you've been lugging around all night like a substitute *dick*?"

Dark, light, dark, light. His face looked so scornful, so savage, and finally, gloriously, *ugly*. Not cute at all, not attractive, just an ugly scornful boy face. I hadn't felt such disgust for a boy since the early days, when they'd tease girls on the playground, kicking us and throwing gravel and raising their voices in high screechy mockery. "They do that because they like you," all the adults said, grinning like pumpkins. We believed them, back then. Back then we thought it was true, and we were drawn toward all that meanness because it meant we were special, let them kick us, let them like us. We liked them back. But now it was turning out that our first instincts were right. Boys weren't mean because they liked you; it was because they were *mean*. This Halloween, we knew better. Everything was different this Halloween. This Halloween, nothing was drawing me toward him except this glorious headache of anger, the sheer agile ease of Natasha's dress against my skin and the heavy wood of the croquet mallet in my hands, ready and obedient. Dark, light, dark, light, dark – I swung and missed.

"*Adam!*" I screamed, and heard all the screams backing me up: Kate, Shannon, all my friends, Natasha screaming in my ear. "*Do something!*"

Adam was still laughing. "This doesn't sound like the kind of talk from a girl who sent me that lovely *postcard!*"

I stopped, staggered, reeling in his sheer dishonesty even now. "You got my postcard?" I said. "You said you never –"

"I was *lying*," he said to me, like it was the easiest thing in the world. He sounded like an exasperated teacher, perhaps some Advanced Biology idiot or a vice principal maybe. A talk-show host. A therapist.

"You *got my postcard*?!" I screamed at him, and his voice rose in schoolyard recess mockery one more time.

"What did it say?" he said, laughing. "Let me think." Laughing, laughing, dark, light, dark, light. He spit on the ground. "Oh, yes, 'Listen what my letters have been trying to tell you is that I love you.'" He stepped into the shade of the tree and stayed there, so the rest of the postcard came out of the dark like the voice of God, or the devil. "'And I mean real love that can surpass all the dreariness of high school we both hate.'"

"*Shut up!*"

He stepped into the light and laughed right in front of me with his mouth wide open, as brazen as only the star of the high school play can be. "*This isn't just the wine talking!*" he shrieked: the punch line. The line where you punch.

I swung *up*, vertically, the way you don't usually swing things. The hit was solid, like the right answer to a test. His eyes widened and his jaw crackled; I watched his mouth as he coughed up blood, tasted it. He stepped back into the shade, then forward again. Dark, light, dark, light. My mallet followed him exactly, waiting for another clear shot, but I wasn't worried. I had plenty of time. The thrill of cold night air swarmed around me like something I was riding, something I could control. For the first time that night I was having *fun*. It was the biggest event of the year. A day to be remembered – a famous day.

"You *bitch*!" he sputtered, still coughing. He spat something on the ground; teeth maybe. He kept moving, stumbling around: dark, light, dark, light. "You *bitch*! You *fat bitch*!"

I inhaled, and stepped into the light myself, blocking it so my shadow fell on him. Dark, *dark*; there was nowhere for him to go. Adam stepped back once and looked at me, and that's the last time I ever saw him alive, I swear.

Vocabulary:

You can't be serious.

Monday November 1st

A new month. I can only remember its opening in fragments. From that moment on, ladies and gentlemen, to the bright slap of Tuesday morning, it's all separate fragments, clear enough in the slide show of my skull but disconnected from everything else, like a chain of bright pearls broken and rolling everywhere down the stairs or like disembodied teeth: individual, personal but *separate*. I have noted them all in my journal like a careful jeweler but cannot attest to their exact sequence. I swear on all I have done that this crazy quilt is the best I can do.

The croquet mallet was stuck in something wet and jagged, like a half-melon. I was unable to pull it out, even with both hands. My own breathing was wet and jagged too, misting in the dark. Tugging and tugging and finally giving up. Stepped back, felt something sharp beneath my feet, like a sprinkler head or maybe bone.
A bloody handprint on a sliding glass door, or maybe just muddy. Little pieces of grass crawling around the

handprint like caterpillars. Kate's face behind the handprint, like she was wearing it.

"OK!" V___ called out grandly, clapping her hands. What time is it? "Everybody go home! Everybody out; go home! The party is over!" My gritty hands on the banister; I knew I couldn't move.

"I can't leave," I whined.

"Not *you*," Kate said in a hurried voice, tense and sounding disgusted. She had a light blue towel in her hands, curled up like a baby. One of those babies that just came out, its eyes still closed and its body limp in the absolute trust of grown-ups. I took Kate's tiny hand.

I thought the music they'd put on was the most boring I'd ever heard: just a simple beat, pounding away like a rapist, with cheesy synthesizer noises washing over it, like an aquarium pump. Wondering what in the world album it was, I walked back into the living room, judging by my view that I was staggering. The stereo was off. None of those electric bar graphs, showing you bass and treble and only-boys-know-what-else, were jumping and skittering like usual. There wasn't any music on. Kate's face loomed in front of me. She was crying. "For God's sake *get upstairs*!" she said. "*Upstairs*! Oh God!"

I sighed at her. "Calm," I said, "the hell down."

Adam stepped back into the shade, then forward again. He spat something on the ground; pearls maybe. Outside the cold night air swarmed around me like something I was riding, something I could control. For the first time that night I was having *fun*, finally after this dreary drunk screaming all night. I was having *fun* and it wasn't even – I had no idea. I felt my own smile bright as headlights, blaring and blaring away, while inside my head I felt a small certainty like a termite biding its time. *Satan is going to kill us. Satan is going to kill us all.*

Natasha pulled my head out of the sink and everything snapped back into place like bright red plastic building blocks. "You know," she said, in a conversational tone of voice I would have fallen for had her eyes not been white coals, "you know, I've heard that turkeys are so dumb you have to drag their heads out of the trough before they drown." She grabbed my hair back like a caveman and wrung it out into the overflowing sink. "But I never thought you were much of a turkey, Flan."

I looked at her; she was looking at me like her room was a mess. Where to start? I blinked and looked around the bathroom. It wasn't the one with books all over it. It was another bathroom. I didn't know where it was. Hopelessly stained guest towels, little soaps in the shapes of endangered animals still wrapped in cellophane, a small glass bowl with potpourri in it – OK, I was obviously still at V——'s house, but what was I doing here?

"Yes?" she said.

"What time is it?" I tried.

She shook her head. "The least of your problems, Flan. Stand up."

I gripped a towel rack, slippery with something. I blinked again. Where was I? No, I mean, V——'s bathroom, but what was going on? "Um –" I said.

"Stand *up*!" she said, cracking. "Hurry up, Flan!" The bathroom stumbled by me, another door opened and I was in V——'s brother's room, everything suspended in time like rooms are when their occupant is a junior at Yale

University. This wasn't helping. Natasha opened the sliding door of his closet and the mirror lurched off left. Prim suits stood in a line like commuters. "Jesus," Natasha muttered, looking at them one by one. She turned back to me in astonishment. "*Don't sit down!*" she yelled, running to me and pulling me off the bed. She looked at the bedspread and tore it off the bed. "*Jesus*, Flan," she said. "Get it off and don't *touch anything!*"

"What are you – what are you *talking about*?" I said, and looked down and realized I had ruined her dress. Rum punch and water were all over it and the fabric seemed saturated with it. *No wonder she's mad*, I thought, but I felt a small rush of relief, realizing it was punch stains. Because if it wasn't punch stains –

"*Get it off get it off get it off!*" she screamed. "Oh, God!" She grabbed me again and the bedroom stumbled by me, another door opened and I was back in the bathroom. "Stand *up!*" she said and I stood up. Downstairs somebody was shrieking; I was therefore upstairs.

Natasha pulled the dress over my head like I was a baby; it slid by me like an eel and left me shivering alone in the bathroom with my hands above my head. I thought Natasha would come back but nothing happened so I lowered my arms. Through the crackle and gurgle of my head came the sound of the water running. Behind the gauzy curtain the shower was running and empty, so taking a wild guess I got in and felt the water wash it off me. I wasn't staying up very well, so I stretched each hand out to balance me: one on the bright clean tile and the other on the shower curtain; I slowly slid down until I was sitting *in* the shower, water spitting all over me, forgotten. I thought maybe I'd just *stay* there but Natasha clawed the curtain back and forced me out of the tub again. I chattered and chattered and suddenly felt myself heaving into Natasha's arms. One of us was crying but I didn't know who.

Natasha leaned over me and turned off the shower. She was wearing a man's suit that was way too big for her and stacked in her hands she had the clothes she'd borrowed from me that night at V___'s party: the plain white T-shirt with a tiny stenciled flower at the center of the neck and a pair of blue jeans. "They're sweaty, but wear them," she said tersely, and threw me a towel.

I rubbed my face and the world went terry cloth for a minute. "I'm sorry about your dress," I said sadly, into the towel. "Is it going to be OK?"

"*No,*" Natasha snarled. I kept rubbing my face, not wanting to meet her eyes. Then I heard her sigh. "It'll be OK," she said, as if to herself, but then repeated it to me. "It's OK," she said, "but listen to me, Flan. Listen to me. Take the towel off."

I took the towel off. The suit made her look less and less ridiculous and more and more OK, glamorous even. She was holding up a paper grocery bag; inside it I could see her ruined dress, curled and coiled like a captured snake. "You've never seen this dress," she said. I was looking straight down into the bag, right at it. "You didn't wear a costume tonight. You've never seen this dress in your life."

I started to laugh but Natasha grabbed my face, turned it to look right at me. With one hand grasping my cheeks and the other pointing right at me, she said it again. "You've never seen this dress."

"What are you talking about?"

"You've *never. Seen. This. Dress!*" She let go of me and my head darted back, like I was startled. I *was* startled.

"What?" I said.

"*What?*" she screamed back at me.

"OK," I said.

"OK *what*?"

"I've never seen that dress," I said, pointing at it. The mirrors were fogging over with the shower, or maybe they weren't; maybe they were reflecting exactly what was going on. "I've never seen it."

Natasha rolled the bag up and put it under her arm. "Put your clothes on," she said. Foggier and foggier.

Suddenly, something grabbed my ankle. I stumbled and put my hand on the damp grass to stop myself from falling. I picked up a baguette, thin and incredibly stale, and beat at the hand until it let go, until it stopped moving, until it was barely a hand.

Natasha had opened the shades so the irksome blaze of dawn was upon me like, I don't know, too much salad dressing. "Today's the day!" she said, straddling me like a rider, or a rapist. "I can't wait! The biggest event of the year." Then I woke up and she was kneeling beside the bed peering into my half-open eyes. "You OK?" she said tenderly. I was grasping the blanket to my chin like a baby, but everything was cold: the gray mist outside, the windowpanes, the floors and walls of the room and my whole body, solid with cold like something stretched out on a slab. I felt like shit. I looked right back at Natasha, who was dressed curiously in a man's suit and sharp perfect lipstick. I looked at her and she looked back at me, sharply, theatrically, until all of a sudden the air didn't feel like a stark glacier, ending our Age as we knew it. It just felt like the morning blues. "I'm thirsty," I said, and shifted under the blanket, looking for a warm spot. "What did I do?" I said. Natasha had put a glass in my hand, so large and cold. She didn't answer my question.

It wasn't the right question. I licked my lips in anticipation, finally, of water, but floating at the top of the glass was a thin layer. Of something. I raised it past my mouth to my eyes; Natasha's face skittered and rippled behind it. Dust was dancing at the horizon of the water, like plankton. My stomach gurgled; I didn't want to sip it. "This water looks gross," I said to Natasha. She was looking at V___'s brother's clock radio.

"I'm not surprised," she said, turning the clock toward me. The bright digital numbers danced in front of my eyes like hot red sparks: HED, DED, DIE, 5IE, 53E, 5:30. It was five-thirty and I was in V___'s brother's bedroom. "It's been sitting around all day. Like you."

When I woke up I found myself in V___'s brother's bedroom, terribly thirsty and still in the clothes I had worn the night before: my white T-shirt with the tiny flower in the center, and blue jeans. Through a dusty glass of water, red sparks of a clock radio were winking at me, but I couldn't read them. I was experiencing what Natasha has been known to call a déjà typhoon – a storm of familiarity, a rush of can't-quite-place-it-ness. There was something right in front of me, something I knew the shape of but couldn't quite know, like I'd just had a baby but hadn't yet gotten to know it, but there it was, suckling away.

Somebody was feeling me up. I could feel the feel of somebody's hand along my very spine, teasing me until the plain white cotton felt like something silky, like a kimono against my skin. I opened my eyes; Yale pennants spun. Outside the window showed moonlight against fog, a dense shrubbery of gray half-light. Somebody was breathing heavily, and their fingers were trembling on my skin. When he kissed me I sucked him in like a fish, taking him down with me. We kissed superhard, and his fingers were still shaking when they slipped under my elastic and across my hipbones, cold and hard as marble. I followed him, grabbed his fingers and slid them inside me. He moaned; it was Gabriel. I grabbed at this: It was my *boyfriend*. My legs were spread so wide it was impossible to take my underwear off; he got them halfway down when they stuck, overstretched like those little wire things that don't always keep bags closed properly. Gabriel needs to cut his nails. I kept thinking things like that the whole time, little sentences. Reduced sentencing. My underwear is ripped and I don't have another pair. In this case it is true about black men. Not being able to remember V___'s brother's name. It hurts. The light is weird in here. Harder. Tasting Gabriel's shoulder, biting down on it. We're not using any birth control. Harder. It hurts anyway. Is somebody watching us? Would I be able to get into Yale? Gabriel breathing in my ear. My hips moving in a way I wasn't planning – instinctively, I guess. The familiar taste of blood. Gabriel's noises and my own. Natasha's unblinking eyes in the dark, like cat's eyes. The hot tip of her cigarette, riveted and bored. The sound of the bed. The sound of us in the bed.

I was sitting on the stained couch with a cup of coffee I wasn't drinking in my hand when the doorbell rang. V___'s doorbell is scrupulously polite, a slight tinkle that just clears the throat in a discreet "ahem"; nevertheless my head split like a melon. I closed my eyes and experienced what I sometimes call a déjà typhoon – a storm of familiarity, a rush of can't-quite-place-it-ness. What was that, a head splitting like a melon? A baguette stuck in it, some weird fruit salad. I got up and answered the door.

317

It was Rachel State, showered and worried. "Hi Flan," she said, looking me over. "How are you?"

I thought it was sarcasm but when I looked down at myself it was genuine concern; I was wearing my plain white T-shirt with a small flower embroidered on it, wrinkled and with a new tear on the shoulder like someone had bitten it. I suddenly felt my hair, like a mess of twigs. Particularly in contrast to Rachel's sleek black ensemble I felt like a mess.

"I'm OK," I said. "Just, you know, getting up. It was quite a party, wasn't it?"

"It's none of my business," Rachel said, looking at the floor.

What? "Weren't you there?" I said.

"It's none of my business," she said again, and I realized she was *beginning* a sentence, "but did Adam sleep here last night?" She raised her eyes and looked at me. In about half a second, she went from The Frosh Goth to a little fourteen-year-old knocking on the door of a house that hosted a party, looking for her big brother like somebody sent into the dark woods in a fairy tale. Which made me the witch, I guess.

"I don't know," I said. "Come on in, I'm freezing standing here with the door open."

She looked wary and embarrassed.

I took a step backward and ran into Kate and Lily. They looked out of breath and were wearing damp aprons. "Hey," I said, "Rachel is here. She's —"

"Adam didn't come home last night," Rachel said. "My mom is raising hell. I'm sorry for coming over." The open door was chilling me through, but I didn't quite have the audacity to reach past her and pull it shut so I just stood there trembling.

"Nobody's here," Lily said quickly.

Rachel blinked. "Have you seen –"

"She's looking for Adam," I told them. "He didn't come home, apparently." Still trembling, I tried to scan back and figure out when I'd seen him last. Laughing in the kitchen –

"Well," Kate said, "he's not here. Only the Basic Eight were invited to spend the night. Everybody else was supposed to *leave*." She was looking right at Rachel.

"I wasn't –" Rachel gestured uselessly. "I just wanted to –"

"I don't think Adam came to the party at all," Lily said.

"Yes he did," I said. "I'm just trying to remember the last time I saw him." I looked curiously at Lily; surely she remembered he was there. Her eyes were wide and bagged; she clearly hadn't slept. Had *I* slept? "Come on in, Rachel," I said. "There's coffee."

"Thanks," she said, giving me a tiny smile. She stepped farther into the house and I walked around her to shut the door. I couldn't remember the last time I'd been this cold, but then again I wasn't remembering much at all. "It's in the kitchen," I said.

"Thanks," Rachel said again, but she couldn't get to the kitchen because Kate and Lily were standing there. They looked at each other and then parted slightly so Rachel could squeeze through. What in the world was going on? Gabriel came through the kitchen door and blocked Rachel from it, his face set and unreasonable. Flora Habstat, of all people, stood behind Gabriel; she looked like she'd been crying. At last, I grabbed the handle to shut the front door and found V___ and Douglas standing there, out of breath. They looked scared raw. "Hi," I said. "Where have you guys been?"

"I know this will be hard to believe, Flan," Douglas said sharply, "but I'm not in the mood for jokes right now."

"He followed me so I could get home," V___ explained.

"Where have *you* been?" I asked.

"*Flan*," she said. Her hands were shaking.

"V___, look who's here," Kate said meaningfully. "Rachel State. You know, Adam's sister."

"Oh," V___ said. She blinked. She put her hand over mine and slammed the door shut. "What are *you* doing here?"

Rachel looked at me, her only ally. "I –" she said. "Did Adam stay here? He didn't – my mom is looking for Adam." She looked around like one of those kittens in a cage they have downtown as part of the Adopt-an-Animal program: Look how helpless, look how cute. Take it home. Everyone was too close to her: Kate and Lily, Gabriel and Flora, standing around her like walls at the zoo. Like a cage.

"It was a *party*," Kate said. "We don't know where he went."

"She's going to kill him," Rachel said quietly, and Gabriel began making a terrible sound. Everybody looked at him, and he covered his mouth though it didn't do any good. He was doubling over. Flora went to him, Kate went to him.

"I'm sorry," Gabriel sputtered, and when he looked up for a minute I saw his red face and knew he was *laughing*. "I'm sorry," he said when he caught his breath.

V___ reached out a hand and whirled Rachel around to face her. "Gabriel's been sick," she said. "He's just hungover, that's all. This really isn't the best time for a visit, Rachel."

"I was just looking for Adam," she said uncertainly.

Kate snapped her fingers. "You know, I think he might have gone home with Shannon," she said. "You know, Shannon, from the choir?"

320

"That's right," Lily said, covering her mouth. I could scarcely hear her over my teeth chattering; there must be another door open somewhere. Maybe the back one, the one to the garden. "He was with her all night. I barely saw him myself."

Rachel sighed. Her brother's friends were acting *weird*. "All right, I guess I'll call her. Can I use your phone?"

"Broken," V___ said promptly, and then shook her head slightly. "I mean, the downstairs phone is broken, and I'm expecting a call from my parents."

"Oh," Rachel said.

"Long-distance," V___ said.

I snapped my fingers. "He's not *there*," I said. "I remember him saying he was going to leave, out the back –"

V___ pushed me away from the door and opened it. Kate and Lily moved forward, forcing Rachel to step quickly toward the open door. It looked like people were moving in for the kill. Jennifer Rose Milton came down the stairs.

"What's going on?" she said, and then assessed the situation instantly. "Flan, would you come upstairs with me?"

"What?"

"I need you for something." Rachel was looking at Jennifer Rose Milton like maybe Jenn had stolen something from her.

I tried again. "Adam's not –" Something brown burned me. Kate had hit my elbow and my coffee had spilled down my white T-shirt, almost to the tiny embroidered flower. I stepped back. The rest of the coffee spilled on the floor. Kate and Lily stepped ahead of me. Gabriel took me firmly by the shoulders and moved me farther back.

"Could I leave through your yard?" Rachel said. "It's a lot quicker to my house. I just cut through –"

"Right," I said. "That's what I –"

"I'm sorry," V___ said, sickly-sweet.

"Sorry," Flora said, agreeing. She stepped in front of me. It was getting hard to even *see* Rachel.

"The garden is closed," V___ continued like a docent.

Rachel wasn't born yesterday. "*What?*" she said. "Will you just let me –"

"No," V___ said. "You weren't invited here. Adam isn't here. Please leave." Gabriel slipped in front of me. Everybody was in front of me.

"Flan?" Jennifer Rose Milton asked. I looked at her but couldn't read what she was saying. "Upstairs?"

"We have *school today*," Rachel said. "My mom wants to know where Adam is. He didn't come home, on a *school night*. Why are you acting like –"

"We're not *acting like* anything," V___ said. They had pushed Rachel to the door and she was looking, finally, frightened. I tried to take a step toward her but Gabriel, gently, pushed me back, toward the stairs. I stepped on the first step and Jennifer Rose Milton moved around me so *she* was in front of me too. I took another step up.

"He's *here*, isn't he?" Rachel said. "*Adam? Adam!*"

Lily tripped over her own feet and stuck a hand out to steady herself. "He's not here," she said, and laughed.

"Where *is* he?" Rachel said. She was out the door and V___ was starting to shut it.

"We don't know," Kate said. "Go find him."

I took another step up and suddenly saw, in aerial view, what was happening just as the door was shutting. Down in the entrance hall it wasn't clear, but from above I could see that everyone was huddling together, staying close and thick between Rachel and me like protective animals. Moving like a flock, to protect one of their own. The whole Basic Eight – Kate, V——, Douglas, Gabriel, Flora, Jenn – moving me away from harm.

"*Where is he?*" Rachel said, and the door shut, and I was safe.

Tuesday November 2nd

I was dozing against the window of the bus, cold and smooth like water, when I heard somebody holding up the line of people boarding. Somebody was inquiring the price of a ticket to Roewer High School, and the bus driver, thinking he was being jerked around (though goodness knows why – he weighs too much to be jerked anywhere), was snapping at her.

"You're holding up the line," he said. "It's a dollar. There's no ticket."

"Oh," she said. I craned my neck to see who this person was, raised by wolves in some San Francisco wilderness and finally escaping by public transportation. A tall hairdo was blocking me. I heard a purse click open and coins drop into the box. Her clunky footsteps coming up the aisle and finally plopping down next to me.

"I can't believe you do this every morning," she said, and I opened my eyes. V—— was on the bus. V——. On the *bus*. "If I ever get my car back, Flan, I'm going to drive you to school every day. This is disgraceful."

"What are you doing here?" I said. "Here I was hoping you'd save me the walk from the stop by pulling up in your gorgeous car."

"My gorgeous car is *gone*," she hissed, scrunching down in her seat like a spy. "We can't talk here, Flan."

"What?" I said, and then her eyes widened. She blinked and smiled at me, then looked around the bus.

323

"That's right," she said in a loud voice. "Stolen. My car was stolen. It's gone. That's why I'm taking the bus." She brushed her hair theatrically from her face. "Stolen."

"That's *awful*," I said. It *was* awful, but why was she telling everyone on the bus? "Um, when did it happen?"

"The last I saw it was at the party," she announced. "I mean, right before the party. And then when I went to drive to school today it was gone."

"Have you called the police?"

"My father is taking care of it," she said. Rays of light were coming through the window at sharp odd angles, branding little triangles and squares on V___'s tired face. "They just got home last night, and boy was I busted. I had to get up at the crack of dawn, just to –"

"*Boy was I busted*? Why are you talking like you're in a TV commercial?"

V___ glared at me, then leaned back in her seat scowling like I'd spoiled her fun.

"V___," I said, "just tell me what's going on." She shook her head. I leaned into her. Her face was dark and furious. I spoke quietly, hoping that was the way she liked it. "V___, I'm sorry. I just – well, I'm just sitting here and suddenly you're *taking the bus*, and now you tell me your car is stolen. Is that it? Your *car*? I mean, I'm sorry it's stolen, V___, but –"

"Hey," Lily said and we both jumped. She was standing up next to our seats, with her cello case next to her like a bodyguard, her notebooks against her breasts. She looked wrecked and not just early-morning wrecked. She looked refugee-wrecked.

"Can I sit down?" she said, and leaned toward us. The rays of light struck her and I saw her face was utterly green. *Really* green, like pale algae was clinging to her. I heard myself gasp. I'd never seen someone *green* like that. "I don't mean to sound like," she swallowed, "an old lady, but I need to sit down."

I waited for V___ to get up but she just sat there, her face still scowling and her eyes far away. V___, ever-polite V___, not giving up her seat for Lily Chandly who was looking like a pond you shouldn't go into. One you shouldn't even touch.

"Of course," I said, getting up and stepping pointedly over V___ whose legs were hanging into the aisle like somebody'd forgotten them. V___ blinked, looked up at Lily and slid over to the window. Lily smiled a small lime smile and dropped into the seat. I put my hand on top of her cello case, to steady it. "I'll take this," I said, but Lily didn't even acknowledge me.

"I don't know if I can make it through the day," she said. "I keep throwing up."

"*We all do*," V___ said tersely. "Shut up."

Lily's face got all puckered like an infant tantrum. "I can't −" she whined, but V___ cut her off. She raised her hand, and for a second it looked like she was going to *hit* Lily. But the harshness of the gesture worked by itself and Lily shut her mouth.

"What?" I said. I couldn't have seen what I had just seen, but I saw it. I think all the tenses are right in that sentence. "*What*?" I looked down at Lily who looked too sick to care. "V___'s just been telling me about her car. Have you heard? It was stolen, sometime around the night of the party. That gorgeous car. Isn't that awful?" I sneaked a look at V___ to see if I was saying the right thing, but her eyes were closed and she was leaning against the window. I looked over at Lily who was blinking at me like *I* was going to hit her. "Lily? Did you hear about it?" Lily looked over at V___, who opened her eyes and shook her head slowly, *no*. "Lily?"

"I can't —" she said, and swallowed. The bus stopped; we were at school. Lily stood up with effort and took her cello case from me. V___ stood up too. Lily walked to the back door of the bus unsteadily while I hovered over her. V___ went to the front; I watched her step down the stairs almost haughtily, not looking back at us. I left the bus first, and Lily followed, stepping down each step like she was in the dark. Finally she was out in the grungy street, in the morning light. V___ hadn't waited up for us and was already striding toward Roewer. Lily blinked at the world; outside her skin didn't have any less of that unearthly green. She took one step and doubled over; I caught her cello case from clattering onto the ground. With a horrible lurching noise she threw up, a mouthful of dark gray thick something onto the curb where it sat like a dirty snowdrift. I put my hand on Lily's shoulder, but V___ didn't even look back. The lurching sound, wet breathing like something going under, struck me in some way, and I stood there, searching my brain for the connection. Some memory. My head was vibrating like a tuning fork, searching the files for the right picture, but nothing came of it, only the dimness of some aquarium dream: gurgle, gurgle, gurgle. Lily gave one more dry heave and then stood up again. She reached into her pocket for a tissue and wiped her face, grimacing at me. She took her cello case and then looked at my hand on her, until I took it off.

"Lily," I said, "you need to go home. You can't —"

"Let's go," she said. Her eyes were dead and white but her mouth was smiling like a bad clown. "Time for school."

"You can't go to school like *this*," I said. "You're *sick*."

"We're having a meeting," she said. "Seventh period, down by the lake. Don't forget."

"What? We all have Millie then. We can't all cut that class to –"

"*Flan*," she said, and started to cry, "we have to go to school."

"OK," I said, and reached out to touch her. She flinched sharply, her hands darting up to mine as if to slap them away. She looked at me and actually took a step back. "OK," I said again, more carefully, and stepped away from *her*. "Just, you know, take it easy."

"We have to go to school," she muttered.

"OK," I said, again. We went to school.

The day itself was uneventful, drifting by like ice floes. Something in Calc. Apologizing to Hattie Lewis for missing class yesterday. I'm sure she suspected something when all my friends were sick too, although Lily throwing up in the hallway just as class let out helped convince her that maybe there *was* a flu going round. Adam wasn't in choir. Pond water under a microscope. Capitalist bell curves rising like tits. And then, for some reason, I ducked Millie's door and trudged to the lake for this big meeting.

Wouldn't you know it – V___ showed up first, so we had to sit there not talking to each other by the side of Lake Merced. Finally I sat up and looked at her taut face. I was astounded to see she was smoking, her dull smoke rising up against the silhouettes of the trees. "V___, I'm sorry," I said. She blinked and puffed. "I don't even know what I was saying, there on the bus." True except for that pronoun. "I didn't mean to upset you, V___. *Please*. I'm very sorry."

She turned to me finally and suddenly, her eyes sharp as the tip of her cigarette. "*You* –" she started in a voice so rough my whole body chilled, down to the cold earth I was sitting on. Then she sighed and shrugged her shoulders, took another drag like a pro. Where did she even *learn* to smoke?

"It's fine," she said, dully. She looked at me and smiled a little. "I guess – I guess it's sort of a rough time."

"Are your parents giving you a rough time?" I asked.

She blinked. "What?"

"Your parents?" I said, and bit my lip. Suddenly I was saying the wrong thing again. "You know, the party?"

Her eyes widened and widened, and the ash of her cigarette sat there, unflicked. "*What*?" she said.

"Hey," Lily said and we both jumped. She was standing up next to us with her cello case next to her like a bodyguard and her notebooks against her breasts. Douglas was behind her, smiling thinly and holding – has everyone been *brainwashed*? – a lit cigarette.

"Hey," V__ said, and burst out sobbing. Her shoulders shook and her cigarette fell to the log she was sitting on, where it nibbled at the damp bark. Douglas crushed it out with his shoe and sat next to her, holding her stiffly in his arms. Lily sat on her other side and stared into space miserably, her cello case leaning against her. Everybody was on the log except me, sitting on the ground. I was not only mystified, I was passé. V__ sobbed and sobbed, in loud raw gulps of sound.

"Cut that shit out right away," Natasha said casually, strolling out from somewhere with Kate and Gabriel. She was smoking too, her dark lipstick staining the filter. Kate was glaring at V__ like a drill sergeant.

"*Natasha –*" Douglas said, whirling around to her.

"She's right," Kate said, sitting on the ground. She leaned back on the log and opened her backpack, took out a notebook and pen. "We don't have time, we can't afford – V__, stop it right now."

"She can't just *stop it*," Douglas said. "She's –"

"*NO!*" Gabriel said, pointing at them. "*No!* Just *stop!*"

I decided not to say anything, sitting on my hands. My body felt so cold. V―― bit her lip and choked back a sob. She was stopping, just like that.

"Thank you," Kate said, with a thin smile. She looked stone-serious but somehow – *eager*.

Gabriel sat down beside me and put a hand on my shoulder, formally. "How are *you*?" he said, looking at me.

"I'm OK," I said, but he was already looking elsewhere. Natasha passed her flask to V――, who took it gratefully and tipped it to her mouth, the faux silver catching the sun. "How about *you*?" I said to Gabriel.

"We'll talk on the way home," he said.

"*Please*," Douglas said. "Whatever anyone has to say, they might as well say it to everybody. It can't *possibly* matter."

"I'm going to throw up," Lily said suddenly. Her face peered over her notebooks, still clutched close, her face still greenish and her eyes tense with certainty.

"Well, do it somewhere else," Natasha said. She was leaning against a tree in this burgundy jumper I'd never seen on her before.

"Yes, *please*," Kate said, folding back her notebook to a blank lined page. I couldn't imagine what we were going to discuss. Lily got up, walked about ten paces to a clump of weeds and heaved into it.

"Can't this all wait?" I said. Gabriel shook his head at me and Kate stared me down like I was out of uniform.

"What?" she said.

"Well, Lily's sick," I said. "V――'s upset –"

"We're *all* upset," Douglas said. "What do you –"

"That's what I mean," I said. "It's a bad time to have a *meeting*, Kate. Let's put it off until –"

She dismissed me with a wave of her hand. "Don't be ridiculous, Flan. I wish Jenn would hurry up."

"And Flora!" Lily called from the weeds. "*Everybody*."

"Well, I wish they'd *both* hurry up," Kate continued. "I don't have much time."

"You have as long as it takes," Natasha said firmly, with a fake sweet icing. "We'd do the same for *you*, dear."

"Shut *up*," Kate said.

"*What*?" Natasha threw her cigarette in the grass.

"*Please*," Gabriel said, as Douglas stood up and crushed it out. "As Flan says, we're *all* upset here, let's just –"

"*We're all upset*?!?" V___ sputtered. "*We? Are all? Upset?*"

"*Please*," Gabriel pleaded again. "Let's just talk about what we need to do."

"Not until Jenn and Flora are here."

"We're here," Jenn said, in a corpse-numb voice. Jennifer Rose Milton and Flora Habstat were standing stiffly as though at attention, their coats dragging on the ground like queens' trains. Flora didn't say anything, and from the look on her face I could tell that was pretty much the plan for the rest of her life. Wrong.

Kate took the cap off the pen and wrote a heading on the paper I couldn't see. Underlining it primly, she looked up and gestured rather formally for Jennifer Rose Milton and quiet little Flora Habstat to sit down. To me Flora's presence indicated that – what do I mean – *adjunct members* of the Basic Eight could come, and I wondered where Adam was. I hadn't seem him for a couple of days, in fact – he wasn't in choir today, and he didn't stay over after the party, I don't think. Everything's such a gurgly blur, fading in and out, dark, light.

330

"All right," Kate started. "If anyone asks, we're planning a party at the Sculpture Garden Friday night. That's why we're meeting today, all right?"

A Sculpture Garden party? I couldn't believe it. "And it can't wait?" I said. "Lily's *sick*, Kate."

"*SHUT UP!*" V—— screamed.

"All right?" Kate continued smoothly, like V—— was some protester being led from the lecture hall. "Friday, eight o'clock, there, we've had our meeting. Now, I guess we just need to hear from some people, so everybody knows what's up. V——, your car?"

"Has been stolen," V—— finished. "I told my dad this morning. Luckily there's been a rash of carjackings in the neighborhood, so he was kicking himself he hadn't installed an alarm system."

"I don't think it's carjacking," Lily said, coming over and wiping her mouth on her sleeve, "if it's just stolen. I think carjacking means somebody forces their way into –"

"*Whatever!*" V—— said. Her lip was trembling.

"It doesn't matter," Kate agreed, settling it. Glancing down she crossed a *t*. What I would give to see what she was writing down. By now it's undoubtedly stored forever in federal files. "It doesn't matter," she said again. "All right? It doesn't matter. The point is that the car is gone, and everything with it."

"It's in a bad neighborhood," V—— said.

"*A bad neighborhood?*" Natasha snorted. "It'll remain invisible there, for sure. That gorgeous car in a *bad* –"

"That's what I'm saying," Douglas said. "The idea is that the cops think it was stolen by, well, *car thieves*. The idea is that he came upon the thieves while they were in the act and they panicked –"

"*We* were the ones who panicked," V—— said. "I don't know what we were thinking yesterday –"

"*If* we were thinking," Lily muttered.

"It doesn't matter," Kate said. "All right? It doesn't matter. We work with what we've got. We had to do something so we did it."

"You sound like Mr. Baker," Gabriel said. Natasha looked at me and winked.

"So the car's in a bad neighborhood," Kate said. "That'll work."

"They'll find it," Douglas said darkly. "It's not like we pushed it off a cliff."

"What in the world," I asked, "are we talking about?"

For a second it looked like Douglas was going to hit me, *Douglas*, right across the face, but then he looked down and his face slackened. "Jesus, Flan," he said in hushed tones like he was in church, or awe. "What do you *think* we're talking about?"

"I don't know," I said miserably.

"Flannery," V___ said, "this is very tedious. We all *know* –"

"I'm serious," I said. "Tell me what's going on. Since that party I've been such a mess. I drank so much of that scorpion punch, and everybody was fighting –"

"Scorpion punch?" Gabriel asked.

"It stang to drink it," I explained.

"I think that's *stung*," Kate said. "Scorpion punch is a good name for it, though. We'll have to remember that for next time."

"Next time?" V___ asked. "*Next time?*"

"Shhh," Jennifer Rose Milton said. "Calm do –"

"There's not going to be a *next time*," V___ shouted. "For *any* of us. Not after everything Flan –"

"After everything I *what?*" I asked. Beneath my skin my memory was playing charades – I knew there had been a party and I knew how many syllables it had, but after that I couldn't make head or tail of that blurry evening, pantomimed in front of me in vague, inscrutable gestures. "Look, everybody," I said. "I'm not being cute here. I can't remember the whole garden party, practically. People were mad at me. I was mad at people. I think I even *hit* what's-his-name, toward the end, as he was leaving. I know I was fighting with him on the croquet field. But after that it's all – *scorpionesque*." Now they were looking at me like *I* was the struggling mime. "Please. I'm ready to apologize or explain or whatever, but somebody has to tell me what's going on. Why are we cutting Millie's class just to talk about a Sculpture Garden party and worry about V___'s car? Plenty of us have cars. If we need to get to the Sculpture Garden, we can take – what?"

Lily had thrown up again, on the lawn in front of her. Green on green.

"Forget it," Gabriel said. "Just try to calm down – *everyone*."

"I *can't!*" Douglas said. Both he and Jennifer Rose Milton were covering their ears and looking at me like I was a horror movie they were far too young for. *For which they were far too young.*

"You have to," Kate said. "We *all* have to. Now calm down, Douglas. You don't see me jumping up and yelling."

"You didn't stuff the body of a friend of yours into the trunk of a car, did you?" Douglas said quietly, and sat down. I stopped breathing, I know I did. I could remember staring into the recess of V___'s trunk, that day she looked for her scarf. Like superimposed slides I was fitting a corpse into it – I could see, dimly, some sputtering red face crushed like an aluminum can, remembered from some movie or something on TV.

"I can't believe we're *doing this*!" Lily wailed. There was still vomit on her chin and her nose was running wildly, stringing down like mozzarella cheese. "*I can't believe –*"

"We don't have a choice," Kate said, looking up from her notebook. "All right? There's nothing we can do. We already decided. The question is, can we get a grip on ourselves and get through this? I say we can. We got through Flan and the fruit flies, and Jim Carr –"

"This isn't the *same thing*," Douglas said. "This is –"

"Why don't you go then?" Natasha said. "Why don't you go, go call the police or your mommy or your fucking Princi*pal* Mokie, OK? Tell them that V__'s car isn't stolen, that it's sitting in some *bad neighborhood* and inside the trunk is a former big man on campus, and that we were all at the party and helped put him there? Why don't you do that? Be sure and put it on your goddamn college applications. You know, that question about what else you have to contribute to the college environs? You could just put *stuff corpses in trunk*!"

"*Stop!*" Lily said.

"You little *faggot*," Natasha snarled. Douglas swallowed. His eyes widened. He put his hand to his neck – the spot I had helped him cover with makeup, each morning.

"We can *do* this," Kate said quietly. Her eyes were lit up, like they were that night in the Sculpture Garden when she was all quiet triumph and organization. She had been waiting for this moment since she'd met us. "This is a real test for us, I think," she said. "If we can get through this, we'll be –"

"Much stronger for it?" V__ asked, raising her eyebrows. "Come *on*, Kate."

"*Stop, stop*," Kate said. "OK, Natasha, the dress –"

"What dress?" Natasha said, looking sharply at Kate.

Kate nodded. "OK. So I take it the dress is –"

"*What dress?*" Natasha said. "I have *no idea* what dress you're talking about, and nobody else does either."

"Well, that's good news," Gabriel said.

"But where *is* the dress?" Jenn asked.

"It *doesn't matter*," V__ said. "Don't you see? We don't know. We *shouldn't* know. Just in case –"

"That *case*," Natasha said, "is not going to happen."

"I can't do it," Lily said, shaking her head.

"We'd do it for *you*," Natasha said.

"Not anymore," Douglas said.

Flora didn't say anything. I didn't either – no one was mad at Flora, so I figured it was the best move.

"Well, there's good news," V__ said, "I guess. My parents wanted to punish me, you know, for the party."

"Did that rack fall?" I realized it was me who'd asked.

"What rack?"

"You know," I said, sensing that this too was the wrong thing to say. "The rack in the kitchen. With all the pots. It looked like it was going to fall."

"What's the matter with her?" Kate asked Natasha.

"No," V__ said. Her eyes were closed. "The rack didn't fall, Flan."

"But what's the good news?" Gabriel asked.

"As punishment," V__ said, suddenly smiling bitterly, "my folks had me mow the lawn. First thing this morning. *Early*."

Everybody breathed some sigh of relief. Kate grinned, even. "And where does the, whatever it is, the *lawn* bag go?"

"Right into the garbage," V__ said. "So everything's OK on that front."

"Was it bad?" Douglas asked.

"We don't have to hear this," Jenn begged.

V—— sighed. "It was, well, OK I guess. I mean, *considering*. It's very *lucky*, that's all. I don't know how much attention the gardener pays when *he* mows the lawn, but if you find a *tooth* –"

Lily threw up.

"*Guh!*" Douglas said, standing up. It had splashed on him a little. "Can we *leave* now, Kate? Is that all there is to this little Friday party meeting? Because I'm supposed to tell you all – I was supposed to tell you in Millie's class – Ron wants to see us all after school for a cast and crew meeting, and I think it's almost after school right now."

"What? Why didn't you say so?" said the courtesan, standing up.

"It seemed like there were more important things," Douglas said dryly.

"Like a *Sculpture Garden party*?" I asked.

"What's *happened to her*?" V—— wailed. "What's *happened to her*?"

"She's just throwing up," I told her, because Lily had doubled over again. She heaved and heaved but came up with nothing, like me.

We were late for the cast and crew meeting. The stage crew sat on folding chairs and the cast sat on the cold floor of the stage because if the cast was going to waltz in late the cast could get their own damn chairs, the crew isn't their slaves, only nobody but the stage crew is allowed in the storage closet because it's dangerous and only trained professionals like Frank Whitelaw and his new girlfriend Cheryl could enter the room safely and grab some fucking chairs. To the disappointment of the crew most of the major members of the cast seemed too distracted to enter into the anticipated fight and just scowled and sat down. Lily Chandly, although technically on the makeup crew, sat down on the stage in solidarity with the cast; Steve Nervo took her chair. Ron stood up and clapped his hands for our attention.

"As you will all hear tomorrow officially," Ron said, "Adam State is missing. He's been missing since your party" – here he glared at us – "almost two days now. Obviously, the play is put on hold, at least until we know what's going on. Keep up on your lines, because I'm sure that Adam is OK, but until he's back at school we won't be rehearsing. But that's not why I called this meeting.

"I called you all here because I think that a person or persons here know where Adam is. If any of your heads have cleared since the party, you'll remember that I briefly attended your, um, *social gathering* Sunday night. Emotions seemed to be running pretty high and I know there was a lot of drinking. That's why I didn't want to contact the police until I talked to you, because I know that you guys don't want your parents knowing all about that party. But Adam's parents are worried. They're frantic. If you can't or won't give me any information, I'll have to drag you guys into it. Is that clear?"

It was dead quiet. Ron scanned us slowly like he was watching a horse race. I looked up and saw all those ropes they need to raise and lower flat wooden backgrounds, thin frayed lines climbing up and up into the darkness, wondering how high they went and if I dared climb them. Then the back door of the auditorium slammed shut and we all jumped and stared into the blackness where the audience sat. I held my breath, half expecting Adam to walk down the center aisle and claim his ticket. "*Cymbeline!*" Do you realize that was only September 14th?

"I know you're worried," he said. "*Everyone* is worried. But I'm trying to arrange things so that nobody gets in trouble, OK? OK. Now, can anyone tell me what happened at the party, with Adam? The last time I saw him was on my way home Sunday night, when he was standing at the bus stop on the corner of California and Styx. He looked upset. Can anyone tell me what happened?"

Nothing emerged from the shadows. The *slam*! must have been the work of a poltergeist or janitor.

Ron sighed. "I hope that somebody in this room will realize the true seriousness of this situation. If someone is hiding Adam or knows where he is, you're in way over your head. I'm going to wait another twenty-four hours and then contact his parents with what I know. I don't want the police to start questioning all of you, I just don't think that's right, but if that's what has to happen that's what will happen. I'll wait twenty-four hours. If anyone wants to talk to me in private you can see me tomorrow in the Theater Office and you can even call me at home tonight. My number is –"

Why do phone numbers in movies and such always have to start with 555? Ron's gone now, his house burned down and I heard very vague rumors about his staying with a friend in Amsterdam during the trial. You can't call him. The phone number I give now will never reach Ron. In defiance of this tripentagonal tradition I will complete the sentence the way it really ended. I know because I was there.

"– 666-7314." Ron put his hand to his head in a theatrical gesture of thinking. "And I want to say this. Figuring out that you're gay is one of the scariest things that can happen to you. You feel like you're alone and that no one will help you. As most of you have guessed," he smiled gently, "I am gay. You're not alone. That's what you should tell somebody who is maybe figuring out they're gay. You can tell them to talk to me." Ron's face was lit with sheer kindness, naive and effortless. He was breaking my heart. Everything was. "You can tell them they're not alone."

Lily, replenished somehow, threw up.

Ron stepped toward her, then looked at us and stepped back a little bit. He had the same look at the party: a sudden realization of bad news. I never saw him again.

"We don't have to clean that up, do we?" called out some fat stage crew boy with long hair.

"You certainly do," Natasha said, but as it turns out the stage area is everyone's responsibility and not just the stage crew's and we should all work together anyway, like the finest theater troupes in the world do.

Gabriel took me home. All the way he kept sighing like he couldn't think of how to start the sentence, and I guess he never figured out how because when we got to my house he killed the engine and just looked at me. Sat there staring until I put my bag on my shoulder and made like I was going to leave. Where was everybody? What were they thinking?

"I'm sorry," I said, because it felt right, chilly there in the car, to apologize for something. For everything, or for whatever people were mad about. Around the corners of my eyes, and high in my head, I felt the weight of all my friends, exasperated and at their wit's end because of something I'd done, and I couldn't even think what it could be. "I'm sorry."

Gabriel smiled faintly and leaned across the gearshift to kiss me. I felt his warmth drip down my body like something in an IV bag. I tasted him like a fix, leaned in to kiss him back, kiss him more, kiss him hard, and then I was just going at it, slurping at him like a thirsty Popsicle. He responded, his breath sharp and sour with the day's worry, and reached down between my legs, not even stopping above the waist like you usually do with boyfriends, you just *do* because that's how it works. He unbuttoned my jeans like he was tearing bread and I was coming as soon as his fingers were inside me, three fingers not even pulling down my underwear, just pulling it sharply aside. I'd never come that fast, not even by myself. I unzipped him and grabbed him sharply, still heaving myself. I ran my hand up and down around him like I was shaking a bottle of salad dressing. I'd never handled anyone so harshly, but it worked, instantly, staining his pants and dribbling on the seat, even a little drop on the steering wheel like a dewdrop or a baby slug. He gave a sharp cry like he'd sat on a shard of something, and then a series of rough grunts before ripping his fingers out of me so quickly I shrieked. Trembling, I buttoned my pants while he looked at me and zipped himself up. I turned to give him a sheepish smile – hot fast fun sex, I thought – but he was just staring at me like he was afraid, a pure dread stare like he couldn't remember who I was, or did remember, but couldn't believe it.

LATER

I found myself sitting on a corner of my bed, curled up against the wall like a creature new and nervous to captivity, when the phone rang.

"Hello?" the creature said.

"Um, we got cut off," Douglas said. "It's me."

"What?"

"Douglas," he said. "We got cut off. The car?"

"What?"

"Hello?"

"Douglas?"

"Natasha?"

"No," I said. "Flannery. We didn't get cut off, Douglas. What do you mean? What car?"

He sighed. "About moving the car to Roewer. Come *on*, Flan. Hello?"

"Douglas," I said. "Who are you trying to call? This is Flan."

"I *know*," he said. Then he didn't say anything.

"Douglas?"

"*About the car!*" he roared. "*About the fucking car!*"

I looked at the phone and tried to figure out what it was screaming at me. "Are we talking about V___'s car again?" I asked it, hesitantly.

"Oh for God's –" Douglas hung up, on himself. What? I looked at my clock; it was 4:00 a.m. What? I stared at the phone for a few minutes, thinking that in a minute something would happen that would make everything click into place. I stared and stared but then I had to bound downstairs because someone was rapping on my door. Rapping on my door, late at night. It was like something in a poem, or one of those hushed moments in early American history: *Those blasted redcoats! Wait a minute while I get my shoes, and then we'll throw tea into the harbor.* "I have to talk to you," Natasha said, panting steam into the 4:00 a.m. sky.

"Do you know what time it is?"

"No," Natasha said blankly, shaking her head. "Get in the car."

"Wait a minute while I get my shoes," I said, but when I looked down I saw I already had them on. "What's going on?"

"Consider it another meeting," she said as I buckled up.

"I can't deal with any more meetings," I moaned.

"You *have* to deal with it," she said. She U-turned; the sky spun. "That's what I'm saying. You're getting out of control, Flan, and – want a cigarette?"

"*No*. Have I *ever* wanted a cigarette? Why is everybody smoking, all of a sudden?"

"I guess they're a little tense," Natasha said, grinning wickedly. The zoo sped by, closed. I figured we were going to the beach. The raw white-gray of the approaching ocean sky was making my eyes throb. Natasha's door was open before we slowed down, slammed shut before we stopped and she was at the shore while I was still fiddling with my seat belt.

I puffed through sand. "It's great to spend time with you like this," I said, when I reached her. We were right at the edge of the ocean. She was staring out, her eyes so far away she was probably scanning Japan. "Natasha?" She didn't say anything, just tapped ash into the foam. Was she angry, was I? "I tried calling you last night," I said. "Nobody answered."

"When I got home I tore the phone out of the wall and threw it out the window," she said, smiling fondly like she was talking about some childhood tantrum.

"You didn't," I said.

She looked me straight in the eye. "When I got home," she said, "I tore the phone out of the wall and threw it out the window. I stepped on pieces of it on my front steps when I left the house this morning."

"That exact thing happened to me one morning," I said, "when I got really sick of a tape and threw it out the window when I was taking a shower." My voice trailed off, because Natasha had stalked off, down the shore. Toward Canada. At a party once, last year I think, at V__'s house, I remember following someone out to the dark garden, the person's face flickering as the light

342

from the party hit it. I can't remember who it was. Now I followed Natasha.

"So," I said, reaching her again, "why'd you throw the phone out the window? Besides the obvious reasons."

"I didn't want to talk to you," she said quietly. The waves crawled toward us. Pale, pale morning tentacles were tinting everything gray and unearthly. Underneath my feet, sneaking through my shoes, was what remains of even the mightiest rocks when they try to go up against the ocean. Somewhere in my head was something I couldn't remember that was making Natasha scowl out to sea like her shipment wasn't anywhere in sight. Like a pearl in an oyster it sat in my head, valuable and wanted. You have to kill the oyster to get it, though.

"Natasha," I said, "*please*."

She blinked and sighed like she couldn't believe it, but she faced me. "Please *what*?" she asked.

"Please tell me what's going on," I said, "please. I – everyone's been so *strange*. Something happened at the party, right? Is that it? Somebody stole V___'s car, or – I can't remember, Natasha."

"If you're lying –" she said.

"I can't remember," I said. I felt the sunken globe within me, hiding in the reeds like a big wary fish, thinking every shadow is a net that will capture it and bring it into the light. So many good poems I'm writing here.

"Well," she said. "Do you remember this boy you had a crush on? He conducted the choir?"

I blinked, clicking the dark world between open and closed like a snapshot. "Adam," I said. "Of course I remember Adam. I haven't fallen on my head, Natasha, I just can't remember the party. Is it about Adam?" I remembered he hadn't been in school, his gaping

343

absence in choir like a lost tooth. "Do we know where he is? Something about why he isn't around?"

She snorted. "You could say that."

"Natasha, *where* is –"

"He's dead," she said simply. She kicked at seaweed like it was as easy as that.

"What?"

She looked at me. "What, did you not hear me?"

"Well –"

"Or was that sentence too complicated for you?" she said.

"Who – how –"

"He's *dead*. Dead, dead, dead, dead, dead. Didn't you learn about it in Econ? The Death of the State?"

"*Stop*," I said, covering my eyes.

"Don't you cry," she said. "I knew you remembered. Adam's dead and he'll always be dead, from now until *we're* all dead and after that, even. Forever dead. So don't start weeping like V___ keeps doing or I swear to God I'm going to throw you to the jellyfish."

"I can't believe this," I said.

"*What* can't you believe? That we all know about it?"

"When did it – how –"

"Remember the thing at the party you *can't* remember?" she said, with all the cruel sarcasm of soap opera matrons. "Well, *then*, that's when it happened. That's when you –"

I screamed, wide open and short like an animal, briefly struck and dead instantly. I didn't hear it, so I don't know how loud it was, but my throat was burning like a first sip of liquor, warm from your dad's bottle when you're no more than nine years old. Shut up, Tert. I tasted blood and realized I had bit my own finger, broken the skin as I tried to keep back the rest of that gaping scream.

Natasha looked at me like I was, I don't know, some creature by the side of the road, hissing and bleeding. Something you're not sure whether you should help it, kill it or leave it alone. "That's when you saw me do it," she said, finishing her sentence uncertainly. "*I* did it. That thing you can't remember is that you saw me do it. Do you remember now? *I* did it, Flan. That's why I had to hide my dress. It was covered in – well, do you remember now? Flan?"

I looked at her. The truth of her story was slipping around me like a borrowed shoe. A little big. Not shaped to my foot. But wearable. Fitting. "No," I said, "I don't remember."

"Well it's true," she said primly, exhaling. My finger aimed my blood at the ground, stinging and vibrating at my side. "I killed Adam, Flan. And now we have to work fast, because, well –"

"You don't want to get caught," I said. Three blood drops were in a sloppy row on the damp sand in front of me like little scarlet saucers.

"Right," she said, relief bright and sharp in her eyes. She was talking faster like she'd made up her mind. "That's why V__'s car – well, it's not *stolen*, not really. We're *saying* it's stolen. We just –"

"*Adam's* in the trunk?" I said. "That's what Douglas meant yesterday? He meant you guys stuffed *Adam* –"

"It's not like it sounds," she said.

I blinked. "How is it not like it sounds?" I asked.

She blinked. "Well, OK. It *is* like it sounds." We both giggled nervously. "It's *just* like it sounds. We – well, not *me*, I was getting rid of my dress. But Adam was put in the trunk, and Douglas and V__ drove her gorgeous car to –"

"Why did you have to get rid of your dress?" I asked.

345

"There was –" She gestured like she was wiping her hands on an apron. "All *over* him. *Me*. I mean, it was, well –"

"*Evidence*," I said.

"*Messy*," she said. "To a bad neighborhood. They drove the car –"

"But they'll find the car, won't they? I don't get it," I said. Still not being able to remember this gave me a cushioned pad, so I could talk about things like they weren't already happening, like it was some TV movie. Which of course it *is*, now. "Why did you put the bod – Adam – whatever – in the trunk of V___'s car? They'll find the car, and then they'll –"

"That's why I'm talking to you," she said. "We've got to think of something, Flan. When we all saw you were freaking out –"

"I wasn't *freaking out*," I said. "I just didn't –"

"We need *everybody* for this," she said. "Kate's organizing it, of course, she's such a – well, I shouldn't complain. They're getting you out of it, but –"

"*Me?*"

Natasha bit her lip. "Don't you see, Flan? We shouldn't have done the thing with the car. They'll *find* the car, and then they'll –"

"Why did you put it in the car in the first place?"

"We *had* to," she said defensively. "There was still a party going on when you ran in, screaming and with blood –"

"*Me?*"

"Yes," she said. "You'd *seen* me, and I guess some of the – so, anyway, we quickly ended the party, and we had to get rid of – well, for safekeeping –"

"And now," I said, "he's in the trunk of V___'s car in a bad neighborhood, is that right?"

"Well, not anymore," she said. "Douglas and I moved it to the student lot."

"At *Roewer*?" I asked incredulously. "Have you gone mad?"

Natasha seesawed her hand, *so-so.* "Actually there's a method behind it." She looked at my finger and then at the sand. "Does that hurt?"

"You know, oddly enough I can't seem to concentrate on my finger injury because I'm suddenly seized with the notion that we're all going to go to *jail!*" I said. Panic was running out of each strand of my hair so it must have been sticking out like static. I spread my arms out wide. "What are we going to *do*?"

"*Something*," Natasha responded instinctively, and then looked at me. "Look, if they found V___'s car in some neighborhood they'd just suspect *us*. If Adam's – death –"

"*Murder*," I corrected. "You *killed* him, Natasha."

Her gorgeous hand seesawed again. "It doesn't matter. The point is that now the car will be found at Roewer, so *anyone* could be suspected. Not just you."

"*Me?*" I blinked and I felt the bullet slide into the chamber, or cock the gun or whatever I mean: *click into place.* I saw myself, clearly, a scorned woman drunk and angry at a party. Hell hath no fury etc.

"I mean, not just *me*," Natasha said quickly. "Don't worry. As Kate would say, we can *do* this."

"They're going to suspect *me!*"

She twisted a strand of her hair around her sharp, stern finger. "No they won't," she said quietly. "Not with the car at Roewer. Now it could be *anyone* who did it, don't you see? If we all work together –"

"Natasha, *why* did you – *how could you*? I'm sorry, Natasha, but I don't think a *high school clique* can –"

"We *have* to," she said. She stopped moving and looked at me, slit-eyed. "*I'd* do it for you," she said.

"How do you know?"

"We did it when you let those fruit flies go."

"Oh," I said. "*Well. That's* comparable."

"I'd do it for you," she said again.

"*How do you know? How do you know* you'd do it for me?"

"Believe me," she said. And then: "Please."

As the sun rose the beach just got uglier and uglier. What had looked like rocks, in the foggy dim, were broken Styrofoam coolers. Dog mess mingled with lazy seaweed dotting the landscape like spent condoms. The roar of the traffic was hitting its stride, easily competing with God's ocean, and everywhere, everywhere were bits of broken glass. "Natasha, why did you do this thing?"

"He's a dick," she said. "*Was* a dick. I don't know. Baker's Rule, or something."

"You know, Mr. Baker was talking about *math*."

"I don't know," she said again. I could almost see her, in full detail. Almost clear as day. How long had we been here? Past the shore the ocean sat, waving listlessly, and past that there wasn't anything. With the clouds so low you couldn't see anything at all. Any boats or islands were obscured in the foggy air, so that not even the horizon was evident anywhere, just the sea leaking into a smoky nothing. "Our lives are over," I said. Some *thing* in my head rose to the surface and threatened to pop like one of those domes of lava you see in active volcanoes, near boiling. A watched pot. All my friends, my best friend, me: we were incredibly screwed. "Our lives are –"

"I heard you," she said quietly. "Will you help me?"

She had stepped so close to me that when I looked at her I saw the texture of her lipstick, stretched and cracked slightly from talking. She was vulnerable. "*Would* I?" I said, reducing the proceedings to a joke from which I could always get a laugh. The grimy water stretched out, almost catching my foot. The drops of blood were washed away like a symbolic moment only writers are sensitive to. *To which they're sensitive.* "Would I? Would I?"

Wednesday November 3rd

I was dripping in my towel, opening my drawer, when the cancer hit. A black clump of memory, a little velvety bubble of carbonation, stretched against the confines of my skull, squatting and sulking like a bad plum. Everything I've forgotten is still balled up behind my eyes, inscrutable and sensitive to the touch, a cold, impenetrable marble of truth. I've already taken four aspirin.

There in my drawer I found my plain white shirt with the small flower embroidered on it. At the party Natasha was dressed like me, remember? "I want to wear something *regular*," she said. "But, you know, sarcastic regular. Ironic. You know, for Halloween." There the shirt was, stark clean, blinking white. If Natasha had been wearing my shirt, why had she burned the dress? It was a mistake, I was sure, that we'd pay for later.

I was already running late but I decided to look for Natasha's nail file and give it back to her, thinking I should try to set this jigsaw as right as I could and return things to their proper places. My tumor throbbed in my head as I overturned sofa cushions and peered underneath tables but it wasn't there. It wasn't there. You remember the nail file, don't you? The one with the claw at either end, one claw striking a faint bell in my head and the other stretched out into the ether, invisible and irrevocable. Like – *shit!* – the bus.

Millie and Jennifer Rose Milton were running late too, Millie applying her makeup in the rearview mirror at the red light where I stood shivering. "Get in, get in," she called, but Jenn just glared at me.

"I don't want to interrupt anything," I said cautiously, as Jenn looked on, her lips taut and tight. That's right, taut *and* tight.

"We've already been *un*interrupted," Millie said. "I forgot to set my alarm. I don't know what's gotten into me. Or *Jenn-Jenn*, for that matter. I found her asleep on the *floor* of her room, in yesterday's clothing."

"*Yesterday's clothing?*" I asked, mock shocked. "How passé, Jenn."

Millie shrieked with laughter; even little Jenn-Jenn snorted and turned to roll her eyes at me. "Oh Flan," Millie said, capping her lipstick with a brisk click. "No wonder you're a writer. You always have a line."

"Yes, well," I said. I couldn't think of anything to say.

"Oh, I've been trying to ask Jenn-Jenn this, but she's been so *touchy* lately." Millie spoke lightly, but I saw her meet Jennifer Rose Milton's cold eyes in the mirror. "We need to choose a new opera. Do you have an opinion on *Tosca* versus *Faust*? Hard to choose between murder and the Devil, eh?"

Lightning could strike anytime now. Any time at all would be fine.

"Flan?"

"Um –"

"*Shit!*" Millie said, jamming on the brakes. We all nodded forward, like praying Muslims. Traffic was stalled in front of school. For some reason the student parking lot was blocked and the parking guards were waving people away with useless arm sweeps. "What *is* this?" she said. "The faculty lot's full again, and we're not allowed in the student lot – where are we supposed to park? The union's going to go *crazy*."

We were inching closer and closer to the entrance of the student lot. There was a small crowd of people, mostly students, with a few impatient teachers trying to herd everyone out of the way. But what was going on? The parking guards kept waving away, and cars were trying to inch out of lanes, trying to turn around in driveways. Then suddenly somebody tall moved, and a flashing red light shone in my eye, spinning DANGER and explaining the backup. We inched closer. Policemen waved us through, their eyes squinting in the fog-filtered sun, their jaws set in an official grimace. Occasionally they'd call out something inaudible, but you know what it was. What it always is. Move along, move along. There's been a problem. The police are here. The culprits will be hung.

Jennifer Rose Milton and I glanced at each other. My stomach dropped like a cartoon anvil. "Maybe we should get out of the car," she said hesitantly.

"Yes, OK," Millie said, looking distractedly in her rearview mirror. Yellow police tape was being unwound and wrapped around posts and trees like some big kite had tangled itself up in my high school.

Jennifer Rose Milton opened the door and jammed it into V——'s chest. "Oof," she said, holding her stomach. "*Watch* it."

"Sorry."

"Well, *watch* it."

"She said she was sorry," I said, still marveling that somebody had actually said "oof" out loud, like we were in a comic strip.

"Fuck you," V—— said, looking at the cops. I guess it wasn't a comic strip; I guess it was reality. In a comic

351

strip V__ would have let loose a string of asterisks and exclamation points.

"V__!" Millie said amazedly.

"I was just kidding," V__ said, halfheartedly remembering herself. "I'm sorry, Millie. My car was stolen and now they found it."

"It was *stolen*?" Millie said. "That gorgeous car? That's awful. Jenn-Jenn, you didn't tell me V__'s car was stolen."

"V__'s car was stolen," Jennifer Rose Milton said stonily.

"But *now*," V__ continued, her dark eyes on me, "it's in the student lot."

"I'm confused," Millie said. A car behind us honked. "You all get to homeroom and we'll talk about it later. I've got to find parking, preferably within a five-mile radius. Oh, V__ – do you have an opinion about the next opera we do? We were talking about *Tosca* versus *Faust*. Hard to choose between murder and the Devil, eh?"

"I don't know," V__ said. "It doesn't matter, I guess."

Honk. Move *along*, Millie. "OK," Millie said, looking at V__ curiously. "I'm glad they found your car, V__."
HONK. Millie moved off and we walked to the sidewalk.

"Flan?" V__ asked with elaborate casualness. "Do you mind telling me what exactly the car is *doing* in the student parking lot?"

I was trying to remember what Douglas had said. "Douglas and Natasha moved it."

"Why?" Jennifer Rose Milton said.

"Ask them," I snapped. Why was everything about *me* all the time? I opened the door of the school; inside it was pandemonium. Kids were yelling and yelling, while teachers waved their hands above their heads and the loudspeaker squawked something. A locker crashed open and somebody's life toppled out: books, papers, photographs, all trampled beneath everyone's expensive shoes. Some people were crying, and others were shouting; suddenly a knotted whirlpool appeared in the crowd as somebody, her hands over her face, became the center of attention. Mokie, his glasses crooked on his face, pushed his way through the crowd violently, actually thrusting people aside like they were clothes of the wrong size, muddling the rack. He reached the person everyone was swarming over, and grabbed her. Her hands slapped him, each one a tiny wicked claw like Natasha's emory board. Mokie grasped her by the shoulders and began to move her like a shopping cart; she turned around and I saw it was Rachel State. Her eyes were wide open and raccoonishly made up, her face was gummy black with all her Goth makeup melting under her brother's death. Her mouth was open in a drowned-out howl. Mokie dragged her to his office door, opened it, shut it behind them.

"They must have opened the trunk," I said, and Jennifer Rose Milton glared at me and put her finger to her lips. With difficulty we made our way up the stairs where the din was quieter and better organized. Clumps of students were seated in circles on the floor, leaning against lockers. A few of the more star-struck freshman and sophomore girls were crying, but mostly everyone was talking very fast, spreading the crumbs of gossip in grating high voices. It was the sort of scene I always pictured going on inside Kate's brain.

Right on schedule Kate ran up to us, with a wan Douglas scurrying after her.

"*There* you are," she said to me. "Douglas was just telling me this whole thing was *your* idea."

"What?"

"Moving the car," she said. "Why didn't you keep it in the bad neighborhood?"

"Natasha —"

"You know," Kate said, "it doesn't matter. This will speed up everything, anyway."

"What are you talking about?" Douglas asked. "You're turning into a basket case, Kate. Just like Flan. We're all — incredibly *fucked*."

What happened, I wondered, to all the intricate and resonant words we always used? Now we were savages. Now we were so savage.

"No we're not," Kate said. "You're forgetting Ron Piper. He saw Adam at that bus stop. California and Styx. No matter how suspicious we look, he can verify our innocence."

"California and Styx are parallel," Douglas said.

"No they're not," Jennifer Rose Milton said.

"Yes they *are*," he said. "Think about it."

"*You* think about it."

"It *doesn't matter*," Kate said. "The point is that he'll back us up. Ron will —"

"I'm not so sure having Ron provide an alibi is going to work." Jennifer Rose Milton swallowed, her wan face rippling. "*Maman* said she heard that Ron was the last person to see Adam — the teachers are gossiping about this as much as the kids — but that it doesn't make him beyond suspicion. It makes him the *center* of suspicion. *Maman* asked me if I thought he had anything to do with it. I said of course not, but she went on and on. You know, Ron's gay, and why was he at a party with teenage boys —"

"That's absurd," Kate said. "It wasn't 'a party with teenage boys.' It was more than —"

"She said," Jennifer Rose Milton plowed on, "that she felt Ron had been a little too close to us over the years

354

anyway, and now it looked like he was *really* mixed up in something. She said that the school board really took a chance hiring a gay man and that now it looked really – I just think that Ron is not going to be as unimpeachable – is that the word I mean? – he's not going to be as unapproachable – as *effective* a witness as we want. Particularly now that V___'s car –"

"*Why did you move my car*?" V___ cried. "That's what *I* want to know. Flan, *why did you* –"

"It wasn't me," I said. "It was –"

"*Please*," V___ said in ugly disgust. Kate was shaking her head at V___ and watching me carefully.

"How did you even get the *keys* to V___'s car?" Jennifer Rose Milton asked.

"*Please*," V___ said again. "She got them the same place she got Lily's *glasses* and Douglas's *hat* and my *silk scarf*!"

"Shhh," Kate said. "This isn't helping, V___."

"Or Gabriel's *pocketknife*," V___ cried. "Or *your sweater*, Kate!"

"V___!"

"How did this happen?" V___ asked, suddenly quiet. She was biting her lip and I was so close to her I could see all the bites she'd made on her lip, like little astronaut footprints, tiny foreign dents claiming the moon forever. We'd never be the same again.

"Come on," Kate said. "We'll talk about this later."

"No," Douglas said. "V___'s right. Flan, I want *you*, right now, to tell Kate what you told me about why we should move the car."

I just stood there. Once again I was supposed to say something. Once again the slippery creature I was riding, the neat boxcars of *what happened*, had submerged quietly under the dark water gurgling in my head, the cancer humming like some appliance in my skull. All the props were moving over, tossing like sleepers: the clean white shirt in my drawer this morning, the missing nail file, all the secret items on my top shelf suddenly in plain view of everyone. In my gurgly dreams an incomplete croquet set was spread out on the lawn in front of me next to a short row of bloody teeth and eight shiny pearls. I had the clues but I didn't know the mystery. "I don't know," I said, finally.

"Come *on*," Kate said again, like she hadn't expected anything to come of this interruption. "We have an all-school assembly, and I think we should be there to hear what they found."

"We *know* what they found," Douglas said, but Kate shook her head again.

"We can *do* this," she said.

The auditorium was overcrowded past overcrowded, with harried teachers trying to herd everyone everywhere. I ran into Natasha, literally and *hard*. "*Watch* it," she said to me even when she saw who I was. Kate, Douglas, V____ and Jennifer Rose Milton were right behind me but suddenly those incredibly fat twin boys who always wear hooded sweatshirts got between us and soon it was Natasha and me sitting together. I craned my neck to try to find the other B8ers, but almost immediately the lights dimmed ominously, turning the auditorium hysteria up just one more notch.

Mokie stepped up to the podium. His glasses were still crooked on his face and he was still an idiot, but panic was coming off him like steam rising off Lake Merced in the mornings. "Children," he began into the mike and a short tantrum of indignation roared back at him. "*Students*," he corrected himself hurriedly. "We have called this all-school assembly to correct rumors that have been going around this morning that something terrible has happened. Something terrible *has* happened. As you all know –" Mokie coughed and looked offstage, then nodded. "As you all know, here is Principal Bodin with an important announcement."

Bodin waddled on. His light blue blazer was buttoned and his hands were on his hips so the collar was haloing around him like a cobra hood. There was the scattered clatter of a few people clapping, for some reason.

"Hello," he said. "This is Principal Bodin. Is everyone here? Everyone?"

"No," Natasha muttered.

"Unfortunately," Bodin said, "we've had what I would call some terrible news. We *all* would call it that. It is tragic. I regret to inform you of this terrible announcement. That is why we are having an all-school assembly to come together as a community" – he swallowed and held a closed fist to his rib cage – "as we did previously and have always done."

That's when everybody knew that what was darting around school was true – somebody was dead. And some people knew who it was. A large teenage wail rose up from the masses; instinctively the bossiest teachers stood up and marched up and down the aisles waving their hands horizontally to shut everybody up. They looked like umpires: *Safe! Safe!* If they only knew.

"It's true," Bodin said, looking down. "Here to talk to you more about it is – we're very grateful to have – Dr. Eleanor Tert. You know her from her work on the all-school survey, and some of you have had the honor of individual interviews. Without any further – for more on this subject –" Bodin gestured emptily out toward us like he was tossing us crumbs.

357

The curtains parted slightly like late-night television. I swear the grumble of the auditorium sounded like a timpani roll. Everyone clapped and there she was.

Hello, children. The last time I was here I was here to talk to you about a story.

My story.

I hope that some of you remember the story of my addiction and triumph. If not, you can read the book. But that isn't important. Today I am here to talk to you about *your* story.

Today in the student parking lot the body of Adam State was found inside the trunk of a stolen car. He had been missing almost a week, and the police told me he was dead most of that time. I have also been told that Adam was one of the brightest boys here at Roewer and was on the cusp of a brilliant future. Barring any addictive behaviors of his own he could have become an incredible person, and we all mourn him.

His death is not what worries me, however. What worries me is the *way* he died. Adam State was killed in what looks distinctly like a Satanic ritual. The body was brutally mangled and wounded, and there was a talisman decorated with claws which was found protruding out of Adam's eye. Although this artifact is normally used as an emory board, I believe – and law enforcement officials believe as well – that it is a Satanic object.

A friend to all of us was found dead this week. Whether he was killed by a Satanic cult here at Roewer or by somebody else at some other place doesn't matter in the slightest. What is important is that Satan has entered this world of Roewer High

School as a phony solution to the pressures you face. I was in high school, so I know the pressure you are feeling, and I'm here to tell you to join me and say no to Satanism and survive! That's what I'm here to tell you! Cults are not the solution! I am the solution! Listen to me! My name is Eleanor Tert and I am here to help you all! Thank you.

The auditorium was in full evangelistic roar. The floor rumbled with all the stomping feet, shaking loose some of the gum that had stuck there for years. The house lights burst on. The umpires were walking up and down the aisles again but nobody felt safe. With a horror-movie-shower-scene scream Sweater-Vest Shannon stood up and ran toward the stage, where Tert made little shooing motions. "*Please!*" Shannon said. "*Please!* He *died!* Everyone *dies!* Everyone *dies!*" Tert walked back through the curtains after floundering for a while to find the opening. One of the guidance counselors was trying to say something into the microphone, but with a loud *pop!* it shut down and she walked back offstage, wobbling from a broken shoe. "Everyone *dies!*" Shannon shrieked, alone in the front of the auditorium. Why wasn't anybody helping her? "Everyone *dies!*" Some people started laughing, tinny and shrieky like it was being torn from their throats by fishhooks. "*Dies! Flies! Lies!*" I stood up; it was clearly time to leave. Some geometry teacher – the balding one Gabriel had sophomore year, I think his name is Treadmill – tried to block me from the aisle but I darted past him.

"I've been looking for you, Flannery Culp." I turned around and there was Hattie Lewis, her crazy-quilt dress matching her crazy-quilt eyes. The assembly let out, and I walked toward her, upstream, as everyone else ran to class.

"I'm really sorry about the *Myriad* lately," I said. "I know I've been a bad literary magazine editor."

"That isn't why I'm looking for you," she said. "I've been worried about you. The faculty gossip says that you and the others are somehow involved in this ghastly business with Adam and Mr. Piper."

"Adam and Mr. Piper?" I said.

"Apparently there was some *business* going on there." Hattie shuddered. "Mr. Piper always seemed a little suspect to me, but I never thought – the school board really took a chance with him, you know?"

"Yes," I said. Doors slammed. I was late for something or other.

"Adam's poor mother was down here this morning, and she's contacting some of the other parents who have always had *concerns* about him. They're really angry and I don't blame them, of course. I just hope that nothing gets out of hand. Flannery, did you ever notice Mr. Piper do anything that was at all –"

"No," I said. "*Never.*" I remembered, suddenly, a ride home in the rain. A late rehearsal and a grateful sophomore – me. Ron would have never tried anything like that – I mean with a *boy*, of course he didn't try anything with *me* – and now what would happen to him? And – I found myself crying – to us?

"Oh, dear," Hattie said, like she'd dropped something. Her hand reached toward my shoulder but didn't reach it.

"*When?*" I cried to her. "*When* will I be wise? You always said it would happen, but –"

"*Hush,*" she said, her hand still hovering. She reached into her kooky purse for a tissue. "*Blow,*" she said sternly, handing it to me, and I did. "Soon," she said, finally answering. "Soon, dear, but right now you have a few difficult days ahead of you."

360

"*Ahead* of me?" I cried.

"I'm afraid so. The police are undoubtedly going to talk to you all. *Flannery*, surely you must know it just wasn't proper to have him at one of your parties. Goodness, you're *trembling*, Flannery. Are you ill?"

"Scared," I said. I felt my teeth chattering.

"What's to be scared of, really?" she said mildly. "I know you're upset, Flannery, but try to get ahold of yourself. It will make everything easier. Just tell the police whatever you know. Do you want to talk about it with *me* first?"

"I'm scared," I whispered. Her hand reached toward me again and finally, finally, found my shoulder. I exhaled for the first time in months, breathed in the good air.

"Scared to talk to me?" she asked. "Flannery, *honestly*. This is an upsetting matter, a very upsetting matter, but it's not like you're going to get *caught* or *in trouble* or anything."

"I won't?" I said, biting my lip. "Promise?"

"*Flannery*," she said, astonished and smiling. "*No*, dear. *No*. What on *earth* – ? How could you even *think* such things? Didn't you learn, as a child, that the police are our friends?"

I giggled at that, looked down at the filthy floor.

"After all," she continued smoothly, "it's not as if *you* had anything –" Our eyes met and with that English-teacher wisdom she saw it, right through me like a glass-bottom boat. All the creatures at the sandy bottom of myself, scuttling around. Predators, afraid to be caught. Afraid to be prey. She jerked her hand back from me so hard my neck snapped. From behind a classroom door students tittered politely at some teacher's joke.

"*Oh*," she said, and stepped back.

"Mrs. Lewis –" I started, reaching for a laugh. "You've misunder – this is a misunder –"

"*Oh, oh,*" she said, and cupped her face in her hands.

"Mrs. *Lewis*!" I cried. "*Please.* Let me –"

"*Oh, oh, oh,*" she said, and she was crying. She stepped back, one step farther. Two steps. "*Oh, oh, oh,*" she said, perfect syllables of grief, well formed and grammatically, morally, academically, athletically, socially, correct.

"Mrs. – ," I heard myself say. The class, safe behind closed doors, laughed again. The hallway was echoing with her funny run and she was gone from me, like a dear lost item, a single pearl clattering forever down stairs.

And you know the rest of the day. When the police made an official statement about suspected teenage Satanic cults the national news picked it up, so when Mr. State and other men screeched their cars to a halt and ran down the street and kicked in the windows and lit the gasoline all the cameras arrived in time to see Ron's house not yet extinguished. "Fucking devil faggot killed my son," said the hysterical State when the microphones reached him, before the police grabbed him, before the lawyer got him off. No charges were pressed. He was hysterical and Ron wasn't even home, the house was well insured and the dogs ran out the puppy door into the crowded street yipping at the blaze. The flames rose bright on everyone's screens, flickering lipstick red and traffic-cone orange and Lord knows what else, depending on how your television's color was. It was probably on in those electronics stores, where rows and rows of the same broadcast glare at you so you can compare reception. You can compare the ruddiness of Mr. State's face, or the darkness of the angry silhouettes, still waving fists even as the police dragged them away. The tint of the flowers on the neighbor's robe. He was a good man. This is a quiet neighborhood. We never knew he was a cultist. The exact shades of brown on the suit Dr. Tert wore to the studio that night, giving her commentary. The black hue of the charred remains, providing a background the next morning for the newscaster to purse her lips disapprovingly but sympathetically. An America hungry for justice and tired of the way children are getting gunned down even in good neighborhoods, or stabbed, by Satanists, in a stolen car. An angry father. A known homosexual. It is true he hasn't been charged with anything but he did admit to being at what was now being called the Fatal Party. The call for a National Youth Curfew. Why people don't go to church anymore, and what that is doing to the next generation. What inside sources say. What neighbors say. What Dr. Tert says. More after this. We are interrupting this program. We regret to inform you. We are going live at the site. Live at the school. More after this. More after this. More, they promise me, there's more, there's plenty more after this.

Thursday November 4th

When I woke up the television was still on and my neck was noose-stiff. I was still in yesterday's clothes. I stumbled out of the chair and turned off the morning hosts who were chatting in clean suits and scrubbed faces. The door was knocking – I mean, someone was knocking on the door.

"Nice outfit," Natasha said when I opened the door. "Something about it seems familiar, though. Get in the car, Flan."

I moved the flask so I could sit down, took a swig, and stared down at my sleep-wrinkled clothes thinking suddenly of that smooth white shirt with the embroidered flower in the center, unruffled in my drawer. "You know," I said, "speaking of nice outfits, why is the white shirt you –"

Natasha reached over and pulled out the cigarette lighter from the dashboard. Its tip glowed lava-hot. "We *weren't*," she said, "speaking of that."

OK. "Where are we going?"

"The lake." Kate, Jenn, Douglas and Gabriel were already there, standing around looking cold and cross, and Lily was already throwing up.

"Top of the morning to you," Natasha said.

"Shut up," Douglas said.

"Sounds like things are starting off well," Jennifer Rose Milton said. She'd clearly been crying.

"What's wrong?" Kate asked.

"What's *wrong*?"

"Besides, you know, the obvious. Everything."

"Nothing. *Maman* and I had a fight this morning. She – I can't –"

"Let's all sit down," Kate said, soothingly and sternly. "This feels like a cocktail party, and besides, we don't necessarily want to be spotted meeting together secretly before school, do we?"

We all sat down. Jenn wiped her eyes. "Kate, I can't go on like this much longer. Millie is just *grilling* me, and I don't know what to say. I have *never* had a real fight with *Maman* until last night." She was crying. "*Never*."

Natasha lit a cigarette and passed the pack around. "Then it was about time. Can we get started, Kate?"

Kate lit her cigarette; everybody, *everybody* was smoking. Even Lily had wiped her mouth so she could light up.

"We have to wait until V__ gets here," she said.

"I bet she doesn't show," Douglas said. "She's really seemed a wreck lately."

"Not like the rest of us."

"She'll show," Kate said.

Jennifer Rose Milton took a long drag, still heaving from sobs and smoke. "What is going to happen?" she asked.

"You just *never know*," Kate said, "what's going to happen."

"That's for sure," Gabriel said, sitting next to me and smiling oddly. "I mean, just maybe a month ago –"

"Can we *please* skip the clever conversation until all of this is over?" Lily said. "I'm sorry, I just don't have the stomach for it."

"What *do* you have the stomach for?" Natasha asked.

"*Natasha –*" Douglas sputtered. "If it weren't for *you* –"

"Stop, stop," Kate said, clapping her hands. "Can we start this?"

"You said we'd wait for V____," I said. "And Flora's missing too."

"Shut *up!*" Gabriel yelled, "*Shut up!* We are all trying to get *out of this,* and all you can do is make jokes!"

"I wasn't joking," I said, astonished.

"Forget it," Kate said. "Let's start."

"*No!*" Gabriel said, and stood up. "I want to say this! We've never had a chance to really *say* this! Flan –"

"*Sit down!*" Kate said. "And *shut up,* Gabriel. We can't do this if everybody's going to be joking or arguing or crying or *throwing up*" – she pointed dramatically at Lily – "we can only do this if everybody just *sits down* and *shuts up* and listens to *me, me, me.*"

Natasha opened her mouth and started to say something, but Kate met her gaze and topped it and even Natasha, my brave Natasha, shook her head, took back her cigarettes and didn't say anything anymore.

"Now," Kate said, "so far I think things are going as well as can be. They found Adam in the car, of course, but nobody's talked to any of us, right? So they must have believed Ron when he –"

"Does everybody *know* what happened to Ron last night?" Douglas asked. "His *house burned down*, Kate."

Kate blinked. "So?" she said.

"So I think we might be fucked," Douglas said.

"No, no," Kate said.

"What Douglas means," Jennifer Rose Milton said gently, "is that Ron might not be as – what's the word I'm looking for? – unimpeachable a witness as we had first thought. I believe I mentioned that yester –"

"Ron's house means nothing," Kate said. "I mean, of course it means something to *Ron*, but it doesn't mean anything to us. What should matter to us – the *only thing* that should matter to us – is –"

"V___'s still not here," Lily said, suddenly. "We shouldn't have started without her."

"Hi," V___ said, and we all jumped.

"Um, hi," Gabriel said. "Sit by me."

"I have something to say," she said, and sat by Gabriel. I looked around the clearing: Gabriel, V___, Douglas, Kate, Lily, Jennifer Rose Milton, Natasha. Remember that. That's how we sat. Gabriel, V___, Douglas, Kate, Lily, Jenn, Natasha, me.

"Then *say* it," Kate said, "because we have a lot to –"

"I want out," V___ said, "of this life."

We all looked at one another: Gabriel, V___, Douglas, Kate, Lily, Jenn, Natasha, me. *What* did she say?

"I can't do this anymore," she said. She was fiddling with her long-gone pearls, which weren't there. She was fiddling with imaginary pearls. "I'm a wreck, and it isn't worth it. It would be better if the curtain just came down on this and we all got whatever we deserved or –"

"You think we'd get what we *deserved*?" Kate said.

V___'s hands were shaking. "I can't do it," she said. "I can't. I'm going to tell."

"I don't think that's your decision to make," Kate said.

"*What*?" V___ said. "What do you – *I just can't*, Kate! Don't make me."

"She can do it if she wants," Gabriel said.

"*No*," Kate said. "No she can't."

"I agree with Kate," I said.

"Well of course you do," Gabriel said, actually moving a few inches away from me. But we stayed in the same order, though: Gabriel, V___, Douglas, Kate, Lily, Jenn, Natasha, me.

"No," I said. "I *do*. We all got into this, and –"

"No no no no no no," Lily cried, putting her hands over her ears. "*No*! V___ is right, we *can't* do this. We have to –"

"We most *certainly can* do this," Kate said. "Everybody needs to *calm down*. We're not just doing this for Flan anymore. We're doing it for *all* of us. We're *all* –"

"For *me*?" I said. A white pillar of fury streamed through me. Everything was on *my* shoulders again, here in this important semester. Everyone *expecting*. Everyone *awaiting*. I was sick of it. "For *me*?"

"*Yes*," Jennifer Rose Milton said, and I saw that even she was angry, her beautiful skin coloring and her pretty-girl eyes hooded like she was taking aim. "*Yes*, Flan. Like Gabriel was saying – *trying* to say – just a few minutes ago. Nobody's had a chance to just *say* it. Nobody's been able to just *say* –"

"*We can* do *this*!" Kate shouted. She had the look in her eye when you kick and kick at the door and it doesn't open, when you write a boy letters and letters and he never loves you, not 'til the day he dies. Not even then. The fucking handkerchief. "*We can* do *this*! *We can* do *this*!"

"*Nobody here*," Jennifer Rose Milton said, "has just been able to just say what the deal is! That we –"

"Why don't we just say it, then?" I asked. "Why don't we just –"

"So *say it*!" Gabriel said, and pushed me *hard*, on the shoulder. "Why don't you just tell us why exactly we're all here, what exactly went on? Why don't you just explain it to us, tell us *why*, Flan?"

"I will," I said. "I'll say it. There's nothing so complicated about it. One of our friends committed a murder. Killed somebody we all knew, killed somebody I was in love with, beat him to death right there at one of our parties." I found myself giggling a little bit, the audacity of everything hitting me for the first time. The black marble in my head was bursting wetly, like it was never a marble at all but a bulging bubble in tar. Popping at its own pace, at its own time. Easy as that. "We didn't want her to go to *jail*, remember? We all *love* her, and we know it was, at least partially, an *accident*. That's why we are here, is that what you want to hear? We're all in this together, and that's why! Just face it: Mr. Adam State, handsome senior, big man on campus, adjunct member of the Basic Eight was killed by our glamorous friend Natasha, and now we're all –"

"Who?" Douglas asked simply, blinking.

Simply. The planet turned *over*, and the light shone in such a way as it hadn't for a long time, not since I don't know when. There's a point, every Saturday morning, where the cartoon character keeps running until the land ends and he's suspended in the air. He looks at the camera, suddenly suspicious of what he's been walking on. Sometimes he waves. Then gravity takes over and the joke finishes in a burst of dust on the canyon floor, the character crushed into whatever geometric shape the writer thought would get the biggest laugh. I looked around at my friends and a little figment in my head just melted away. There they all were. There wasn't Natasha. Never had been. Just a few minutes earlier I had been running, and although I didn't know where I'd end up I thought I knew what I was running on, but now I looked around at my friends and saw that the joke was reaching punch line. The line where you punch. The rest of it you know – the trial, the television and all that tiresome, tiresome speculation, digging under rocks we never noticed, much less put anything under – but a small sliver of the story is still mine to tell. Gravity took over and I saw that Gabriel was there, and V——, and Douglas was there next to Kate, and Lily was there, and Jennifer Rose Milton had always, always been there. But next to her was someone else. Always had been. The Basic Eight, after all, had always been the Basic Eight, and now Flora Habstat was looking right at me as easy as counting on your fingers. And perhaps even more surprisingly, she spoke.

"I'm going," she said, and she got up and started walking back toward Roewer High School. "I'm going to –"

From across the street, in some athletic field, somebody blew a whistle.

LATER
You're surprised? *You're* surprised? How do you think I felt? Even now, flipping through the rest of my journal here in my pod, trying to find anything left worth typing

for you, even now I'm still surprised. In the TV movie, I think, this revelation will be immediately followed by a montage, with pop ballad accompaniment: Natasha and I at a café, at the movies, in her car, on the beach, switching clothes, and finally Natasha beating Adam to death while I looked on, cowering by the tree and covering my ears as blood and teeth flung from his head and landed in the grass beside me. *Ohhhh*, the viewing audience will say. She was alone the whole time. We've been lied to. We want a refund.

I can't give one to you. I feel the same way, indignant, alone, left without anything to stand on. Everybody wants a friend with *panache*. Everybody wants somebody to drag them to the mirror and say, look, Kate's fatter than you. I didn't ask her to come; she told me she was there. She made all those Bloody Marys, gave me all those swigs for courage, sat and planned strategy with me over lattes for more hours than I can ever count. She found all the best bands before I'd even heard of them, taped their albums for me so I'd know what to listen to when we drove around together, late at night, with the wind in our hair. I thought I knew my friends. But you always learn the hard way: She said she'd always be there for me but was gone the moment I needed her most. *Anybody* could have healed my little cut on my back, from Carr yanking on my bra. But only Natasha could arrange things so that I wouldn't end up alone with only a snapshot to keep me company: Kate, leaning on an armrest rather than sitting on the couch like a normal human being, placing herself (symbolically, in retrospect) above us and looking a little smug, serving out a four-year sentence at Yale, V—— right next to her, fingering her pearls. V—— must have snuck into the bathroom sometime that evening to redo her makeup, because she looks better than anyone else, better than Natasha even, and that's saying a lot. Lily and Douglas, snug on the couch, Lily between Douglas and me as always, Douglas looking impatiently at the camera, waiting to continue whatever it was he was saying, Gabriel, his black hands stark against the white apron, squashed into the end of the couch and looking quite uncomfortable, beautiful Jennifer Rose Milton standing at the couch in a pose that would look awkward for anyone else who wasn't as beautiful, and stretched out luxuriously beneath us all, Natasha, one long finger between her lips and batting her eyes at me. It's humiliating to have her brought out like that, for everyone to see: just a stripe of blank carpet at the bottom of a photograph.

To go back and edit a journal, to find her scrawled on every page, impossible to ignore, undeletable, breaks my heart. I can't do it. Too much in my life has been reread like that, dramatically reinterpreted, and it always puts me in a bad light. It's like finding a trail of handkerchiefs dropped across early October, until you have to conclude that Adam was always going to be dating Kate, and never me, until just before he died. It's like having your sloppy handwriting on an all-school survey blown up and projected on a wall, the typed questions rippling on the arm of the prosecutor as he picks out his favorite parts while you, by law, must remain silent. It's like Dr. Tert holding up an earring that she stole from your top shelf and talking at length about talismans. Leaders of Satanic cults, you see, often horde personal items from all their acolytes so they can cast spells on anyone who disobeys them. "The claw-hand nail file, obviously, belonged to Adam." When you hear the new explanation all the original ones slip away, intangible, until you can't remember why you had all that stuff on your shelf in the first place, or exactly who it was who took the rest of the absinthe and mixed it into a cup of fruit punch. It's like going back to your locker, opening it and dropping everything into your gaping bag until it bulges at your side. Once, all these things in your locker meant something – that economics textbook you've barely touched since you covered it, that shiny flask you borrowed from your best friend, that long-overdue library book – but now I was just emptying my locker. Now they were just all the things I was taking home with me as I left school for the last time.

Hanging around the front entrance to Roewer High School were Mr. Dodd and Mr. Baker, and both of them were smoking and laughing at some joke. My backpack was heavy on my shoulders from clearing my locker out – I figured now was as a good a time as any. I was stunned that it wasn't even time for homeroom yet, but I guess that time drags when you're not having any, *any* fun.

"Hey Flannery," Baker said. "Larry, do you know Flan?"

"I believe I do," he said, looking right at me. "You'll be late for homeroom, honey."

"So will you," I said, "*honey*. Besides, I'm not going."

Dodd looked at Baker, who rolled his eyes. "And why not?" my homeroom teacher asked me.

I sighed. Now that I'd said it once I was getting a little tired of it. "Because," I said, "because *I*, Flannery Culp, beat Adam State to death with a croquet mallet, and now I'm going home to wait for whatever happens in these situations."

"What do you mean?"

I sighed, again; Dodd always was so *slow*. "I mean, I don't know if they send cops, or call my parents, or the principal or Dr. Tert or what. See you later, gentlemen."

I'd walked about five steps when Baker's hand grabbed my shoulder, right in the bruisy place where my boyfriend Gabriel Gallon had pushed me. "What?" I said.

"What?" *he* said.

"What?"

"What were you talking about, back there? Were you serious? Are you – are you serious, Flan?"

I looked down the blank space of the sidewalk, in front of my high school. Once upon a time, during stressful conversations, this glamorous girl named Natasha would just appear, with all the right words and the right gestures, and great legs and a shiny, shiny flask. But right now there were just some students arriving for what this girl used to describe as same shit, different day. One of them had a big black box that was playing a new song by a band I hadn't heard of. "Yes," I said. "I guess what I am is *serious*. I really did it."

Baker opened his mouth, a little geometric shape I couldn't give the formula for to save my life. "You –"

"*You*," I said. "*You* told me to, Mr. Baker. *You're* the one who always said, 'Do *something*.' It was your *rule*."

Baker blinked. How streamlined I can make these sentences, how tidy and clean. Baker blinked. "That's not what I meant," he said. "That's not what I meant *at all*."

"Well," I said, shrugging. My heavy bag went up reluctantly, groaning, the squeak of its plastic straps poking the gurgle in my head, the sound of Adam's lungs filling and heaving with his own blood. "It doesn't matter now."

Baker stepped back. More kids were arriving, and not just at Roewer; every moment, all over the world, more and more kids and what are *you* going to do about it? "That's not what I meant *at all*," he said, redundant as only teachers can be. So this is what he was springing on me, as I went home to wait for my life to end: I've disappointed my Calc teacher. "Flannery, that's not what I –"

"I know," I said. I looked down the sidewalk and for a second a glint of a forest-green dress threatened to appear, out of the gray morning like a phantom from fog. But then there wasn't anything, and then, as I kept staring, I couldn't even remember what I was looking for. What I needed was right in front of me somewhere, but I was spacing out, momentarily. Forgetting myself. What was it, what I was looking for?

"Flannery –" he said, and the bell rang just as I found it. *For what I was looking*: the seven of clubs.

EPILOGUE

Hello, my name is Eleanor Tert, a therapist and doctor. Perhaps you've read my books or seen me on TV with my good friend Winnie Moprah, another doctor. Through my work, I try to help people reach a better understanding of themselves and others, and make a better life.

You've just read the diary of Flannery Culp, the famed teenage Satanic murderess who led her cult, the Basic Eight, to notoriety this year with the murder of Adam State. Adam isn't really presented fairly in Flannery's version of the events, so I hope that through the integrity of our media you all know the *real* Adam. Adam State was one of the most popular boys at Roewer High School, and at the time of his murder he was on the cusp of a dazzling future: college, and then undoubtedly a brilliant and lucrative career, perhaps raising children of his own. From all I know of Adam he would never have done some of the things Flannery talks about.

I must object, too, to the presentation of myself and my work in the diary, particularly in the first speech I make at Roewer's all-school assembly. To try to dismiss me merely because of my past addictions is to do me a grave injustice; the writer Edgar Allan Poe, Flannery notes, took absinthe and yet is still a respected novelist and short story writer in America and elsewhere. What particularly angers me is that the sixth-period Advanced Shorthand class at Roewer was instructed to take complete notes on my speech as a classroom exercise; Flannery easily could have obtained a copy of the word-for-word transcription rather than relating it from memory, tailor-made to her own point of view. And I won't even comment on her presentation of my all-school survey without the statistical justification and analysis which precedes and follows all such surveys I do. I will just say that to deny me my full say on the matter is what I consider to be Flannery's *other* great crime. Like James Carr, who remains in a coma, I have been blocked from telling my side of the story. For more of my thoughts on this matter see my book, *Crying Too Hard to Be Scared*, which is much more thorough on the subject.

I was asked to write this epilogue to explore some of the more remarkable things to be found in what is regarded by Dr. Moprah and myself to be one of the most important documents on teenage Satanic murder to appear in this century. First off, of course, is the matter of Flannery's parents. David and Barbara Culp are well-respected members of their community and were considered to be model parents by all who knew them. David is a radiologist and Barbara teaches networking, so they were able to provide for Flannery all the comforts of an upper-middle-class Jewish home in San Francisco. Both of them have many hobbies and insist that they have had no more than a passing interest in the occult. We all saw the coverage of this event and will always remember their somber faces as they supported their daughter through the trial, and nursed their private grief at home. Having moved to Florida after the verdict, they ask that their whereabouts not be disclosed.

There is also the much-maligned Flora Habstat, whom I have met and counseled many, many times. Due to client confidentiality I cannot discuss Flora at any length, but suffice to say that she is a bright, beautiful, thoughtful, intelligent, attractive, creative and life-loving human being. There is nothing at all in her personality to suggest that she is a "bitch," and with a good fitness and diet program she keeps quite thin. All in all I am very proud of her and only hope that she will be allowed to tell *her* side of the story once this book is published, perhaps on television.

Lastly, of course, is the mysterious Natasha, Flannery's confidante. Who is she, really? In researching Flannery's life as part of my position as creative consultant for the TV movie *Basic Eight, Basic Hate*, I researched Flan's early life and found two prospective "Natashas" to whom Flan may have found an extreme attachment. One is Natasha "D." (her last name has been changed), a girl in Flan's first-grade class. A janitor at Pocahontas Elementary School (which was then Martin Van Buren Elementary) remembers that Flan and Natasha "D." were "unusually close, almost best friends," for at least the first few months of first grade, whereupon the "D." family moved to Plano, Texas, due to her father's position as an executive. Natasha "F.," nee "D.," said in a brief telephone interview that she does not remember Flannery, nor did she know who I was.

The other Natasha, Natasha "V.," may be closer to the mark. Natasha "V." worked at Camp Boyocorpo during one of the two summers Flan attended as a camper and was assigned to Flan's bunk as a counselor-in-training. Who knows what whispered confidences or other activities may have gone on during those starlit nights? In any case, Natasha "V." became a lesbian with serious self-esteem issues. Shortly after I appeared on the Winnie Moprah show, Natasha "V." sought me out for professional help, and during one of our early hypno-imaging sessions this revealing connection rose to the surface.

Whatever her source, Natasha's importance cannot be overemphasized. What Natasha did, Flannery did – Adam's murder, Carr's poisoning, the drinking, talking back in class – so Natasha's actions can be seen as an imaginary manifestation of Flan's *dark side*. Like a shadow, Natasha performed the actions Flannery was afraid to admit wanting to perform. Luckily this whole sequence of events was put to a stop before it was too late, and hurrah to Flora Habstat for that.

In conclusion, I wish to draw your attention to a passage from the end of Flan's diary: "More kids were arriving, and not just at Roewer; every moment, all over the world, more and more kids and what are *you* going to do about it?" Flan's desperate question is obviously a cry for help, though despite several letters I have written to her, she refuses to see me even for a minute. But it is also a call to action. Indeed, more and more kids are arriving, and not just at Roewer; high schools everywhere report dramatic overcrowding. In short, teachers and administrators are getting more and more overworked and unable to deal with the myriad of problems that challenge today's teens academically, athletically and socially. So the responsibility falls on you. Peter Pusher, in his remarkable book *What's the Matter with Kids Today?: Getting Back to Family Basics in a World Gone Wrong*, suggests that the answer lies in prayer, but I would suggest (with all due respect to Peter) that we take our solution one step further: Moral Watchfulness.

Moral Watchfulness is a combination of different concepts, and each one needs further explanation. "Moral" because society is nothing without morals. Teach your children – and other people's children, if you have no children of your own – the importance of right or wrong.

To do so, you need to arm them with the weaponry of morals. In addition, you need to be "Watchful." Be *Watchful* for signs of Satanism. Be *Watchful* for absinthe abuse, even casual absinthe abuse. Perhaps you need to give your children my all-school survey, and interpret it accordingly. I may be creating a workbook. Finally, you need to combine both "Moral" and "Watchful" (*ness* is just a suffix) into an aggressive strategy to make sure our children don't end up hanging out with the Basic Eights of this world.

Remember, our world is at the equivalent of first semester senior year – the most important semester for our future. Read this diary, not for the true-crime thrills all of us crave deep within us, but for the important lesson it teaches us all: Flannery Culp, and people like her, are neither fish nor fowl but are living, breathing human beings, as real as I am. Thank you.

Vocabulary:

CUSP	THOROUGH	RADIOLOGIST
MUCH-MALIGNED	MORAL	WATCHFULNESS

Study Questions:

1. Dr. Tert says: "To try to dismiss me merely because of my past addictions is to do me a grave injustice." Write one paragraph agreeing with this statement, and another paragraph disagreeing with this statement.

2. Which model for Natasha do you think is more likely, Natasha "D." or Natasha "V."?

3. Do you, deep within you, crave true-crime thrills? Why or why not? Do you think you would be a better person if you used Dr. Tert's strategy of "Moral Watchfulness?" Why or why not? Do you think

Flannery's version of the story of the Basic Eight is correct? Why or why not? Do you think Dr. Tert's version of the story of the Basic Eight is correct? Why or why not? Was Dr. Tert even there? Why or why not? Why or why not? Why or why not?

4. Ness is a suffix. Name at least four other suffixes.

An excerpt from Daniel Handler's new novel *Adverbs*, on sale now...

COLLECTIVELY

SALTWATER TAFFY IS I GUESS MADE from salt water and a whole bunch of sugar, spun or woven or beaten into a substance they sell down by the boardwalk. If you're in San Francisco, as this love story is, you can head south and see it being made in a shack, next to the shack where they sell tickets and next to the shack where they fry up calamari and give it to you for a price. Just follow the signs. You can't miss the signs they put up.

This is love, saltwater taffy. Pretty much everybody has had some. Somebody offers it on a day when you have nothing to do, and most likely you'll take it and put it in your mouth. It unites us, saltwater taffy, but whose favorite is it? Who likes it best? Just about nobody. So why do we eat it? This love story is about this style of love, this sweet thing that exists unasked for, that everybody eats out of the same bag. But also it is about what it says on the shack. I was there myself, and the large sign said: COME IN AND WATCH US MAKE IT.

I did not want to. Some things are private, no matter how many people know about the sugar and the spinning and such, and this love story is about that part of love too.

There's a song called "Please Mr. Postman" or maybe it's just "Mr. Postman." The postman always had it in his head. It was one of the downsides of his job, that and vicious dogs. He explained this to his son as they reached a flat part of the hill, which like a bunch of things was a false ending. If you had a bird's-eye view you could see there was more to it. The postman in effect had a bird's-eye view, from all the days of climbing this hill with mail for everybody.

The son's name was Mike. It was Bring Your Daughter to Work Day, which after much debate had been changed to Bring Your Child to Work Day, to make it more inclusive. It was fairer this way, it united more people, so the postman had Mike with him on his route.

"Most people think it's just delivering mail, just finding the right house and slipping it into the slot," the postman said, "but there's more to it than that." He started to list some things about his job Mike might not know, more or less off the top of his head. Mike sort of listened. "Everybody gets mail, is the thing. No matter where they live. Mail unites us, son, and at a time like this with volcanoes and wicked men we need that."

"My teacher says the volcano thing isn't true," Mike said.

"She would, that teacher of yours," the postman said. "Teachers used to be city employees and they never got married, and now look. They still are. But in my day we all had to stand up and say the same thing to the flag on the wall. Do you do the pledge?"

"I don't think so," Mike said. "I don't think we've had that yet."

"In my day you always did," the postman said. "We would all stand up and say the same thing about indivisible. Blah blah the state of this country. Blah blah blah,

blah blah blah blah, Mike. Blah blah blah blah business addresses, or blah blah blah private homes."

Mike wasn't listening, except perhaps a little bit. His father's voice was like the dull sound of the sea. "What?" he said. "What's private homes?"

"You know what private is," the postman said, slipping some mail into the slot. "You can't go in unless you ring the doorbell and someone lets you in."

"Like vampires," Mike said. He was going through a thing about vampires.

"*Not like vampires*," the postman said. "You're not listening, Mike. We've talked about this. We hope this guy will let us come in and—"

"What's the best part of your job?" Mike asked. This was part of the report he had to write, which would be read halfheartedly by his teacher as she shared a bottle of chianti with her spouse whom she loved.

"I've been *saying*," the postman said irritably, pointing to the next house. "Pay *attention*. The fellow at 1602 is the best part. You're gonna meet him. You're gonna love him. He's a great fellow. Handsome, and pretty tall, and he's made something of himself. I can't wait to see him again."

"A guy? That's the best part?" Mike asked.

"Yeah it's the best part," the postman said, and stepped up to 1602. The house looked like any other house, home to somebody, not to you. It had paint on the outside of it, and windows on the walls. Mike had scarcely any curiosity about it at all. "We're all together on this, Mike. We're all on the same page. You're gonna love him. I love him. I love him like a root beer float. And you're gonna love him like saltwater taffy."

Mike, like a bird, had headed south once. He had walked down the boardwalk, where the taffy is made in small buildings and shops. The sea had nudged his feet and it had been very hot and sweaty outside. He had read the signs, everything they put up for him to read, but still he was unprepared for the man who opened the door. Love can smack you like a seagull, and pour all over your feet like junk mail. You can't be ready for such a thing any more than saltwater taffy gets you ready for the ocean, or Bring Your Child to Work Day prepares you for the lonely times of going to work. But Mike wasn't going to have any lonely times. Not lately, or not in the immediate future. No way, with a door opening like this one.

"Can I help you?" the fellow said, and Mike just loved him. Why wouldn't you? Mike loved this fellow on the spot, like his father said, particularly his necktie and the way that he grasped his hair with one hand, distractedly, as he looked out at his postman. Love flowed through Mike and stuck to the roof of his mouth like a sticky

sticky sweet, this fellow from 1602, this man who suddenly showed up on the route and opened the door.

"Hello!" the postman said. "Hello! This is my son. I wanted him to meet you and he did too."

"Um, hello," the fellow said.

"We both totally think you're a great guy," the postman said. "We both love you. We just want to come in for a minute."

"It's not really," the fellow said. "It's not really a good time."

"Just for a minute," the postman insisted, and Mike nodded in agreement. "I have to continue my route because everybody wants their mail, but if we could just come in for a minute, so my son here could get to know you. It's Bring Your Daughter to Work Day. Be a sport, will you be a sport?"

"I guess so," the fellow said, and gave them the benefit of the doubt with an open door. The postman held the fellow's packet of mail out and then flipped it back toward himself and his son.

"I won't give you your mail," the postman said playfully, "until you let us in for a few minutes."

"I already said okay," the fellow said sharply, and Mike flushed a bit. This is love, and the trouble with it: it can make you embarrassed. Love is really liking someone a whole lot and not wanting to screw that up. Everybody's chewed this over. This unites us, this part of love. Mike walked through the door into 1602 and just beamed at this fellow, all smiley with admiration and liking him a lot.

"Make yourselves at home I guess," the fellow said, and just past the door was a sort of living room kitchen combo where Mike could see the fellow cooked and ate and sat on a sofa and put his feet up on a table with magazines. Mike didn't care which ones the fellow sub-scribed to, because Mike subscribed to the fellow. "I was just going to excuse myself," the fellow said, adorably, "when the doorbell rang."

"Okeydokey," the postman said and led his son into the room to sit. The fellow at 1602 left, and the two visitors suddenly realized there was a woman in the room with them who had been concealed by a floor lamp.

"Hello," the woman said. Her name was Muriel.

"Oh my," the postman said, half-rising from the sofa. "I didn't realize he already had company."

"Yes," Muriel said. "We're having something of a re-union, actually."

"Reunion?" the postman said.

"Here," the woman said, and reached over to the pile of magazines. On top was some mail including an opened envelope.

"Oh, I couldn't!" the postman said. "Not someone else's mail. Put that in your report, Mike. Don't read other people's mail. Your teacher will love that."

"It's okay," Muriel said, handing it over. "Read it."

The fellow at 1602 washed his face more than necessary, as we all do. First Muriel, now the postman and his son. He looked at his wet face in the bathroom mirror. Why was this happening? Why love, today? But nobody ever answers that one, guy. He reached for a towel as the doorbell rang again.

> Dear Joe,
>
> I have reason to believe that you are my baby and that I am your real mother. When I was 16½ or 17 I got pregnant and I gave the baby to your parents and said they should never tell anybody. They didn't. You were my little boy, made of sugar and spice and everything nice. I named you Joe for obvious reasons, and as the years went on I was very lonely so I hired two detectives to find you, the source of my regret. I don't want money or anything. I'm a normal person like everybody else and I just want to get to know you because you are my baby, baby.
>
> Love,
>
> Muriel, your real mother

"Sooo," the postman said, handing the letter back. "The guy's name is Joe."

"I like the name Joe," Mike said.

"Who doesn't?" the postman said. "And you're Muriel? Well, all I have to say to you, Muriel, is congratulations."

"Excuse me," the fellow said, walking through the room. "I have to answer the doorbell." The fellow kept walking, amazed at his own decision to pretend he hadn't heard what they were talking about. It wasn't true, in any case. The fellow at 1602 looked exactly like his father and overall the letter was suspect. Last week he had received a letter on the same stationery telling him he had won a prize and it was signed "Muriel, your prize deputy." He hadn't answered that one, and now he was thinking both letters were limp ruses to get into the house. But now Muriel was in the house. She was in the house and all she wanted to do was sit on his sofa and get to know him. Where did he work? Where did he find that tie? Did he grow up happy with his fake parents? This is love, the plain truth once you get inside. Like a peacock, we all show off with the plumage. Come in and watch us make it! But then it's just the same story, sugar and spice all spun up. We're all mostly salt water. Love is candy from a stranger, but it's candy you've had before and it probably won't kill you.

"It's just hitting me," the postman said as soon as the fellow was out of the room, "that the name Joe is never on the envelopes I give this guy."

"I have no idea if his name is Joe," Muriel confided with a whisper. "I made up the whole letter, just about. I just love this guy. I love him. I love him and I want to get to know him."

"I know," the postman said. "Isn't he a peach?"

"I love him," Mike said, "and I've only known him for a few minutes."

"That's how it goes," the postman said. "It's like a miracle. You're lucky it was Bring Your Daughter to Work Day. Let's look at his books."

The three lovers shared a look and got a case of the giggles. There was no competition amongst them but otherwise there was nothing unusual. The books too were nothing unusual: something by Alice Walker, for instance, a very popular author, and several books on things that interested him. They say love is in the details, that it's the little things that make a person special, but then why are the love songs so alike? It's your smile, it's your eyes, I love your eyes and your smile. I like to go to the beach with you, but really the beach is so interesting and pretty that you could take anyone to the beach. The girl singing that song "Please Mr. Postman" just wants a letter from some fellow, and you just make up who the guy is. You're encouraged to do so, to draw up the details that bring you to love him, so why shouldn't you go to his house, where the details live? That's what the guy who delivers the organic box told himself, as he turned off the same song on the radio and stopped his truck at 1602 and rang the doorbell for obvious reasons.

"Just for a minute," the fellow at 1602 said with a sigh. "I already have three people here."

"I didn't want to insist," said the guy who delivers the organic box. He was holding a box of heavy cardboard, filled with organic fruits and vegetables and other products. The gentle hump of a mango, the perky celery, and a plastic container of yogurt were peeking out of the top of the box like they wanted to be with this guy, just lay eyes on him for a few moments, his pretty eyes. "It's just that I think you're totally super and I want to get to know you."

"Get in line," the postman said, and nearly everybody laughed.

"Do you guys love him too?" the delivery guy said, putting the box on the counter.

"Hell yeah," Muriel said. "I love this fellow like he's my own baby."

"I like his necktie," Mike said.

"We're all on the same page, clearly," the postman said, putting a book back where it belonged.

"I've been watching this guy for like six months," said the fellow who delivers the organic box, pointing to the fellow at 1602 with an eager open palm. "Ever since I got on this delivery route. He's a terrific guy."

"I love him," the postman said and winked at Muriel.

"Who doesn't?" the delivery guy said. "He's the rat's pajamas."

"It's cat," Mike said. His teacher's unit on idiomatic expressions had been almost a complete waste of time.

"I knew it was some animal who had the pajamas," said the fellow who delivers the organic box. "*Cat*. I'll have to remember that. Now, where do you keep your blender?"

"Call him Joe," Muriel said. "It's a name I made up for him, a term of endearment. Try it."

"Where's the blender, Joe?" the delivery guy tried, but he'd already found it, in a cupboard. There are only a handful of places where a blender is kept. If you live with someone romantically, for years even, you could switch to a new person and find their blender within moments.

"Look," the fellow finally said, and everyone looked. He fussed with his hair in that way people love and gave everyone a little smile like he didn't really mean it. "All this is very strange for me."

"Like you're walking on air?" Mike asked.

"No," the fellow said. "Another kind of strange."

"It can't be any kind of strange," said the guy who delivers the organic box. "You asked for it."

"I did not *ask for it*," the fellow said.

"Sure you did," the guy said. "Every week I deliver organic food right here to this house. Look, we have tomatoes, mangoes, beautiful kale, homemade salsa, wild clover honey, celery and fennel and potatoes, and a thing of organic yogurt from the dairy down the highway. Look at all the flavors here. I bring you them because you want to eat them. You signed up for it, Joe."

"And I give you your mail every day," the postman said, "except Sundays and holidays. Why shouldn't I think you're terrific, and stop by to tell you so?"

"I'm putting you in my report," Mike said. "It's for school."

"That's not the same thing," the fellow said.

"The hell it isn't," Muriel said. "I love you like my own son and you don't want me in your house?"

"Yeah, it's my house," the fellow said. "You all seem like nice people, but I'm going to ask you to get out of it. Get out of my house."

"Don't be silly," the fellow who delivers the organic box said. "I'm making you a mango lassi."

"You'd better make a pitcher," the postman said, craning to look out the window. "We got someone else coming up the front steps."

"What the—" the fellow said, but the doorbell rang and he had to go answer it. Once more, this is love: it rings and you open up unless it looks like an ax murderer.

"Maybe it's his wife," Muriel said. "I'd love to meet her."

"Who wouldn't?" the delivery guy said. "I bet I'd love her too. I'm certain of it, in fact. This is going to be delicious. They drink these in India, like at a wedding or if they're feasting. Mangoes, yogurt, a little lime juice if I can find it. I found it!"

"My my," said the first of the three women who walked into the room. It wasn't his wife. None of them were. All of the women were somewhat old and they lived in the neighborhood. "What a lovely room!" she said. "I love how it flows from the kitchen to the living area, and I love you!"

"I knew he would have a fantastic room," said one of the other women, "because he is a fantastic person."

"Come in, come in," the postman said. "The fellow who delivers the organic box is making us all a pitcher of Indian drinks. Stay for a moment and we'll drink a toast—to Joe!"

"What are you adding, clover honey?" one of the

women asked, looking over at the blender. "It looks like this is going to be very unusual."

"Well, I suppose it's a somewhat unusual situation," Muriel said.

"I for one am glad," said one of the older women, and perhaps because of her age the fellow who delivers the organic box turned off the blender and everyone gave her the floor. "I had a story I was going to tell," she said. "I was going to say that I had a rare disease of some sort and I needed comfort. Or that I was anxious for my mail and that I saw the postman go into this house and not come out and so I couldn't wait anymore or I wanted to make sure nothing was wrong. But I'm not anxious for my mail. I'm healthy as a donkey, and no one writes me, just companies hungry for money. Dear Valued Customer, they say, but I know better. Who gets real mail nowadays?"

"It's not donkey," said the fellow at 1602. "It's *horse.*"

"Joe gets real mail," Muriel said, and lifted her letter from the table. "I wrote him a real letter."

"Then read it to me," the woman said. "Or make Joe read it. Tell me a story to pass my time. I find you interesting, Joe, so nearly everything you say will be interesting too. I love you. I could say I'm lonely but that's not the only reason. So many days you passed me by, see the tears standing in my eyes. You didn't stop to make me

feel better by leaving me a card or a letter. Mister Postman, look and see if there's a letter in your bag for me."

"I hate that song," said the fellow, but let's be honest:
that song is an enormous hit. It's most certainly part of
a hit parade, and everyone loves a parade. Joe found, to
his mild amazement, that he was having trouble not
singing along with the love song that was now in the air.
"I want you all to leave," Joe said, but he was still ador-
able to the whole crowd. "This is private property and
you're in flagrant disregard."

"Flagrant disregard, get him," Muriel said, or clucked.
"Let your mother tell you something, Joe."

"I don't want you to tell me anything," I said. "I'm
not—I'm not the terrific guy you keep telling me about.
I'm not made of sugar and spice and everything nice.
I'm made of rats and snails and puppy-dog tails. I lie
sometimes. I have broken people's hearts. I'm looking
for love, I'll admit that, but now that it's here in abundance, I'm afraid of commitment and I want you, please,
to leave me."

"It's not rats," Mike said, and bit his lip.

"Now look," said the postman. "You've upset my kid."

"Why are you here?" the fellow from 1602 said.

The postman threw the packet of the fellow's mail on
top of his other mail on the table in the guy's house. "I'll
try to explain," he said, and then he tried to explain the

idea that's here. It's an idea we're more or less stuck with. Isn't love a sharing? Isn't it opening your bag of sweets and passing it around, or whipping something up out of groceries you brought to someone else's house? And if it's a sharing, then you have to share it. Love makes the world go round, the hit songs collectively tell us, and the world is full of people you don't know and might as well be nice to because they won't leave. Some of the people you won't like, but every day we wait for the postman and he hardly ever brings something good. Let us love you, the postman was trying to say, this time let everyone love you, but this kind of talk wasn't really his style, so he just said, "We love you, guy. It's your eyes and your smile and your necktie and shoes. You are terrific and we love you, and you're a sport, so be a sport. Take a mango lassi and drink with us." For in the hubbub of things the fellow who delivers the organic box had easily found glasses for eight. They were fancy glasses, not ones the fellow used often due to their delicacy, but why not use them now, even if they break? Why not fill them while they last?

"We love you, man," the postman said, and held out a glass like you'd hold out a bag of something made by the sea. We all want what's in the bag. You'd have to be crazy not to take some. Have you ever had a mango lassi? Thick down the throat, crazy orange, delicious and happy if you like that sort of thing? What else can a fellow do, in the grip of mango and yogurt and fruit, spun up into a substance just like love? It *is* love. It's a part of it.

"Come on, Joe," Mike said, and Joe reached out and closed his hand around something sweet.